THE
LIAR'S
CHILD

BOOKS BY SHERYL BROWNE

The Babysitter
The Affair
The Second Wife
The Marriage Trap
The Perfect Sister
The New Girlfriend
Trust Me
My Husband's Girlfriend

'swap', each donor giving a kidney to the other person's intended recipient, but Kay wasn't entirely sure she understood all the details. She needed to talk more to Poppy's consultant, to be clear in her mind exactly what options they might have should her tissue typing exclude her as a suitable donor. She hoped to God that she was.

Matt squeezed her tighter as a shudder ran through her. 'I'll chase the biopsy up when I get in,' he promised. 'I'll text you as soon as I have any information. Meanwhile, since going into work naked might cause a few raised eyebrows, I suppose I really ought to put some clothes on.'

Kay smiled, amazingly. She did love this man, who tried so hard to cajole her from her deepest dark thoughts. He was right to. Dwelling on what the future might bring wouldn't help Poppy. It wouldn't help him. She needed to put on a brave face for their sakes, which she certainly wouldn't have been doing if she'd charged into Poppy's room looking terrified. 'Only in appreciation,' she assured him, sliding a hand down his back to give his rather enticingly firm buttocks a cheeky pat.

'If that's a proposition, I may just have to take you up on it,' he whispered close to her ear.

Kay snuggled further into him. That suggestion sounded most definitely enticing. She longed to lie safe in his arms, where the worries and cares of the day would once have drifted away. They'd found intimacy impossible lately, though, each carrying their own guilt, imagining that they were responsible for Poppy's illness.

'In case I haven't mentioned it lately, I love you, Mrs Young,' he murmured. Lifting her chin, he pressed a soft kiss to her lips, and then rolled his eyes in wry amusement at Poppy's timely intervention from the landing.

'Mummy,' she called worriedly. 'It's time to get ready.'

'Damn. Foiled again.' Matt sighed in mock despair and disappeared discreetly back to the bathroom a second before Poppy charged through the door.

'We have to get our skates on, Mummy,' she informed Kay, her little face serious as she mimicked what Kay so often said to her on a school morning, school not always being Poppy's favourite place. 'I have to take the things for my project in today.'

'Oh my God!' Kay's eyes sprang wide. 'I forgot all about your project!'

'Uh oh. All hands to the pump then?' Matt asked from the bathroom.

'Please,' Kay called, skidding after Poppy back to the landing. 'It's a sensory project. They're doing the sense of touch this week.'

Pouring cereal out for Poppy with one hand – Shredded Wheat, which happily she loved and which was healthily low in potassium – Kay made coffee with the other. She was taking a quick glug and debating the wisdom of sending her daughter into school with an egg for her project – it was definitely smooth, but possibly impractical unless she hard-boiled it –when Matt came into the kitchen. 'Okay, Mission School Project, what do we need?' he asked, rubbing his hands together in a show of enthusiasm.

Poppy downed her spoon, almost falling off her chair as she scrambled to run and greet him. 'Something smooth,' she said as he bent to sweep her up. 'And something else that feels different, like, um …?'

'Fur?' Matt suggested, hoisting her high in his arms and then pretending to buckle under her weight.

'Yes!' Poppy laughed delightedly and clung to his neck.

'Ta-dah,' Matt said, producing her penguin plush soft toy from under his shirt.

Poppy leaned back, making wide eyes at it. 'But I can't take all of him in.' She knitted her brow dubiously. 'I have to put it in my workbook. He'll get squashed.'

'Ah.' Matt knitted his brow in turn. 'How about if I surgically remove just a tiny piece of fur from under his wing where no one will see it?'

The frown in Poppy's forehead deepened. 'Will it hurt him?'

'Not at all,' Matt assured her. 'He won't even notice. I'll tuck him up in your bed afterwards until you get home to check on him. Okay?'

'Okay.' Poppy nodded, satisfied.

'So what else do you need?'

'Something …' Poppy had a think, and then reached to place the palm of her hand against his cheek. 'Prickly.'

Kay laughed. 'I think Daddy's face might get a bit squashed if you put that in your workbook,' she pointed out, going across to the under-sink cupboard and fetching a scouring pad. 'How about this?'

'That will work.' Poppy nodded maturely.

'Good thinking, Batman,' Matt said, winking at Kay as he lowered Poppy to the floor. 'So, what else?'

'We have to find lots of different textures,' Kay supplied, checking the wall clock as she hurriedly finished packing Poppy's lunch box.

'Something spongy maybe?' Matt suggested.

He was obviously thinking of the bathroom sponge. 'Top of the class, Dr Young,' she said, smiling over her shoulder.

'I'll go and snip a bit off,' Matt said with another wink, and about-faced back to the hall.

'Brilliant. Thanks,' Kay called after him, and then, to Poppy, 'Right, young lady. You have five minutes to brush your teeth and get your shoes on, or we'll be late.'

She was grabbing coats and pushing her feet into her boots when Poppy came back down the stairs, closely followed by Matt. Helping Poppy into her coat, she cursed as her phone rang from the kitchen. She was so distracted lately, she thought, she would forget her head if it was loose.

A second later, Matt appeared from the kitchen with the phone – and the lunch box, which she'd also almost gone without. 'I didn't get to it in time,' he said, handing her the lunch box but hanging onto the phone as she reached for it. 'I checked who it was, though,' he added, scanning her eyes, confusion in his own. 'Jason.'

'Oh.' Kay glanced down, taking hold of Poppy's hand. 'Right. I'll, um, call him back later.'

Matt didn't say anything for a second. Then, 'Why's he calling you?' he asked.

She looked back at him, unsurprised by the suspicion in his eyes. She'd gone out with Jason briefly before Matt, and had detected an undercurrent of tension between the two brothers ever since. After a violent altercation between them almost six years ago, they were as estranged as it was possible for two brothers to be. Matt couldn't even bear to hear Jason's name spoken, and had rudely cut his father off when he'd tried to update him on his brother's life out in the States.

'Because he wants to meet Poppy,' she answered truthfully, a nervous knot tightening her stomach. He'd actually called her more than once, wondering how she was. She hadn't called him back, texting him instead to say that *they* were fine, and suggesting it wasn't a good idea for him to be contacting her.

Matt continued to study her, a telltale tic playing at his cheek, indicating he wasn't impressed. 'Why?' he asked shortly.

Opening the front door, Kay urged Poppy out before her, then glanced back at him. 'Because he hasn't seen her,' she whispered, feeling uncomfortable under his unwavering gaze. 'He is her uncle, Matt, and he's back from the States now.'

'Why ring you, though?' Matt pressed, his eyes filled with doubt. 'Specifically, I mean? He's only been back two weeks, according to Dad.'

'I don't know, Matt.' Feeling under attack, and not sure why, Kay turned away. 'Possibly because you wouldn't have taken his call?'

Once Poppy was safely in school, Kay drove home on autopilot, her mind on the whispered provocation that had incited the normally placid Matt to such uncharacteristic violence towards his brother, which had resulted in the estrangement between them. It had taken all her willpower to quash the tears that had threatened as she left him this morning with the same thunderous look in his eyes she'd seen all those years ago. The situation between Matt and his brother had been relegated to history, but she was bound to feel emotional. She couldn't give in to the tears that seemed to be perpetually threatening, though, especially in front of Poppy. How much would that rock her daughter's little world? How much would Jason reappearing in their lives rock Kay and Matt's world? Matt was right to be suspicious. After so long, why was Jason insisting on seeing Poppy, on calling *her*, which he must know would only reignite hostilities?

Arriving home, she pulled out her phone, debating whether to ring him back. Her heart sank as she realised he'd left a voicemail. Having recognised his brother's number, Matt would doubtless have played the message back. Tentatively Kay listened to it.

'Hi, Kay,' Jason said cheerily. 'I just wondered if you'd given any more thought to what we discussed? It would be nice to meet Poppy, get to know her.' There was a pause as he seemed to ponder, then, 'Call me when you can. It would be nice to see you too, obviously.'

God, no wonder Matt had been agitated, realising she'd been talking to Jason behind his back while he flatly refused to have anything to do with him. But how was she to avoid speaking to him when he called her?

A confusion of guilt and apprehension rising inside her, she tried to think what to do. As she debated whether to send Jason a curt text or completely ignore him, she heard Matt's phone ringing.

He must have left without it, she realised, distracted by his brother's untimely call. She would have to call the hospital, offer to drop it off. Aside from the fact that he'd said he would text her, he needed to be contactable at all times in case of emergencies.

Pushing aside the niggling worry about Jason and what his agenda was, she climbed the stairs and headed for the bedroom, guessing that was where Matt had left his phone. It rang again as she neared where it lay on the dressing table.

She picked it up and answered. 'Matt's phone. Kay speaking.'

'Oh, hi, Kay. It's Emma here, from the renal department,' the voice on the other end said. 'Matt called earlier about scheduling the tissue testing. I'll probably see him later, but just in case I miss him, can you tell him I'll get it organised for as soon as possible?'

Kay frowned, a new worry worming its way into her head. He was organising the tests without talking to her first? 'Yes, no problem,' she said, working to keep her tone even. 'Actually, as you've rung, do you mind if I ask you something?'

'Shoot,' said Emma. 'I'm happy to help with anything I can.'

Kay inhaled deeply. 'What do the tests involve exactly? Matt will no doubt fill me in later, but just to put my mind at rest meanwhile …'

'It's not as worrying as it sounds, honestly,' Emma assured her. 'It just involves a simple blood test. They'll be looking at certain principal proteins involved in the process of getting rid of viruses. It sounds a bit complicated, but I can get the consultant to call you if … Hold on. Talk of the devil, Matt's just come through the door. Do you want to speak to him?'

Kay hesitated, not sure what she would say to him, which was ridiculous – she'd never been nervous around Matt. 'Yes please,' she said. 'I need to bring him his phone.'

'It's Kay,' she heard Emma say. 'She's asking about the tissue tests and what they involve. I'm probably not best qualified to answer.'

Matt came on after a second. 'Hi,' he said. 'I'll email you a leaflet. It should explain everything. There's something in there that might give you cause for concern. If we need to talk about it, it would probably be a good idea at this juncture.'

'Oh, right. Thanks,' Kay answered uncertainly. What did he mean? Wasn't the whole thing cause for concern? She'd been about to ask why he'd gone ahead with organising the tests without consulting her, but sensing he was in a rush, she thought better of it. 'I could collect the leaflet,' she suggested. 'I was going to bring your phone in on the way to uni. I thought you might need it.'

'No need,' he assured her. 'I'll swing by later. I should go. I have early surgery to prep for, a newborn with congenital heart disease. I need to be focused. Talk later.'

Kay stared at his phone in bemusement as she realised he'd ended the call. He hadn't mentioned whether he'd had a chance to speak to the consultant about Poppy's biopsy yet. Confused, she made her way slowly back down to the hall to get her own phone. Was he being off with her? No, she was imagining it. He was obviously busy. And with a newborn baby to operate on, he would absolutely need to be focused.

A thousand nervous butterflies thrashed around in her stomach as she waited for the leaflet to arrive. Taking a fortifying breath, she quickly scanned it, and then dropped to the stairs to study it more thoroughly. It explained that the proteins, called HAL antigens, would each be given a number to identify them, and that Poppy could have inherited three of those numbers from each parent, but that she couldn't inherit a number that neither parent had. If her number sequence included a number that Kay or Matt didn't have, it could preclude them as a good match. Her blood pumping, Kay read on:

It is important for you to understand that tissue typing is similar to what is sometimes called 'paternity testing'. That is, the results may help to confirm (or not) the biological parents of the child. We ask that you consider this carefully before agreeing to the test. As a family, you would need to decide who should be told if the results are unexpected. That is, if the tests were to show that one or other of you is not the 'blood parent', would both of you, one of you or neither of you want to be told?

Kay's heart flipped. Was this what Matt had meant might give her cause for concern? She read the last section over again, and then laughed at the absurdity of her train of thought. He couldn't be hinting that he suspected she … *No.* It was preposterous.

CHAPTER TWO

'So, A. S. Byatt's *Possession: A Romance* …' Glancing down at her scant notes about the book she'd asked her students to study as part of their Reading into Writing module, Kay faltered. She'd had hours to prepare for her creative writing lecture since dropping Poppy at school, but hadn't been able to concentrate. Try as she might, she couldn't understand why Matt would have warned her about the contents of that leaflet. Was he really doubting her loyalty, when *he* was the one with the history of withdrawing from their marriage? After that ill-fated family wedding six years ago, the root of the rift with Jason, he'd disappeared for a whole week. He hadn't gone to work, hadn't answered his phone … Kay had been beside herself with worry. Later, when things were back to normal, she'd forgotten about it, dismissed it as a blip in their marriage, caused by Jason, who seemed to be the only person who could wind Matt up and clearly revelled in it. But now he seemed to be doing it again, withdrawing from her, not being honest with her about the basis of his anger.

Her mind reeled back to the wedding and the awful violent confrontation between Matt and Jason. She hadn't even wanted to go. She'd been feeling emotionally fragile and should have made her excuses, but the bride was one of Matt's cousins on his mum's side, and she felt he needed her support. He'd lost his mum so tragically. It had been years ago, when he was just ten years old, but she was aware he found it hard to see that side of the family. Nausea rose inside her as she recalled the events leading up to Matt knocking his brother unconscious – or at least those memories that hadn't been lost in the sea of alcohol she'd consumed, largely because the inevitable baby question had been asked once the service was over. With the bride obviously expecting, her dress designed to show off her bump, the occasion had been ripe for it.

So many times people had asked her if she and Matt were going to hear the patter of tiny feet soon. So many times her heart had bled icily into her stomach when they had. They couldn't have known, because she hadn't told anyone, but she had been desperate for a child. After delivering a baby whose tiny heart had stopped beating at just sixteen weeks, she and Matt had tried so hard for another. Two years of tests, procedures, tears, IVF and loss had followed – all of it bearable only because of their love for each other, the belief that one day it would happen. She'd tried hormone therapy, drugs to kick-start her ovaries, fertility drugs, acupuncture … everything.

Just weeks prior to the wedding, she'd been full of hope, sure that this time her prayers had been answered. Fate had had other plans, leaving her feeling bereft again, as if she were grieving the loss of a child, yet there'd been no child. How could she explain that to strangers? How could she explain that every time her hopes were dashed, she felt inadequate, vulnerable, exposed? She couldn't – couldn't bear to even share it with Matt. She'd worked hard at hiding how wretched she felt, because he would have blamed himself. He wouldn't have said so, but that was what he would have thought. She knew he blamed himself for his mother's death.

Once at the wedding, she'd tried hard to brush off her bleak mood, but the combination of little children belonging to other people running gleefully around and the alcohol had made her tearful. Feeling woozy, she'd headed precariously out of the hall to the loos. She hadn't realised that Jason had followed her until he reached to steady her halfway across the hotel foyer.

'Whoops,' he'd said, both hands on her forearms as he steered her around to face him. 'I'm sensing a little over-indulgence.'

'I'm fine,' Kay had assured him, shrugging him off and stepping away from him, only to find herself reeling backwards. Realising she'd drunk so much she couldn't seem to coordinate properly, she'd been grateful for his help to the lift. Inordinately grateful for his help to her room, by which time the walls were spinning vertiginously. If not for Jason, she might have passed out on the landing.

She vaguely remembered being fearful of Matt finding Jason in their room as he helped her to sit woozily down on the bed, assuring her he wouldn't mention it. She'd assumed he understood why she wouldn't want Matt to know. It was bound to look suspicious, after all, even though she'd only gone out with Jason for a couple of months, before realising that she didn't actually like him that much.

Finding herself alone in the bed the next morning with the duvet tangled around her and a horrendous hangover starting to kick in, she'd forced herself down to breakfast to look for Matt. He'd seemed a little moody, distracted. Wondering whether he, or someone else, might have witnessed the silly drunken kiss Jason had attempted as they'd stepped into the lift, she'd told him about that. Now she was wondering whether Jason had mentioned that he'd helped her up to the room, implying that there might have been more to it. Something had caused Matt to react uncharacteristically violently that morning, to the horror of the other guests who'd stayed over. To this day, because he refused to discuss it, she didn't know what it was that Jason had whispered to him.

'Ahem.' Someone coughed pointedly, dragging her attention back to the lecture room. Realising her students were waiting for her to go on, she swallowed back the sharp constriction in her throat.

She shouldn't have come in today. Shouldn't be dwelling on all this now. Her energies and emotions should be focused on Poppy.

'Sorry. I lost the plot,' she joked feebly, and made an effort to pull herself together. She loved this job, despite sometimes feeling as though she wasn't really qualified for it. After all, some of her students were better writers than she could ever be, and she only had short stories on her CV. 'So hopefully you've all had a chance to read the book. What were your thoughts? Is it a love story? Does the title have more than one meaning?'

'It was *all* about possession in my opinion.' Amelia, a bright, pretty latecomer to the course, spoke up. 'In the modern concept of the word, the biggest possession, for me, was Ash's possession of Christabel,' she went on, giving Kay some much-needed breathing space. 'Ash claims to respect her freedom, that being her physical independence and her reluctance to become embroiled in relationships, which she feels will stifle her independent thought and therefore her ability to write, and then makes ceaseless demands on her time through his letter-writing. He's basically trying to control her.'

Well, that should open up the discussion. Kay breathed a sigh of relief. She was trying to formulate an intelligent response when she was saved by the bell, or rather the fire alarm, which she guessed was the weekly drill. 'Could I have your essays in by Wednesday?' she called, as seats were hurriedly vacated. 'And don't forget there's a masterclass on …' She stopped, realising she was talking to retreating backs, apart from Amelia, who lingered despite the shrieking alarm.

'Thanks for the notes.' The young woman approached her with a shy smile.

'No problem.' Kay smiled warmly back. She'd given her a few notes on previous modules to help her catch up, that was all.

'Byatt's novel is quite interesting, isn't it?' Amelia commented as Kay cast an eye around for her handbag, which she'd dropped somewhere as she'd rushed into the lecture room. 'I suppose I'm reading it with a modern take, having had experience of a controlling relationship myself.' She paused to pick the bag up from under the table next to the lectern. 'But then, haven't many of us?'

Kay eyed her curiously.

'I mean, being cheated on in a relationship is a form of control, after all, isn't it? Men thrive on it because they're making you feel lesser, don't you agree?' Amelia held her gaze as she handed her the bag. Up close, her eyes were amazing. Outlined with an unusual mushroom-coloured eyeliner and peering out through a tangle of jet-black hair, they were slate grey in colour, projecting a quiet confidence. Quite mesmerising. Her perfume was unusual, too, jasmine-fragranced.

'It's a big subject,' Kay said, deflecting the question, because it actually was. 'We should have more of a chat about it sometime.' Collecting up her paperwork, she nodded the woman towards the doors as the fire alarm continued to scream.

'We could chat about it now,' Amelia suggested as they headed along the corridor towards the exit. 'I thought, as we're finishing early, we could maybe go for a quick drink?' She looked back at Kay hopefully. 'It's just, with my being new to Worcester, I haven't got to know that many people yet.'

'I'd love to.' Feeling for her, Kay smiled. She was probably feeling lonely. 'I'm keen to pick my daughter up, though. She's been poorly, so …'

'Oh, right, not to worry.' Amelia nodded understandingly. 'I just thought I'd ask.'

She looked a bit despondent, Kay noted, and felt bad. 'We could go for a drink one evening,' she offered, as the woman held the exit doors open for her. 'I don't have a babysitter, though, so I'd have to make sure my husband's home. He's a doctor, paediatrics, specialising in neonatal intensive care, so he sometimes gets caught up.'

Amelia brightened. 'That would be brilliant. As long as you're sure it won't cause you too much hassle.'

'It won't,' Kay assured her. 'We'll sort something out after our class on Wednesday,' she promised. 'I'd better get off.'

'Great.' Beaming her a smile, Amelia made to leave, then stopped and turned back. 'How old is she?' she asked. 'Your little one?'

'Just five,' Kay said, and glanced down, tears suddenly close to the surface as she was reminded how fast those years had flown.

Amelia nodded. 'She has a very special daddy,' she announced, and headed off.

What an odd thing to say. Kay's brow furrowed as she watched the woman walk away. She supposed she was referring to Matt's job. And he *was* special. Kay loved him – for what he did, for who he was, which was the polar opposite of Jason. The two were similar physically, with piercing blue eyes and dark, brooding good looks that seemed to attract females like bees to honey. Jason, though, was the complete opposite of Matt in nature, confident and brash where Matt was quiet and modest. He could never resist winding his brother up. The two of them had issues that she suspected went back to the death of their mother, for which Matt blamed himself. She was sure the conflict between them wasn't helped by the fact that she had gone out with Jason, however briefly. Matt was obviously perplexed by him calling her so soon after he'd arrived back from the US. Of course he would be.

She decided to cook something special and perhaps open some wine tonight. They hadn't had a relaxed evening together for a long time, with Poppy's illness dominating their every thought and conversation. She followed Amelia towards the car park, digging into her bag as she went. *Damn.* Picturing her car keys where she'd left them, on the edge of the lectern, she cursed quietly and turned back.

Her heart dropped as she realised that the nominated fire attendants weren't about to let her back into the building. With the time now ticking by, she had a feeling she was going to be late picking Poppy up after all. Her phone signalling a text as she waited, she checked it and her heart plummeted.

Crisis at the hospital, Matt had texted, clearly having picked up his phone from home. *Not going to get back until extremely late. Sorry.*

There was no kiss. He always signed off with a kiss. Kay's throat constricted, tears welling all over again as insecurities she was trying to bury forced their way back to the surface. She could understand why he would be suspicious about Jason calling her, but he appeared to be angry with her. *Why?* Did he know that his brother had been in their hotel room that night? Had Jason told him, deliberately provoking him? Was that why Matt had seemed to push her away back then? Was he doing the same thing now?

She'd never before doubted that he had been working when he'd said he was, but now she found herself wondering. When she'd found she was pregnant, had he stayed with her out of some sense of duty? No. The notion was absurd. She could see his love for her. It was there in his eyes. She could feel it when he held her after making sweet love together. They hadn't been close in a long time, but he would never have an affair, surely? He would never do anything to jeopardise their marriage, not now, with Poppy so poorly. He just wouldn't.

Unless … She swallowed back the lump, like sharp grit in her throat. Was it possible it was a long-standing affair? If it was something that had been going on for a while, was it that he'd been meaning to end their marriage, but now couldn't bring himself to because of the situation with Poppy?

CHAPTER THREE

Matt had once told her that tears were therapeutic. He'd held her so gently, so sweetly after her mother had died before Poppy was born, telling her tears were a release valve and that she should never be afraid to cry. He'd been lying about that too, she thought, anger surfacing. She didn't feel better for being reduced to tears. Hadn't she already cried enough over Poppy? Whatever he was doing, or not doing, whatever Jason had told him, she shouldn't be feeling like this, torn with guilt, now of all times. Her child needed her to be upbeat, positive, not bloody miserable.

Swiping away the useless tears that had rolled down her face all the way here, stifling the exhaustion that had crept over her after last night's broken sleep, she parked on her friend Stephanie's drive and hurried down the path to the back of the house. Pausing, she tapped lightly on the back door and then poked her head around it. 'Only me.' She smiled apologetically as Stephanie looked up from where she was helping Poppy with her finger-painting at the kitchen table. 'Sorry I'm late, Steph. The fire alarm went off and I managed to leave my car keys in the lecture room.'

'No problem,' Stephanie assured her. 'Come on in. We're having fun, aren't we, Poppy? Messy fun, unfortunately.' She glanced amusedly towards the little girl, who held up her blue-painted hands with a gleeful smile.

Relieved, Kay stepped inside. Her usual childminder had taken a job at a nursery, and Steph had offered to help out. With Poppy's illness, and her being a shy child, Kay would never have been able to bring herself to leave her with someone new.

'How's Matt? Still working all the hours God sends?' Stephanie asked as Kay walked towards the table, only narrowly avoiding getting mown down by Stephanie's two boys as they charged past in pursuit of their yapping terrier.

'Fine.' Jarred by the question, Kay glanced down. 'Afraid so,' she said, taking a breath.

Stephanie gave her a knowing look. 'You wouldn't have him any other way.'

'No.' Kay smiled sadly, suppressing an urge to confide in her friend. Stephanie would probably think she'd gone mad. Kay wondered whether she had. Her emotions were see-sawing all over the place, suspicion pinging around in her head like a pinball machine. Unfounded suspicion. She had no reason to doubt him … apart from the late nights and the fact that they'd rarely been intimate lately. She hadn't looked for reasons, she reminded herself; she hadn't sniffed his clothes for the scent of another woman, or checked he was actually at the hospital – which she easily could have done – or monitored his phone calls and texts. God, how she wished she had looked at his phone today when she'd had the perfect opportunity.

Stop. Closing her eyes, she took another deep breath, trying to stop the incessant thoughts squirming away in her head. 'Thanks for collecting her, Steph. You're a lifesaver,' she said, going across to kiss the top of her daughter's head. 'How's she been?'

'As good as gold. No problems at all,' Stephanie assured her, clearly gathering that Kay was enquiring more about her health than her behaviour. 'She's made a new friend at school, haven't you, Poppy?'

'Really?' Kay was surprised. She'd worried Poppy's shyness might have been exacerbated by her illness making her think that somehow she was different. Even on good days when she was in remission she couldn't race around the playground as the other children did, and had to be well wrapped up when she went out to play, a teacher always keeping a watchful eye on her. They had to be careful that, with her immunity compromised, she didn't catch infections. She had to have flu and pneumococcal vaccinations, which she was aware the other children didn't have. She constantly lost time due to illness and hospital tests, meaning she fell behind in class. There were times when she was sleepy and had to lie down. Days when she might need to go to the loo frequently. Her teacher was golden, but Kay guessed her little girl found those things embarrassing. Right now, she seemed fine, like any other happy child. Kay held onto that.

'Yes,' Poppy answered with a firm nod. 'Her name's Olivia,' she said, sliding from her chair and heading towards Kay. 'But I can call her Liv, because I'm her best friend.'

'Best friends for ever, apparently,' Stephanie added. Seeing that Poppy was about to daub paint everywhere, she caught hold of her and steered her towards the sink. 'They're inseparable, according to her teacher. You do everything together, don't you, Poppy?'

'Uh huh.' Poppy dutifully washed her hands and then skipped back towards Kay, who was ready to dry them with paper towelling. 'She sits next to me. We have lots and lots to talk about. She has Barbie Ballerina, Barbie Doggy Daycare and Barbie Sparkle Mermaid. She has the Barbie Pop-Up Camper, too. I haven't got that one, but we've decided to share because I have the ambulance.'

'Good idea.' Kay smiled with delight as her daughter – suddenly, it seemed, a chatterbox – paused to draw breath.

'We have the same hair, too,' Poppy went on enthusiastically. 'Mrs Weaver sometimes tells us off for talking too much, but she gets us mixed up and calls us by the wrong names. She says we're like peas in a pot.'

'In a pod,' Kay corrected her. 'Well, Liv sounds lovely.' Seeing the excited sparkle in the little girl's eyes, she laughed and pulled her into a hug. 'Shall we invite her round for tea so I can meet her properly?'

'I think you should,' Stephanie suggested. 'And if I were you, I'd make sure to do it soon.'

Hearing the caution in her friend's tone, Kay glanced questioningly up at her. Goosebumps prickled her skin as she saw the warning in Stephanie's eyes.

'Do you want to go and fetch your shoes from the hall, Poppy?' Stephanie urged her, clearly angling to speak privately to Kay for a moment. 'It might just be me, but they're *very* alike,' she whispered once Poppy was out of earshot. 'I really think you should find out more about her. I actually did a double-take when I saw her.'

CHAPTER FOUR

After making sure that Poppy was getting ready for school, Kay went back to the main bedroom to collect her bag. Matt was in the bathroom. His phone was on his bedside table. Halfway across the room, she paused, holding her breath. Telling herself again that she was being ridiculous, she took another step, and then stopped again. There would be nothing there, nothing incriminating to find, she *knew* that. So why in God's name did she feel the need to prove it?

Her gaze flicking towards the bathroom, where the shower was running, she picked up the phone. She tried to fight the compulsion to look at it, but couldn't. If there was nothing to find, there would be no harm done, apart from the fact that if Matt realised she was checking his phone, his trust in her would be broken. Still, she had to do it, if only to put her mind at rest.

Going to his texts, she scrolled quickly through them, seeing nothing out of the ordinary: messages from work, from her, the odd one from his father. She'd scrolled a little further back when the shower stopped and, simultaneously, her heart jarred. *Thanks for last night. Looking forward to seeing you again soon. A xx*

She was wrong. Her blood thrumming, she banged the phone back down, almost dropping it in the process, and whirled around. It was an associate, a colleague. *Not a colleague.* How many colleagues would sign off with two kisses?

Snatching up her bag, she raced for the door, trying to contain her raging emotions. It might be innocent. It *must* be. She had to ask him. Catching a sob in her throat, she hurried downstairs. *How?* How did she ask him in front of Poppy? How did she ask him not to break her heart? Not to break their daughter's?

Hearing Matt come down the stairs five minutes later, she braced herself, still uncertain whether to say anything.

'You're keen this morning,' he commented, coming into the kitchen.

Kay glanced at him from where she was packing Poppy's lunch box. His hair was tousled, his shirt collar askew. She resisted going to straighten it for him as she usually would. He looked more tired than ever. But then he would, she supposed, having come in after midnight. 'I didn't sleep too well,' she said, going back to her task.

She'd already decided not to mention the new little friend Poppy had made, that she was keen to get to the school gates early to meet her. She'd had a mithering sense of foreboding in the pit of her stomach since Stephanie's mysterious comments. She didn't tell him about the new twist in her nightmare either, that this time she'd been able to make out the features of the person lurking in the shadows: Matt's, interposed with his brother's. Would he think her mad if she voiced her fear that it was some kind of prophecy, that her baby girl was in danger from one or both of them because of the history between them?

'Heavy night?' she asked, glancing at him again. 'You look exhausted.'

'Extremely.' Matt sighed, clearly missing the tinge of facetiousness in her voice. 'A prem baby boy with a pneumothorax. It's still touch and go, I'm afraid.'

Kay's heart caught, her thoughts swinging to the little boy she'd lost, perfect on the outside but so tiny, so underdeveloped on the inside he'd had no hope of survival. Poppy had been premature, too. Kay had agonised over that since they'd learned of her illness. She hadn't realised she'd been in labour, dismissing the contractions as Braxton Hicks. Poppy had arrived so quickly, she wondered now whether the lack of oxygen she'd suffered might have damaged her in some way. Despite reassurance from Matt, she couldn't help blaming herself, thinking that she'd failed to keep her baby safe in her womb. Picturing her daughter, so fragile as she lay in her incubator, tubes protruding from her small body, Kay's eyes suddenly filled up and she fought to blink away the tears that were obscuring her vision. Normally she would confide in Matt when she felt like this, overwhelmed by her emotions. She knew he would be the one person who would understand. Yesterday, before suspicion had set in, gnawing away inside her, breeding feelings of jealousy, doubt and mistrust, she would have turned to him. Now, she turned away.

'I'm sorry,' she said, breathing deeply and collecting up the lunch box. 'I know that must be difficult for you.' She tried to dismiss the thought niggling away at her that he might not be telling the truth about where he'd been until past midnight. If he was, he would be hurting; she knew him well enough to know that. During his many rotations in different aspects of paediatrics, he'd always said how important it was to see the child, not just the illness, and had worked at building relationships with his patients. He cared about every single one of them. She couldn't offer him comfort just now any more than she could ask for it, though. If she did, if they talked emotively, her suspicions might spill out, and she was scared of where such a conversation might lead; scared that she might truly be taking leave of her senses.

Hurrying past him without making eye contact, she headed to the hall to call up the stairs, 'Skates on, Poppy. We don't want to be late.'

Poppy, it seemed, needed no chivvying this morning, appearing in a flash from her bedroom, shoes on her feet and her face beaming. Kay's heart swelled with love for her. She'd never imagined she would see her daughter so happy on a school day.

'Careful,' Matt warned her, behind Kay. 'Hold onto the rail, sweetheart. We don't want to be scraping you up off the floor.'

'I am,' Poppy assured him, treading carefully – until she reached the third step up, then, 'Catch me,' she said, pausing to spread her arms and launch herself at him.

Matt caught her, just, murmuring, 'Jesus,' as he did. 'Do you want to give me some warning next time, Pops?' he asked her, relief flooding his features as he swung her round and planted her on her feet. 'Otherwise you'll end up flattening me.'

'No I won't, silly,' Poppy retorted, heading straight for the coat Kay was holding out for her. 'I'm as light as a feather. You said so.'

'Hmm, I'm not so sure about that now,' Matt said, his forehead creased into a doubtful frown as he crouched to zip up the coat and pull her into an embrace. 'I reckon that special diet you're on is making you grow up big and strong.'

'Will it fix me?' Poppy asked, her own little brow creased as he eased away. Seeing the likeness between them, the special bond that existed between father and daughter, Kay's chest ached unbearably. Surely he would never consider breaking that bond?

Matt closed his eyes briefly. 'No, sweetheart,' he said throatily. 'But it will help.'

Getting to his feet as Poppy nodded, seemingly satisfied, he smiled sadly at Kay and leaned in to kiss her cheek. Kay felt herself flinch. She didn't pull away, but the comfort she usually drew from being physically close to him, from the familiar smell of the crisp, clean cotton of his shirt suffused with citrusy aftershave and his own indefinable scent, was gone. It made her want to sit down and weep. Was he being unfaithful? The text she'd seen told her he might be. Yet here he was being perfectly normal, kind and caring. The man she knew him to be. Was she getting things horribly wrong, manifesting somehow her deep fear of losing the two people she couldn't contemplate living without?

'We should go. I need to catch Stephanie this morning.' She moved quickly away from him, grabbing her car keys and turning for the door.

'See you later,' Matt said behind her. 'It might be another long day, so you go ahead and eat. I'll grab something at the hospital.'

Kay's step faltered. *Talk to him. Tell him how you're feeling. Tell him why*, the sensible voice in her head urged her. But still she didn't know how, when he refused to talk about the bone of contention that was once again lodged between them: Jason. And was he likely to have a plausible explanation about a text clearly sent by a female? One with *kisses* attached. Would he even offer one? No, she couldn't do this yet. 'Okay,' she said with a casual shrug instead.

Her chest heavy, she chivvied Poppy onto the drive, waited while she gave Matt a wave and blew him a kiss, which he dutifully caught, and then helped her into the car. Her daughter was up, buoyant and bouncy. She didn't want to do anything to spoil that, not now. Not today.

Making an effort to put her doubts out of her mind, she focused on Poppy as she drove. She'd never seen her so bubbly, chattering on about the toys she and Olivia had in common, the films they both loved. 'Liv's favourite is *Toy Story*,' she said, with an approving nod. 'She has the whole box set.' Noting that her daughter's eyes were filled with awe, Kay smiled.

'She has the Disney Princess box set too,' Poppy enthused as, after parking outside the school, Kay helped her from the car. 'I think we both love that the most, but we think *Moana*'s pretty cool too.'

Pretty cool? Kay blinked in surprise. That didn't sound like Poppy. She actually sounded confident. Her friendship with her new little friend was obviously good for her.

'Can Liv come to tea today, Mummy?' Poppy asked, taking Kay's hand and skipping excitedly alongside her as they walked to the school gates.

'I think it might be a bit short notice for her mummy, sweetheart, but I'll ask, okay?'

Poppy sighed, then shrugged happily. 'Okay, she can come tomorrow.'

She was *definitely* more confident. Kay eyed her in wonderment. Her daughter had been reluctant to ask anyone to tea before now, possibly because she thought they might shy away from her. She fancied this Olivia might be a little miracle. 'So while we're on the subject, what do you fancy for tea?' she asked.

'Pizza!' Poppy exclaimed as, sensing a late April shower in the air, Kay crouched in front of her to fasten her coat higher. 'Liv likes chicken and sweetcorn, the same as me.'

'Does she indeed?' Kay smiled. 'Pizza it is then,' she said, doing a mental audit of the contents of the cupboard. Given Poppy's dietary requirements, she would have to make it from scratch with low-sodium topping and go easy on the cheese, but that was the least of her concerns.

'With chips,' Poppy added with a decisive nod.

'Sounds like a plan, but we might have to have one of your special salads instead. Chips are off the menu for the moment, remember?'

Poppy knitted her brow and had a little think. 'Can we have strawberry lollies for pudding?' she bargained, aware that there was a fresh batch in the freezer. 'I think Liv likes them, and she likes …' She stopped, her eyes growing wide with excitement. 'She's here!'

Kay laughed as Poppy almost fell over her in her haste to run and greet her new friend. Straightening up, she turned around to keep track of her – and her blood turned to ice. The little girl running towards her daughter was the image of Poppy. The same bouncy curls, the same smile. Kay felt the hairs rise on her skin as the girls linked hands and walked towards her. They could almost be twins. 'Hello, Olivia,' she managed shakily.

'Hello.' Olivia beamed her a smile, clearly not nervous about meeting her.

Her heart thumping, Kay warily scanned the girl's face. Her eyes were blue, she noticed, like Poppy's: an unusual, piercing ice blue that mirrored Matt's. A sour taste popped in her throat.

'Liv doesn't think she can come to tea today.' Poppy snapped Kay's attention back to her. 'Her mummy's at work.'

Hell, her mother! Kay hurriedly scanned the playground, but by now the bell had rung and parents were beginning to mill towards the gates. 'Excuse me,' she called to the woman she thought she had seen with Olivia, who was hurrying away, her step brisk, the hood of her parka pulled up and her head bowed. Kay called more loudly as the woman exited the playground, causing eyes to swivel in her direction.

Dammit, she *had* to talk to her. Her head reeled, her mind jerking from one frantic explanation to another. It was impossible, surely, for a child who was her own daughter's double to exist unless they were biologically related. Nausea swilling inside her, she asked a mother she knew to watch the girls into school and flew after the woman.

'Shit!' Rounding the gates to see her climbing into a car, she quickened her pace. 'Stop! Please wait!' she shouted, too late. She ground to a halt, her heart settling like a cold stone inside her as she watched the car whisk the woman away.

CHAPTER FIVE

Matthew

Pausing in the main hospital corridor to study an X-ray, looking for the distinctive cloudy appearance in the lungs of the premature baby born with neonatal respiratory distress syndrome, Matt didn't realise there was someone behind him until she cursed.

Turning around, he found a young female nurse scrabbling about trying to retrieve medical supplies from the floor. 'Sorry,' she mumbled, clearly flustered as he glanced down at her. 'So clumsy of me.'

'No problem.' Matt crouched to help her, breathing in her heady perfume as he did.

Once the equipment she'd dropped was safely gathered up, they got to their feet.

She smiled. 'Thanks.'

'Pleasure.' Matt smiled back. 'Nice perfume,' he commented. Then, realising that might be misconstrued, he added, 'I was thinking of getting some for my wife.'

'I think she'll love this. People are always commenting on it,' the nurse said, appearing untroubled. 'It's the Elegant collection, jasmine and honey. You can get it at most of the big stores, or online, obviously.'

'I'll take a look,' Matt said, and then squinted at her curiously. 'Have we met?' He knew many of the nurses here, but he couldn't remember having seen her before.

'I don't think so. I've only recently transferred here from the Queen Elizabeth in Birmingham. I work nights mostly. Rachel,' she introduced herself. 'I would offer you my hand, but …' She shrugged, nodding towards the armful of supplies she held. 'You're Dr Young, aren't you?'

Matt smiled wryly. 'That's right. My reputation obviously precedes me.'

'It does. You're the hot topic of conversation, in fact. But don't worry, it's all good. The nursing staff love you.'

He laughed. 'I'm relieved. I wouldn't want to be the topic of conversation if they'd decided they hate me.'

'Was that a newborn baby's X-ray you were looking at?' she asked him, nodding at the file he was carrying. 'I couldn't help noticing. I'm curious by nature. That's probably why I ended up dropping everything.'

'That's right. A little boy, born prematurely, unfortunately.'

'Oh no.' Rachel's eyes clouded with concern. 'Will he be all right?'

'I hope so,' Matt said, though he guessed she would know there could be no guarantees. 'He has a pneumothorax, but we're on top of it.'

'Poor little mite. Does that mean you'll have to intubate him?'

'We're going for the nasal prong option at the moment,' Matt explained. 'It's a little gentler than mechanical ventilation and allows a sufficiently high level of oxygen to be delivered. He's doing well,' he assured her.

'He'll be okay then? In the long term, I mean?'

Gathering she was genuinely interested, Matt saw no reason not to share information with her. 'I'm confident he will now, yes. He had a small bleed on the brain, which is quite common in prem babies, but it was mild and won't cause any lasting problems.'

Rachel breathed a sigh of relief. 'That's fantastic. You're amazing, do you know that?' she said, now gazing at him in awe. 'I think what you do is miraculous. Being so dedicated to helping the tiny babies in your care, I mean,' she added, as Matt shifted, feeling awkward under such gushing praise.

'Sorry.' She glanced down and back, her cheeks flushing. 'I didn't mean to act like a fangirl. It's just, I was thinking of specialising in paediatrics. I'd love to work in neonatal care eventually, but ...' She hesitated. 'I'm not sure I could handle it, to be honest.'

Matt noted the uncertainty in her eyes. Pretty eyes, he couldn't help thinking. 'You should go for it,' he advised. 'I'm guessing if you're nursing in the first place you have the right qualities. And I'm sure you could handle it if a tiny human being depended on you being the best nurse you could be.'

'Do you really think so?' She looked hopeful.

He gave her a reassuring nod. 'I do.'

She smiled delightedly. 'Thank you. They were right about you, you know.' Her gaze flicked down again. 'You really are nice.'

'Most of the time.' Matt shrugged. He wasn't perfect. Far from it. And he certainly didn't consider himself a performer of miracles. If he was, his own little girl wouldn't be facing such an uncertain future.

'I can't imagine you being anything but.' She looked him over thoughtfully. 'Can I ask you something? I would completely understand if you didn't have time.'

'Ask away,' Matt said, hoping it wasn't anything that would actually take much of his time, which he simply didn't have.

'Well, as I said, I would really love to work in neonatal care, but I realise it's going to need a lot of hard work and study ...' She paused, looking at him hesitantly. 'I wondered if you might be able to find the odd five minutes, maybe over a coffee or something, to help me out and answer any queries I might have. It's just I find that without the practical application, it's sometimes difficult to grasp the detail.'

Now Matt was the one who was hesitant. He really wasn't sure he could find time that didn't exist, and his coffee breaks only ever consisted of a few minutes taken when he was in dire need of caffeine.

'I honestly would understand if you'd rather not,' she added quickly, clearly noting his reluctant expression. 'I wouldn't be offended if you said no. I have a doctor at the QE who manages to squeeze me in, and I do interact with patients during clinical rotations, under supervision obviously, which helps, but I thought, as I'm going to be doing night shifts here …'

She paused again, possibly to draw breath, and Matt couldn't help but relent. He'd been there himself, struggling to study for his specialty certificate exam, wishing he could be more hands-on, or at least have someone he could informally bounce things off before approaching his own mentor.

'I should let you go,' she said, looking a little embarrassed and crestfallen. 'I've already taken up too much of your time.'

'No, it's okay,' Matt assured her. She was obviously keen. And as long as he made sure they only met in the hospital restaurant or on one of the wards, to forestall any gossip … He'd been on the receiving end of that once before. The clinical lead hadn't been thrilled with the disruption to A&E when the nurse concerned had transferred to another hospital. 'I am pushed for time, as you've gathered, but I'm happy to help out if and when I can.'

'Brilliant.' She practically beamed. 'Um, so how do I get hold of you?'

'Ah.' Matt nodded. Obviously she would need to do that. He was never in one place at any given time, therefore not easy to pin down. 'You could leave a message with my secretary,' he suggested.

'That would be great. Thanks. It's really appreciated,' she said, clearly relieved.

'No problem. I had better get on now, though.' He checked the time. There was an imminent arrival in A&E, called in ahead by the police, apparently: a three-month-old baby caught in the middle of a domestic. He was having to brace himself for it. It made him sick to his gut that any child should have to suffer at the hands of the people who were supposed to love and protect them. 'Look forward to speaking to you more.'

'Me too. Can I ask you one more tiny question before you go?' She batted her eyelashes theatrically, which Matt couldn't help but smile at.

'As long as it's a quick one.' He nodded, though he really was keen to get on now.

'Do you think there's any chance I could maybe stand in and watch the odd operation? I'd be as quiet as a mouse, I promise. It's just that it would really help from a practical point of view.'

Matt thought about it. 'I don't see why not,' he said at length. 'I'll have a word with one or two of my colleagues, too.'

'That would be amazing. It was lovely speaking to you, Matt. Catch you later.' Giving him another radiant smile, she hurried onwards, leaving Matt looking after her, puzzled.

He couldn't recall mentioning his Christian name. Certainly not the shortened version. Presumably she'd heard it from his fan club. He also wondered where she was actually going with the hospital supplies – syringes, scalpels, IV bags and dressings – she was carrying. She appeared to be heading towards the exit. It was out-of-date equipment, he supposed, recalling that the external sealed clinical and sharps bins could be accessed that way.

CHAPTER SIX

Kay

After spending ages trying to access Matt's home computer, using every password she could think of, Kay gave up in frustration. Why was it password-protected anyway? she wondered, going agitatedly back up to the bedroom to make absolutely sure she'd put everything back exactly as he'd left it. He wasn't over-fastidious about the way he arranged his wardrobe, but she would know if someone had been through hers. She knew how she would feel, too: devastated and furious in turn that the person she loved and trusted didn't trust her. What was she doing here, apart from feeling appalled with herself for invading his privacy and going through his personal things? She wasn't even sure what she was looking for; he was hardly likely to carry photographic evidence of another woman in his suit pocket – her heart wrenched violently as she thought of the photo he carried of her and Poppy. She'd thought she might find a forgotten restaurant bill or receipt for some gift that hadn't been for her. There was nothing.

She was going mad. She truly was. If infidelity could drive a person to passionate acts of despair, then Kay felt inches away from just such an act. Was she wrong? No, she couldn't be, could she? She might have been able to convince herself that Matt's behaviour recently was understandable given his rift with his brother, that her suspicious imagination was running away with her, but she'd seen the text on his phone. She couldn't pretend to herself that she hadn't. And what about Olivia? She hadn't imagined her, had she?

She'd factored in that Jason might be involved, carelessly sowing his oats, as he would, but the fact that the girl looked *so* like Poppy … She could be her sister. That was a fact she couldn't escape.

Doing a final sweep of the room, she walked back across it to rearrange the book on Matt's bedside table, which she was sure he'd left at an angle, and then rushed downstairs to grab her car keys and head out to the school. She had to stay healthy, hang onto her sanity. Poppy was her first priority, even if she wasn't Matt's. Her heart ached at the thought, because Poppy *had* always been his first priority – alongside his work. Or so she'd believed.

Her nerves jangling as she waited for the children to come out, she noticed Stephanie walking through the school gates. 'Hi, Steph.' She smiled as her friend approached, and tried hard to pretend that everything in her life wasn't suddenly spiralling out of control. 'How's things?'

'Challenging. When is motherhood ever not?' Stephanie replied with a roll of her eyes. 'One of my two little darlings has been painting – other children, unfortunately. Ben's teacher rang to tell me. I'm expecting to be hauled in and told to sit on the naughty step. How are things with you? Have you found out anything about Poppy's little friend yet?'

'No, not yet,' Kay said lightly. 'She might be coming for tea, though, if her mother agrees.' Pausing, she glanced around the playground. She couldn't see any sign of the woman who'd dropped Olivia off.

'It's inescapable, isn't it, the likeness between them?' Steph mused. 'Uncanny.'

Kay looked back at her to find her friend scanning her face in obvious concern.

'So what do you think Matt will make of her?' Steph ventured warily.

Luckily Kay was saved by the bell again before she was forced to answer that question. She would like nothing better than to confide in Steph, but she couldn't bring herself to say the words that were buzzing around in her head like demented bees. Matt had cheated on her. Had been cheating on her for years. Had she always known it deep down and chosen to ignore it? Suddenly she felt sick to her soul. Her daughter needed her daddy. She might be in remission now, but how long would that last? She couldn't open this can of worms with Poppy so very poorly. Wouldn't that make *her* the selfish one? But how was she to avoid it? she wondered, watching the children spill out into the playground as the main doors burst open.

Apprehension ran the length of her spine as she spotted Poppy and Olivia coming towards her, hands clasped and looking inseparable. Seeing a woman in a green parka heading towards them, her heart lurched. Quickly she caught up with her. 'Hi,' she called chummily.

The woman turned with a warm smile. 'Hi. You're Poppy's mum, I take it. I'm Hannah, Olivia's—' She stopped as Poppy tugged on her hand.

'Can Liv come to tea, Hannah?' she asked, glancing up at her hopefully. 'We're having pizza. Chicken and sweetcorn. Mummy's making it specially. It's Liv's favourite. Isn't it, Liv?'

'Yes,' Olivia concurred excitedly. 'Can I go, Hannah?' She made beguiling eyes at the woman. 'Can I?'

'Well …' Hannah pondered. 'I suppose. I'll have to pick her up at about quarter to six, though,' she said, glancing back to Kay. 'Her mum's expecting her at six.'

'Yay!' Both girls whooped simultaneously. Then, 'What shall we play?' Olivia asked Poppy.

'Barbie dolls!' Poppy decided.

Kay marvelled at how much her daughter's confidence had grown. Poppy was blossoming before her eyes. But as she looked at the girls, heads bent close as they whispered together, icy foreboding crashed through her and her heart froze. Could they really be so similar if they hadn't been fathered by the same man?

'They're obviously keen,' Hannah said. 'I think we might have had tears and tantrums if I'd said no. I'm Olivia's childminder, by the way, as you probably gathered. Nice to meet you. I can see where Poppy gets her looks from. She's the image of you,' she went on, looking curiously at Kay and then turning back to the girls. 'They're very alike, aren't they?'

Kay caught the quizzical look in her eyes. 'I know.' She settled her own gaze on the girls. 'It's amazing, isn't it?'

'Spooky, too.' Hannah filled the ensuing silence. 'I often have people telling me they saw me in such-and-such a place when I was never there. Apparently I have a double walking around town. It gives me the willies, it really does.'

'I think it would me too.' Kay made herself smile and then looked at her watch. 'I'd better get off. I don't want to waste precious Barbie playtime, and I have to pick up some groceries on the way.'

'Gosh, yes. I'd better dash too.' Hannah checked her own watch. 'My sister's coming over with her two little ones and I have loads to do.'

Kay seized her chance. She'd been about to ask for Olivia's mother's name and address, but … 'Why don't you let me drop her back home?' she suggested. 'That will save you a trip and I'd quite like to meet her mother.'

Hannah hesitated. 'I suppose that would be okay,' she decided, after a pause. 'As long as you're sure, and as long as she's home by six.' She glanced again at the two girls, then leaned towards Kay. 'She tends to be a bit overprotective of Olivia. That possibly has something to do with her being a bit frail as a baby. Personally, I would be less inclined to wrap her up in—'

'Frail how?' Kay asked, alarmed.

'A chest infection. I'm not sure of the details, but apparently it wasn't picked up. She seems fine now, though, bouncing with health.'

Kay felt relief flood through her. She'd hardly dared acknowledge the thought, but if the girls were related, then wouldn't there be a high probability of Olivia being a blood match? That she might even be a tissue match? She was terrified of what the girls sharing familial genes might mean for her marriage, but if she'd been tempted to ignore it, she knew in that moment with certainty that she couldn't. If there was the slightest possibility that this little girl could help her daughter should she need a kidney transplant, then she had no choice but to pursue it, whatever the consequences might be.

CHAPTER SEVEN

Matthew

Matt's gut clenched as he examined the baby brought into A&E, noting immediately that her skin had a pale bluish tone and that she seemed to be having difficulty staying awake. According to the mother, she'd also been vomiting. Added to the fact that she was feeding poorly and had previously been brought in with breathing problems and a suspected seizure – all classic symptoms of shaken baby syndrome – it appeared that the child might be a victim of abuse. It wasn't ever clear-cut how these things happened. Sometimes it was because one or both parents were suffering extreme stress and simply couldn't cope. Sometimes, though, abuse was the result of negligence or pure evil, the abuser getting some kind of twisted kick out of it. This was part of the job he hated. He certainly didn't envy the police their role as first responders.

'So what do you reckon?' asked Jess, the female officer who'd come in with the mother.

'I'm not one hundred per cent certain yet, but possibly shaken baby syndrome,' Matt told her, hating that he had to give her the worst-case scenario, but knowing that he was legally required to do so, and that the child's life might depend on it.

'There's some slight bruising,' he went on, indicating the discoloration to the baby's face, which was barely noticeable unless you were looking for it. 'Other than that, no outward sign of injury. There may be other injuries that aren't immediately visible, though: bleeding in the brain, spinal cord damage. We need to do some X-rays to rule out fractures of the ribs, skull and other bones, including any prior fractures.'

'Jesus.' Jess looked as sick as he felt. 'I'd better put a call out to step up the search for the boyfriend.'

'The father?' Matt asked.

'Unfortunately, yes,' Jess growled. 'Just out of prison, proven history of domestic violence, nice amiable sort of guy, you know.'

Matt sensed her frustration and couldn't blame her. So often the legal system left them powerless to prevent abusers doing the same thing over and over again. 'Has the mother offered any information?' he asked hopefully.

Jess sighed heavily and shook her head. 'She's still sobbing her heart out, blaming herself. We're not getting much sense out of her yet.'

Matt glanced towards one of the curtained cubicles, where he could hear the woman crying. He guessed from the injuries she'd sustained herself – severe bruising to her cheek, a fractured wrist – that she'd tried and failed to stop whatever had gone on. Whether the baby was deemed to be safe in her care, though … Christ, he really did wonder at the mentality of people with a predilection for bullying and violence.

Reminded of his brother, whose relentless bullying had finally driven *him* to violence, he breathed in hard, trying to dismiss the recollection and the raw anger the loaded comment Jason had made the morning after their cousin's wedding had evoked. Jason had gone off to the States eventually, grabbed his chance when an opening had come up. Matt had thanked God. He'd had no contact with him since. He wanted nothing to do with him, wished he could be free of him, but doubted he ever would. The suspicion Jason had planted in his mind that day had germinated no matter how hard he'd tried to dismiss it as lies.

On learning from his father that Jason was back in the UK, his heart had sunk to the pit of his stomach. His brother had shown 'remarkable acumen' while he'd been away, apparently, convincing practices and hospitals across the US to invest in Biochem's medically advanced products. In relating Jason's success, his father had clearly been trying to elicit some interest from Matt in his brother's life. The fact was, Matt *wasn't* interested. Jason had bullied him relentlessly when they were children, which could be put down to simple sibling rivalry. If he had resented him in childhood, though, Matt going out with and then marrying his ex-girlfriend had obviously ramped up his jealousy. He seemed to hate him.

'You don't look very thrilled for him,' his father had commented, obviously disappointed at Matt's indifference. Matt had felt for him. With his recent unstable angina diagnosis, their father wanted the rift between them to close. He was probably hoping that Jason would eventually take over the running of the company he himself had been a founder member of, and that the two brothers would get on. Matt couldn't see a time when *that* would happen. He'd never really hated anyone, but he didn't like the person his brother was. Now that Jason was back to 'crack' the UK market where Biochem's current operating officer had failed, however, he might not be able to avoid him. Jason would be dealing with NHS hospitals, seeping into the fabric of Matt's life. He'd already started. He'd come home after five years and the first person he called was Kay. Why? How the bloody hell could Matt ask her about it without seeming to be making accusations? With Poppy so ill, he couldn't bring himself to do that. For her sake, he had no choice but to maintain the facade.

'I'd better go and check how she's doing.' Nodding towards the cubicle where the baby's mother was still quietly crying, Jess pulled his attention back to the crisis before them. 'Will you get someone to grab me when you have any further info?'

'Will do,' Matt promised. Turning his gaze back to the baby girl, he couldn't help but be reminded of the first time he saw Poppy. As he'd gazed down at her, drinking in her softly curled eyelashes, her perfect Cupid lips, he'd felt something shift inside him. She'd stolen his heart completely. He'd sworn then he would kill anyone who harmed her. Jason should be made aware of that.

CHAPTER EIGHT

Kay

Kay's stomach churned with apprehension as Olivia carried her plate carefully across the kitchen to hand it to her. 'Thank you, Mrs Young. That was scrummy,' she said politely.

'Call me Kay.' Kay smiled, her apprehension growing as she met the eyes of the girl who could easily be her own child's sister. 'As you're Poppy's "best friend in the whole world",' she said, quoting Poppy's words on the drive home, 'we should be friends too, shouldn't we?'

'Yes.' Olivia nodded happily, her eyes straying towards the chocolate mug cakes Kay had made as a treat. They were low in fat and made with sweetener, but surprisingly tasty.

'Do you like chocolate cake, Liv?' Kay asked her.

'Uh huh.' Nodding fervently, Olivia widened her eyes, looking so like Poppy, Kay's heart missed a beat. They were related. They had to be. She studied her intently, possibly a little too intently. Looking uncomfortable under the scrutiny, the girl dropped her gaze, and Kay warned herself to stop. She was an innocent, just a child. She'd done nothing wrong.

'Finished, Mummy,' Poppy declared, having made a great effort to eat all her food – because Olivia had cleared her plate and she didn't want to be seen to be doing differently, Kay guessed. Having Olivia as a friend was definitely good for her.

'Excellent.' She smiled encouragingly as, following by example, Poppy carried her plate over to the dishwasher too.

'Can we have our cakes now?' she asked eagerly, her eyes also travelling towards the chocolate treats.

'Ooh, I should think so,' Kay said, then laughed when the two girls whooped in unison.

'And then we can play Barbie Doggy Daycare in the Wendy house,' Poppy enthused, skidding back to the table with Olivia as Kay carried the cakes across.

'As long as you wrap up warm,' Kay reminded her. Her daughter was definitely blossoming in the other girl's company, confident and carefree, which was something Kay had longed to see. She was happy, the nervous uncertainty gone from her eyes, the too-adult reassurance that was there whenever she thought her mummy and daddy were worried about her. Whatever happened, Kay realised, she couldn't do anything to damage this relationship. To do that might be to damage her daughter.

Once the girls were dressed appropriately and huddled safely in the Wendy house, she went back inside and grabbed her laptop. Sitting at the kitchen table where she could keep an eye out of the window, she set about googling the phenomenon of unrelated twins. Trepidation gnawing away inside her, she browsed various sites, finally settling on an article that explained how any two people taken at random shared approximately 99.5 per cent of their gene sequence. Everyone was related on some level, she read; even total strangers could share as much DNA as cousins. There were many photographs, showing people from opposite sides of the world who were completely unrelated, yet with the same face shape and features. But Poppy and Olivia weren't on opposite sides of the world, they were here in the small town of Tedbury in Worcestershire. What were the chances? Minuscule, she knew. The two of them must be related, fathered by the same man.

Feeling hot and clammy, she buried her head in her hands. She had to talk to Olivia's mother. But once the woman knew who Kay was, was she likely to confirm that Matt was Olivia's father? If she did, how would Kay then tell her about Poppy's situation? She had no idea where she would find the strength to go through with this, but she *had* to establish who this child was.

It might destroy her marriage. A marriage that had been good. Or so she'd thought. One that was still good. Or so she hoped, even now. Had she truly deluded herself so badly? All these *years* … She stifled a wretched sob. How could her marriage ever have been good if Matt had had an affair with another woman, made a child with another woman at the same time Kay had fallen pregnant with Poppy? Whatever their relationship had meant to her, it obviously hadn't meant anything to him.

Did she believe that? That Matt was the sort of man who would lie and cheat and deceive? That he cared so little for her? In her heart she didn't, but in her head … She had to do this. There might be no going back for her and Matt, no way to go forwards, yet it might save her daughter. She couldn't walk away from it.

CHAPTER NINE

Amelia

Exhausted after too many hours on her feet juggling her job and her uni course, and wondering whether she was truly capable of achieving what she'd set out to, Amelia felt the need to touch base with her mum. As she walked into the hospice, she steeled herself, still finding it hard to accept that her mother was here. She approached her room and found the door open. The staff had just brought in evening tea, but her mother sat staring vacantly out of the window, probably unaware the tea was there. Lost in her memories, she often didn't even register her daughter's presence.

Tugging in a breath, Amelia forced her face into a smile. Her mother gave no indication she had even noticed her presence. Crouching beside her, Amelia took hold of her hand, tracing her thumb softly over the back of it. The skin was almost translucent, like thin tissue paper. Her mother's face was sallow, her eyes yellow, more noticeably than the last time Amelia had visited. She was clutching a familiar framed photograph in her other hand, the one she kept close and seemed to gather some comfort from. She would become agitated if it was out of her sight for long.

Amelia gave the hand she held a small squeeze. 'How are you, Mum?'

Her mother's gaze came slowly to hers, her expression confused, as if she couldn't quite place her. Amelia scanned her face, her heart aching. She looked much older than her age. Like someone whose mind might have been ravaged by dementia rather than deep-rooted grief.

Her mother stared at her for a long, curious moment, then asked, 'Is your sister coming?' It was the question she always asked.

Amelia's heart splintered. She clearly recognised her daughter, but she wasn't the daughter she longed to see. Trying hard not to mind, Amelia buried her own grief. 'No, Mum. Not today. She's studying. Maybe tomorrow.' She smiled encouragingly, as she usually did, allowing her mum to hold onto the hope that Kelsey would come.

Her mother seemed to accept that, answering with a small nod. There was a flicker of something in her eyes, though, a question, as if she were trying to catch hold of the memories that floated frustratingly out of her reach.

Amelia hoped she never did. She was glad she'd spoken, at least. Often she didn't, continuing to stare into the distance instead. She was somewhere else, somewhere her nightmares wouldn't haunt her. Unable to cope with what had happened, her mind had simply closed down, just as her kidneys and her liver had. Some people would think she'd brought that on herself, drinking far too much for far too long. She was only five foot three, just sixty years old. Her system simply couldn't take the alcohol she'd poured into it. It had been her way of coping, her crutch, what had got her through after their dad died. She had blamed herself for his suicide. It was after losing Kelsey that she really hit it hard, drinking everything she could get her hands on, anything that would blot out the pain. She hadn't been a bad mother, abusive or rolling drunk. Comatose sometimes, but never aggressive. A functioning alcoholic, Al-Anon had told them. Kelsey and Amelia had tried to make her stop drinking, Kelsey most of all, because she'd had more patience than Amelia ever had. Amelia had learned patience since. She was an expert now at being patient.

'Would you like me to fetch you some more tea, Mum?' she asked, aware that the cup she'd been brought was growing cold. It was something to do, something to say to fill the silence.

'It's her birthday soon,' her mother replied absently.

'I know.' Amelia never forgot her sister's birthday. In times past, she and Kelsey would have done something together: gone to the pub or out nightclubbing, or maybe just stayed in watching a film together, depending on finances. All that had changed when *he* had come into her sister's life, pushing Amelia out. Kelsey hadn't been able to see that he'd been working to alienate her, that he'd wanted her all to himself. Until the day he'd got bored with her, of course, and then he'd just walked away, because men could.

'I'm not sure what to buy her.' Her mother's panic-filled eyes came back to hers.

Amelia swallowed back the shard of grit in her throat. 'I'll choose something,' she said, forcing a smile.

'But not a skateboard.' Her mum's expression was alarmed suddenly, her mind shooting way back to when Kelsey and Amelia had both been given skateboards for Christmas. Their mum had expressly forbidden them to go into the town centre, where the other kids were street skating. They'd gone anyway, although they could barely balance on their boards. Kelsey had ended up with a broken arm after falling. 'You could have fractured your skulls!' their mum had yelled. She'd been furious; the skateboards had been confiscated. Amelia understood now that she'd only been looking out for them, but they'd hated her then. She didn't hate her now. She just wished she'd been able to carry on looking out for them.

'Not a skateboard,' she agreed, humouring her. 'Some jewellery, maybe.'

'Earrings.' Her mum nodded decisively. 'She likes earrings.'

She had, until she'd stopped wearing jewellery because *he* hadn't wanted her to wear anything that might make her look attractive to other men.

Amelia eased the photograph from her hand as her mum fell silent again, her mind plainly having moved on, or further back. Amelia was never sure where she might be. Two teenage girls looked back at her out of the frame, both wearing dangly earrings, both with their mousy manes highlighted bleached-blonde, both smiling, each determined that, despite their humble background, they would make something of themselves. They'd had their hair done together, done everything together. Sworn they would be there for each other for ever, sisters supporting each other, protecting each other. They'd made their pact shortly before this photograph was taken. But Amelia had failed her sister. She hadn't protected her. Hadn't known how to stop what she could see happening before her eyes. She'd begged Kelsey, pleaded with her, but in the end she hadn't been able to persuade her to stop seeing him.

She winced inwardly as she recalled how Kelsey had screamed at her, her face livid, her violet eyes wild. 'It's you who's the controlling one. Why can't you just accept that I'm in a serious relationship? We're not joined at the fucking hip, Amelia. I want my own life!' All this her sister had said, careless of the pain she was causing her. Her mind had been poisoned against her. She hadn't seen Amelia as her friend any more, the one who truly cared for her, who always would. She'd seen her as the enemy, the person who would come between *him* and her.

Closing her eyes, Amelia felt her throat thicken, bitter regret kicking in as it did every time she remembered Kelsey the last time she'd seen her. She hadn't wanted to leave her after that heartbreaking argument, their final words to each other. She'd sobbed until she thought her heart would break, wanting to hold her and never let her go. She couldn't, of course. The bond between them had been broken. Kelsey hadn't meant to be so cruel. She hadn't been responsible for the hurtful words that had spilled from her mouth. She'd been manipulated, her mind twisted.

Amelia hoped in her heart that Kelsey would forgive her, that she would realise that what she was doing now, she was doing for both of them. It was taking all her energy, but she would achieve her aim. It was time for her to put things right. Kelsey would see then how much she did love her. More than a man who'd used her only for his own satisfaction ever could. He would realise the enormity of what he'd done, that he had to pay. Kay was nice, friendly towards her. That would make things easier.

'I have to go, Mum,' she whispered, leaning to press a soft kiss to her cheek. 'I'll come again soon.'

There was no answer from her mother, but Amelia saw her fingers move softly over the photo when she placed it back in her lap, as if caressing Kelsey's face. She was doing this for her mother, too, although she would never know it. That thought saddened her to the depths of her soul.

CHAPTER TEN

Matthew

Climbing out of his car, Matt approached the house with trepidation. There was a distance between him and Kay that hadn't been there before. It was all his delightful brother's fault for reappearing and trying to insert himself into their lives. Did he have any idea what they were going through? What Poppy had endured, and would have to endure in future?

Kay hadn't mentioned it, but shooting off that leaflet about the tissue typing in a fit of pique would no doubt have exacerbated the situation. It was a juvenile thing to do. He'd promised himself he would bury the past, and then had pointedly dug it up again. Couldn't he have at least softened the blow? Added a note, making her aware it was a standard information leaflet? Kay wasn't stupid, far from it. She would have read between the lines, got the not-so-subtle message. After years of refusing to acknowledge what his brother had told him, telling himself he could live with it, why was he handling this so badly? Because he knew the truth would have to come out, and he wasn't sure he could handle that.

Now he had to break the news that, having considered Poppy's steroid resistance, along with the series of biochemical tests they'd carried out, the nephrology consultant had rescheduled her biopsy for as soon as possible, while she was still healthy. How would Kay take it? How would Poppy deal with it? Bravely, he suspected, wondering not for the first time how it was that children could sometimes be so caring of their parents' feelings when parents were so bloody inept at considering their children's. Matt didn't often pray, but he had today, hoping that God would see fit to answer his prayers and allow his daughter to thrive, to blossom into the beautiful woman it was obvious she would become. He could hardly bear to contemplate how he would cope if her kidney function suddenly declined or her kidneys failed completely. To keep her healthy, she would need albumin injections to make up for the protein lost in her urine, diuretics, antibiotics to help fight infection, plus growth hormone injections. Her diet would need to be rigorously monitored, which would fall largely to Kay, since he worked such godawful hours. Ultimately, removal of one or both kidneys would follow, and then dialysis until transplant became an option, assuming a suitable match could be found, something they would have to pray for. He smiled wryly as he recalled Rachel's unwarranted praise, her imagining that what he did was miraculous. Christ, what he would give to be able to perform a miracle right now.

Pushing his key into the lock, he opened the front door and stepped into the hall, and was surprised when Poppy didn't run to greet him as she usually would. She wouldn't be expecting him, he reminded himself, going straight to the kitchen – where Kay shot up from a chair at the table so fast she almost gave him a coronary.

'Bad timing?' he asked, glancing narrowly from her to her laptop. He wondered whether Jason had also started emailing her.

'No.' She reached to close the lid. 'Just tweaking my timetable,' she said, turning away from him to put the kettle on. 'What brings you home so early? You're never normally here at this time.'

Matt walked across to her. She seemed tense, edgy. Was that any surprise, though, given his attitude and the leaflet he'd sent her? He debated the wisdom of delivering the news about the biopsy now. A young mother had gone into premature labour, possibly too premature to make the baby's survival viable. She was on her way to the hospital now and he would need to be there. Kay would have questions he didn't have time to answer. 'Where's Poppy?' he asked, trying to gauge her mood.

Kay moved away from him towards the sink. 'In her Wendy house,' she said, nodding towards the garden and then grabbing mugs from the dish rack. 'I didn't want to be overprotective, and the weather's quite mild, so …'

She turned to face him, her eyes filled with anxiety, then moved away, turning the tap on, swilling the cups, which were obviously already clean if they were in the rack.

Matt felt his heart sink. She was finding things to do to avoid looking at him. 'Are you okay?' he asked. 'You seem a bit … agitated.'

'I'm not agitated.' Kay glanced at him over her shoulder. 'I'd say it was you who was agitated, Matt. Apparently angry with me because your brother called me rather than you. Being short with me on the phone yesterday when I'd actually called offering to put myself out and bring you your mobile.'

Guilt kicking in, Matt took a step towards her. 'I know. I didn't mean to … Look, I'm sorry. It's just that Jason calling—'

'Did you want to see Poppy?' Kay asked, turning to face him. 'She's not long gone out, but I can go and fetch her.'

Matt squinted at her. That was a swift change of subject if ever he'd heard one. 'No, don't worry,' he said tiredly. 'I'll go out and—'

He stopped, cursing silently as his phone rang. The ringtone told him it was the hospital calling, which couldn't be worse timing. 'One second,' he said, pulling it from his pocket.

His registrar confirmed that the young mother had arrived, and it looked as if the baby was also imminent. 'On my way,' Matt told him. Ending the call, he eyed Kay apologetically. She looked wary, which he frankly didn't understand.

'An emergency?' she asked.

'Afraid so.' He drew in a breath, and decided against telling her what the emergency was, thinking it too emotive a subject right now. 'I'll try and get back early. We'll have a chat then.'

'That would be nice.' Kay smiled shortly. 'I won't hold my breath, though, given the emergency.' She nodded towards his phone as he pocketed it.

And now Matt was definitely confused. Was that sarcasm in her tone? Had he done something to kick this whole thing off? Yes, he'd reacted badly to his brother calling, but he'd done nothing to warrant what had happened at that damn wedding. Apart from failing to give her the child she'd so desperately wanted, he reminded himself, swallowing back the bitter taste in his mouth.

'I should go,' he said, hopelessness washing through him. He'd fought for her once, fought his brother, fought his jealousy, his inclination to do what he wanted with whoever he wanted, just as Jason did, which everyone else seemed to think acceptable. He didn't think he could keep fighting, not if it wasn't him she wanted.

Kay held his gaze for a second. Matt was sure he could see tears in her eyes, but for the first time in a long time, he didn't know how to react. Were they tears of regret? Sympathy? His gut wrenched. Were they falling apart? Now, with Poppy's future so precarious? All because Jason had swung back into town? He wasn't sure he believed it. Had no idea how he would deal with it. 'Kay …' He moved towards her again.

Kay looked away, towards the hall, as the landline rang. 'You need to go,' she reminded him. 'And I need to get that. I'm expecting a call from the university.'

Wiping a hand over his brow in frustration, Matt turned around to watch her go, then headed after her. He hesitated at her PC, his eyes flicking to the hall; then, feeling not great about doing it, he eased the lid up and woke the laptop.

Seeing what she'd been looking at, he furrowed his brow, his confusion mounting. Why on earth would she be searching sites about unrelated twins? Course material? he wondered. At least she didn't seem to be swapping emails with Jason. He supposed that was something. Should he check her email?

No. Sucking in a breath, he closed the lid. They needed to talk, he knew they did. If this was the start of what he'd been dreading might happen one day, then they had to. The truth was, though, he was too terrified to broach the subject. What if she truly didn't want him? If she preferred Jason and always had? Where would that leave Poppy? Yes, Matt worked too many damn hours, but his daughter was everything to him. She needed the stability of having her father in her life, now more than ever. She needed him here.

Did Kay? He'd thought she did. His chest constricting, he glanced at her as he walked past her to the front door.

Her dazzling emerald eyes were full of hurt, but she met his gaze and smiled tremulously at him, which confounded him, dissipating the anger unfurling inside him. Did she love him? Had she ever? How could he ask her?

CHAPTER ELEVEN

Kay

Blissfully unaware of anything amiss, the girls were chattering happily in the back of the car as Kay pulled up in front of Olivia's house. Her nerves were in shreds, not least because of Matt arriving home while Olivia was yards away from him outside, *and* while she was researching information she wanted to keep from him, at least until she knew more. She couldn't make accusations without knowing she was on firm ground. Yet she almost had. He'd been hurt by the sarcasm he must have heard in her tone when he'd said he would try to get back early. She'd been on the verge of confronting him. Asking him exactly why he was treating her like *she'd* done something wrong. And what would she have done then? Fetched Olivia in from the garden and paraded her in front of him as evidence? How unfair would that have been on the girl, on Poppy? And what would *he* have done? Offered up some kind of explanation? Denied any knowledge of her? Did he even know about her? The thought occurred that he actually might not. In which case, where did they go from there?

Swallowing back her apprehension, she surveyed the property, an ordinary detached house on a pleasant suburban road, much like their own. Not the sort of house you would imagine might feature in your worst nightmare.

'Ready, Liv?' Arranging her face into a bright smile, she twisted to check on her.

'Uh huh.' Olivia reached to unbuckle her belt. 'Can Poppy come to play at my house tomorrow, Kay?' she asked, her eyes wide and beguiling, and so like Poppy's that Kay's heart squeezed painfully inside her.

'I think that depends on your mummy, sweetheart. She might have other plans,' she pointed out with a regretful smile.

'Will you ask her, Mummy?' Poppy piped up. '*Please?* She's bound to say yes if you ask her.'

Kay wasn't so sure about that. This meeting wasn't going to be easy for either of them. Suddenly she wasn't sure she could go through with it. She was tempted to simply drop Olivia off and drive off. Take Poppy and run away from all of this. But there was no way to run away from her illness. She was here to establish whether Olivia was related to Poppy. Given how closely related she suspected she was, she might be the best match possible. This meeting could offer an opportunity for her daughter but might also mean the end of her marriage at a time when Poppy needed stability in her life. She needed her daddy. Kay felt a sharp stab of pain as she imagined them splitting up and Matt leaving. She needed her husband, too. Was Matt aware of how much? Of how much she loved him? That she could never imagine a day when she wouldn't? 'We'll see,' she said, her throat tight. 'I'll have to have a little chat with her first.'

'Oh. Okay.' Poppy shrugged. 'Can I come with you and play with Liv while you're chatting?' she asked, perfectly reasonably.

Kay's heart fluttered with anxiety. Poppy was already scrambling to unfasten her belt. She could hardly tell her she had to wait in the car. She'd rather her daughter wasn't here at all, but there'd been no way to avoid bringing her. 'Come on then, but best behaviour,' she warned her.

Once out of the car, Poppy and Olivia raced on ahead of her up the garden path to the front door, while Kay's feet dragged like lead weights beneath her. She sucked in a fortifying breath as the door swung open and a woman appeared, smiling expectantly.

Kay studied her curiously. She was in her late thirties, possibly even her early forties, and looked very businesslike, dressed in a stylish suit and wearing her caramel-coloured hair in a short stylish cut. She was not what Kay had expected. But then she wasn't sure what she *had* expected. Someone younger than herself, she supposed, exuding sexuality, unlike Kay, who felt distinctly unsexy. Was she? Was that why their sex life had waned, and not because of the worry, guilt and exhaustion, as she had imagined?

Gathering herself, she said nervously, 'Hi. I'm Kay, Poppy's mum, and I, um …' She faltered, seeing the woman's smile disappear as she glanced down, looking confusedly between Poppy and Olivia. 'Do you think we could have a quick chat?' she pressed on, hoping the woman would glean that they very much needed to.

The woman hesitated, and then replied, 'Of course.' Her smile was tight now, as if she too was girding herself for whatever Kay had to say. 'Hello, Poppy. It's lovely to meet you,' she said, stepping back from the door.

'It's lovely to meet you as well, Mrs Taylor,' Poppy replied, remembering her manners as she and Olivia filed past.

'Please come in.' The woman's eyes returned to Kay's. Although there was uncertainty in them, there was no hostility as Kay had feared there would be.

'Right, girls.' Closing the door, she clapped her hands. 'Who's for milkshake?'

'Me!' both girls said in unison.

'Actually, Poppy can't.' Kay's heart sank as she guessed how disappointed her daughter would be. 'She's on a special low-sodium diet, so I have to be careful to check the ingredients,' she explained.

'Oh.' The woman frowned sympathetically. 'How about just milk then, Poppy?' She smiled encouragingly down at her. 'I have some home-made cookies, too. They're definitely low salt and sugar.'

'Can I, Mummy?' Poppy checked with her, and Kay thanked God that her daughter was so easy-natured, even now, when she had every right not to be.

'Sounds perfect.' She gulped back the lump of emotion she was dangerously close to giving in to.

'Upstairs, then, girls,' the woman urged them. 'Wash your hands, and then you can show Poppy your room, Liv. I'll bring the milk and cookies up. Don't make too much noise though.'

'We won't,' Poppy and Olivia assured her in synch as they both charged excitedly up.

'I'm Nicole,' the woman introduced herself once the children were safely on the landing. Her eyes held Kay's, quietly assessing her.

'Pleased to meet you.' Kay shook the hand she offered. 'I think.'

'Quite,' Nicole responded stiffly, and turned to lead the way to the kitchen.

It was a contemporary, functional room, but no less homely for that. With a combination of black and grey cupboards, splashbacks and worktops, a large wooden island in the centre and splashes of colour everywhere, it looked cosy and inviting. Kay suspected it reflected Nicole's personality. Who was she? Did Matt sit at the island with her, sharing intimate dinners? All those times he'd said he would eat at the hospital, or else grab a takeaway, had he been here instead?

'It's uncanny, isn't it, the likeness between them?' she commented, as Nicole moved efficiently around, extracting milk from the fridge, cookies from a cupboard.

'Very,' Nicole answered sparingly. She stopped halfway across the kitchen, a laden tray in her hands and her eyes again holding Kay's, a long, searching look this time, causing goosebumps to prickle her skin. 'I'll just take this up.' She nodded towards the stairs. 'Grab a seat. I'll only be a minute.

Seating herself unsteadily on a stool at the island, Kay scanned the drawings fastened to a corkboard on one of the walls. A five-year-old's depiction of her world: colourful rainbows and houses, stick people with smiling faces. All innocuous, yet so like Poppy's drawings, Kay's heart wrenched afresh. Her gaze settled on one picture in particular, of a square house, a bright yellow sun rising above the red roof. Two stick people holding hands outside it, a small one and a tall one. The tall one wore a triangular skirt. This, then, was Mummy. Where was Daddy? Why wasn't he in the picture?

'She's very talented, isn't she?' Nicole came back into the kitchen, startling her.

Kay composed herself. 'She is.' She smiled, and paused, then forced herself to open the conversation there would be no turning back from. 'I bet her father's very proud of her.'

Nicole came around the kitchen island to face her. Her expression was inscrutable, her eyes narrowed as they searched hers. She didn't sit down. 'There's no father on the scene. I'm a single parent. Olivia's adopted,' she added bluntly. 'Before you say whatever it is you've come to, you should know she means the world to me. Are you her mother?'

CHAPTER TWELVE

Matthew

On his way back into the neonatal unit, Matt looked up as someone called to him along the corridor. 'Evening. Anything interesting?' Rachel said brightly, coming towards him. 'The case notes you were engrossed in.' She indicated the file he'd been studying as he eyed her in confusion.

'Oh, right.' He nodded. 'Sorry, I was miles away.'

'So I gathered. Nothing too worrying, I hope?'

Wiping a hand over his face, Matt attempted to concentrate on anything but his home life, which almost overnight seemed to be falling apart. 'It is, I'm afraid.' Realising that Rachel was looking at him expectantly, he explained, 'A baby boy born at twenty-five weeks.'

'My God.' She stared at him, shocked. 'But that's under six and a half months.'

Matt nodded, swallowing tightly as he pictured the child, so small, yet fighting for life. He dealt with premature babies on a daily basis. His heart had wrenched when he'd seen this child, though, the reminder of the son he and Kay should have had hitting him like a physical blow to his chest. Poppy hadn't been quite so premature, but still she'd had to fight hard for her life. He and Kay had clung to hope, clung to each other. When the future had seemed so unbearably uncertain, their consolation was that they'd had a deep understanding of each other's pain and fears. He'd thought they did still, up until recently.

'Sorry,' he said, drawing in a breath. 'I'm a bit distracted.'

'I'm not surprised.' Rachel looked him over sympathetically. 'Do you think he's going to make it?'

'I, er …' Matt kneaded his forehead, wished to God that the thoughts rattling around in his mind would stop. He couldn't allow himself to be distracted, not while he was here. The people he worked with depended on him to do his job to the best of his ability at all times. The patients did. This child did. 'Honestly, I'm not sure,' he admitted. 'We managed to resuscitate him, but babies born so early have a low chance of survival. Even then, they can often end up with profound disabilities. The need for twenty-four-hour care and precise calculation relating to that care is constant.'

Rachel nodded, understanding. 'Poor you,' she said, reaching out to him. 'It must be so difficult for you, wondering what their futures might be.'

Matt looked down at the hand she'd placed on his arm, trying not to read anything into it. It was a gesture of comfort; that was all. 'More difficult for the parents,' he said, acutely aware of the pain they would be going through. 'The hardest part of the job is not being able to promise them they'll leave with a healthy baby.'

'That must be so awful for them after all the anticipation. Awful for you, too. I'm so sorry, Matt,' Rachel said, her eyes filled with concern.

'I deal with it. You have to.' Matt smiled his appreciation – and then, realising it was perhaps inappropriate to be appearing to be so intimate with a young, attractive nurse in the middle of a hospital corridor, stepped back a little. 'All we can do is our best. Sometimes it's just not enough.'

'Are we able to offer them ongoing support?' she asked.

'We have a support package in place,' he confirmed, guessing she would be feeling for the parents leaving the hospital to cope alone with their grief. 'Though we can only advise them to seek help. We're here to offer support through the difficult decisions while they're at the hospital, obviously.'

'Do you advise them about those decisions?' she pursued.

Matt hadn't the heart to put her off. She was obviously keen to understand the various aspects of neonatal care. 'No.' He shook his head regretfully. 'The decisions are ultimately theirs to make. We try to support their hopes for their child, whilst also trying to manage them. We also have to be advocates for the child, of course. So, yes, it can sometimes be difficult emotionally.' He sighed and glanced towards the neonatal unit, thinking he should discreetly extract himself.

'Well I think you're an absolute saint,' Rachel announced. 'I really don't know how you do it. Working such long hours, as well. You must be totally exhausted.'

'Sometimes.' He shrugged. He actually felt fit to drop, in desperate need of sleep – dark, dreamless sleep preferably. 'The rewards of the job outweigh the downsides, though.'

'A saint, definitely,' she repeated with a fervent nod.

'I'm not, I can assure you. I make mistakes. Get upset and angry, just like anyone else does.' Matt recalled the time he'd been far from a saint, drowning his sorrows after leaving the hotel that morning after the wedding, imagining it would dull the pain. It hadn't. Sleeping with someone he hardly knew in an attempt to hurt those who'd hurt him, imagining it would make him feel better. It hadn't. He'd actually felt pretty disgusted with himself. He had no idea how Jason did it: treating people like shit and then walking glibly away.

'But you keep it in check, because you have to,' Rachel suggested.

'I, er … try to, yes.' He glanced awkwardly away.

'Are you okay?' she asked, sounding concerned. 'You seem a bit jaded.'

'I'm not,' he assured her. 'Not with the job. It's just …' He hesitated, warning himself to be careful how much he divulged.

'Your daughter?' she hazarded.

He felt his heart wrench. She obviously knew about Poppy. He shouldn't be surprised. News travelled fast, particularly during the night shift. He nodded. 'She has her biopsy soon,' he confided. 'Naturally I'm a bit apprehensive.'

'As you would be. I'm sure she'll be fine.' She smiled sympathetically. 'She's in the best hands.'

She was. Matt was aware of that. Not his, unfortunately, renal medicine not being his area. Even then, he would probably be deemed too emotionally involved. It broke him inside every time he thought about it.

'You know, you can always talk to me, Matt,' Rachel added uncertainly. 'I know sometimes it can be difficult to confide in those closest to you about how you're feeling.'

'I, er …' He paused, checking his phone as it beeped with a text.

No need to rush back, Kay had sent. *Poppy and I are at a friend's. She's fine. X*

Matt's heart hitched. Which friend? he wondered. Jason? 'Thanks.' Forcing a smile, he pocketed his phone and looked back at Rachel. 'I'd better get on.'

'Oh Lord.' She smiled apologetically. 'Yes, of course. Sorry, I'm detaining you. Maybe we could catch up later over a quick coffee break?' she added hopefully. 'I have a few questions. That's if you're not too busy to take a break and don't have to rush off home or anything.'

'No.' Matt smiled ruefully. 'I'm in no hurry to rush off home.'

CHAPTER THIRTEEN

Kay

'*Adopted?*' Kay stared at Nicole in shocked disbelief. She was sure she knew her husband well enough to know he would never have condoned such a thing – assuming Olivia was his, assuming he knew about her. Perhaps he didn't. It was entirely possible. Might he have had a one-night stand or some quick fling? She felt a smidgeon of hope that what they'd had together – still had, she thought – might survive if that were the case. He was a good man, she knew that without a doubt, but he was human. Olivia was the same age as Poppy, so she would have been conceived around the time of that awful wedding. Matt had acted so out of character, the violence he'd shown towards his brother a side of him she had never seen before or since. And then he'd disappeared, showing up eventually uncommunicative and withdrawn, working late. It all added up.

Her heart raced, her mind racing faster, as she tried to think what to do. She couldn't just dismiss the fact that he'd had a child with another woman, whatever his involvement with her – a child who'd ended up being placed for adoption, for goodness' sake. She couldn't just shrug and say, *Ah well, it doesn't matter.* It did. She *had* to find out what had happened, find out for sure that Olivia was his. How could she face him with it otherwise? Poor Olivia. She must have had such a bleak start in life.

'Does she know she's adopted?' she asked, praying that Nicole wouldn't refuse to discuss it with her. Why should she, after all, but for the existence of Poppy?

Looking her cautiously over, as if gauging how much to tell her, Nicole drew in a breath. 'No,' she said, shaking her head. 'I intend to tell her one day, but …' Glancing guardedly at Kay again, she breathed out a sigh and then, concerned no doubt that the girls might overhear, walked across the kitchen and closed the door.

Coming back to the island, she looked at Kay full on, her eyes troubled and uncertain. 'How do you tell a child of any age that her mother abandoned her? Literally dumped her and walked out of her life without looking back?'

'Dumped her?' Kay was struggling to get her head around any of this. 'Where? When?'

'Olivia was just a month old.' Nicole's face creased into a frown. 'The one small credit to her, I suppose, was that she at least left her where she would be found: at the City Road Hospital. She was well cared for, it seems, but she had a chest infection, which had possibly been missed. I suppose that might have been why the mother felt unable to cope, but we'll never know, will we? She simply walked away. Washed her hands of her.'

The City Road Hospital? But that was where Matt worked, where he'd done his ward rotations and completed his specialty training. Why would she have done that unless … *Had* Matt known? Had he abandoned the mother? No, the Matt she knew would never do that. But then she would never have believed he would cheat on her either. Kay's heart ratcheted up a notch.

'It might have been different if she'd given her up at birth, but how does a child ever come to terms with the fact that the woman who'd nursed her for the first month of her life abandoned her without an apparent second thought? Which brings us to the question of the father.'

Kay looked up at her sharply.

Nicole studied her for a long, hard moment and then seated herself opposite her. 'If you're Poppy's birth mother, which I presume you are, and clearly not Olivia's mother, then given the striking similarity between the girls, I'm thinking they were fathered by the same man. I'm assuming you're thinking the same?'

'I ... don't know what to think,' Kay admitted honestly. 'Matthew, my husband, he has a brother. It's possible that he ...' She trailed off. She was groping for explanations, making excuses for Matt. The girls were so alike, she was struggling to believe they'd been fathered by different men, even brothers.

Nicole nodded slowly. Her eyes narrowed again; she studied Kay carefully. 'And do either of them know of Olivia's existence?' she asked, after an agonisingly long moment.

Kay dropped her gaze. 'As far as I know, no,' she said, knotting and unknotting her fingers on the island before her.

Nicole said nothing for a second. Then, 'And Matthew ... your husband ... is he the father of your child?' she asked, point blank.

Kay swallowed against the acrid dryness in her throat. 'Yes,' she whispered, leaving the woman to make her own assumptions.

'Do you think he will want to have contact, should he become aware of her existence?' Nicole now sounded wary.

'Honestly?' Kay locked eyes with her. 'I don't think Matthew would ever do anything he imagined would be detrimental to Olivia. He's a neonatal specialist. He devotes his life to children. He would never countenance doing anything that might harm a child's welfare.'

'He sounds very noble. You obviously know him well.' Nicole studied her a second longer, and then looked away and got to her feet. Kay watched her walk across to the kettle. Flicking it on and retrieving two cups from the cupboard, Nicole faced her. 'What's wrong with Poppy?' she asked, blindsiding her. 'You said she was on a special diet. Why?'

Kay's heart lurched. She'd tried not to hold on to the idea that had popped into her mind when she'd realised that Poppy and Olivia might be half-sisters. The reality was, though, that in the absence of any other suitable living donor, should Poppy's condition worsen to the point where she might need dialysis, Olivia might be her only hope.

'She has allergies,' she said, deliberately vaguely. She didn't feel she could share how serious Poppy's condition was without alerting Nicole to the fact that there was a possibility she might need a transplant. If the shoe were on the other foot and she were presented with such a situation, would she be willing to offer up her child as a donor? She doubted it. Her first instinct would be to protect her own child. Nicole might even try to discourage the friendship, which would break Poppy's heart. Olivia's, too. No, she couldn't tell her everything. Not yet.

The other woman looked her over pensively. 'You should know that Olivia is very dear to me, Kay. The most precious thing in my life. I have a secure income, so I wouldn't want to pursue the father regarding maintenance payments. I wouldn't want him to do anything that would destabilise my daughter. As for the future, I can't speak for Olivia. She may want to find out who he is, in which case I wouldn't try to stop her. I think it's a case of crossing those bridges when we reach them, though, don't you?'

Kay didn't know how to answer. She tried to banish the thought, but it was there in her head. It wouldn't go away. What if Poppy reached a bridge she couldn't cross without Olivia's help? She wanted to ask, but she couldn't, not without alerting her.

'What about the girls' friendship?' she asked instead, alarm rising inside her as she realised that, after what Nicole had just said, she might not want the friendship to continue for fear of Matt seeing Olivia.

Nicole hesitated before answering. 'I wouldn't want to do anything that would be detrimental to my daughter either,' she said eventually. 'Or to Poppy. They've obviously bonded. We should be careful about the timings of their play dates in future, though. At least for now.'

Kay breathed a sigh of relief. Losing her special friend would devastate Poppy. She was also relieved on another level, and felt incredibly two-faced and selfish about it. The girls continuing to see each other would buy her time. Time to get to know Nicole better. Time for Nicole to come to know Poppy and realise that she might hold the key to her *having* a future.

CHAPTER FOURTEEN

Nicole

Holding Olivia's hand as she waved her friend off, Nicole watched the woman drive away. Closing the door, she turned to her daughter. 'She's lovely, isn't she, your new friend?' she said with an approving smile.

'She's my best friend.' Olivia nodded fervently. 'Can she come to play again soon, Mummy?' she asked, skipping ahead to the lounge.

'Absolutely,' Nicole promised her.

'And can I go to Kay's house to play with Poppy there sometimes?'

'I don't see why not,' Nicole said. She wasn't entirely sure about that, but she was definitely having to cross bridges as she got to them. She noted how Olivia had addressed the woman by her first name. Clearly she liked her. Nicole could see why. She'd quite liked Kay herself, despite the news she'd come to deliver. God, why hadn't she known about Poppy, a child so similar to her own it was impossible they weren't related? Because she'd rarely taken Olivia to school or collected her, single parenthood demanding she work full time and devote too much of herself to her job. She tried not to begrudge Kay her husband. She clearly had worries, but even so, she didn't realise how lucky she was having someone in her life to share the financial burden as well as the responsibilities of parenthood.

She'd lied about her own personal finances. She actually hadn't got a penny to her name, but pride had stopped her mentioning that in front of a woman who was obviously well off, given her husband's job. Her heart caught as her thoughts went to her own husband. Even struggling with his devastating illness, he had been torn with guilt that he couldn't provide her with a child. They'd tried right up until the end. She'd wanted to use the samples they'd stored, but of course funds wouldn't allow her to pay the fertility clinic bills. Steven had bitterly regretted that he hadn't had any insurance in place and had suddenly become uninsurable. She hadn't cared that he'd left her in debt – she'd had to give up her job back then, of course, to nurse him; that was never in question. She had cared about this house, though, the place they'd originally chosen together with a family in mind. To have given it up would have been like saying goodbye to him all over again. She might never have been granted adoption of Olivia without it. Now she was desperate to hang on to it. She couldn't countenance the thought of living in some small flat. A child needed space to grow, a garden.

After Steven had gone, she'd managed to bring the mortgage payments up to date, working two jobs: her day job at the estate agent's and a night job at a restaurant. She'd managed somehow. She couldn't do two jobs now, of course, and she'd had to remortgage recently, wanting Olivia to have all that a child should have growing up. That was a worry. She supposed, given her circumstances, she shouldn't feel ashamed that she was struggling. If she sought advice, though, she was sure that advice would be to sell her house, although there was little equity in it now. No, that was out of the question. She had to find a way to hang on to it.

She glanced at her daughter as she scrambled into her favourite corner of the sofa. Olivia meant more than her life to her. She *was* her life. She couldn't let her down, relocate, take her out of school, away from the friend she'd made, no matter how shocking Nicole had found Poppy's existence.

'Right, you have half an hour of TV before bed,' she said, clapping her hands and arranging her face into a bright smile for her daughter's sake.

'Scooby-Doo!' Olivia decided delightedly, clutching her special furry throw and snuggling up.

Nicole picked up the remote and went to CBeebies, selecting *Scooby-Doo and the Beach Beastie*, which she hoped wasn't too scary for bedtime. 'I'll join you in a minute,' she promised. 'I'm just going to check we're all locked up.'

Tucking the throw warmly around her daughter, she kissed the top of her head, then made her way back to the kitchen, where she picked up her phone from the work surface. Some might view her fierce pride as an encumbrance. Perhaps it was, preventing her reaching out for help when she needed it. She'd become self-sufficient. She'd had to. But could she really let pride stand in the way of Olivia's future stability?

Selecting her texts, her thumb hovered. She took a deep breath, glanced upwards and made her decision: no, she couldn't. Looking back to her phone, she keyed in a message: *I met Kay and little Poppy today*, deliberated for a second longer – and then pressed send.

CHAPTER FIFTEEN

Kay

She was trapped. It wasn't the walls of her house that were closing in on her, but the mirrored walls of an elevator. The air inside was stifling, the aftershave assaulting her senses, heavy and cloying. His eyes scanned her face, piercing blue, darkening to cobalt, full of desire as he locked his gaze hard on hers. His hands were mapping the contours of her body, one sliding up the inside of her thigh, his mouth closing over hers, his tongue prising her lips open, urgently searching and probing. Matt? His breath hot on her breasts, she twisted her face to glance in the mirror, and her stomach turned nauseatingly and then plummeted violently as the lift jarred for a petrifying heartbeat before plunging her into new depths of hell.

'No!' Gasping out a sob, Kay woke with a jolt. 'Matt,' she cried, reaching for him, as she always instinctively did. He wasn't there. There was no indent in his pillow. His side of the bed … she ripped back the duvet … cold. But it was morning, she realised. He hadn't come home.

He'd *texted* her. Sifting through the fog in her head as she scrambled from the bed, she recalled the short, soulless message. *Emergency at the hospital. Not sure when I'll be back*, was all he'd said. She grabbed her phone from her bedside table. There were no further messages. No explanations. He hadn't come *home*. Where was he? Who was he with?

Trying to banish her nightmare, to convince herself that it was just a bad dream, that it wasn't prophetic or significant, she flew to Poppy's room to check on her. For all her reassurances to herself, she couldn't shake the blood-freezing terror that had gripped her as the lift fell. Why were the dreams coming so frequently? What was happening to her? Her heart still thudding erratically, her hand trembling as she reached for Poppy's door handle, she paused. Confused and disorientated, she took a second to compose herself, to be the mummy Poppy needed her to be, and then pushed the door open.

'Matt?' She stared in surprise. He was here. He'd obviously slept on Poppy's bed, an arm protectively around his daughter, who was curled into the crook of it. A turmoil of emotion assailed her. Why hadn't he woken her?

He stirred as she walked towards him, throwing his other arm across his eyes as the daylight from the landing window shone in. Easing himself up, careful not to wake Poppy, he rubbed the heels of his hands against his eyes. 'Sorry. I disturbed her when I came in,' he said, climbing gently off the bed. 'She said she was feeling scared, so …'

He'd stayed with her, trying to keep his little girl safe. He loved her. With his whole heart and his soul he loved her. Would he really have deserted a child, another baby girl just weeks old, if he'd known about her? Kay couldn't make herself believe he would ever do that.

'Daddy?' Blinking sleepily, Poppy stirred. Clearly she'd sensed the absence of him, as Kay had. She swallowed, her heart fracturing another inch as she considered a future without him. How would she ever explain to her daughter that her mummy and daddy weren't together any more? She wasn't sure he didn't want to be with her, whether he was cheating on her or not, although she couldn't escape the text she'd found on his phone signed off with two kisses. No woman would do that unless they were close, intimately so. She couldn't escape the fact that he had cheated in the past, either. Olivia had to be his daughter. Could she accept it if he explained it away as a mistake? No child should ever be that. Kay had lived with the knowledge that she was a mistake in her own father's eyes. She wouldn't ever forget the hateful thing he'd said as he'd left. 'I never wanted a fucking kid in the first place!' he'd spat, slamming the door so resoundingly behind him that the walls shook. Her mother had tried to dry her bewildered tears, to convince her that it was his wife he didn't love, not his daughter. But Kay had heard him. She'd tried not to let it mar her life. Her mother had loved her enough for both of them, but it had hurt, knowing that her father had been so indifferent to her birth.

'Morning, baby girl,' Matt said softly, smiling down at his daughter. 'Did we sleep well?'

'Uh huh.' Beaming a smile back at the father she adored, a man Kay truly believed would give up the air he breathed for her, Poppy sat up. 'I didn't have any more bad dreams,' she said, closing one eye as she squinted up at him. 'You did, though, Daddy. But you were okay,' she assured him seriously. 'I stroked your cheek and you went back to sleep.'

Matt laughed throatily and bent to sweep her up. 'I thought I felt a little angel snuggling up to me,' he said, hoisting her high into his arms.

His gaze drifted to Kay and they were connected for a second, each contemplating a word he'd always used naturally, but which took on new connotations now, reminding them of their daughter's fragility. That connection was vital, as vital to her as it was to Poppy, yet there was a vast space opening up between them that Kay didn't know how to cross. She was too frightened to even attempt to.

'So, are we looking forward to school today?' Matt turned his attention back to Poppy.

'Yes,' Poppy answered enthusiastically, rather than with her usual uncertainty.

'Really?' He grabbed her dressing gown. 'Well, that's excellent news. So why the change of heart?'

'Because Liv loves going to school and I love Liv,' Poppy informed him. 'She makes it lots more fun.'

'Does she indeed?' Matt widened his eyes in surprise as he carried her to the landing. 'And who's Liv?'

'My best friend ever in the whole world,' Poppy provided assuredly.

'In the whole world, hey?' Matt chuckled. 'She's obviously a very special friend, then. I'm going to have to meet her, aren't I?'

Watching them go, Kay felt the foundations of her world shifting beneath her. Her life was rocking. The walls were crumbling, and there was no way to stop them. Things could never go back to the normal she'd been striving for just a short while ago. It was impossible. Olivia coming into her life had taken her normal away.

Following them out, she waited until Matt had set Poppy down in the bathroom, then caught his arm as he made his way to the bedroom. 'Matt, can we talk?' she asked him, her stomach tying itself into nervous knots.

He looked her over quizzically. 'About?'

'The tissue testing, the biopsy. Things in general. I thought we could maybe talk later. That you could make an effort to get back.'

His mouth twitched into a short smile. 'I do make an effort, Kay,' he said, despair obvious in his voice. 'My patients tend not to get ill only between the hours of nine and five, though.'

'I know.' Kay felt wrong-footed and defensive all at once. 'I do know that, Matt. I just think we should—'

'Would these "things in general" we need to talk about have anything to do with Jason?' Matt cut in, blindsiding her completely.

'What?' She laughed, confused. '*No*. It's to do with us. Our future. Poppy's future.'

He looked away, a cynical smile now playing at his mouth. 'Not the past, then?'

Kay was growing confused. Did he *know* what it was she wanted to talk about? Clearly he realised the past had some bearing on it. 'Yes,' she said, with a combination of relief and trepidation. At least now the door was open.

'I see.' He nodded contemplatively. 'Have you spoken to him again?'

He was still talking about Jason. Why was he so damn obsessed with him? Did he imagine she was flirting with him? She stared at him, torn now between anger and bewilderment. What was the *matter* with him?

'I just wondered whether you'd returned his call?' Matt asked, a question mark in his eyes as he searched hers.

'No,' Kay answered flatly, holding his gaze.

'Right.' A pensive frown crossed his face. 'Well, just so you know, there's no need. I'm going to call him today and arrange to meet up with him. Now, sorry to cut this short, but I have to go. I have work to do. Nothing pressing. Just major surgery on a sick baby, but I'll make an effort to get back early, rest assured.'

Stunned by his abrasive sarcasm, Kay watched him walk on into the bedroom, dragging a hand agitatedly over his neck as he went. Why was he doing this, shutting her down, turning things around? She'd never seen him like this. She'd thought she knew all there was to know about him. Quite plainly, she didn't.

CHAPTER SIXTEEN

Later that day, Kay trailed into the university, her thoughts on Matt, his obvious anger, his defensiveness. Why would he be defensive if he'd done nothing wrong? Heading to her assigned classroom, she jumped as Amelia appeared at her side, seemingly out of nowhere.

'Morning.' Amelia smiled cheerily. 'Oh dear.' Her smile slipped as she clearly noted Kay's flustered expression. 'Sorry, I saw you from the stairs. I should have thought before leaping on you like that. I hope I didn't scare you.'

'No,' Kay lied – she'd scared her half to death – and offered her a small smile back. 'I was distracted, that's all. My mind on other things, you know.'

'But you're all right?' Amelia asked, catching the door Kay held for her and following her in.

'Yes, fine, why?' Hurrying to her desk, Kay glanced back at her. The other students were already seated, waiting expectantly for her to get under way.

Amelia came around to the front of the desk. 'You look exhausted,' she said, scanning Kay's face worriedly. 'As if you haven't slept a wink. You know, if you ever need a shoulder … A problem shared is a problem halved.'

'Thanks, but I'm fine, honestly,' Kay assured her.

'Okay,' Amelia said, with an easy shrug. 'We can always chat later if you do need an ear.'

'Later?' Kay asked, confused.

'That drink we were going for? I thought we could go to the Dog and Whistle on the high street. They serve bar snacks there, if you fancy it?'

Oh no. Kay had said they would catch up some time, but they hadn't fixed anything. Had they? With so many things coming at her, she was getting muddled, but she was sure she hadn't actually said she would go out this evening. She couldn't possibly. Aside from the fact that she had no sitter for Poppy, she was desperately praying that Matt would get back, that they could talk about Olivia, however hard that conversation was going to be. 'I'm sorry, Amelia,' she said apologetically. 'I—'

'It doesn't matter,' Amelia cut in, and although she smiled, Kay saw a flicker of annoyance behind her eyes. She was about to say more, suggest they rearrange, when the woman spun around and walked away from her.

Feeling uneasy, Kay took a minute, delving into her bag to retrieve the questionnaires to help with character creation she'd prepared for a previous class. Deciding she was probably being paranoid with all that was going on in her life, she collected herself and glanced up at her students. 'So, we're looking at characterisation today,' she started.

Walking to the front of her desk, she seated herself on the edge of it. 'On that subject, I thought it might be an idea to think about scriptwriting.' That drew a few curious looks, since hers wasn't the Scripting and Staging module. Amelia was definitely looking at her curiously, her eyes fixed so intently on her that Kay began to feel slightly uncomfortable.

Unhitching herself from the desk, she decided to circulate instead. Having someone staring at her wasn't helping her concentration. 'Think about your characters,' she went on, 'and ask yourselves, are they flat? Uninspiring?' She gave them a second, and tried not to look in Amelia's direction as she walked, feeling her gaze following her around the room.

For goodness' sake, get a grip, she warned herself. Where else was the woman supposed to look? Taking a breath, she pushed on. 'Depth of character is often an issue in storytelling. I'm referring to scriptwriting because film producers want to see real three-dimensional people in scripts, not two-dimensional, unrealistic people. After all, if they could cast a cardboard cut-out of, say, Jake Gyllenhaal in a movie, why would they shell out millions of pounds for the real Gyllenhaal?'

'I wouldn't mind a cardboard cut-out of Jake Gyllenhaal,' one young female student cracked. 'I think he would be quite inspiring propped up in my bedroom. Those sultry eyes.' She sighed dreamily. 'They definitely have it.'

'Might be a little distracting, though, Emma?' Kay suggested, her mouth curving into a small smile. 'Anyway, Jake's eyes aside, if you have a character without all the traits that make them human, be they sultry looks, charming smiles, annoying habits or secrets, then the actor can't make them come alive. Likewise, the reader might be able to *picture* your character, assuming you've described eye and hair colour – which isn't always necessary, as we've discussed before – but they won't identify with or *feel* them.'

Turning from the back of the room, she noted that Amelia had twisted in her seat to follow her progress. She was winding a strand of hair around her forefinger, definitely staring at her, a little furrow in the middle of her brow. Was she scowling, or simply concentrating?

Kay looked away, attempting to stay focused as she walked to the front of the room. 'Our characters need three different dimensions in order to jump off the page,' she continued, grappling to hold onto her train of thought. 'Two elements will give us our basic character: their personal life and their occupation. If those two elements are in conflict, we've already made them interesting. The super-organised mother, for instance, whose personal life is a mess. By adding a third element, you're adding another dimension. What eccentricity or defining character trait makes her come alive? Does she hate her life? Her husband? Her kids for – as she might see it – stealing her dreams and forcing her into a mundane existence? What does she do about it? Murder her husband? Does she have serial affairs? Does her husband?'

She faltered, her heart jolting as she was reminded of her own situation and how powerless she felt to do anything about it, knowing her daughter's future happiness was at stake. Was Matt having serial affairs? Or was it just one? If so, was it a long-standing one? Sucking in a breath, she forced her personal problems aside and pushed on. 'Is she a serial murderer? Is he? What is her secret? What makes the reader relate to her, to want to know more about her?'

Pausing, she breathed a sigh of relief as she noted the students busily scribbling notes. Apart from Amelia, whose gaze now seemed to be drilling into her.

Quickly handing out her questionnaire, she asked the students to list everything about their character, from the basics – name, marital status, children, occupation – right through to fantasies, worst vice and best virtue. She finished by reading the last question out loud. '*What is their secret?* That, for me, is the defining character trait and also pivotal to the story.'

Leaving them to ponder their characters, she sat down at her desk, busying herself with preparation for her next lecture and making sure not to look in Amelia's direction. After a lively discussion about diversity and inclusivity, prompted by a question by one student, she was relieved when it was time to call a close to the class. As hard as she was trying to stave it off, exhaustion seemed to be catching up with her.

'Have a think about that last trait on the list,' she suggested, as chairs were scraped back. 'I look forward to hearing some fascinating secrets next time.'

Realising that Amelia was taking her time, rising slowly and strolling towards her, Kay turned to gather her things from the desk. It might well be paranoia at play – God knew she was feeling paranoid lately – but she was beginning to feel wary of the woman.

'Do you have secrets in your relationship, Kay?' Amelia asked, pausing at her side.

Kay caught her breath. 'None that I know of,' she said lightly, focusing on her task rather than on Amelia. She was uncomfortable under her scrutiny, and given the way she was feeling generally about the state of her marriage, she could do without a conversation on this subject, even though she'd introduced it herself.

'Hmm? You're sure about that, are you?' Amelia enquired.

'What?' Kay's gaze snapped up.

Amelia narrowed her eyes. 'Well, they'd hardly be secret if you knew about them, would they? I mean if, say, Matthew, were having serial affairs, he wouldn't tell you about them, would he?'

Kay's chest lurched, confusion coursing through her as Amelia drew her gaze languidly away and strolled out of the room. She grappled to grab her paperwork, swiping half of it from the desk in her haste.

Damn. Crouching, she scrambled to retrieve it, then left it and flew after the woman. 'Amelia?' she called, skidding into the corridor. 'Amelia!' She spun on her heel, gazing around, but Amelia was nowhere in sight.

CHAPTER SEVENTEEN

Matthew

'We're monitoring her twenty-four hours a day,' Matt assured the father of the baby born at twenty-five weeks. The man's complexion was pale. He looked exhausted. Clearly he was sick with worry. Matt wished he could offer him more, but for now, all they could do was help the baby's small organs to function. 'Why don't you try to get some rest?' he suggested.

'Thanks, but we prefer to be here, if that's okay?' Smiling sadly, the man glanced back to his wife, who had hardly moved from the neonatal unit, despite a difficult birth.

Matt understood. They needed to be by their child's side, even though he'd managed to secure them a room across the road, thanks to a charity providing accommodation for parents of premature babies. He knew how they felt. He knew also that if fervent prayer could get their baby through, he would survive. 'I'll keep you up to date with any relevant information,' he promised, hating his powerlessness, his inability to do anything now but pray silently himself.

'Thanks,' the man repeated, 'for everything you've done for Clare and for little Leo. And for levelling with us. At least we're prepared ...' He faltered, swallowing emotionally.

Matt felt his heart ache for them. Did being prepared for the worst-case scenario help? He doubted it. Because of his job, he and Kay had been fully aware of the facts when their son, David – named after Matt's father – had been so devastatingly premature. And again when Poppy had arrived worryingly early. He didn't think knowing what the outcome might be for her had prepared them any better, particularly Kay, who'd already suffered the unbearable grief of having to let go of a child she'd given birth to. His own grief over David had been different. Kay had fallen in love with the child growing inside her. He hadn't realised how powerful his love for Poppy would be until he'd seen her. To have lost her then would have crucified him. It would destroy him to lose her now, to lose Kay, which he might well do if he couldn't keep a rein on his emotions.

Quashing thoughts of his personal issues, which were in danger of affecting his judgement, he turned his attention back to the father. 'I like the name you've chosen,' he said, aware that they'd decided quickly because they wanted to get the child baptised.

The man managed another small smile. 'We thought something strong.' He glanced again at his wife, who was wiping a silent tear from her cheek. 'He's certainly made an impact.'

Swallowing back a lump of emotion of his own, Matt placed a hand on the man's shoulder. 'He's a fighter,' he said. He was wary of giving them false hope, but miracles did happen. Despite apnoea of prematurity, meaning that Leo had stopped breathing, and subsequent bilateral intraventricular haemorrhages due to lack of oxygen to the brain, he was strong, a determined soul in a tiny body.

As he left, Matt watched the man go to his wife, threading an arm around her, drawing her to him, and felt his heart stall. It could have been him and Kay sitting there, looking down at Poppy. 'I should have taken better care of her,' Kay had whispered, as if she were somehow responsible. She'd felt guilty because she'd dismissed her signs of labour as Braxton Hicks and hadn't called him. He'd watched, feeling as useless as he did now, while she struggled with her misplaced shame. He'd tried to reassure her, told her how much he loved her. She'd said she loved him too. Had she? Did she? How did he ask her without raking up things he'd promised himself he never would?

The unit seeming suddenly too claustrophobic, he sucked in a breath and headed for the nurses' station. He needed to take a break, get out of here for a while, where everything was too stark a reminder of all that might yet be taken away. Conferring with Leo's full-time nurse, he emphasised that they should call him straight away if there were any developments, and left the baby in their capable hands. Going to his locker, he grabbed his jacket and headed for the hospital exit. He found himself drawn to the children's ward on the way, in the hope of catching Rachel there. Because, having taken up her suggestion that they meet for a coffee last night, he'd found her easy to talk to, he supposed. He'd steered clear of emotive, personal issues, but Rachel was astute. She'd sensed his concern about the premature baby, and tried to reassure him that Leo's parents would know he was doing his absolute best for them.

She noticed him now as he went into the ward, smiling in his direction.

Matt made coffee signals with his hand.

'Two minutes,' she mouthed, beaming him another smile and sticking up her thumb.

Should he be doing this? Agreeing to meet her to discuss work-related issues was one thing, but seeking her out for a casual coffee moved it a step beyond a strictly professional relationship. Or might be deemed to. He possibly shouldn't, but he couldn't deny it was refreshing to see someone smiling around him, to be able to drop his guard for a while. It occurred to him then to wonder whether his guard had always been up, whether he'd been subconsciously waiting for the life he'd built with Kay to unravel.

CHAPTER EIGHTEEN

'So the initial blood tests exclude you as a donor?' Rachel asked, studying him carefully over the coffee she was stirring.

'Unfortunately, yes.' Matt dropped his gaze, picking up his cup and swirling the contents contemplatively around as the bewilderment and inadequacy he'd felt when he'd found his blood type ruled him out washed through him all over again. Devastated didn't begin to describe his feelings when Poppy's consultant had called him to deliver the news.

'But you're going ahead with the tissue typing?'

He nodded. 'In case there's a possibility of a paired exchange, should it come to that.' That was what he'd told Kay. It was the truth, but not his whole reason for going ahead.

Rachel didn't pursue it and Matt was grateful for her tact. Whenever he went down this road, his emotions were way too close to the surface. 'Do you have a photo of her?' she asked.

Matt picked up his phone and scrolled through his photos. Finding a recent picture of Poppy with Kay, both of them smiling and carefree, he handed it to her, his heart wrenching as he did. Would Kay ever look at him that way again, rather than warily, as she had been doing recently, or else not at all? She was hiding something; he'd lived with her long enough to realise that. She'd seemed on the verge of telling him earlier. She might well do so this evening, if he got back early. The fact was, though, as much as he wished she would be honest with him about her feelings for him – what they were all those years ago when they'd almost fallen apart, what they were now – he really didn't want to hear it.

'Oh, she's just gorgeous. She definitely takes after her father.' Rachel smiled, an approving twinkle in her eyes as she looked up at him, and Matt felt his heart wrench afresh. 'And is this your wife?' she went on, perusing his phone interestedly. 'She's gorgeous too, isn't she?'

'She is,' Matt agreed. He would feel like an idiot admitting it to anyone, but he'd had a crush on Kay since they were kids living next door to each other. Open-faced and pretty without seeming aware of it, she'd had a vulnerable quality about her that masked a strength she probably didn't know existed. She always seemed to be looking out for her mother or younger children in the school playground. He'd fantasised about kissing her when he'd hit his teens. When he'd come back from university to find her serving behind the counter at WHSmith one Saturday, he'd been stunned. He'd had other girlfriends, but she was the one who had captured his heart, right there and then. Her eyes, a myriad of forest greens peering out from under a wild tangle of blonde hair, had danced with amusement when she'd noticed his tongue-tied embarrassment. He hadn't felt capable of stringing a sensible sentence together. He had gone to the store several times over the following few weeks. He'd never purchased so many books in his life, but though he'd fantasised about doing a whole lot more than kissing her, he'd struggled to find the courage to ask her out.

It hadn't taken Jason long to move in on her – Matt guessed he'd realised he was besotted from his many visits there – and Kay had ended up going out with him. She'd soon seen through the superficial charm, though, to the man Jason was. He was a control freak, a bully. Always had been, always would be. He wanted everything his own way, or no way, and he wanted everything for himself. Matt had been surprised when she'd agreed to go out with him a few weeks after ditching Jason. After all, he was Jason's brother, and she might have imagined they were similar. Now, he couldn't help wondering whether she had ever actually finished with Jason or whether he still had some kind of emotional hold over her. Why else would he contact her? Why would she convey to him it was okay to? More worryingly, why would she not tell her *husband* about it?

Looking back at Rachel, he found her studying him curiously. 'You know, Matt …' she hesitated, looking him over sympathetically – obviously she'd picked up on his maudlin mood – 'my friends tell me I'm very good at relationship advice. If you ever need a shoulder …'

Matt smiled his appreciation. About to steer the subject away from his personal problems, he almost spat out his coffee as his major problem, in the form of Jason himself, walked into the room.

'Mind if I join you?' He strolled across to their table as Matt stared at him in shocked disbelief. 'Or is three a crowd?'

Waiting for him to drip more unsubtle innuendo, Matt sighed and closed his eyes. He didn't think it would take him long.

'So how are we, little brother?' Jason asked, as if he would be remotely interested. 'Still working all the hours God sends, I see.'

Matt resisted a rude retort. 'Fine,' he replied with a despairing sigh. He supposed he would have to introduce him. 'Rachel, this is my brother—' he started.

'Jason Young,' Jason cut in, extending a hand to Rachel. 'The better-looking one,' he quipped, as was his wont.

'Hi, Jason.' Rachel reached to shake his hand, her expression slightly bemused as she glanced between them. 'Nice to meet you. Are you a doctor here at the hospital?

'Nope.' Jason sat down, whether they minded or not. 'Senior partner at Biochem Pharmaceuticals,' he said with a self-important smile. 'Here to make sure the hospital is supplied with the world's most medically advanced products.'

Rachel glanced again at Matt. He gathered from her expression that she wasn't sure whether to look impressed. Matt definitely wasn't. Jason had been back two minutes and he'd already promoted himself to senior partner? Was their father aware of this, he wondered, and that Jason was doubtlessly counting the days until his retirement so he could run the whole show?

'You're a nurse, I see.' Jason smiled his most charming smile and settled his eyes on her. Also probably his sights. 'What area of nursing are you in?'

There he went, pretending rapt interest. Matt had no doubt that it was part of a chat-up technique. 'I have to go,' he said, glancing at his watch and getting to his feet. 'I need to check on a patient.'

'Matt, hold on …' Jason came after him as he walked towards the exit. Reaching him, he caught hold of his arm, and Matt immediately felt his hackles rise.

'Look, I just wanted to ask you if we could bury the hatchet.' Jason shrugged as Matt turned to face him. 'Call a truce for the old man's sake. He's not getting any younger.'

Matt squinted hard at him. *Right.* What utter bullshit. Jason didn't want to call a truce for their father's sake. It was for his own sake, to make him look like the returning hero in their father's eyes, willing to forgive and forget, rather than the manipulative bastard he was. Matt knew what it was his brother did want, and he was bloody sure it wasn't his friendship.

CHAPTER NINETEEN

Kay

'Do you want me to drop her off at school?' Matt asked, coming through the back door from the garden as Kay raced around the next morning. Poppy's school project had moved on to naturally found smooth objects. She still had those to find and her lunch box to pack. It was also a good reason not to stand still too long so she didn't have to look Matt in the eye. She didn't like what she'd seen there when she'd tried to suggest they sit down and talk: anger and irritation. Her stomach tightened, tears rising in her throat as she thought about it. Matt hadn't come home early, citing emergencies at work yet again as his excuse. He'd probably never intended to.

'You're going in late, are you?' She answered his question with one of her own, her heart rate ratcheting up as she realised that if he did the school run, he would be bound to meet Olivia. Poppy would be bursting to introduce her to him. Kay was working on the assumption that he didn't know of her existence, or else had no knowledge of her upbringing or where she lived. Either way, he would be shocked. Either way, it would bring things to a head that she wasn't ready to deal with. She was scared of the lies he might tell her. After all, he'd done a bloody good job of lying to her until now, professing to love her. She hadn't seen much evidence of that in his eyes lately.

No, she couldn't risk Matt seeing Olivia yet. Although she knew it was incredibly unlikely, she was still harbouring the hope that Nicole might at least consider putting Olivia forward as a donor for Poppy. She hated herself for thinking that way, but wasn't she bound to when her little girl's life might be at stake? She had to think ahead, in case Poppy's health deteriorated suddenly. If she and Matt turned out to be unsuitable donors, what options would that leave them? They could ask Jason to take the tests, but he might not be willing and could also turn out to be unsuitable. In that case, they would have to join the donor register, meaning years of waiting, with no guarantee even then. Siblings had a high chance of being an exact match or half-match, she'd learned that much. Olivia might only be Poppy's half-sister, but it would be hope where there might be no other hope. Surely Nicole would consider that. She had to talk more with her. Right now, though, the important thing was that Poppy's happiness, her security, might be at stake if Matt were to meet Olivia. Matt could keep his secrets, have his affairs – her heart keeled at the thought – until Poppy was able to deal with them.

'I don't have anything major scheduled and my registrar is covering my rounds,' Matt said as Kay busied herself loading the dishwasher, 'so I thought I'd take a step back this morning. Smooth objects,' he said, offering her two large pebbles as she finished stuffing the breakfast dishes in and turned around.

Her emotions too close to the surface, she hesitated for a second. 'Thanks.' She swallowed, her eyes flicking to his and away again as she took the stones from him. She still couldn't bring herself to look at him full on.

'No problem,' Matt said quietly. She could sense his quizzical gaze on her. She desperately wanted to feel his reassuring arms around her, but didn't dare go near him. Could she bear to be in his arms, imagining he'd been with another woman? 'So, would you like me to take Poppy in?' he asked again. 'I thought it might give you time to catch your breath.'

Kay turned away to wash the pebbles. 'I've arranged to talk to her teacher to check on her diet,' she said with a shrug. 'I have a dental appointment straight after, and then I promised Steph I would pop over. Thanks for the offer, though.'

'Right.' Matt fell silent for a moment. 'I actually thought we might …'

'What?' Kay felt a flutter of nerves as he trailed off.

'Nothing.' She heard him draw in a breath behind her. 'It's just …'

'Damn, the time.' Kay dropped the pebbles on the draining board and snatched up the towel to dry her hands. 'I bet Poppy's nowhere near ready.'

She was heading for the hall when Matt stopped her, catching hold of her arm. 'Slow down,' he urged her. 'You're running yourself ragged.'

'It's what I do in the mornings, Matt,' Kay reminded him. Hearing the curtness in her voice, she cursed herself for it. She didn't want to provoke an argument. Bickering in front of Poppy was the very last thing she wanted. 'Poppy needs chivvying on, you know that.'

'What, even though she has a new best friend ever in the whole world? I thought she was looking forward to going in now.'

Kay looked at him at last, to see his mouth curving into a sad smile. He would break her heart. He would smash it completely. Learning that he didn't love her, that he hadn't in a long time, would do that in an instant. Quickly she averted her gaze, glancing past him to the hall. 'She still needs help with her shoes,' she said feebly.

Again Matt fell quiet. Then, 'I'll go,' he offered, sounding deflated.

'Thanks,' Kay said again, feeling as if there were an iceberg between them and no way to break through it.

'No problem. I know I'm not here as often as I'd like, but she's my daughter.' Matt sounded so dejected now that Kay felt as if someone had reached inside her and twisted her heart. She wished she could make the pain stop. Make it all go away. She couldn't. Nor could she ignore it. She would have to face it sooner or later. But not now. Not today.

Matt turned away from her towards the hall, then stopped, his shoulders tensing. 'You were right,' he said. 'We do need to talk.'

Kay's heart banged against her chest. *Sooner, then.* 'When?' she asked, her throat closing.

'Tonight?' He shrugged. His look was apprehensive as he glanced back at her.

With no hope of choking a response out, Kay nodded quickly and turned away, on the pretext of collecting Poppy's lunch ingredients from the fridge.

She waited until he was climbing the stairs before she let the tears fall. Perhaps the dreams were a prophecy after all. Her marriage was crumbling and so was Poppy's safe world. How could he do this?

CHAPTER TWENTY

Watching her daughter go safely through the school doors, Poppy skipping happily alongside Olivia, Kay felt fresh tears prick the back of her eyes. Tears of fear, frustration and anger. Anyone who didn't know Poppy was ill would never imagine what she was going through, the painful infections they worked to keep at bay, the tests and hospitalisations. All she might have to go through. What was she going to do? The girls were surely half-sisters, she couldn't ignore that. If Poppy were healthy, she wasn't sure how she would have tackled the situation with Matt. All she did know was what her instinct was telling her, and that was to tackle it slowly. To consider everything, her daughter above all.

They would have to talk soon, though. Somehow they would have to have that conversation. Whatever the outcome for them, with his knowledge Matt might be the one person who could persuade Nicole to at least find out if Olivia were a suitable match.

Swiping away a tear that plopped down her face, she turned around and headed back to the road, forcing the odd tremulous smile at other parents as she went. Her head bowed as she tried to work out a way to approach the subject with Nicole, and with Matt, she made her way slowly back to her car. She was in danger of losing the man she had always loved. Even through the trials life had thrown at them, she'd loved the kind, caring person she knew him to be. Her baby girl … was there a real danger she might lose her to this illness she seemed powerless to do anything about? She couldn't bear it. Even the thought caused such a physical reaction inside her, she couldn't breathe. She was caught like a deer in the headlights, not sure which way to turn for fear it was the wrong way.

She was nearing her car when someone called her name, causing her to start.

'Kay!' Jason called again, dodging traffic as he crossed the road towards her. 'I've been trying to catch up with you. I've rung you a couple of times, but—'

'I know.' Kay turned away, pressing her key fob. He'd rung her more than a few times. Even when he was living in the States, he'd called her. If Matt knew, he would be furious. She stifled an ironic laugh. He *was* furious. At first, she'd thought she understood the rivalry between them, the rift that had ended in such terrible violence; it was because she'd once gone out with Jason. But now she wondered if Matt was more like his brother than she'd realised, wanting to have his cake and eat it, wanting to control her – who she saw, her emotions – whilst doing exactly what he liked.

Jason caught her arm as she reached for the driver's door. 'I just want to talk, Kay. To see how you are.'

Kay scrutinised him through narrowed eyes.

'I never got a chance to talk to you before I left. I was worried about you. After what happened at the hotel, I mean. Things weren't great between Matt and me, and I …' He stopped, shrugging embarrassedly. 'Look, Kay, it shouldn't have happened. I acted badly and I just wanted to apologise.'

Kay continued to stare at him, scarcely able to believe it. Not only was he apologising, which was a first, but far from the cockiness she'd always seen in his eyes, he looked contrite, actually concerned. How had that happened? He'd never been able to accept in the past that Matt was the man she wanted to be with. He'd clearly always been jealous of all that Matt had accomplished.

Jealous of the fact that he'd apparently won Kay from him. Jason had once said he loved her. He didn't. She suspected he wasn't capable of loving anyone but himself.

'Your scepticism is showing,' he joked, but again, there was no conceit in his eyes, only remorse. Was this the same person she'd gone out with? 'I've changed, Kay. Learned the value of love and relationships.' He shrugged once more, sadly this time.

Kay searched his face. Seeing tears now in his eyes, she was utterly stunned.

'I had to. My girlfriend, Crystal, she was ill, and I, er …' He stopped, wiping a hand over his face as he glanced down. 'I lost her.'

Kay's heart flipped over. *Oh no.* 'You mean …?'

He nodded sharply, pinched the bridge of his nose. 'She had a heart problem, inherited, hypertrophic cardiomyopathy. She was, well, living a normal life, but then she got sick and …' He broke off, his voice cracking.

'My God, Jason, I'm so sorry.' Kay's heart went out to him. Hesitating for a second, she reached out to him, her natural inclination to hug him.

Jason nodded and squeezed her back hard. 'I'm okay,' he said, easing away. 'Life can be a right bitch sometimes, can't it?' He laughed cynically. 'I didn't actually intend to tell you all that, but … It was seeing you again, I guess. I'm struggling to keep the emotion in check, you know.'

Kay nodded. She understood that completely. 'If you need anything… To talk any time …'

'Thanks.' Jason smiled appreciatively. 'I'm not sure Matt would be thrilled if I took you up on it, but thanks for the offer.'

Kay wasn't sure what to say.

'I'd better let you get off. I have an appointment anyway.' He nodded back to his car. 'I just wanted to check you were okay. I guessed Matt wouldn't welcome a call from me, so …'

'I am,' Kay assured him with a small smile. What else could she say? Burdening him with her problems wouldn't help how he was feeling.

'You look good,' he commented.

Kay glanced down, her cheeks flushing. She hadn't taken a jot of notice of how she looked lately. It hadn't felt important.

'See you around.' He reached out, just briefly, brushing a straggle of hair from her face, then pushed his hands into his pockets.

Kay felt dreadful for him. She wished there was something she could do. Maybe she could convince Matt to talk to him, at least give Jason a chance to try to put things right between them. He had changed, though she would never have believed it in a million years if she hadn't seen the evidence with her own eyes. 'I'll ring you,' she said, 'and I'll speak to Matt. Suggest that you two meet up and have a chat.'

'I won't hold my breath.' Jason smiled ruefully. 'I doubt he'll even want to see me.'

CHAPTER TWENTY-ONE

Matthew

Well, well, his brother was multitalented, obviously. Not only was he Biochem's shit-hot sales rep, but it also seemed he was qualified in dentistry. Kay had lied to him, right to his face. Quite clearly her 'dental appointment' was with Jason. A potent mixture of jealousy and fury boiling inside him, Matt watched the intimate exchange between them and felt sick to his soul.

Jesus. And there he'd been, feeling guilty about his own failings. He laughed cynically. He'd been a prize idiot, hadn't he, trying to convince himself that what had happened between them at the wedding was some mental aberration on Kay's part. To put it in the past and concentrate on building a future with her. He'd been determined to do that once Poppy was born. *No looking back* – it had been his mantra. But it wasn't the past, was it? It was happening now, right under his nose. *This* was why she couldn't even look him in the eye. She was seeing Jason.

Swallowing back the shard of glass in his windpipe, Matt started his car and pulled away from where he'd been parked several cars down on the opposite side of the road. They wouldn't notice him, he guessed. They were too busy gazing into each other's fucking eyes.

He'd thought she had more taste. How could she do this with *Jason* of all people? *Why* would she? Because he himself was never there for her; he answered his own question. Because Jason was back and all too ready to slide into his place, offering her what Matt couldn't. He wouldn't care that Kay was his brother's wife. On the contrary, he would get some perverse kick out of it. Some immature satisfaction from shafting him. He always had.

Matt's mind snapped back to the worst day in his childhood, the accident that had ramped up his brother's merciless bullying and made Matt wish it were him who was dead. Even now, when he closed his eyes at night, he could still hear his brother's mocking tones as he'd sat next to him in the back of their father's car. Matt had been determined to ignore him, Jason equally determined not to let him.

'Give us a listen,' he'd said, leaning across to twang Matt's earphones from his ears.

Wincing, Matt had made a grab for them as Jason dangled them tauntingly just out of his reach. 'Give them *back*.'

'Aw, poor little Matt.' Jason only held them higher. 'Is he going to cwy then, hey?'

Matt had been furious. Humiliated, as he always seemed to be. 'Stuff off,' he'd muttered. At which their mother had twisted in the front passenger seat to face them.

'Matthew! Language!' she reprimanded him. 'And you, Jason, act your age, for goodness' sake.'

'*What?*' Jason had splayed his hands, his face a picture of innocence. 'It's not me, it's him. He's nicked my Walkman. His is bust.'

'Liar,' Matt mumbled, his stomach tying itself into an angry knot.

'I'm not. *You* are.' Jason gave him a low V sign.

'Enough!' their father shouted furiously. 'Matt, do not *ever* let me hear you using foul language again. Understand?'

Matt had felt his throat tighten. Why did his father always take Jason's side? he wondered. But he knew really. Dad had always been disappointed in him. At least, that was how it had felt then. Whenever he'd looked at him, it was as if he couldn't quite work him out, as if he were mystified because Matt preferred to have his head stuck in a book rather than being out doing 'man's stuff' with him and Jason. Matt hadn't much enjoyed football, whereas his brother was always putting the boot in. He hadn't much liked fishing, either. He'd felt sorry for the fish flapping about with bloodied hooks skewering their mouths. Jason had revelled in that, calling him a 'big girl' and a 'sissy'. Their father would look at Jason reprovingly, but he'd never told him to stop. His ethos was that big boys should fight their own battles.

Hunched in his seat, Matt had seen his brother's gaze flick to the rear-view mirror, and knew he was checking to make sure their father wasn't watching before making a grab for the Walkman. Matt had decided that this time he *would* fight his own battle and stand up to him.

Sure enough, a second later, Jason lunged for it. 'Let *go*,' he'd hissed, grappling to wrench it out of Matt's grasp. When that failed, his eyes narrowed menacingly; he'd prised Matt's fingers away from it, wrenching them sharply backwards, but Matt had been adamant he wasn't going to let go, or cry. He would only be labelled a wimp if he did. 'I said, *let*—' Jason had stopped, gawping in surprise as the cassette deck sprang open and the cassette flew out, a long worm of snarled brown tape spewing out after it. 'Now look what you've done,' he'd gasped, his mouth hanging open in feigned shock. 'You've gone and broken it.'

'I didn't. *You* did.' Tears sprang from Matt's eyes despite his best efforts to stop them. It wasn't Jason's Walkman. It was *his*.

'Idiot,' Jason had cursed, banging the side of Matt's head with the heel of his hand. 'Mum, look what he's—'

'I said, *enough*!' Their father glared over his shoulder, his face puce with rage. 'What the bloody hell is wrong with—' The words had died in his throat as the oncoming car hit.

Matt sucked in a breath, feeling it over again, the bone-jarring impact, the impossible velocity thrusting him forwards, punching the air from his lungs. A split second's deafening silence followed, silence so complete he swore he could hear the soft beat of a passing bird's wing. Then came the high-pitched screaming, the raucous twisting and grinding of metal against metal. He could taste it, the coppery, salty taste in his mouth as he'd bitten down hard on his tongue; he could smell the petrol fumes and the acrid smoke that seared the back of his throat. A dull heartbeat later, he heard his father's anguished roar, the blood-freezing primal cry of a wounded animal, his brother's desperate scream: 'You *killed* her. You fucking *killed* her!'

His mother's lifeless eyes followed him as he was led away from the wreckage; that was the part that made him want to sob now like the ten-year-old child he'd been. But he couldn't. He hadn't cried then. Hadn't cried since.

'*Shit!*' Realising he'd jumped the lights, he yanked the steering wheel hard left, pulling the car into the kerb, to a cacophony of horns blaring behind him.

His hand shaking, he wiped away the sweat beading his forehead, tried to slow his rapid breathing. What in God's name was he doing, driving like a madman? His daughter needed him. He'd thought his wife did. He'd thought she loved him, thought he'd seen it in her eyes. That was what had got him through the nightmare his life had turned into after that *fucking* wedding. He'd made himself believe it, because he'd wanted to.

And then Jason had come home, the man who could apparently never forgive him for their mother's death, for taking Kay away from him. Now, it seemed, he'd decided he was going to take her back. For Jason, it worked like that. If he wanted it, he simply took it. But Kay wouldn't go. Would she? *Right*. He'd just seen the evidence with his own eyes. Then there were the calls. And the lies. The evasiveness.

He had to talk to her. And what then? What if she confirmed it? Matt wasn't sure how he'd handle it. He was sure, though, that if his brother had chosen this moment in Poppy's life to try and take away all that was safe from around her, he would fight him. No way was he about to stand aside and allow him open access to his daughter. Kay needed to be aware of that much. It simply wasn't going to happen.

CHAPTER TWENTY-TWO

Kay

Going into university a little early, Kay caught sight of Amelia walking across the quad towards the library. Still perturbed by the remarks she'd made after the last class, as if she knew what was happening in Kay's marriage – which she couldn't possibly – she decided now might be a good time to have a quiet word with her.

The way Amelia had been watching her the other day hadn't been with rapt interest in the subject matter. She'd been scrutinising her, and Kay had definitely felt uncomfortable. And that remark about Matt being hardly likely to tell her if he was having serial affairs was far too much of a coincidence. She had even referred to him as Matthew and Kay certainly couldn't recall having mentioned his name. She remembered the comment Amelia had made the first time they spoke. 'She has a very special daddy,' the woman had said, after their brief conversation about Poppy. Kay had thought it was an odd thing to say at the time, but had dismissed it, thinking she was referring to Matt's work as a neonatologist. Playing it over, though, it sounded almost as if she knew him. Then there was the text, signed off with two kisses. Sent by someone with the initial A. She might well be being paranoid now, given recent events, but she was starting to think none of it was coincidence.

Sprinting after the woman, she followed her up the library steps, only to be frustrated by the security checks. Amelia was on the other side of the reception area as Kay approached the barrier that would allow her through to the library. She was climbing the stairs to the first floor. Kay could hardly yell across to her.

Pushing through the automated gate, having twice inserted her identification card the wrong way round, she flashed her pass at the security guard and headed quickly towards the stairs. Bounding up them, she spotted Amelia approaching the doors at the end of the corridor leading to the reference section. 'Amelia,' she called.

Amelia didn't respond, disappearing through the doors instead.

Kay took a breath. Aware of where they were, she hadn't called that loudly. It was possible she hadn't heard her.

Reaching the doors, she followed her through and glanced around. Amelia was nowhere to be seen. Puzzled, Kay checked the reading rooms and various tables, then between the bookshelves, finally slowing at the creative writing section, where she found Amelia browsing. She appeared absorbed as Kay approached her, oblivious to her presence.

'Hi, Amelia,' she said pleasantly.

Amelia started, looking alarmed at first, and then surprised. 'Kay!' she said, now appearing delighted, which threw Kay completely. 'I didn't expect to see you here. I thought you came in later.'

'I do normally,' Kay answered, keeping her voice low. 'I had one or two things I needed to catch up with, though.'

Amelia's eyes lingered for a second. Then, 'Ah,' she said, with a small nod, and turned back to the titles she was perusing.

'Searching for something in particular?' Kay enquired.

Amelia furrowed her brow thoughtfully. 'Something that might give me a clue how to set out my assignments,' she said with a forlorn sigh. 'I'm keen to crack on with my critical response to *Possession*, since it's a subject that's so close to home, but I'm hopeless without a clear structure.'

Kay glanced at the books, then plucked one she was familiar with from the shelf. 'This might help,' she said, offering it to her.

'Brilliant. Thanks.' Smiling, Amelia reached for it.

'You mentioned you'd been in a controlling relationship,' Kay ventured. 'That must have been difficult for you.'

'Not me. My sister,' Amelia said, leafing through the book.

'Oh.' Kay studied her profile as she turned back to the shelves. 'She must have been badly affected. For you to be so concerned about her, I mean.'

Keeping her gaze fixed on the bookshelf, Amelia took a second to answer. 'He possessed her,' she said eventually. 'Just like Ash in the book, pretending concern for her. He wasn't concerned for her, he just wanted to own her. My sister couldn't see it, though, like Christabel. She seemed totally unaware that he was stealing her identity. She changed completely. He controlled everything she did, everything she said, everything she was, eroded her confidence until there was nothing left of her. I tried to tell her, but ...'

Kay sensed she was upset as she tapered off, and felt for her. It explained why she'd identified with the text she'd set. 'I'm sorry. That must have been hard for you to stand by and watch,' she said, choosing her words carefully. 'Is she all right?'

'Not really,' Amelia said.

Kay noticed her body stiffen, the sudden tense set of her jaw. 'You seem angry.'

'I am. Very.' Amelia turned to her, and Kay felt goosebumps prickle her skin. Her expression was stony. For a split second, her eyes became flint-edged and so dark as to be almost black. And then it was gone, as if she'd internally shaken herself, her face softening into a smile. 'So, how's Matthew?' she asked.

Poleaxed, Kay stared at her. Was she playing some sort of game with her? If so, it was far from amusing. 'How do you know my husband's name?' she asked, counselling herself to stay calm.

Amelia's smile changed to an expression of bemusement. 'You mentioned it. How else would I know—'

'When?' Kay cut across her.

Amelia knitted her brow. 'When we were talking. I can't remember when exactly, but—'

Kay wasn't buying it. God knows, she was muddled lately, but she was sure she'd never mentioned Matt's name. 'Why did you ask me if there were any secrets in my relationship, Amelia?' She held her gaze, though she felt far from brave. She felt like weeping with uncertainty and frustration. What was going on here?

Amelia shook her head, seemingly perplexed. 'Because you'd just been talking about secrets being a defining character trait. I was curious, that was all,' she said.

'When I told you there weren't, you asked me if I was sure,' Kay reminded her. 'You talked about my husband having serial affairs.'

'Hypothetically.' Amelia laughed bewilderedly. 'I mean, men usually are the ones having affairs, aren't they? I thought we might discuss it further. But clearly you didn't want to, so …'

Kay squinted at her. Amelia had walked away. Walked out of the classroom and vanished. She must have heard Kay calling after her. 'It was too personal a comment,' she pointed out, feeling incredibly confused and close to tears. 'I'm struggling to understand why you would presume to make it.'

Amelia looked at her in bafflement. 'It wasn't meant to be. Married people do keep secrets from one another, don't they? They have affairs, as you pointed out. It was just an innocent comment, Kay, on the subject in hand. There's really no need to be so defensive.'

Defensive? She was being no such thing. 'Do you know my husband?' she asked. It was the question that had wormed its way into her head that day and wouldn't go away.

Amelia scanned her face, tears welling in her eyes. Kay was struggling now to believe they were genuine, to believe anything she said. 'Have I done something to upset you, Kay?' she asked shakily. 'You seem very agitated.'

'I said, do you *know* him?' Kay demanded.

Amelia was backing away from her, her expression fearful. 'Why are you so angry with me, Kay?' she asked tremulously. 'I don't understand. I really like this course. I thought we were getting on, but suddenly you seem so hostile.'

'Hostile?' Kay's stomach dropped. 'I'm not being anything of the *sort*.' She took a step towards Amelia and then froze as someone placed a hand on her shoulder. Her blood turned to ice as she turned around to discover it was the security guard.

'You're creating a disturbance, madam,' he said, looking her over, unimpressed. 'I'm afraid I'm going to have to ask you to leave.'

Kay swallowed, deeply humiliated. She'd raised her voice. She hadn't realised she had, but she had. Why had she done that? Why was her whole world suddenly unravelling? 'But I work here,' she pointed out, a hard lump expanding in her chest.

'Nevertheless,' the man answered, his expression uncompromising.

Behind him, all eyes were turned in their direction. Students were whispering to each other. Another member of staff was looking on, horrified, and Kay wanted to curl up and die.

CHAPTER TWENTY-THREE

Amelia

The clouds were bulbous and low, the charcoal-grey sky as bleak as her mood. Glancing around, making sure there was no one else in sight, Amelia placed the simple spray of spring hyacinth on the ground, then straightened up and tugged her leather jacket tighter around her. It did little to keep out the biting wind that was slicing across the open fields, chilling her to the bone. Rain threatened, the earthy smell of damp wood and grass hanging heavy on the air. Hearing the distant rumble of thunder, she looked back to the darkening skies. It was clearly about to bucket down. She didn't have a brolly. She didn't care. It wouldn't have been much use in these conditions anyway.

Glancing behind her, she could see the harsh glow of office lights shimmering through the branches of the trees surrounding the field. She was sure someone would spot her one day, a solitary figure silhouetted against the flat landscape. She wasn't sure she cared about that much either now. She'd had to come. She felt closer to Kelsey here.

'She's upset. I feel bad about that,' she said, seemingly to the wind, but she knew in her heart that her sister could hear her. She did feel bad. Kay *had* been upset, but was that any excuse for judging her without knowing anything about her? 'It's not her fault, though, is it? It's his,' she continued out loud, not expecting answers other than those she imagined in her head. Kelsey would agree with her now, Amelia felt sure. Her eyes had been opened. Except they weren't there any more, the orbs beneath her eyelids eaten away until there was nothing but soulless empty sockets where laughter once danced. Amelia would never look into them again. Never whisper shared secrets late into the night. Never dance with her again like no one was watching.

'I miss you,' she murmured, sinking to her knees, careless of the bumpy ground beneath her, the wet mud that would soak into her jeans. She turned her face upwards as the heavens opened, allowing the fat plops of rain to spill down her cheeks and mingle with her tears. She wished it would sweep her away. That the water, pure and fresh, running in rivulets down her neck to her breasts, could wash away her pain and her grief. Why had she done it? Why hadn't Kelsey listened to her? 'Why did you desert me?' she asked aloud, swallowing back the unbearable pain in her chest.

But she knew the answer. Love was a powerful thing, dangerous. Kelsey had been besotted, sucked in by him. She'd lost all sense of self. It hadn't been her fault. She'd been blind. And she'd been swept away, too emotionally entrenched to realise she was drowning.

The sound of a car engine firing up snapped Amelia's gaze away from the flowers she'd arranged, saddened by the knowledge that they would rot here too until she came back to replace them. 'I should go,' she said. 'I'll be back soon. Please don't be lonely.'

Kissing her fingers, she pressed them to the ground, and then pulled herself quickly to her feet to make her way back across the fields to where her own car was discreetly parked in a disused side lane. Her phone alerted her to a text as she walked. She retrieved the phone from her jeans pocket and checked it, and her mood lifted.

I'm not sure I want to be involved in what you're suggesting. We should probably speak on the phone, was all the message said. She hadn't thought she would get back in touch after the last text Amelia had sent, suggesting that she should seek support for her child, at least financially; she'd been racking her brains wondering how to physically approach her, yet here she was. Her interest had obviously been piqued.

Relieved, Amelia jogged the last few yards to her car, slipping wetly into the driver's side, where she paused, ducking down a little as a flashy car slid past the T-junction ahead of her, and then called the number.

'We might do better to meet in person,' she said as soon as the woman picked up. 'It's safer that way, and I have something to show you.'

CHAPTER TWENTY-FOUR

Kay

Checking that Poppy was still engrossed in an episode of *She-Ra and the Princesses of Power* – her absolute last five minutes of TV before bed – Kay went to the kitchen. Leaving the door slightly open in case Poppy needed her, she picked up her phone to call Jason, even though she knew what Matt would think about it. A pulse of tension tightened between her temples as she wondered where he was. She'd done something she rarely did, and checked up on him. She'd rung the hospital, pretending she couldn't reach him on his mobile and casually enquiring whether he was around. The switchboard had tried to locate him, eventually putting her through to a nurse on the neonatal unit, who told her she thought he'd left for the evening. What was she supposed to make of that? What excuse would he have when he came home?

Still, she felt guilty ringing Jason, aware that Matt didn't believe the contact between them was innocent, thinking she had ulterior motives. She was aware, too, that she wasn't calling Jason solely to check he was okay after the awful thing he'd told her about his poor girlfriend. She had an ulterior motive, which made her feel doubly guilty. What choice did she have, though? She was scared. Terrified that Matt might allow the history between them, the animosity he felt towards his brother, to cloud his thinking.

That he would be too stubborn to approach Jason as a possible donor match.

Where did that leave her? Was she supposed to not contact Jason because Matt didn't want her to, because his pride might be wounded? He wasn't that shallow, she knew he wasn't, but that was how it looked from where she was standing. She couldn't put Matt's feelings before her daughter's health. There was simply no way she could ignore another avenue, any avenue. Poppy was her daughter, the child she'd given birth to. Matt should understand.

Listening to Jason's phone ringing out, her heart pumped. She felt as if she were living on a knife edge, her nerves in shreds, as evidenced by her behaviour in the library. How had so many things gone horribly wrong so quickly? How was her marriage apparently in peril, while her daughter was so sick? She didn't feel she could cope. Some mornings, in the early days after Poppy had become ill, she would arrive home to the empty house after dropping her at school and would just want to sit down and weep like a baby. Now, she felt that if she allowed herself that release, she would never stop. She had to pull herself together. Her darling daughter was coping. Kay had no right to feel sorry for herself.

Hearing Jason's voice message kick in, she was about to hang up when he answered. 'Kay … I didn't think you would call,' he said, his tone a mixture of surprise and pleasure.

'I thought I would check on you. I wondered how you were doing?' Kay tried to quash her guilt. She did care – how could she not, after what he'd told her? – but he hadn't treated her well when they were together. He certainly hadn't treated Matt well over the years. She needed to bear that in mind.

'Okay, you know.' Jason paused. 'A bit lonely, if I'm honest.'

Kay felt her heart squeeze. Of course he would be, after going through such a terrible tragedy out there in the States on his own and coming back here to the hostility that still lingered between him and his brother. 'We could go for a coffee sometime, if you'd like?' she suggested.

'I'd love to,' Jason said, sounding more chipper. 'Gazing at you over it would certainly cheer me up.'

Feeling immediately uncomfortable at the quip, which sounded more like the old Jason, Kay didn't answer.

Jason evidently picked up on her discomfort. 'Sorry. Old habits,' he said, sounding contrite. 'You can't blame a man for trying.'

A man who'd not long lost his girlfriend under awful circumstances, Kay resisted pointing out. And with a woman who was married to his brother. She felt herself wavering, wondering whether this really was a good idea.

'It's just me, Kay. The way I am,' Jason went on. 'You know what I'm like, glib when I probably shouldn't be. It's my way of coping, smiling through the sadness, if you like. Don't judge me too harshly.'

She paused before answering. 'Perhaps you should try being serious once in a while,' she suggested. 'If you don't want people to take you at face value.'

He went quiet. Then, 'I know. I'll try,' he said. 'I'd like to talk seriously to Matt. Apologise. But I guess he doesn't want to hear it.'

Again, Kay felt for him. She wished Matt would meet with him. She knew he would struggle to come to terms with the fact that she and Jason had been in touch, but Poppy had to be their first consideration, above all else. He should be the one reaching out to his brother, building the relationship in case Poppy needed Jason as a donor. 'There's something I need to talk to you about,' she said hesitantly, feeling it would be unfair of her not to mention it up front. She didn't want to appear to be playing on his emotions, though perhaps she was.

'I'm all ears,' Jason responded, his tone jovial again.

'Soon,' she added.

'Right. About?' he asked, a curious edge now to his voice.

Kay took a tremulous breath. 'I have a problem. Something I need to ask you about.'

'Problem?' Jason sounded guarded. 'What kind of problem?'

Hearing a sound in the hall and guessing Poppy might be about to appear, Kay avoided answering. 'I can't discuss it now. Poppy's still up. Do you think we might be able to meet tomorrow? If you're free, that is.'

'Of course,' Jason assured her. 'Where?'

'Costa in the town centre. And Jason, please don't tell Matt,' she added.

'If you'd rather I didn't …' He sounded intrigued now.

Kay swallowed back another lump of guilt. 'I'll see you there, one o'clock.'

'I'll be counting the minutes,' Jason quipped.

She really wished he wouldn't. His flippancy, his innuendo around her, which she knew had riled Matt endlessly, wouldn't make his attempts to mend fences with him any easier.

Turning away from the window as she hung up, her heart leapt into her throat. 'God, you scared me,' she said shakily, seeing Matt looming in the doorway. How long had he been standing there?

'I'm not that alarming, am I?' Matt smiled, but there was something behind his eyes. Wariness? Kay couldn't quite read it.

'No.' She offered him a smile back, and tried to slow the palpitations in her chest. 'It's just that I wasn't expecting you. You're never normally home this early.'

'I grabbed the opportunity.' He walked towards her and brushed her cheek with a kiss. 'I thought maybe we could sit down and …' He stopped, his brow furrowing as he looked her over. 'Are you okay? You look a bit pale.'

'I'm fine. It's been a long day.' Kay forced another smile. She'd felt shock ripple through her entire body when she'd realised he was there. Now she felt disorientated, caught out. 'Poppy had a good day,' she announced brightly.

The furrow in Matt's brow deepened. 'Right,' he said, with an uncertain smile. 'Well, that's good isn't it?'

'Yes, brilliant,' Kay agreed, and then almost died when he asked, 'So, who were you speaking to on the phone?'

'Just Steph,' she said, averting her gaze. She couldn't look at him and lie to him. She shouldn't *be* lying to him. She should just tell him she'd been speaking to Jason. But that would risk him accusing her of deceiving him, and she was sure she would explode with all that was pent up inside her if he were to do that.

Glancing back at him, she found him scrutinising her carefully. 'Is there a problem?' she asked cautiously.

'No.' Moving away from her, Matt shook his head. 'I thought I heard my name mentioned, that's all.' He looked questioningly back at her.

Kay's heart plummeted. 'Yes, I, um …' She faltered, and then sighed with relief as Poppy appeared in the doorway, giving her a little more breathing space to try to work out how to talk to him about Olivia; how to convince him to put personal grievances aside and speak to his brother. Matt knowing she was in communication with Jason wouldn't smooth the way to him doing that.

'Daddy!' Poppy cried delightedly, charging across the kitchen towards him.

Matt turned around, just in time to catch her as she hurled herself at him. 'Hi, baby girl,' he said, sweeping her up. 'And what face are we wearing today, hey, smiley or sad?'

'A smiley face,' Poppy assured him, locking her arms around his neck. 'I haven't been tired or poorly once.'

'Really? Well, that is good news, isn't it? The best I've had all day.' His voice hoarse with emotion, he hugged her hard to him. Seeing him close his eyes and realising he might be close to tears,

Kay swallowed back the hard lump expanding in her chest. He gave such a huge part of his life over to his patients, but he lived for his baby girl.

Poppy eased back after a second. 'Liv stays with me when I do get tired,' she told him. 'Mrs Weaver says she can because she's my special friend. She reads me a story.'

'Does she?' Working visibly to compose himself, Matt smiled. 'Well, she *is* a special friend, isn't she?'

'Uh huh.' Poppy nodded. 'Mrs Weaver thinks we're so close we could be sisters.'

Oh God. Kay felt herself tense.

'Liv thinks that would be really cool,' Poppy babbled innocently on, 'because then we could live in the same house and—'

'Come on, chatterbox,' Kay interrupted. 'Daddy's tired, and you have to give your teeth a good brush before bed.'

'Oh *Mummeee.*' Poppy screwed up her face. 'Just five more minutes.'

'No more minutes, young lady,' Kay answered firmly. 'It's already way past your bedtime. If you don't go to sleep soon, you *will* be tired in the morning, and then you might not be able to go to school and see Liv at all.'

'Eek.' Poppy turned alarmed eyes to Matt, and then squeezed her arms around his neck and planted a fat kiss on his face.

Matt laughed. 'Do you want me to take her up?' he asked.

'No,' Kay said quickly, possibly too quickly, wary of the conversation continuing upstairs. 'Why don't you grab us a drink instead?'

Matt nodded and made an apologetic face at Poppy. 'Better do as Mum says, or we'll both be in big trouble,' he said, kissing her cheek and lowering her gently to the floor.

Holding onto his hand, Poppy hesitated. 'Will you drive me to school tomorrow, Daddy?' she asked, causing Kay's heart to catapult into her mouth. 'You could see Liv then.'

Matt glanced regretfully down at her. 'I'd love to, but I have to go to work early, sweetheart.'

'Oh.' Poppy looked disappointed. 'To look after a poorly little baby?' she asked him.

'Yes.' Matt's smile was heart-wrenching. Kay willed her daughter to come to her, but there was no way to interrupt this moment between them.

Poppy blinked sadly. 'Will you give the baby a kiss for me?'

'I will, I promise.' Kay heard his breath catch.

'And one from Liv, too.' Poppy gave him a firm nod, and finally let go of his hand to take hold of Kay's. 'Night, night, Daddy.' She gave him a little wave.

'Night, night, precious girl.' Matt smiled and waved back. 'No more bad dreams, okay? Think about happy things.'

'I am,' Poppy said with another resolute nod. 'I'm going to think up a story about Barbie Ballerina to tell Liv. We take it in turns. It's my turn tomorrow.'

'Excellent,' Matt said. 'You can tell us in the morning. Maybe it will stop Mummy's bad dreams too.' He glanced at Kay, holding her gaze for a second before looking away.

'Excellent,' Poppy repeated, happily following Kay, whose heart was thrumming a prophetic warning in her chest. Nothing could stop her bad dreams, not with her world about to be turned upside down.

CHAPTER TWENTY-FIVE

Kay was halfway through Poppy's bedtime story when her heart stalled. *Her phone.* Panic rose inside her as she pictured it where she'd left it on the kitchen table. She didn't think Matt would snoop on her, but still, she didn't feel comfortable leaving it there. 'Do you mind if we finish this tomorrow night, sweetheart?' she asked, reaching to brush her sleepy girl's fringe from her forehead. 'Mummy's feeling a bit tired too.'

Poppy looked surprised for a second, and then snuggled down. 'No.' She yawned widely. 'I can think up my own story to tell Liv instead.'

'Good idea.' Kay leaned to press a kiss to her cheek. 'Night, night, angel,' she whispered.

'Night, night, Mummy. Love you bigger than the world,' Poppy murmured, her eyelids already growing heavy. Kay felt a huge surge of relief. One of the side effects of the steroids Poppy had to take was insomnia, which added to the tiredness that would wash over her in the middle of the day. At least tonight she looked as if she would sleep.

'Love you too, darling.' She smiled sadly. *With my whole life.* If only God would accept it in exchange for her baby's, she would offer it in an instant.

After tucking Poppy in under her duvet, she walked quietly to the door, eased it to, then flew down the stairs into the kitchen –

and froze, the knot of nerves inside her tying itself tighter as she looked from Matt to the phone he held in his hand.

'It rang,' he said, his tone flat.

Kay's eyes snapped back to him, and she knew. Before he confirmed it, she knew who had called, what he was thinking. His eyes were as dark as thunder.

'Jason,' he added after an interminably long minute. 'I didn't answer it. He sent you a text. He wonders whether you could make it one thirty instead of one o'clock.'

Her stomach turning over, Kay considered lying. For the sake of Poppy just upstairs she considered it, but dismissed it. This had gone too far. She couldn't stand here, the accused, not when his suspicions were so wide of the mark, when her motives for speaking to Jason were motives he should share too. 'I called him,' she said, folding her arms defensively across her chest.

'Right.' Placing the phone down on the table, aligning it precisely with the edges, Matt studied it for a long, loaded moment. 'And were you going to mention it at some point?' he asked coldly. 'Just out of interest?'

'Of course I was. I …' Kay closed her eyes. 'God, this is *ridiculous!*' she snapped, unable to contain her emotions any longer, to bear the weight of everything. She needed him on her side. Not this juvenile behaviour. 'It's to do with Poppy, for goodness' sake. I'm seeing him because of Poppy. Why else—'

'I gathered!' Matt yelled over her.

Kay froze. He'd never raised his voice. He'd lost his temper, but she couldn't remember a time when he'd ever shouted like that. His face was rigid with anger. She felt the tears rising, her throat closing. So, she'd once gone out with Jason for a bit. Drunkenly kissed him at a wedding. It meant nothing next to what she had with Matt. He must know that. He *did* know that. What had she done that was so *wrong*?

'Were you ever going to tell me, Kay?' he asked, his voice more subdued. Still, though, his fury was palpable.

Kay swallowed painfully. 'Tell you what?'

'You weren't, were you? You were just going to pick right up where you left off. Christ, I've been a complete idiot, haven't I?' He laughed, a short, hollow bark, then pressed his thumb and forefinger hard against his forehead and turned abruptly away.

'What in God's name are you talking about?' Kay followed him to the hall. 'Matt, stop. We have to talk.'

He paused. 'Not here. Not now,' he said, his eyes flicking towards the stairs.

'Yes, now.' Kay was struggling to hold on to her own temper. 'We need to sit down calmly and—'

'Am I not a good enough father to Poppy?' Matt faced her. 'A good enough lover, is that it? What, Kay? You need to tell me, because …' He stopped, blinking hard at the ceiling. 'I have no idea what I've done.'

'Really?' Kay felt tears spring to her own eyes. 'I find that very hard to believe, Matt. And while we're on the subject of who's done what, I've done *nothing* to deserve any of this.'

Looking away, Matt shook his head, emitting another cynical laugh.

Kay felt her blood boil. She'd promised herself she wouldn't do this, not with Poppy in the house, and not until she'd spoken again with Nicole, but he was forcing her hand. Was that what this was all about? 'You are aware I know, aren't you?' she asked him.

Matt looked back at her, his eyebrows raised. 'Know what, precise—'

'Daddy,' Poppy called from the landing. 'What's wrong?'

Matt's gaze shot in her direction. He took a step towards the stairs. But Kay was faster, flying up them towards her daughter.

Hoisting the little girl into her arms, she heard the front door close.

'Where's Daddy going, Mummy?' Poppy whispered.

'He has an emergency, sweetheart.' Kay held her close, pressed a kiss to her cheek and breathed in the special smell of her. 'He'll be back soon.'

She felt her heart crack as she carried Poppy back to her bedroom. She had no idea whether he would be back. Why he was so furious if he'd gathered she was talking to Jason about Poppy. Shouldn't he be relieved that she was? Shouldn't *he* be the one feeling guilty, because he hadn't spoken to him when he damn well *should* have? What in God's name was happening to them?

CHAPTER TWENTY-SIX

Matthew

'Dr Young …' Hearing someone calling him as he fumbled with the coffee machine in A&E, Matt tried to shake the sleep from his head. His hope was that copious amounts of caffeine might dilute the whisky he'd consumed before he'd fallen into an alcohol-induced sleep on one of the on-call beds in an empty side room. He'd meant to have one drink. It had turned into one too many. It had been a bloody stupid thing to do. It hadn't helped. Far from dulling the pain, all it had done was bring his marital problems into sharp focus, his focus being on his brother, who was the cause of them. It had been particularly stupid to choose the pub close to the hospital to drown his sorrows in. If word got around, speculation about why he'd been there drinking alone would be rife. The last thing he needed was his colleagues gossiping about his private life and imagining they might have to tiptoe around him. Coffee, however, he did need. *Dammit*. He cursed silently, giving the machine a shove with the heel of his hand as it swallowed his money without producing the goods.

'Matt!' Whoever had been trying to get his attention shouted across the reception area.

Matt snapped his gaze up to see one of the newly qualified doctors racing towards him. 'It's Leo Cooper,' he said breathlessly. 'He's bradycardic. We've tried—'

'Shit.' Matt abandoned the coffee and headed fast for the corridor leading to the neonatal unit.

'What's his heart rate?' he shouted back as he ran.

'Below fifty,' the young doctor answered, close behind him. His voice was strained. Having not yet started his specialty training, he would probably be panicking. Matt was panicking too. Below fifty was way too slow for a newborn, even when sleeping. Why the bloody hell hadn't he checked on the child earlier? At least gone straight to neonatal as soon as he'd woken? Because he'd been too busy feeling sorry for himself, as if that would help cement his crumbling marriage. Because he hadn't been capable. Christ, what was *wrong* with him?

Bursting through the NICU doors after sanitising his hands, he could see immediately that the baby was limp. 'How long has he been struggling?' he asked, taking over from the nurse who was checking the tube delivering extra oxygen through Leo's nose. His heart missed a beat as he noted the baby's bluish skin tone, indicating cyanosis, meaning his oxygen levels were dangerously low.

'Just a few minutes,' she said. 'I noticed his breathing was noisy, so I immediately checked for signs of distress. We tried to get hold of you, but—'

The cardiorespiratory monitor alarm sounded over her. She hadn't needed to finish her sentence. They hadn't been able to get hold of him. He'd been sleeping it off, his phone going unanswered because he hadn't even heard it ringing. His thoughts had been all on himself. Not on this child. Not on his own child, who needed him to be functioning and there for her as much as this baby did – as he'd promised his parents he *would* be. *Dear God, please don't let this happen.* Rubbing the baby's back, arms and legs, trying to stimulate him into breathing, Matt swallowed back the lump lodged like a stone in his throat. Leo's lips were blue, his nail beds were blue … *Please don't let him die.*

His own heart rate slowing to a terrified thud, he shouted instructions to intubate. Mechanical ventilation was something he'd wanted to avoid in order to minimise inflammation to the baby's lungs, the danger of bronchopulmonary dysplasia. Now there was no other choice.

Seconds later, he attempted to fix his focus where it should be and pass the endotracheal tube down the baby's throat. He couldn't do it. He blinked away the sweat from his eyes. The airway was small, but he'd done this a thousand times, yet he couldn't … His hands were shaking. *Jesus!* He blinked hard. *Help me!* Sweat wetting his shirt, he sucked in a sharp breath and tried again. The relief from the team working diligently around him was tangible when he finally succeeded. Matt's was so overwhelming, he felt his entire body grow weak.

Allowing himself to breathe out, he stepped away, giving the junior doctor room to take over under supervision. His, for what it was worth. He'd rarely felt less capable or in control.

'You should try and get some rest,' the man suggested, glancing up at him after a second. Matt noted his expression, a combination of sympathy and puzzlement. It was no surprise that he was puzzled, having been forced to race around the hospital looking for Matt, and then finding him looking the worse for wear, trying to force coffee out of the machine. He guessed he would also have noted the tremor in his hands, as if he might be suffering alcohol withdrawal symptoms. The realisation hit Matt like a sledgehammer: he probably was.

CHAPTER TWENTY-SEVEN

Kay

Kay waited nervously to be put through to the director of the MA in creative writing. She'd hardly ever taken time off at short notice, unless it was for Poppy. The university had been extremely understanding whenever Poppy had had a hospital appointment or had been unwell. Now she was lying to them. She had no choice. She simply didn't feel capable of containing her emotions around Amelia. After finding Matt's side of the bed empty this morning and realising that this time he really hadn't come home, the last thing she wanted to do was meet with Jason either, but she was beyond desperate now to find out if he could shed some light on what she now realised must have been eating away at Matt for some time. What it was Jason had said to him all those years ago that had driven him to violence. If he was truly contrite, he would be honest with her, surely. She also wanted to broach the subject of Poppy's potential need for a donor, and find out if he was willing to put himself forward for testing. She had to. The prospect of there being no suitable living donor, should Poppy need one, terrified her.

Feigning a tummy bug once Professor Simons answered – about which he was sympathetic – she was about to end the call when he stopped her. 'Actually, Kay, I was hoping to have a bit of a catch-up with you,' he said, his tone guarded. 'Do you think you could give me a call, as soon as you're well enough, obviously, so we can organise a meeting?'

'Of course,' she said, knitting her brow worriedly as she wondered what it was he wanted to 'catch up' about. They'd finalised her timetable two weeks back and there was nothing else outstanding as far as she knew. 'Was there something in particular you wanted to discuss?'

Professor Simons hesitated for a second. 'I have to say it as it is, Kay,' he said, now sounding awkward. 'Something's been brought to my attention, an incident in the library,' he went on, causing genuine nausea to rise inside her. 'I'm sure it's nothing that can't be cleared up, but I thought we should perhaps have a little chat.'

Kay's breath caught in her chest. Amelia had spoken to him? Dear God, had she *reported* her? 'Right. Yes, fine,' she managed tightly, whilst scrambling through her mind for a way to defuse whatever she might have said to him. 'I'm not sure what it's about. I am aware that one of my students has latched on to me a little bit, but she hasn't been that much of a problem so I thought it was probably best to just leave it for the moment.'

Professors Simons paused again, ominously. 'We'll talk about it when you're back to full health. Give me a call. Meanwhile, get some rest.'

'I will,' Kay said weakly. She stared at her phone in shocked disbelief as he hung up. *This* on top of everything else. What had Amelia told him? A new wave of panic unfurled inside her. She'd never imagined the university would invite her to take up the position of visiting lecturer. She hadn't felt qualified, but had tried her damnedest to earn the trust they'd placed in her. She loved her job, the one time when she wasn't incessantly worrying about her sick child and could use her intellect. Amelia must know that by mentioning what had happened between them she would be putting Kay's future in jeopardy. Why had she done it? Why did every aspect of her life that mattered to her seem under threat? She felt as if she were losing control of everything. Losing her mind. How had this happened? *Why?*

'Mummy, are we leaving now?' Poppy tugged on her arm as she stood, disorientated and stupefied, in the hall.

Realising her daughter was already in her coat and ready to go, Kay dragged her stunned gaze from her phone. 'Yes,' she said quickly, aware that Poppy was keen not to be late to meet Olivia, which only exacerbated her feelings of bewilderment. Her life was crumbling. It felt as if it was being dismantled brick by brick, and no matter how hard she tried to hold the walls up, she couldn't. Soon they would bury her.

'Sorry, sweetheart.' She tried to still the nerves grinding inside her and concentrate on her daughter, who was tugging urgently on her sleeve. 'Mummy just had to ring work. Won't be a sec.'

'We have to hurry, Mummy. Liv will be waiting.' Poppy turned for the door as Kay reached to grab her coat and bag from the newel post while hastily checking her phone in hopes of a text from Matt. Nothing. Her heart slid icily into her stomach. He'd texted her once last night in response to her messages begging him to come home, or at least call her. It had been crushingly short. *Needed at the hospital* was all he'd said – no preamble, no signing off with a kiss, as he normally did. Had he even been at the hospital last night? Kay felt panic mushroom inside her as she wondered whether he might have left her. Surely he wouldn't, not with his daughter's health so precarious? Unless … The thought had occurred to her last night, when he'd seemed to be instigating an argument she didn't want to have, that he might have made up his mind to go. *No.* She would have known. She *would* have. But she didn't know all there was to know about Matt, did she? Quite obviously.

Her throat tightening, she blinked back the tears stinging her eyes and hurried to fumble the front door open. She felt as if she were falling apart. She *wouldn't*. Determinedly, she swiped at her cheeks and helped Poppy into the car. Whatever the future held, she had to stay in control. For her little girl's sake, she had to do that. Climbing into the driver's seat, she started the engine and steeled her resolve.

Poppy chatted incessantly as she drove, mostly about Olivia. Kay's heart almost stopped beating when her daughter told her what she and Olivia had decided to do together when they grew up. 'We're going to be doctors and look after little babies,' she said with a confident nod. 'Just like Daddy.'

Forcing an encouraging smile, Kay tried to work through the jumble of thoughts in her head. What was she going to do? What *could* she do? She had to find out what Jason had said to Matt on that dreadful day of their confrontation, which might help her understand what her husband was so afraid of. But even if she did, if Jason were honest with her, how would that help save her marriage? It couldn't explain away Olivia's existence. Couldn't excuse anything. Frantically she searched for a way forward, a shred of hope that she might be able to save her marriage. She couldn't see any.

Soon Matt would meet Olivia. He would realise that she was his daughter, and then what? Might he want a new family with her? She knew now that he had kept a big part of his life from her – he had been unfaithful once, maybe more than once. She couldn't shake the feeling that he was seeing someone now. Could it even be Olivia's birth mother? Whoever she was, she mattered enough for him to throw his marriage away. Kay didn't think she could survive it, but she would. She would have to. Her child's health and happiness depended on her. She would fight through this. She would fight for her child. She would fight Matt if she had to. She wouldn't let him destroy her psychologically with his games, the deceit she'd never believed him capable of. She would die to keep her child safe if it came to it. It was that simple.

CHAPTER TWENTY-EIGHT

Approaching Costa Coffee along the pedestrianised high street later that afternoon, Kay instantly spotted Jason seated at a table outside. He smiled when he saw her, looking so like Matt it broke her heart another inch. She'd once thought they were as alike as chalk and cheese personality-wise. It was strange how appearances could deceive. How could she have been so taken in by Matt, so completely in love with him? The part that broke her heart most of all was that even now, knowing he had been unfaithful to her, she still loved him. Had it been just one affair, a moment of madness, maybe, just maybe, there would have been a way to get through it, but this … His being so cold and distant with her, staying away from home. Her mind went to the text on his phone. He was seeing someone else. He had to be. Lying to her. Keeping so much from her. *Did* he know about Olivia? Keeping that from her was possibly the cruellest thing he could do, especially now. She didn't know him, did she, not at all. How could she fight for him when he clearly didn't want her, when he had hurt her so badly?

Jason stood to greet her as she approached the table. 'Hey, how are you?'

'Fine.' She arranged her face into a smile. 'You?'

'Getting through.' He shrugged. 'One day at a time, you know.'

Kay had an inkling. She'd had to force herself out of bed this morning to face another day full of fear and uncertainty. If not for Poppy, she might not have done, preferring to stay cocooned under the duvet until the darkness had gone away. 'Do you mind if we go inside?' She nodded towards the Victorian building the coffee shop was housed in. There was no reason she shouldn't be meeting her brother-in-law for coffee in the normal course of things, but things were far from normal. She didn't want anyone she knew seeing them. God forbid Matt should. The coffee shop had three floors, which should afford them some privacy.

Once through the doors, she made her way to the top floor, glancing quickly around to check for familiar faces before taking a table at the balcony overlooking the ground floor, where she could observe people coming in.

Walking towards the table behind her, Jason stopped a yard or so away. 'Er, do you mind if we move? It's a bit … draughty here.' He glanced nervously towards the balcony, and Kay was perplexed for a second until she noticed his suddenly pallid complexion. Of course, she remembered, he was scared of heights. Thinking it better not to comment, she picked up her bag and moved to a table in the corner.

'So, assuming you're not here because you've finally realised you married the wrong man, what can I do for you?' Jason asked, planting his coffee on the table and sitting down opposite her.

'Don't, Jason.' Kay dropped her gaze to the table.

'Hey.' He reached across to squeeze her hand. 'I'm joking, Kay.'

Biting back her tears, she looked at him angrily. 'Like you were joking after the wedding? Is that what you were doing then, Jason, having a joke at Matt's expense? Again?'

Jason looked uncomfortable. 'It's hardly my fault he reacted the way he did,' he answered with an evasive shrug. 'He needs to chill out and stop taking himself so seriously. He always has done. Even as a kid, he—'

'What did you *say* to him?' Kay snapped over him. She didn't want to listen to this. Knowing that Matt had carried guilt about what happened to their mother since he'd been ten years old, guilt compounded by Jason claiming the accident had been his fault, she couldn't believe he would bring up the subject of their childhood.

'Nothing.' His expression astonished, Jason splayed his hands.

Kay pushed her chair back, ready to walk away.

Jason reached for her forearm. 'Okay,' he said, relaxing his grip as she stayed where she was. 'Okay, I did wind him up. I regretted it afterwards; considerably, actually.' He smiled wryly, his hand going to his jaw. 'But it was a joke, Kay, just that. It wasn't even anything that emotive. Christ knows why he flew off the handle the way he did.'

Kay waited, her gaze hard on his, her breath stalled in her chest.

Jason sighed. 'All I said was that you'd soon get bored with him.'

Kay shook her head, confused. It was bad enough, but … 'Was that all?' she asked.

Jason shrugged again. 'It was enough, obviously. I suppose it hit a raw nerve, possibly something to do with the fact that he was feeling inadequate anyway, with the situation between you two. I mean, not being able to …'

Have a baby? Kay finished mentally as Jason's eyes flicked awkwardly down and back.

'I'm sorry.' Jason tugged in a breath, blew it out slowly. 'I don't mean to sound uncaring, Kay. I do care, about you *and* him. You know I do. I just want to move on, that's all. Matt doesn't feel able to, obviously – he won't even see me – but … I don't know. I was hoping you could forgive me for whatever part I played in what happened, even if he can't. I need my family, I guess. Maybe I needed the jolt of losing someone else I was close to to wake me up to the fact, but there it is, I do.'

Kay scanned his face with a mixture of incredulity and uncertainty. Was he telling the truth? She still couldn't reconcile Matt's reaction with what Jason insisted he'd said. He was claiming now that he needed his family. She felt a spark of hope light inside her.

'Your family needs you too,' she said, bracing herself to tell him how much, to ask him whether he would take the tests.

'Not you, though?' Jason said, derailing her.

Kay was taken aback, not sure how to answer.

'You really do love him, don't you?' He searched her eyes, sadness and disappointment in his.

'Of course I do,' Kay assured him, confounded. 'We have a child together. We're good together.' *Were*, a voice screamed in her head. She tried desperately to ignore it, to not let anything show in her expression that might lead Jason to think otherwise. He seemed to be being honest, genuinely trying to reach out, but she couldn't take the risk that he would feed anything she said back to Matt.

'I know.' He held up his hands in contrition. 'I know. I'm sorry. That was too personal. It's just … I didn't think he was good enough for you, Kay. I still don't.'

Flabbergasted, Kay said nothing. This was a bad idea. She should never have come.

'He's not perfect, you know,' Jason said, breaking the following awkward silence.

Kay's head snapped up. 'Which means *what* exactly?'

'Nothing.' He glanced away. 'It's just … I saw him. The week after the wedding.'

The week he was missing. 'Jason, *what*?' She studied him hard, noted his uncomfortable expression, and her stomach tightened. He knew something. Something about what Matt had done, where he was during that week – and possibly who with. Clearly he'd been unable to tell her because he would be branded a liar, jealous of Matt, the man who would stop at nothing to wind him up. 'Jason, you need to tell me what you're talking about.'

He drew in a tight breath. 'He's not the saint everyone thinks he is, that's all. I can't say any more. I doubt you'll believe me anyway. You need to talk to Matt. Ask him.'

CHAPTER TWENTY-NINE

Kay almost didn't go to her appointment with Professor Simons at the university. The last person she wanted to run into was Amelia. Her emotions were still fraught after her meeting with Jason on Friday, which she'd cut short for fear of spilling everything out to him when he refused to tell her more. But how would it look if she didn't turn up? She couldn't just pack in her job.

She was so exhausted, though. So confused. She'd lain awake last night, and the night before, wondering where she and Matt would go from here, her mind reeling from one possible bleak scenario to the next. Despite what was happening between them, she'd worried where he might be over the weekend. He'd said there'd been some major surgical emergency at a sister hospital on Saturday. To her shame, she'd rung the hospital to check up on him and found he was there. He'd come home late, undressed quietly, slipped into bed trying not to disturb her. She wasn't sure how she managed to stifle her tears when he hadn't reached to hold her as he used to do. He'd gone to the hospital on Sunday, citing a baby in distress. He hadn't come back last night. There'd been complications, he'd texted to tell her. She'd imagined him sleeping in one of the empty beds in the hospital, as he sometimes did after working impossible hours. The thought that he might not be there had struck her like a low blow to the stomach. The most soul-destroying scenario of all, that he might have been spending the night with another woman, had robbed her of any sleep she might have managed.

A chill of apprehension running through her, she headed through the university reception and straight to the toilets to check her appearance before going up to the classroom where Professor Simons had said he would be. With dark circles under her eyes and having tugged on the first clothes that came to hand, she looked like she felt, a complete mess. Definitely not the in-control person she wanted to be. She stepped back and surveyed herself in the mirror. Her hair was hopelessly knotted and sticking out Medusa-like in all directions. Matt had been right, she did look pale, insipid against Amelia with her perfectly made-up face, her flawless complexion and her messy bob of raven hair. Her heart dropping as she realised she couldn't do anything about it now, she hurried out and back across the foyer to the lift, trying hard to focus on the reason she was here rather than the muddled thoughts going around in her head.

Stepping out on the third floor, she headed for the classroom where the professor would have just finished his Creative Non-Fiction lecture. She was relieved he'd suggested they meet there. At least it felt less like she was being summoned to the headmaster's office.

Tapping on the partially open door, she poked her head around it. Finding him on his own, she braced herself.

'Ah, Kay …' Smiling, he beckoned her in and stood to greet her. It was a reserved smile, she noticed, not his usual exuberant welcoming beam. 'How are you feeling?'

'Much better, thanks,' Kay assured him, walking across to him. 'It was just a twenty-four-hour thing, I think.'

'Good, good.' His face creasing into a thoughtful frown, he pulled out a chair for her.

Kay sat, her heart beating a rapid drumbeat in her chest.

Lacing his fingers on the desk in front of him, he offered her another not over-effusive smile. 'You're feeling all right generally, though, are you?' he started, surprising her.

'Yes,' she answered guardedly. 'Why?'

Professor Simons looked slightly awkward. 'I couldn't help noticing you've been a little distracted lately,' he continued, his eyes troubled as he looked her over. 'I was wondering whether you might be struggling with any component of the course module.'

Kay was taken aback. It was true she had been distracted, but her work hadn't suffered because of it, she was sure. 'No,' she replied, warning herself to stay calm. 'I'm actually finding it quite stimulating. I'm sure you'll find the students are too.'

'And everything's all right with little Poppy, is it? You know, you can always take time out, Kay, if you—'

'Yes.' She spoke quickly. 'Sorry,' she apologised, realising she was talking over him, but ... Did he really have her down as someone who wasn't coping? True, inside she felt as if she were drowning, but she'd tried so hard to do her job to the best of her ability. 'She's doing really well,' she said, less forcefully. 'Though it is an ongoing situation, obviously.'

Professor Simons nodded understandingly. 'So, this incident in the library ...' He paused, his gaze flicking worriedly over her. 'Was it something to do with the course?'

Kay felt her stomach drop. He wouldn't be at liberty to tell her what Amelia had said. He was leaving her to tell her side of the story, presumably, from which he would draw his own conclusions. 'We're talking about the conversation between myself and Amelia, I assume?'

He answered with a small, reluctant nod.

Kay drew in a breath. 'I came across her in the reference section,' she began cautiously. 'She was looking for something that would help her structure her assignments.'

'And you offered to help her?'

'I did, yes,' she confirmed, feeling as if she were in the witness box offering her own defence. 'We're looking at Byatt's *Possession* in class. She was keen to get on with her critical response. She started to discuss it, relating it to her own experience regarding coercive relationships.'

Professor Simons nodded again, his expression pensive.

'Unfortunately, she made a comment about my personal circumstances, and to be perfectly honest, she's already said one or two things I found disturbing. As I mentioned on the phone, she does seem to have rather latched on to me, possibly because she's a little lonely. I thought it prudent to cut the conversation short. That's pretty much it. It's not something I feel I can't handle,' she finished, with what she hoped was a competent smile.

'And you don't have any personal problems you might have hinted at in front of her?' Professor Simons asked, resting his chin on his hands as he scrutinised her carefully.

Kay hesitated. She hadn't shared anything, but the fact that he'd mentioned it clearly indicated that he thought she might have.

'I'm just trying to establish why things would have escalated, Kay. Why you might have felt compelled to raise your voice and act perhaps a little more aggressively than you might normally.'

Aggressively. Kay felt her anger spike, and then quashed it, realising she probably had done – and that reacting angrily now to defend herself would confirm it. 'No. I don't have any personal problems. Absolutely not.'

'I'm not judging you, Kay,' he said sympathetically. 'We all have problems from time to time.'

'Well, yes,' she conceded. 'But even if I had, I wouldn't discuss them with my students. That would be totally unprofessional, wouldn't it?'

'Quite.' Professor Simons appeared to ponder. 'A bit of a personality clash then, possibly.'

Kay felt uncomfortable with that, but thought it might bring a close to a conversation she had no wish to prolong. 'Possibly.'

'I'll have a word with the student concerned,' he decided. 'See if we can't smooth things over.'

Kay wasn't very happy about that either. It sounded as if she were the one who'd rumpled things. 'Thank you,' she said.

'I'm sure it will all sort itself out. There's been no official complaint made,' Professor Simons said, his tone attempting reassurance. 'Try not to worry too much. I'll get back to you if we need to discuss it further.' He got to his feet, indicating that the conversation was over, for now.

Kay nodded and stood. Walking to the door, she stopped and turned back. 'Can I just ask who brought the incident to your notice?' she ventured. 'If it was one of the library staff, I'd like to apologise for any nuisance that might have been caused.'

Professor Simons looked uneasy. 'I'm afraid I can't disclose a confidence, Kay.' He shrugged apologetically.

'No. No, of course not.' She forced another smile and headed on to the door. It was Amelia. Obviously. Was it also Amelia who'd left the telling text on Matt's phone? She had thought at first it was impossible. How likely was it that she would be a student here and involved with her lecturer's husband? Yet now she was growing more and more sure that Amelia knew him. But why was she doing *this*?

CHAPTER THIRTY

Matthew

Matt watched in frustration as one of his newly qualified doctors struggled to carry out a nasogastric tube placement, failing on his second attempt to pass the tube into the stomach through the nose and throat.

Noting the panicked look on the man's face, Matt sucked in an agitated breath and moved to take over. 'Take a break,' he instructed him.

'I've almost got it,' the man answered. He was sweating profusely and quite clearly wasn't going to be able to complete the procedure without risking harming the infant, despite having undertaken the task in a simulated setting and therefore deemed competent to work under direct supervision.

'Almost isn't good enough, is it?' Matt growled. 'For God's sake, take a break before you cause someone serious injury.'

'Right.' The man stepped back. 'Sorry, I, er … I think my nerves got the better of me.'

Matt looked at him. He was pale, clearly shaken, not least by Matt reprimanding him so aggressively in front of colleagues, including the clinical lead, who'd shot Matt a not overly impressed look. He knew he'd handled it badly. It was because he was tired, because his personal problems were playing constantly on his mind, preventing him doing *his* job competently. Hadn't he almost messed up recently, and not through lack of experience, but because he'd been drinking, for God's sake?

'Nerves can cost lives, Dr Stokes,' he reminded the man, moderating his tone, though it was too late. The damage was done.

Completing the procedure, he left the nursing staff to finish up and headed for coffee, feeling in need of stimulants to help him keep focused.

'Dr Young.' Angela Meakin, the clinical lead, stopped him halfway across reception. 'Quick word, if I may?'

Matt sighed inwardly. He guessed it was about the dressing-down he'd just given Stokes. He felt bad about it. He would find him and apologise, try to bolster the man's confidence, though he clearly did need to practise again in simulation.

'What was that all about?' Angela, who was compassionate but known not to take prisoners in her attempt to run a tight ship, got straight to the point, giving him a withering glance before he'd even got through the door of her office.

'Sorry,' Matt apologised. 'I'm a little tired, I guess.'

'I gathered.' She looked him over less ferociously. 'Did you have to embarrass him like that, though?'

'It was a basic procedure,' Matt said in his own defence. 'But no, I didn't,' he admitted, running a hand wearily over his neck. 'I'll find him and have a word with him.'

'Do that. He's a good doctor. It's your job to guide and supervise, not put him off. We all make mistakes, after all, *don't* we?'

Hearing the pointedness in her tone, Matt glanced down.

'I heard what happened with Leo Cooper. It's you who needs to take a break, Matthew. I thought I could pack a change of clothes in the bags under my eyes, but I could pack my entire wardrobe in yours. Is this about your little girl?' she went on, before he could respond. 'She has her biopsy soon, doesn't she?'

'She does.' Matt swallowed back the emotion he was aware was all too close to the surface.

'Have you spoken to Kay about how you're feeling?'

'I, er … Not at length, no,' he managed, his throat thick.

'Go home, Matt,' Angela suggested, her tone more sympathetic. 'Talk to your wife, get some sleep, and come back refreshed.'

Matt answered with a small nod and turned to the door, gulping back the bitter taste in his throat as he did. Sleep simply wasn't an option. He'd lain awake when he'd gone home on Saturday night, knowing that Kay was awake next to him. He'd wanted to turn to her, to hold her and reassure her. How was he supposed to do that feeling she wouldn't want him to? As for talking to her, apart from the need to communicate about Poppy, he was beginning to wonder whether there was any point.

CHAPTER THIRTY-ONE

Kay

Kay headed home after her meeting with Professor Simons feeling emotionally depleted. Approaching the house, her heart stalled when she saw Matt's car parked on the road outside. Why would he be here at this time? Parking her own car on the drive, she climbed out, apprehension gripping her stomach as she walked hesitantly to the front door. Her hand shaking, she fumbled the key into the lock, pushed the door open and then froze as she noticed the overnight bag on the hall floor.

Stunned, her gaze shot to the stairs, where Matt was paused halfway down. 'Matt?' she said, her voice emerging a dry croak.

He drew in a visible breath and continued on down. 'I have a conference. I'll be staying over for a few nights,' he said, answering her unasked question. He was avoiding looking at her.

'A conference? At this short notice?' Kay stared at him, incredulous.

He raked a hand through his hair. 'I need some time to think things through. I can't be here, Kay. Not for a while.'

She felt her heart twist painfully as he picked up the bag, glancing at her briefly before walking past her. Kay stayed where she was, glued stupefied to the spot. Fear and anger galvanised her into action as she heard the front door open behind her.

'Matt!' She whirled around. 'Don't you dare walk out. Don't you *dare*. You need to tell me what the *hell* is going on. You owe me that much. You owe it to Poppy, for God's sake.'

He wavered, his back towards her as he glanced down at the car keys in his hand, weighing them pensively for a second, then turned slowly. 'I could ask the same of you, Kay. But the thing is, I don't think I could bear to hear your answer. Or the lies.'

'*Lies?*' Bewildered, Kay searched his face. 'I've never lied to you. Not *ever*. I don't understand what—' She stopped, her heart going into freefall as her gaze was drawn past him.

'I hope I'm not interrupting anything,' Jason said from where he stood outside the open front door.

A cynical smile curving his mouth, Matt shook his head. 'You're sure about that, are you, Kay?' he asked her.

'I could always come back,' Jason offered, looking Matt nervously over as he turned back to the door.

'No need,' Matt said abrasively. 'I'm just leaving.'

'Matt, *don't*.' Kay rushed after him as he all but pushed past his brother. 'Please come back.'

His step faltered. He waited a beat and then turned slowly to face her. 'I meant to tell you, I have the date for Poppy's biopsy,' he said, his eyes full of crushing hurt as his gaze travelled from her to Jason and back. 'I'll text you.'

'Matt!' she called after him as he strode on to his car.

But he wasn't listening. Climbing into the driver's side, he slammed the door, gunning the engine and driving erratically away from the house.

Utterly confused, Kay turned back to the house to see Jason looking open-mouthed at Matt's disappearing car. 'He was obviously thrilled to see me, then.' He sighed despairingly.

'What in God's name were you *thinking*, just turning up here?' Kay turned on him in frustration.

'I came to apologise,' he said, looking hurt. 'You left the café in such a hurry, I gathered I'd upset you. I didn't intend to do that.'

'So you turn up here, *now*, even though you and Matt haven't seen each other in how many years? You must have known it would cause problems, surely?'

He splayed his hands innocently. 'I didn't think he would still be so pissed off with me. I didn't even know he would be here. I wouldn't have come if I had, particularly if I'd known what kind of reception I would get.'

'You must have seen his car,' Kay pointed out.

'I didn't know what car he was driving. I haven't had much to do with him, have I? His choice, not mine,' Jason reminded her.

Kay felt her bluster deflate. It wasn't his fault. It was Matt, twisting things out of proportion to justify his own behaviour. Because he wasn't man enough to admit to what he'd done, had been doing. She'd never imagined she would think that of him. All he had to do really was utter four words: *I don't love you.* That would have done; that would have been enough to end things, rather than crucifying her slowly like this.

'So where is he going?' Jason asked, his interest clearly piqued as he sensed trouble between them. 'I noticed the overnight bag.'

'To a conference,' Kay told him, guessing he wouldn't believe it any more than she did.

He nodded thoughtfully. 'For what it's worth, I didn't intend to upset him either. But that's not difficult, is it, when he can't bear to be in my company for more than two seconds?'

'Look, Jason,' Kay pressed a hand to her forehead, 'I'm sorry too. I know you've been through a lot, but … It's just that things are difficult here at the moment.'

'I gathered.' He searched her face, his own full of sympathy. She wished he wouldn't. Her tears were too close to the surface. One kind word and she felt sure she would break down and sob.

'What Matt said as he left,' a frown creased his forehead, 'something about Poppy's biopsy, what did he mean?'

Kay's stomach tightened. She had to tell him, whatever Matt felt. Jason might be a match. She wasn't sure what the percentages were in favour of male to female donors, and she had no idea whether he would even put himself forward for testing, but her first priority was her daughter's health. 'They're looking for changes in Poppy's kidneys,' she said quickly. 'They think she has secondary nephrotic syndrome arising from an infection. The thing is …' She faltered. He might say no – it was a huge thing she was asking. The way she was feeling, she really wasn't sure how she would handle it emotionally if he did. 'She might need surgery,' she pushed on. 'Ultimately, her kidneys might fail and … We're struggling to cope with everything right now, as you might imagine.'

'I see.' Jason nodded at length, his expression now one of deep concern. 'Will you let me know how the biopsy goes? Obviously if there's anything I can do …'

'There is.' Kay latched on to that. 'You could take a test to see if you're a blood match. It's just a simple blood test, no more than that.' She blurted it out before her courage failed her. 'It might never be needed. I mean, there might never be a need for you to take it any further, but if they had it on record, then …'

She stopped. She was rambling, sounding desperate. She was, but desperate also not to scare him off.

Jason studied her, his expression now a combination of shock and surprise. He dropped his gaze after a second, his frown deepening, then, 'Okay,' he said, looking back at her. 'If you need me to …' He shrugged, but there was no flippancy in the gesture, more worry and uncertainty – and Kay could have kissed him.

'Thank you.' She allowed herself to breathe out and moved to hug him instead.

'No problem,' Jason said, holding her gaze for a long, lingering moment as she looked up at him. 'I should leave. I have an appointment.' He smiled regretfully. 'We'll talk soon. And you're right, I have been through a lot. If I'm honest, I wondered how I would survive it sometimes. I did, though. We do when we know those we love most need us to be strong. I want you to know, though, if you need someone, I'm just a phone call away, okay?'

Kay inhaled hard to stop her tears from falling. 'Thank you,' she managed, her voice strained. She didn't resist when he pulled her closer. It wasn't Matt, the man she'd given her heart to, who'd decided to crush it in the cruellest way possible, but she needed a hug just then.

CHAPTER THIRTY-TWO

'Can we go and play in the Wendy house, Mummy?' Poppy asked as soon as they were back from school.

Kay looked her over worriedly. Her teacher had said she'd seemed more tired today than usual. Also that she'd 'popped to the loo' quite frequently. That might be due to the diuretics, which were supposed to make her pee more often to help rid her little body of excess fluids, but it might be due to an infection, in which case she might need antibiotics. Kay tried to quash the panic blooming inside her. 'I don't know, darling. Mrs Weaver said you've been tired today. And it's not that warm outside. We don't want you catching a cold, do we?'

'But we're boiling, aren't we, Liv?' Poppy puffed out a breath and wiped an arm melodramatically across her brow, as if swooning from the heat.

Kay couldn't help but smile at her theatrics, but was she play-acting? She pressed the back of her hand to Poppy's forehead. It didn't feel warm, but she should take her temperature, she decided, just in case.

'And you've had no pains in your tummy?' she double-checked, scowling just enough to let her daughter know she had to tell her the absolute truth, no matter how much she wanted to play with Olivia. The two girls were practically superglued to each other. Kay thanked God that Nicole seemed okay with their friendship continuing, allowing Poppy a play date at her house and now a reciprocal one here. It couldn't have been an easy decision. Nicole didn't want to do anything that might rock Olivia's world, and Kay understood that completely; she desperately didn't want Poppy's world rocked either, and knew her daughter would be distraught if she lost Olivia's companionship now.

'Please, Mummy?' Poppy wheedled. 'We have our Barbie Ballerinas all set up. We're playing Greatest Dancers, aren't we, Liv?'

'Yes.' Olivia nodded enthusiastically, then looked at Kay, a flicker of worry in her eyes. 'Don't worry, Kay,' she said, her little face serious. 'If Poppy gets cold I can give her my jumper, because I'm quite warm really.'

Kay smiled. 'Thank you, Liv. That's a very kind offer,' she managed past the lump in her throat she couldn't seem to swallow. Olivia was so like Poppy, with that same precocious emotional maturity and sense of responsibility. It was breaking her heart.

'Does that mean we can?' Poppy asked eagerly. 'I have my good-luck charm to keep me safe.'

Kay looked at her, puzzled, as Poppy delved down underneath her shirt to produce a silver pendant.

Kay peered at it. It was a tiny four-leaf clover. Her eyes shot from the pendant to Poppy's face. 'Who gave you this?' she asked her.

'A lady,' Poppy answered.

'One of the mummies,' Olivia added. 'She said she hoped Poppy got better soon.'

Kay was taken aback. She hadn't realised her daughter's condition was general knowledge. But then, children chatted, she supposed, as did their mothers. It was a thoughtful thing to have done, she supposed, but still, it was a bit strange for someone to have approached Poppy and given it to her directly. 'Whose mummy was it?' she asked.

Olivia knitted her brow. 'I'm not sure, but we've seen her before, haven't we, Poppy?'

'Uh huh.' Poppy nodded confidently. 'Can we go out and play now, Mummy? *Please?*'

'You can,' Kay relented. 'But only for half an hour,' she tacked on as the two girls whirled around in unison and headed for the back door. 'I'll be out in a minute to take your temperature, Poppy,' she called after her, but they were gone in a flutter of childish excitement.

She closed her eyes, praying fervently that there wouldn't come a day when her daughter might be too sick to even climb out of bed, let alone want to venture out to the Wendy house, which was her favourite make-believe place, especially since finding a little friend to share her magical world with.

Attempting to pull herself together, she made a mental note to make enquiries about the thoughtful mother, then tugged off her jacket and grabbed her phone, intending to text Matt as she went upstairs for the thermometer. Whatever the situation between them, he should know if Poppy were to show any worrying symptoms. She'd taken a step towards the stairs when the hall phone rang behind her.

She hesitated as she recognised the hospital's number on the caller display. It wouldn't be Matt. He would ring on his mobile if he wanted to speak to her. Thinking it might be something to do with Poppy, she attempted to still the anxious butterflies in her tummy as she answered with a nervous 'Hello?'

'Kay?' a female voice said. 'It's Angela Meakin, clinical lead at the hospital. I wondered whether I could have a quick word with Matt? I'm assuming he's switched his mobile off since I suggested he get some rest.'

'Rest?' Kay repeated, alarmed. Was that why he'd come home? But Matt rarely took unscheduled time off. Only ever in an emergency or when he was too ill to function, which wasn't often. 'He's not back yet. I think he mentioned he might pop in to see his father today. He might well be there,' she lied, preferring not to hint at the trouble between them. 'Is he not well?'

'It's nothing to be concerned about,' Angela assured her. 'He's been a bit tired lately, that's all, which is no surprise with all you're both going through. I think he may have been pushing himself a little too hard. And he's clearly worried, possibly blaming himself.'

Kay felt her heart drop. 'Blaming himself for what?' she asked.

Angela hesitated before answering. 'The thing about doctors is that they do tend to blame themselves in situations like this,' she said, 'thinking they should be able to fix things, particularly where a child is involved. Given the seriousness of Poppy's illness, I imagine guilt is also contributing hugely to his exhaustion.'

'And the biopsy will definitely tell us how serious it is?'

'It will be helpful,' Angela replied. 'Her consultant will be able to tell you more.' Again she paused. 'Did Matt not discuss this with you?' she asked, her tone wary.

'Yes, he did, but to be honest, I didn't really take it all in. I'll have a chat with him later,' Kay assured her. 'Would you like me to get him to call you back?' she added quickly, wanting to end the call. Recalling the tissue-typing leaflet Matt had emailed her without any prior discussion about the contents, she felt extremely close to tears. They were due to go together for the tissue test, but if Matt had failed the blood match test, was there any point in him being tissue typed? She didn't know all the answers. She *needed* answers. She needed to know what was going on in his head *and* in his heart.

Once Angela had signed off, assuring her that she would catch up with Matt later, Kay dropped heavily to the stairs. Where was he? If his clinical lead was worried about him, he must be in a terrible state. Why had he stormed out the way he had? To find the comfort he must badly need in someone else's arms, quite obviously. She was wondering about the initial 'A', wondering also if she'd got things horribly wrong about Amelia, when she heard the back door open.

'Mummy … Mummy, where are you?' Poppy called. 'Mummy?'

Kay snapped her attention towards her daughter as she came into the hall. 'Sorry. Here, darling. I'm here.'

'Why are you sitting on the stairs?' Poppy asked, her forehead knitted perplexedly.

'I was just on the phone,' Kay said, attempting to pull herself together.

'Was it bad news?' Poppy asked, the little furrow in her brow deepening as she approached.

Realising she must look as worried as she felt, Kay shook herself. 'No, not bad news. Just university stuff,' she added, her voice catching as she took in her baby's concerned face. Poppy's intuition was strong. She always knew when there was something wrong, whether with her or with Matt or between them. Kay couldn't let this hurt her. She *wouldn't*. But how could she stop it? 'I'm just tired, sweetheart, like you.' She smiled tremulously.

'Shall I hug it better?' Poppy asked, her expression uncertain.

'Mmm, yes please.' Kay choked the words out, squeezed her tears back and hugged her daughter close as she wrapped her small arms around her.

'Did you want something, sweetheart?' she asked, easing back after a second to smooth Poppy's hair from her face.

'Could we have a drink?' Poppy asked. 'It really is warm outside, Mummy.'

Her stomach turning over, Kay felt Poppy's forehead again. She was hot. *God*, she needed to focus. 'Of course you can. You go and call Liv and I'll make us all one.'

As Poppy went back to the garden to fetch Olivia, Kay flew up the stairs. She knew what she had to do. The girls were siblings. She was as certain of that as she could be. Matt would know of Olivia's existence soon; she couldn't hide her for ever. She'd asked

Jason to take the initial blood test, but given that Matt wasn't a suitable blood match, it was possible his brother might not be either. Which left just her, and if her tissue-typing test didn't turn out favourably, then she too would be excluded. She had to talk to Nicole. First, though, she had to take Poppy's temperature. How could she have forgotten? And how could she ever forgive Matt for being so selfish as to walk out when his daughter needed him so badly?

CHAPTER THIRTY-THREE

Matthew

Not wanting to go back home, feeling sick to his soul as he considered what the future might hold, Matt sat in the hospital car park watching people come and go, patients and visitors arriving, day staff emerging from the main entrance, night staff going on duty; everything was seemingly normal. How could the world still be turning, he wondered, when he felt as if the ground had been ripped from beneath him?

He was still trying to digest what was happening. He felt as if he'd woken up one morning in a parallel universe. His whole life had shifted off kilter, everything that made him who he was drifting away from him, and he had no way to hold on to it. She'd lied to him; she kept right *on* lying to him. She was seeing Jason. *Why?* Jesus! He was falling apart, short-tempered with his colleagues, not concentrating when he needed to be totally focused. Risking people's lives. Children's lives. Did she not care? Banging the heels of his hands against the steering wheel in frustration, he cursed furiously, then leaned his head back against the headrest, breathing slowly as he tried to calm his erratic thinking.

Clamping down hard on thoughts of possible future scenarios, he braced himself and sent a brief text to Kay, informing her when the biopsy was – just a week away – then pushed his door open. He needed to go inside and get this thing done. The consultant looking after Poppy had agreed to meet him and take the necessary bloods for his tissue-typing test. Kay would still need to have her test. And then … he had no idea. He couldn't go home, not tonight. There was simply no way he could deal with it.

A hard lump expanding in his chest, he smiled ironically. His brother had always wanted to take everything that mattered away from him. Now he'd succeeded, spectacularly.

Going through the main reception, hoping not to bump into Angela, who would no doubt question him as to why he was here when he should be at home, he headed for the stairs that would take him to the renal department. Reaching the stairwell below, he paused as he heard someone calling after him. Rachel, he realised. She was a nice person, thoughtful, genuine, but he needed not to be distracted right now. He'd been terrified of doing this, of the results it might yield. Now, though, he guessed it didn't matter. His marriage was crumbling, exacerbated by his inability to keep turning a blind eye. He'd been so fucking *stupid*. No, not that. He'd been in love, prepared to sit it out and wait. He didn't need this, the DNA tests to tell him what he already knew. He'd always known. What hurt most was that Kay must know now that he did.

'Matt,' Rachel called again, descending the stairs after him. 'Do you think I could have a word?'

Matt closed his eyes, took a breath to compose himself and then turned around. 'I'm in a bit of a hurry, Rachel.' He smiled apologetically. 'Can it wait?'

'Yes, sorry.' She glanced awkwardly down. 'No problem. I'll catch you tomorrow. I'm actually on my way home now, so …'

Noting her troubled expression, Matt looked her over, concerned. She seemed pale, tearful. 'Are you okay?' he asked her. 'You're not ill, are you?'

'No.' She smiled tremulously. 'I, um, got a bit spooked just now in the grounds, that's all. There was someone following me and, I, um …'

Matt's heart jarred. '*Following* you?'

'I wasn't sure at first. I thought I was being neurotic, then …' She stopped, clutching the neck of her uniform as she glanced at the ceiling, clearly trying hard not to cry. The neckline was torn. Matt squinted at her. Were those finger marks on her throat? *Jesus Christ.* His gut tightening, he reached for her, threading an arm around her and urging her towards him.

'He grabbed me,' she blurted, burying her face in his shoulder. 'I thought he was going to … I'm so sorry, Matt. I managed to get free and I ran back to reception, but I was so scared he was following me. And then I saw you, and …'

'Hey, hey, it's okay. You're safe now, I promise.' Matt held her closer. 'Come on, we need to get you somewhere more comfortable than the stairwell. Find you a hot drink and get someone to check you over.'

Rachel snatched her head up. Her eyes were shot through with sheer terror. 'You won't leave me, will you?' she asked him.

'No, I won't leave you.' Matt smiled, though the anger that had been building up inside him was in danger of exploding. 'I'll wait and drive you home afterwards, if you'd like me to.' It would mean rescheduling his test, but he didn't think that would be too much of a problem. Under the circumstances, he definitely wouldn't feel comfortable leaving her.

She relaxed a little. 'I'd like that very much,' she said, wiping a hand under her nose.

As Matt eased away, his eye caught a shadow on the stairwell above them. It was gone in an instant. There'd definitely been someone there, though, as evidenced by the door back to the main reception clanging shut.

CHAPTER THIRTY-FOUR

Kay

'You're sure you're not feeling poorly?' Kay asked Poppy, tucking her duvet up to her chin. 'No tummy pains or feeling sick?'

'I'm sure, Mummy.' Poppy held her gaze, wisdom beyond her years in her wide blue eyes. It was as if *she* were the adult, reassuring the child. In that moment, Kay wished that she was; that she could be consoled in the arms of the mother she'd lost. Where was Matt, the man who'd held her and helped her put the broken pieces of her heart back together when she'd felt so bereft? She needed him. Poppy needed him. He must know how profound the effect of his abandoning her now would be on her.

Swallowing back a new kind of grief, one she'd never thought would be inflicted on her by the man she loved, she reached to smooth Poppy's hair from her forehead, checked her temperature with the back of her hand, then hummed 'Frère Jacques' – her favourite babyhood lullaby – to her until her eyes fluttered closed. 'Night, night, my darling,' she whispered, kissing her cheek lightly and easing herself off the bed.

Once in the kitchen, she poured herself a large glass of wine and was about to take a sip when her mobile rang. Thinking it was Matt, she grabbed the phone up from the work surface. *Jason*. Hesitating for a second, she accepted the call. She hoped to God that now he'd had time to think about the blood test and all that might follow, he hadn't changed his mind.

'Hey, how's it going?' he asked, his tone still as concerned as it had been earlier.

'Okay.' Kay closed her eyes, relieved, and then took a breath. 'We have a date for the biopsy. Matt texted me.' The text had been brief in the extreme. Just the date, nothing more. He really did seem to want to hurt her. 'It's just a week away.'

'Christ, that soon.' Jason sounded taken aback. 'I'm sorry, Kay. You shouldn't be going through all this on your own. I take it Matt's staying over at his conference?'

'He, um …' Kay's heart squeezed painfully. She had no idea what Matt was doing. Pride wouldn't let her admit that, though, not to Jason. 'Yes. It's an important one, apparently. I'm sure he'll be back as soon as he can, though.'

'No doubt.' There was a cynical edge to Jason's voice, as if he didn't quite believe it. 'Well, if there's anything I can do, just let me know.'

'There's nothing,' Kay assured him. 'I'm just grateful you've agreed to take the blood test.'

'Like I said, it's not a problem. It's the least I can do. I only wish Matt had asked me, for Poppy more than me. Pride really is a stubborn bugger, isn't it?' he finished with a sigh.

Kay immediately wanted to jump to Matt's defence. The fact was, though, she couldn't. This *was* about Matt's stubbornness. She would never have believed he was a man who would put his pride above his daughter's life. She couldn't believe, either, that he wasn't exploring all possible avenues for a donor. *Did* he know about Olivia?

'It is a big ask, though, Jason,' she said, wanting to draw the conversation away from Matt to Poppy and what might happen in future. 'You do understand what might be involved, don't you? I would understand if you felt you didn't want to go through with it.'

Jason paused before answering. Then, 'Do you honestly think I wouldn't put myself forward when it might save Poppy's life?' he asked her kindly.

'I …' Kay was lost for words. 'Thank you,' she said finally – inadequately, she felt.

'Do you think Matt will be okay with it, though?' Jason asked after a second.

Kay understood his concern, since Matt had made it so obvious he wasn't prepared to even consider burying the hatchet between them.

'It's just, I can't see him being thrilled with the idea, judging by his attitude earlier,' Jason went on.

Kay's heart plummeted. 'So you won't do it unless he agrees?'

'I didn't say that,' he said softly. 'I just don't want to cause any more trouble between you two.'

Kay laughed wryly. 'You'd be hard pushed to do that,' she said, then immediately wanted to reel the words back in. She was bewildered by Matt's behaviour. Right now, she was furious with him, but she didn't want to denigrate him in his brother's eyes.

Jason paused for another interminably long moment. 'Of course I'll do it,' he said eventually. 'Whatever our differences, Matt and I are just going to have to put them aside, aren't we?' he added, leaving Kay gobsmacked.

When had he become so caring? So intuitive? When he was out in the States, watching the woman he loved slip away from him, she reminded herself. Yet he hadn't gone on about it, playing the sympathy card. He'd been quietly stoical, trying to manage his emotions, getting precious little support from those who were supposed to be closest to him. She'd been so preoccupied with her own problems she'd hardly asked him how he was coping. She'd misjudged him. Convinced herself he hadn't got a heart. That he was incapable of caring. Quite clearly he was.

CHAPTER THIRTY-FIVE

Curled tightly on the sofa, her thoughts on Matt and where he might be, who he might be with, Kay jumped when the doorbell rang. With no idea who would be calling at this time of night, she went cautiously to the window. Her heart did a somersault as she realised it was Jason's car parked outside.

What on earth …? Matt would be far from pleased to find him here. But then Matt wasn't here, was he? And Jason might be in need of someone to talk to – he must be, to call at this late hour.

Quickly she went to the front door, pulling it open before he could ring the bell and wake Poppy.

'Jason?' She looked at him worriedly. 'Are you all right?'

'Fine.' He shrugged, his expression not very convincing. 'It's you I'm concerned about, being here on your own with so much to deal with.'

Kay was surprised, and touched. It was sweet of him to be worried about her. She looked at him standing on her doorstep, his hands thrust into his pockets, and couldn't help thinking he looked like a lost soul. He probably felt like one, his country of birth like an alien place to him after so long away.

'I'm not on my own,' she said, her eyes flicking towards the stairs as she pulled the door wider, inviting him in.

'I know.' He smiled and stepped inside. 'But I figured my shoulder is probably a bit broader than Poppy's, assuming you might need one.'

Smiling, Kay led the way to the kitchen. 'Tea or coffee?' she asked him. 'Or do you fancy something stronger? I have some red wine open.'

'Wine would be great. Thanks.' Jason smiled appreciatively. 'Just what the doctor ordered.'

Kay poured him a glass and decided to have another herself. 'It strikes me it might be you who's in need of a shoulder,' she said, looking him over carefully. He looked so terribly sad, dark circles under his eyes indicating he hadn't been sleeping, and no wonder.

Jason dropped his gaze, took a sip of his wine and then placed the glass next to him on the work surface. 'I'm okay,' he said, running a finger contemplatively around the rim. 'It's just … I miss her,' his voice cracked, '*so* much.'

Bewildered for a second by this genuine emotion from a man who'd once seemed incapable of it, Kay wasn't sure what to do, what to say. But then, seeing him press a finger and thumb hard against his eyes, her heart bled for him, and instinctively she reached out, offering him what she guessed he badly needed. 'I know.' She shushed and comforted him as he leant into her hug. 'You're bound to. You can always …'

Talk to me, she'd been about to say, when the words died in her throat. 'Matt!' she exclaimed, shocked, and pulled away from Jason as if she'd been electrocuted.

Matt said nothing. He didn't need to. The look in his eyes said it all.

Nausea roiling inside her, Kay scanned his face. His complexion was chalk-white, the anger emanating from him palpable. How long had he been there?

Jason spoke first, breaking the charged silence hanging in the air. 'Matt,' he said, wiping a hand over his face and stepping apprehensively towards him. 'We weren't expecting you.'

Matt gave a strangled laugh, dropped his gaze and pinched the bridge of his nose hard. 'Clearly,' he said, looking back up to lock murderous eyes on his brother. 'The door's that way,' he said, nodding shortly in that direction.

'Hold on, Matthew. Before you go off on one, this isn't how it looks,' Jason said.

Kay flinched, knowing it was possibly the worse thing he could have said.

Matt said nothing, but kept his eyes firmly fixed on his brother.

'Kay called me earlier. I was concerned about her,' Jason went on, attempting to explain but only succeeding in making things horribly worse.

Kay stared at Matt, her blood pumping with fear, terrified at how he might react.

'I have no idea what you think you're doing here, but you need to leave,' Matt growled. 'Now!'

'What *I'm* doing here?' Jason shook his head scornfully. 'I might ask you the same question, little brother, since you obviously decided it was a good idea to leave Kay to deal with all the shit she's going through on her own.'

Matt's eyes narrowed dangerously.

'But then you obviously have more important things to attend to. Giving pretty young nurses thorough examinations, for instance,' Jason continued, apparently uncaring of what the consequences might be.

'Jason, stop,' Kay warned him, noting Matt's thunderous expression. 'Please just go.'

'What the hell are you blathering on about?' Matt asked, eyeing his brother with open contempt.

'I *saw* you!' Jason jabbed a finger at him. 'Right there on the hospital stairs with that pretty brunette. Not very discreet, were you, Matthew, considering you're supposed to be a doctor?'

Kay's heart flipped in her chest. She looked confusedly between the brothers as they eyeballed each other for a heart-stopping moment.

Then Matt moved, swiftly. His temper exploding, he grabbed Jason's collar in his fists, hoisting him bodily upwards. 'You just don't know when to back off, do you?' he seethed.

'Stop!' Kay screamed, flying towards them, attempting to prise Matt away – to no avail. He wasn't hearing her. Wasn't seeing her. Terror gripped her stomach like a vice. He looked as if he might kill Jason. 'Please stop,' she begged him.

After a petrifying moment, Matt relaxed his grip, tearing his gaze away from Jason and taking a stumbling step backwards.

Kay moved towards him.

'Don't.' Matt shrugged her off. 'Just don't,' he grated, his expression now somewhere between shock and fury.

He looked as if he'd been punched in the stomach when he heard Poppy's voice behind him. 'Mummy, why are you crying?'

Kay dashed towards her, but Matt was quicker, spinning around to sweep her up. 'Mummy's not crying, sweetheart,' he said gruffly, holding her close. 'She—'

'I have a cold, that's all. Uncle Jason came to bring me some medicine,' Kay improvised, her heart breaking for her baby. For all of them. How had this happened?

Matt glanced from her to Jason, visibly trying to compose himself. 'And now he's leaving,' he said hoarsely, his eyes pivoting to the door.

Jason hesitated, then nodded, thank God. 'That's right,' he said, smiling for Poppy's benefit. 'I have to get home now. And I think you should be sleeping, shouldn't you? Bye, Poppy,' he said. 'It was lovely seeing you.'

Poppy looked at him uncertainly, clearly wondering who this uncle was who was suddenly in her life. 'You too, Uncle Jason,' she said after a second, tightening her arms around Matt's neck.

'Night, Kay.' Jason smiled apologetically in her direction and then headed past Matt, making brief eye contact as he went. 'Nice seeing you too, Matthew,' he called over his shoulder.

Matt didn't answer, heaving in a breath instead, breathing out only when he heard the front door close. 'Come on, precious girl,' he said shakily, his attention on Poppy. 'Let's get you tucked back up in bed. We don't want you getting overtired, do we?'

'No.' Poppy shook her head. 'But …'

Matt noticed her hurriedly dropped gaze, as did Kay. 'But what, sweetheart?' he asked her, his face concerned as he scanned hers.

Poppy's huge blue eyes travelled worriedly back to his. 'I think I might have wet the bed,' she said in a tiny voice.

Oh God, no. Kay felt the ground shift beneath her. Because she'd heard raised voices? Or …? She exchanged frightened glances with Matt.

Matt swallowed and nodded and looked back to Poppy. 'Not to worry,' he said, pressing a soft kiss to her cheek and carrying her back towards the stairs. 'We'll just tuck you up in the big bed and maybe get you some medicine too, hey?'

Kay followed them up, but hesitated outside the main bedroom door. He would call if Poppy needed her. Right now, she sensed he needed to be alone with his daughter. Her heart palpitating like a terrified bird in her chest, she went to Poppy's room to strip her bed, praying as she did so, listening to Matt gently reassuring his daughter. He wouldn't leave her. She knew he wouldn't. He would always be there for Poppy. It was just his wife he wanted to leave. What had Jason meant about Matt and a nurse on the stairs? What was wrong with her baby? Dear God, she couldn't do this. She *couldn't*.

Fear like a cold stone inside her, she went to the airing cupboard, and felt herself physically jump as Matt emerged from their room.

'She's asleep,' he said, closing the door quietly behind him. 'I gave her an anti-inflammatory. She may need antibiotics. We should do a dipstick test and check her temperature first thing in the morning.'

Kay nodded. There were a thousand questions zooming around in her head, but her mind was too stultified, her throat too parched to ask any of them. Feeling utterly depleted, she glanced down, swiping a tear from her cheek. He didn't move to hold her, help chase her fears away, as he would have done such a short while ago. Kay guessed that spoke volumes.

'She doesn't seem to be in too much discomfort,' he went on. 'I'll sleep in the spare room. It will give you and Poppy some space. Wake me if you need to.'

Kay felt the broken pieces of her heart pierce her chest like a knife as she watched him walk away.

CHAPTER THIRTY-SIX

Matthew

Up early the next morning, Matt had managed to get hold of Poppy's consultant. 'Her temperature is almost normal, but her protein levels and blood pressure are definitely on the high side,' he told him. He could feel Kay's nervous tension as she hovered behind him. 'She's passing urine infrequently. I've given her penicillin to be on the safe side, but … What's your thinking, Peter?'

His colleague hesitated before answering. 'Obviously we can't be sure yet, but it's looking more like it could be secondary childhood congenital syndrome. Possibly chronic kidney disease,' he said sympathetically, confirming what Matt had so desperately hoped he wouldn't.

'Right.' Squeezing the bridge of his nose, Matt breathed in deeply. 'So … what's our next move?' he asked, willing his voice not to crack.

'We'll need to check for elevated levels of creatinine and urea nitrogen in the blood, which would indicate reduced kidney function,' Peter informed him. 'We have the biopsy scheduled. We'll go ahead with that and organise some urgent renal imaging. As for the future … I have a free slot first thing tomorrow. Why don't you swing by and we'll have a longer chat and look at her treatment plan then? Meanwhile, if there's an emergency, I can always be contacted.'

'Cheers,' Matt said, sounding reasonably normal for a man whose heart was splintering inside him. 'I'll do that.'

'No problem,' Peter assured him. 'Meanwhile, it might be an idea to make sure you and your wife have had all the relevant tests so we know where we are should we need to consider surgery.'

Matt drew in another sharp breath. 'I'll get it sorted, organise us some appointments.' Finishing his call, he turned to Kay to find her staring at him, wide-eyed and terrified.

'They think it's chronic kidney disease, don't they?' she whispered, her complexion ashen.

Matt nodded, his own voice failing him. He wanted to hold her, to somehow protect her; desperately wanted to be held by her. Yet for the first time ever, he didn't know how to.

'We need to run the tissue-typing tests.' He hesitated. What was she thinking? Why in God's name didn't she just *tell* him?

Kay didn't speak. Wrapping her arms around herself, she answered with a defeated nod instead, and closed her eyes.

Seeing the tears wetting her cheeks, her shoulders slumping as if the strength had drained from her body, Matt moved towards her, wanting to do something to bridge the widening gap between them. As he reached out, though, she pressed her hands to her face.

'I'm sorry. So sorry,' she murmured.

His heart hitching as she gulped back a sob, Matt quashed his own warring emotions and wrapped an arm around her shoulders, easing her gently to him.

'I'm sorry,' she repeated wretchedly, her forehead pressed to his shoulder.

What for, Kay? Matt's chest constricted. What was she sorry for? He looked up at the ceiling, blinking hard to hold back his own tears. Feeling the closeness of her, he acknowledged the fear that had dogged his thoughts for over five long years. Losing her would break him. Losing his daughter would surely kill him. He just wasn't strong enough to bear it. 'Talk to me, Kay,' he urged, his voice catching. 'Please just tell me—'

He stopped as Poppy called from the landing. 'Mummy, I can't find Luna Lamb.'

Her snuggle toy, Matt realised, as Kay pulled instinctively away from him.

CHAPTER THIRTY-SEVEN

Kay

Distracted, worried to death about Poppy, and about Matt, who'd promised faithfully to get back as soon as he could, Kay snatched up the landline, thinking it might be him or the hospital calling. 'Hello? *Hello?*'

Frustrated when no one answered, and thinking it was an international sales call, she was about to hang up when someone spoke. 'Kay?' a female voice said tremulously.

'Yes,' Kay confirmed, her heart catching. The voice sounded familiar. A hospital receptionist or staff nurse? she wondered. Fast on the heels of that, she wondered why they would sound so cautious. Her heart rate rose as her mind played graphically through the possible reasons. Poppy was tucked up warmly in the big bed watching CBeebies. She'd just checked on her. But Matt, where was he? Please God don't let him have been driving erratically. She recalled how he'd skidded away from the house when Jason had turned up.

'I had to call,' the woman said, as Kay tightened her grip on the phone. 'I wanted to check you were okay after what happened.'

Amelia? Kay was taken aback. She didn't know whether to be astounded that she would call her, or annoyed. What had happened between them was Kay's fault, undoubtedly. She was the tutor. She should have handled the whole thing more professionally, perhaps even have spoken to the professor herself. But for the woman to call her here at home? She couldn't quite believe she would do that. 'Why are you ringing, Amelia?' she asked her. 'Where did you get this number?'

'Online. It's listed,' Amelia said, sounding surprised.

Was it? It was possible. Kay couldn't honestly remember.

'I was calling to apologise,' Amelia went on quickly, astounding her further. 'I really was talking hypothetically about your situation, Kay, but I realise now how it must have sounded. I know you're dealing with a lot, with your little girl being poorly, juggling work and … I'm so sorry that I've added to your troubles. I shouldn't have got so upset. It's just, I don't have anyone else – no family, and not many friends in the area yet,' she went on, talking so fast Kay felt breathless. 'I thought we were friends, and then … I messed up, obviously. I always do, opening my mouth without thinking. Anyway, I just wanted to say I was sorry.'

She stopped at last, and Kay tried to coordinate her thoughts. 'It's fine,' she said reluctantly, though she wasn't sure it was, or that *she* was. She was still perturbed by the comments Amelia had made. And the fact that she had reported Kay to the director of the course, knowing she might be putting her career at risk …

'So, can we still be friends?' Amelia asked hopefully, putting Kay more in mind of an uncertain teenage girl than a grown woman. She was clearly lonely, though; her first instincts had been right about that.

'We'll have a chat when I come in, though I'm not sure when that will be,' Kay replied, thinking it better not to add to Amelia's guilt and say that she wasn't sure she actually still had a job. 'My daughter's really not well just now, so I might have to take some leave.'

'Oh God, Kay … I'm sorry,' Amelia said again. 'If there's anything I can do …'

'There isn't.' Kay didn't think she would be taking up the offer of going out for a drink with Amelia any time soon, but she couldn't help but feel some compassion for her. She obviously felt wretched. 'But thanks for the offer,' she added.

'No problem,' Amelia assured her. 'Anything at all. If you need anything bringing in, or for me to sit with your daughter for a while, just shout.'

Kay really didn't think she would be taking her up on that either, but it was kind, she had to concede that. Perhaps she'd misjudged her. Perhaps she was misjudging everyone – Jason, Matt. As bad as that thought made her feel, she held on to a sliver of hope that her suspicions about Matt might be unfounded – until she remembered Olivia, and the comments Jason had made last night. He couldn't have made it any plainer that her husband was cheating on her.

'I will,' she said, a fresh wave of unbearable hurt crashing through her. 'I'd better get off and go and see to Poppy.'

'Of course, sorry,' Amelia apologised again. 'Shall I give you my number?'

'Oh. Yes please.' Kay found herself swept along by the woman's enthusiasm, and noted the number down as Amelia reeled it off.

'Speak soon,' Amelia said. 'It wasn't me who reported you, by the way. Professor Simons spoke to me, but I just wanted you to know it wasn't me who made the complaint.'

Kay frowned as she ended the call. She'd been sure it was Amelia. The professor's expression had confirmed it. Hadn't it? But if it wasn't her … Kay's heart sank as she realised she really had misjudged the woman, badly.

CHAPTER THIRTY-EIGHT

Matthew

He needed to pull himself together. Up until recently, he and Kay had been strong, a unit, unanimous in their determination to do their absolute best for their daughter. When he'd learned she was pregnant with Poppy, he'd made up his mind there would be no looking back. He loved his daughter with his whole heart and soul. He simply wouldn't know how to live without her. And Kay? Even knowing she'd been lying to him, he still loved her. He'd never stopped loving her. The question he desperately needed the answer to if he was to hold onto the hope that there might be a way forward was: did she love him back? It had been impossible this morning, but he *had* to talk to her, beg her to be honest with him before the tissue test results confirmed his fears. First, though, he needed to establish what the hell his brother was up to.

Parking in the Biochem car park, he noted his father's car in its usual spot in the bays reserved for directors. To the right of it was his brother's new car, a flash white BMW 4 series convertible – a company car, no doubt. He hadn't been slow getting his feet back under the table, had he? Good old Jason, he was probably in there right now, convincing his father, who really should be thinking about retiring, that the company would be in safe hands with their top sales executive at the helm.

Climbing out of his car, he walked up to the large contemporary glass structure. Built five or so years ago, it had been designed by an award-winning architect to reflect the company's success. Biochem's shares had taken a dip in the market around that time, however, and the construction might never have been completed without the indomitable Jason Young's input. Jason seemed to forget that it was their father who'd truly built the company, with hard work and sweat, and Matt doubted the staff would be delighted about him taking over at the top. His brother had worked on his facade, but underneath, he was the same manipulative bastard he'd always been. As a teenager, Matt had seen him in action. Any girl who succumbed to his spurious charms would end up being miserable, expected to ask how high every time he said jump. Jason was a bully, doubtless due to his own insecurity – which, if he stopped long enough to think about it, he would realise was basically down to people not much liking him.

'Hi, Matt.' The receptionist jarred him from his thoughts, smiling as he walked in.

'Hi …' He stopped, grappling for her name, embarrassingly, since she'd obviously remembered his.

'Laura,' she supplied, seeming not to mind that he couldn't recall it. 'How's that gorgeous daughter of yours? Poppy, isn't it?'

'Yes, Poppy. She's doing okay, thanks,' he answered, smiling appropriately. He didn't really want to get into a discussion about her illness, not here.

'You'll have to bring her in again sometime,' Laura suggested. 'David never stops talking about her.'

'I'll do that,' Matt promised, but now a new worry gnawed away at him. His father didn't see Poppy as often as he would like, but he doted on her. What would all this do to him: Poppy's condition deteriorating, his family fractured further? David suffered from unstable angina, which put him at high risk of having a stroke or heart attack. He was on all the right medication, but had yet to have a stent inserted to keep his arteries open. The last thing Matt wanted was to cause him any stress.

'He's in a team meeting at the moment.' Laura nodded towards the boardroom, where his father held regular meetings, his aim to keep his staff engaged and on board. 'He should be finished shortly,' she added. 'Do you want me to poke my head around the door and tell him you're here?'

'No, don't disturb him.' Matt smiled appreciatively. 'It's actually Jason I've come to see.'

'Ah, right.' Laura's face fell. Clearly she wasn't a member of his brother's fan club either. 'He has a meeting with one of the sales team. He should be finished shortly. I'll let him know you're here, shall I?'

'How about I just go on up?' Matt suggested.

Laura looked hesitant. Matt guessed she was concerned about letting anyone past without Jason's permission. Fortunately, she was distracted as someone came into reception behind him. The fire officer, he gathered. His father had mentioned there were concerns about the cladding on one of the side walls of the building. Jason had yet to do something about it, apart from arguing with the insurers, saving money obviously being a priority above the safety of the employees. Matt doubted his father would concur.

Indicating that he was going up, he left Laura to it and took the stairs to the second floor, walking through the outer communal area to the office at the back he assumed Jason had reclaimed – the biggest office, as befitted his status. Approaching it, he could see through the glass that he was still in his meeting. A fraught meeting, judging by the raised voices: Jason's, mostly. 'All you had to do was close the deal. What were you thinking, for Christ's sake, leaving without getting him to sign on the dotted line?'

Matt hung back, watching his brother, who was on his feet, eyeballing the recipient of his tirade furiously.

'He needed to confer with his colleagues,' the other man offered in his defence. 'He had to discuss funding. I did my best, but there was no way he was ready to—'

'In which case, you convince him this drug will *save* him money.' Jason cut angrily across him. 'Improving patients' health means fewer patient visits, meaning doctors and nurses have to spend less time with patients, meaning they'll have to spend less of their budget employing *staff*. It's not fucking rocket science, Davies.'

'Right. Sorry.' Davies shrank back in his chair.

'Sorry?' Jason squinted incredulously at him and then threw his hands up in despair. 'For fuck's … I give up. Just get out, will you, before I really lose it.'

'Do you want me to make another appointment?' the man asked tentatively.

'No, I do not want you to make another bloody appointment,' Jason growled, dropping moodily back into his chair. 'You need to be able to close a deal, Davies, to stay on my team.'

Matt offered the guy a smile of commiseration as he walked out of the office and past him. His expression one of deep humiliation, Davies barely looked at him. Matt felt for him, but no job was worth taking that sort of abuse for, surely? Then again, he might well have people dependent on him. Swallowing back his contempt for his brother, who wouldn't give a damn about anyone's personal circumstances, he walked the short distance to the office, knocked perfunctorily on the door and went straight in. 'On form, I see,' he commented, making no secret of the fact that he'd heard the exchange. He guessed several people in the outer office had as well.

Jason glanced at him warily, as Matt had expected after their last confrontation, and then back to his PC. 'He asked for it, useless prick, putting a major contract at risk.'

'Right.' Matt closed the door. 'He's on commission only, presumably?'

'And?' Jason's eyes drifted briefly back to him.

'I'm assuming that means he leaves without a penny.'

'Not my problem,' Jason muttered.

'He might have a family. Kids,' Matt pointed out.

'Like I say, not my problem.' Jason shrugged. 'I set the deal up for him. He had it handed to him on a plate. If he can't do the job, he's no use to me. I'm not running a charity.'

He wasn't running …? Matt smiled sardonically. 'You really don't give a toss about anyone, do you?' He walked across to the desk, shoved his hands in his pockets and studied Jason hard. 'About *anyone*.'

His brother eyed him tiredly. 'Which means what?'

Matt scanned his face. It was there: the same contempt Jason had always had for him. As a kid, he'd consoled himself with the fact that his brother was contemptuous of everyone, probably to compensate for his own shortcomings. Beyond a certain age, he'd rarely challenged him. Now that things had taken a new twist, though, he had no choice. 'What were you doing at my house?' he asked him.

Jason looked momentarily uncomfortable. 'I told you, I spoke to Kay on the phone. She seemed down, unsurprisingly, since you were otherwise engaged, fondling nurses on the stairs. Bit desperate, if you ask me. I mean, there are plenty of beds around the place you could have utilised, aren't there?'

Matt swallowed back his disdain. It had obviously been Jason at the top of the stairs. Had he been there on business, he wondered, or just spying on him? 'That comment you made after Anna's wedding, was it a lie?' he asked.

A puzzled frown crossed Jason's face. 'Do you want to enlighten me?' He leaned back in his chair, looking bored. 'I haven't got the faintest idea what you're talking about.'

Matt knew very well he knew *exactly* what he was talking about. Pulling his hands from his pockets, he planted them on the desk, leaning forward to lock his eyes hard on his brother's. 'I need to know whether you were *lying*,' he enunciated slowly, wanting to make damn sure that Jason knew he meant business.

There was something else in Jason's eyes now, a flicker of apprehension. Then, shaking his head scornfully, he pushed his chair back. 'You're talking about your girlie tantrum, aren't you?' He laughed derisively. 'Christ, little bro, you really do have a complex. I was winding you up. It was a joke; that was all.'

Matt noted the hand he was running over his jaw. Reflecting on the damage he'd inflicted when he'd had his 'girlie tantrum'? He hoped so. Hoped the bastard realised he had no regrets, that he wouldn't hesitate to inflict the same damage again, that he'd been dangerously close to doing just that last night. Fixing his gaze meaningfully on his brother's, he walked around the desk.

'Oh dear.' Jason looked at him uncertainly as he stopped in front of him. 'We really are angsty, aren't we? Did we get out of the wrong side of bed? Or did the sexy little nurse not deliver the goods?'

Matt tried to ignore that, just as he had tried so hard to oust from his head the taunt his brother had delivered at that damn wedding. He couldn't. He never had been able to. *She whispered my name when she came.* The words twisted his gut violently, just as they had then. The kiss he'd witnessed as they'd stepped into the lift … He should have followed them. He hadn't. Nauseous to his soul, he'd drowned his sorrows instead, which made him every inch as weak as his brother thought he was.

Jason broke eye contact after a second. 'Leave it, Matthew,' he warned him. 'I was joking. It's history. Just let bygones be bygones, will you? I have work to do.' He made to rise from his chair.

'You despicable piece of *shit*.' Fury white-hot in his throat, Matt clutched hold of Jason's shirt and hauled him from the chair.

'Jesus Christ!' Panic flooding his eyes, Jason attempted to shove him away. 'What the hell are you *doing*?'

'What I should have done years ago.' Matt breathed in hard, trying to get past the rage in his head, the deep desire to see his brother dead.

'Matt?' He heard Laura's shaky voice from the doorway and felt himself waver. *Stop*, the rational part of him willed him. *Can't.* He felt his jaw clench. He wanted to kill Jason. Some primal urge deep inside was driving him; he really wanted to *kill* him.

Jason's eyes swivelled towards Laura. 'Don't just stand there, for fuck's sake! Call security!'

'Matthew! What the *hell* is going on?' His father's shocked voice reached him. He would be stressed, upset. Matt groped for his sanity, closed his eyes and sucked in another long breath, held it. Finally, his fury dissipating, he breathed out.

He didn't see it coming, his brother's forehead cracking blindingly into his, sending him sprawling. Disorientated, blood oozing through his fingers, he didn't realise his father had sunk to his knees, until he heard Laura screaming.

CHAPTER THIRTY-NINE

Kay

'She doesn't look too bad now,' Nicole observed as the two girls scooted upstairs, Olivia chattering away, filling Poppy in on what she'd missed at school today. They were clearly delighted to see each other. Their teacher was right: they were two peas in a pod.

Kay had brought Poppy over to see her friend, but she also hoped this could be an opportunity to speak directly with Nicole about the possibility of Olivia becoming a donor. Olivia couldn't make the decision to help Poppy herself; Nicole would have to bear the responsibility of that, but Kay prayed she might consider how Olivia would feel if she and Poppy were separated by Poppy's illness. How badly she might be affected if she lost her best friend completely. She couldn't count on Jason. Even if he were a match, the animosity between him and Matt was so intense, she no longer knew if Matt would be able to accept him as a donor.

'It was a good idea to bring Poppy round. Olivia's been missing her.' Nicole smiled, but again there was that curiosity that Kay had seen before. She knew Kay wasn't telling her everything. Nicole might be the girl's adoptive mother, but she would do anything to protect her daughter from a perceived threat. Clearly she suspected that the existence of a little girl who looked so like her daughter might be such a threat, bringing things into her life that were hitherto unknown. Specifically, the man who'd fathered her.

'I'm just making a coffee, if you fancy one?' Nicole offered, plainly gathering that Kay hadn't just called so the girls could catch up.

'I'd love one.' Kay smiled, relieved. She had to tell her the truth about Poppy's condition. She owed it to her to do that anyway, for Olivia's sake. She also had to be honest about why she'd called. She prayed that Nicole would see that Olivia might provide hope for Poppy's future; that she might be the key to her even *having* a future, and that she would at least consider putting her forward for testing.

'I thought you might. You look as if you need one. It's not easy, is it, keeping a sick child entertained?' Nicole glanced over her shoulder as she led the way to the kitchen, the same wariness now in her eyes that Kay had also seen before.

'No.' Kay's gaze flicked down. 'Once she's up and about, there's no stopping her. That's why I rang. She was driving me mad asking whether she could come and play with Olivia.'

'She's welcome any time.' Nicole nodded her towards a seat at the island.

'As Olivia is at ours,' Kay assured her, although Nicole had insisted that Olivia should only have short visits to her house, and only when she could be sure Matt wasn't there. 'It's just that the place is such a mess with the decorators in, I thought it would be easier to bring Poppy here.'

Nicole nodded, glancing at her as if she didn't quite believe her as she went to put the kettle on. Was she really that bad a liar? Kay's thoughts went to Matt, the lies he must have told her that she hadn't picked up on. Her heart started its downward trajectory again as she realised that, though it was obvious he loved Poppy with every fibre of his being, he had never loved *her*, not as a man should love his wife.

'Coffee. Nice and strong.' Placing two mugs on the island, Nicole brought Kay's mind back to what she was doing here. It was time for them to talk. Nicole had clearly realised already that she wasn't there solely to allow Poppy and Olivia half an hour's play together.

'So, these allergies …' Drawing up a stool, Nicole sat opposite her. 'What are they, exactly? It might be a good idea to let me know, assuming Poppy's going to be spending a little more time here.'

Kay glanced down, taking a second to summon up her courage. She prayed fervently that what she had to say wouldn't impact the girls' friendship. She thought not; Nicole seemed bigger-hearted than that. At least she hoped so.

'She has a kidney disease,' she said, glancing cautiously back up.

Looking utterly stunned, Nicole took a second to digest what she'd said. 'And it's serious?' she asked, scanning her face questioningly.

Kay hesitated. 'Yes.' She shrugged disconsolately, feeling hopeless and helpless all at once. She was Poppy's *mother*. She should be able to help her. 'They have certain tests to do, but …'

'It could turn out to be life-threatening?' Nicole probed.

Unable to squeeze an answer past the sudden constriction in her throat, Kay nodded and wiped away the tears that sprang to her eyes. 'There's damage to the kidneys, originating from an infection. They'd hoped the kidneys might recover, but I think now they suspect the damage is permanent. She's due for a biopsy, but …' She faltered. 'She might need dialysis, and then … if her kidneys fail, she might need a new kidney …' She heard the sob in her own voice, but struggled on. 'It would have to be someone who was a match. If the girls are related—'

'Oh no.' Nicole reached for her hand. 'I'm so very sorry, truly I am, but …' She paused, studying Kay with a mixture of sympathy and guardedness.

Kay's heart sank. 'Buts' were rarely a good thing.

'I have to be honest, Kay,' Nicole went on. 'You might think I'm being brutal, but …'

Kay braced herself. She knew what she was going to say. Wouldn't she say the same herself?

'… as I mentioned before, Olivia is the most precious thing I have.' Nicole stopped, appearing to gather herself. 'My husband died,' she continued quietly after a second.

Oh God, no. Kay felt herself reel. 'I had no idea. I'm so sorry,' she offered, feeling devastated for her.

Nicole nodded sadly. 'It was a good while back now. Cancer.' She paused reflectively. 'When we found out it was terminal, we tried desperately for a child. Steven even stored samples at the fertility clinic for me to keep trying after he'd gone. It didn't work.'

Kay closed her eyes. What was she doing here, forcing this woman to relive her memories, which could only be compounding her pain?

'Being accepted as an adoptive parent, being offered Olivia,' Nicole went on, 'it was as if I'd been given a miracle, a reason to keep going. That's why I'm so concerned about her natural father having access to her. What if he should try to take her away from me? I would die before I let that happen, or any harm come to her. I'm sorry, Kay, but if you're looking for a living donor for Poppy, I'm not sure I could ever give permission for that, even if it turns out the girls are related.'

Kay nodded, understanding. It didn't stop her heart from breaking. It had been a faint hope, after all, and in order to make it happen, she would have had to introduce Olivia to Matt, bringing old secrets into the open and slamming the final wrecking ball into what was left of her marriage.

CHAPTER FORTY

Nicole

Nicole felt awful watching little Poppy and her mother leave. She wanted to help. Of course she did. If she could give away one of her own organs to save the little girl, she would, but she couldn't offer up her daughter. She didn't know enough to understand what the implications might be, but she had to stand by her decision. As much as she would like to, she couldn't help Poppy. It was out of the question. She could never put Olivia's health at risk.

'Why are you sad, Mummy?' Olivia asked her, catching her by surprise as she came from the lounge, where she'd been waving Poppy off at the window.

Nicole quickly wiped away an errant tear that had spilled down her face. 'I'm not, darling,' she assured her, crouching down to pull her into a firm hug, 'The wind whipped my hair into my eyes, that's all.'

'Oh.' Olivia gazed uncertainly at her as Nicole eased back. 'I thought you might have been sad because Poppy is poorly,' she said, her beautiful innocent blue eyes flecked with obvious concern.

Nicole was taken aback. Presumably Poppy had told Olivia about her illness. How much did Poppy know? It broke her heart imagining what might be going through the little girl's mind, what might now be going through her own daughter's mind. 'I am sad for her, sweetheart,' she said. 'But I'm sure Poppy will be better soon.' She didn't know what else to say to make her own little girl feel better.

Olivia nodded, but her look was uncertain. 'We made some secret wishes. I wished I could make Poppy better,' she confided.

'Did you now?' Nicole laughed, though her heart squeezed at her daughter's natural open-heartedness. Was she being selfish, wanting to protect her own child above another?

But she couldn't allow it. However mature Olivia appeared to be, she wasn't old enough to understand any of it. She wouldn't be old enough at fifteen or sixteen, let alone five, to make a decision not knowing what the consequences would be for herself if she were to become ill. And Nicole could never make that decision for her.

'I tell you what, why don't we make a get-well card for Poppy?' she suggested, forcing a bright smile. 'We could find all her favourite things online and print them onto a card, and we could fill it with lots and lots of hearts and kisses. What do you think?'

Olivia considered for a second, then nodded. 'Doggies,' she said. 'Poppy likes cute furry puppies. And ballerinas and sparkly things.'

'Then we'll make sure to find lots of sparkly things too,' Nicole promised, leading Olivia to the kitchen to set her up at the island with her laptop.

Two hours later, every available space on the card peppered with kisses, Nicole popped the card into Olivia's school bag to take in tomorrow, and then encouraged her upstairs to get ready for bed. There were no protestations. Olivia was keen to see Poppy and present her with the card in the morning. The two little girls loved each other. Nicole knew she could never bring herself to stop her daughter seeing her new friend, although she was terrified that while Olivia was at Kay's house, her husband might meet her. She couldn't have him involved in her life, especially now.

Once Olivia was safely tucked under her duvet, she pressed a soft kiss to her forehead and went down to the kitchen. Walking across to her knick-knack drawer, she retrieved the note she'd tucked in there. It had been pushed through her door just after her house had been broken into about a week ago. Nothing much had been taken – just a few trinkets. Olivia's christening bracelet was the thing she'd been most upset about. Her paperwork had been strewn about, though, including her bank statements.

Unfolding the note, she reread it: *I know who she is. I know who her father is. He's extremely well off. It could be to your advantage. We should meet.*

Nicole screwed the note up and walked across to the bin to stuff it deep inside. She'd promised herself she wouldn't contact the woman, but she had, texting her and then talking to her on the phone. She wished now that she hadn't, that she hadn't got involved with any of it.

The woman had denied it, but it was quite clear in Nicole's mind that she'd been the person who'd broken into her home; she'd had access to her bank statements and was therefore aware of the fact that she was struggling financially. She'd seemed aware also that Nicole would be reluctant to allow Olivia's natural father access to her – she'd reinforced Nicole's determination not to allow that. Nicole had listened to her suggestions as to how she could provide Olivia with everything a mother should. She wished with all her heart now that she'd told her she wanted no part of it and walked away, but with Olivia's future to consider …

CHAPTER FORTY-ONE

Kay

Kay stood in the queue at the coronary care unit, holding tightly to Poppy's hand and willing the person ahead of her to hurry up. Leaving Nicole's house, she'd tried to ring Matt, needing to touch base with him, to tell him Poppy had improved slightly with no sign of a temperature. She'd needed to hear some kind of hope in his voice – for their precious girl, for them. She'd tried him several times. He hadn't responded to her calls or texts. She'd tried to get a message through to him here at the hospital, and had been devastated to learn about David. She'd rung Biochem to find out if Jason could shed any light on what had happened, and had been horrified when the receptionist told her that Matt had been there, and that the two brothers had come to blows.

'Is Daddy working here now, Mummy?' Poppy asked, tugging on her sleeve.

Realising how bewildering all of this was for her, Kay turned her attention to her daughter. 'No, sweetheart. Daddy doesn't work on this ward.'

Poppy went quiet for a moment, obviously pondering why they would be here otherwise; then, 'Is Daddy poorly, Mummy?' she asked, her voice tremulous.

Realising that her little girl could see through the open door of a side room, where a man lay in bed, attached to tubes and monitors, looking terribly poorly, Kay's heart skipped a beat. With all she'd had to endure, what she might have to endure, staying in for tests and infusions, Poppy shouldn't be seeing *this*.

'Daddy's not poorly, darling.' Crouching down, she hugged her close, wishing to God she'd been able to get hold of Stephanie, who would have taken Poppy in a flash. 'Grandpa is a little bit poorly, though,' she explained gently, easing back to gauge her reaction, 'so I thought we would come and be here to give your daddy a hug. I think he's bound to need one, don't you?'

Poppy nodded, but still her eyes were clouded with concern. 'Is he as poorly as that man?' she whispered, glancing uncertainly back to the side room.

'No, darling, not as poorly as that man,' Kay assured her, giving her another squeeze and hoping to God she wasn't lying to her little girl.

Finally at the desk, she told them who she was and asked after David.

The nurse she was speaking to eyed her hesitantly. 'He's just come out of surgery,' she said, her eyes drifting cautiously down to Poppy. 'Dr Young's with him. Would you like me to get someone to tell him you're here?'

Oh God, no. Was she saying that David was too sick for Poppy to see? Kay tried to think. She wanted Matt to know she was here, but she didn't want to drag him away from his father if he needed to be with him. If David really was bad, then … Her stomach twisted with anxiety. How could she establish how ill he was with Poppy looking on, her eyes like saucers and her radar on red alert?

'No, don't bother.' She managed a smile. 'I'll wait here for a while, if that's—' She stopped, her gaze snapping towards the doors a short way down the corridor as they swung open. Her heart jolted when she saw it was Jason banging through them, coming out of the ward, clearly upset. Realising that he didn't appear to have noticed her, she stepped towards him. 'Jason?'

He looked up, distracted, and then focused on her.

'David, is he …?' She faltered, her throat catching.

'He's doing okay,' Jason answered tetchily. 'No thanks to Matthew. I have no idea what you see in him, you know, Kay. The man's a complete—'

'*Jason!*' Kay dropped her gaze meaningfully to Poppy. 'Don't. Please.'

Getting the message, Jason nodded apologetically. 'Dad's doing as well as can be expected,' he said, moderating his tone. 'He's had bypass surgery. He's not out of the woods yet, though.'

'I'm sorry,' Kay offered, realising how upset he must be. 'Is Matt with him?' she asked, glancing past him towards the doors he'd just come through.

'He is. He was there at Biochem when it happened, performed CPR, saved him, I guess. He, er, came to see me.' Jason glanced cautiously at Poppy. 'Things got a little … fraught.'

Kay felt the knot of apprehension tighten inside her. 'I gathered. I spoke to Laura.'

'Christ knows what possessed him.' Jason sighed, and ran a hand wearily over his neck. 'Do you want to go through and see him?'

'I'd like to, but …' Kay indicated Poppy.

'You go. Poppy can stay with me, can't you, Poppy?' He gave her a reassuring smile.

Poppy looked worriedly at Kay. Jason crouched down in front of her. 'You're right to hesitate,' he said. 'You don't know me that well, after all, do you? But you know I'm your dad's brother, right? I've just been with your grandad. He's doing okay, I promise.'

A small furrow forming in her brow, Poppy studied him cautiously.

'How about you stay out here and help me play a game on my phone while your mum goes to check on him and make sure your dad's okay?'

Poppy glanced at Kay again, looking for permission. Kay could tell by the excited glint in her eyes at the mention of phone games that she wanted to stay with Jason. 'She's been a bit poorly today,' she said, keeping it low-key for Poppy's benefit.

Jason frowned in concern. 'In which case, I'd better take good care of her, hey, Poppy? She'll be okay with me for five minutes,' he said, glancing back to Kay. 'And we are in the safest place.'

Still Kay was hesitant. She knew she would have to let Poppy out of her sight at some point, but she was reluctant to do so.

'I think you might have to help me choose a game, though, Poppy,' Jason went on, pulling his phone from his jacket pocket and frowning perplexedly at it. 'I'm pretty rubbish at most of them. Okay with you, Mum?' he checked with her.

Kay deliberated. He was really trying. And Poppy was obviously keen. She hadn't got the heart to say no. 'Just for a few minutes,' she relented, bending to smooth Poppy's fringe back and kiss her forehead. 'And you're to stay right here,' she said to Jason, who nodded, understanding that she wouldn't want Poppy far out of her sight.

'Yes!' Poppy whooped. 'There's an app for kids' games,' she told Jason seriously.

'You'll need to show me where.' He looked convincingly clueless. 'Third door on the left,' he said to Kay, and extended his hand for Poppy.

Once she could see that they were seated in the waiting area, Kay headed quickly through the swing doors and along the corridor. She had to see for herself how David was. And Matt. He hadn't mentioned Jason's visit to the house before he'd left this morning. The fact was, though, he'd hardly spoken to her other than to liaise about Poppy. He'd hardly looked at her, and she needed him to. She needed to see what was in his eyes. Approaching David's room, she attempted to still her nerves, and then stepped quietly through the open door.

Matt was standing by his father's side, a hand placed over one of his. David's hands were secured, she noticed, her heart sinking, presumably to stop him pulling his breathing tube out. There were tubes everywhere, disappearing under the sheets. One protruded from his chest, draining off fluids, she guessed. Another was inserted into his arm, connected to a drip. 'How is he?' she asked softly.

Matt glanced in her direction, hardly seeing her for a second, Kay felt. He looked utterly exhausted. He had blood on his shirt – her heart twisted – and his face was almost as pale as his father's. Kay prayed with all her might that David would get through this. Matt would blame himself if the worst happened, just as he'd blamed himself for his mother's death. It would crush him. She couldn't bear to think of him hurting, even though he'd hurt her so much.

'He's stable,' he answered her finally. 'We'll know more once he wakes up.'

'What happened?' she asked, willing him to look at her.

'Heart attack,' he answered quietly, and then fell silent again.

It was clear he didn't want to say more. He was devastated, plainly. She couldn't open an impossible conversation between them now. 'Poppy's here,' she ventured after a second, thinking that might distract him from whatever guilt he might be carrying.

Matt did look at her then, surprised.

'I couldn't get hold of Stephanie,' she explained. 'And you weren't answering your phone, so …' She stopped. *I was scared*, she didn't add, but he must know that she would have been, both for him and for David. 'She's in reception, waiting to give you a hug.'

Matt frowned. 'In reception? But who's …' He stopped, his expression turning to one of astonishment. 'Don't tell me you've left her with … *Jesus*, you have to be joking.'

Seeing the flash of fury in his eyes, Kay felt her heart boom a warning. 'He offered to watch her while I came in,' she said quickly. 'I needed to see you. I—'

'After everything that's happened?' Matt spoke over her, his voice thick with emotion. 'You're seriously telling me …' His face was a kaleidoscope of emotion: incredulity, incomprehension, agitation. He emitted a strangled laugh, and then his eyes darkened. 'We need to talk,' he said, glancing back to his father, then turning to stride past her to the corridor.

Confusion and fear clogging her throat, Kay raced after him.

He'd stopped a short way down the corridor, his back towards her, kneading his temples. Hearing her approach, he spun around to face her. 'Just tell me one thing,' he said, his voice low. She could feel the heat of his fury as he glared at her. 'Did you love me?'

What? She squinted at him, confused. Of course she'd loved him. She—

'Ever?' he grated.

'Yes!' she responded fiercely. 'I've *always* loved you. Why would you think I didn't after all we've been to each other? All we've been through and done together? I don't understand. Matt, please—'

'Like having a child together, you mean?' he cut in acerbically, and Kay was left utterly speechless. 'You're not even going to deny it, are you?' he said after an excruciatingly long second.

Deny *what*? What was he *talking* about? She searched his face, stunned.

'So there it is.' His eyes drilled into hers. 'God, I've been a prize idiot, haven't I?' Tearing his gaze away, he looked up at the ceiling.

Kay's heart somersaulted in her chest. She reached out to him, but he moved away. Sucking in a breath, he glanced towards the viewing panes in the swing doors, through which Poppy and Jason were visible, and then back to her, looking as nauseous as Kay felt.

'I can't do this, Kay,' he said, swallowing emotionally. 'But that's okay, isn't it?' He laughed, a short, bemused laugh. 'He's back now, isn't he?'

It took a second for comprehension to dawn. When it did, it hit Kay like a freight train. He actually believed that she was still in love with Jason. He really did. Was *that* why he'd been unfaithful to her, possibly was still being unfaithful? 'Matt, you need to listen to me.' She took another step towards him.

'Don't.' He held out his hands, freezing her to the spot. 'I'm not doing this, not here.'

'But you *have* to listen. I'm not—'

'For fuck's sake!' Matt's face was rigid with anger. 'My father is *yards* away. He almost died! Do you really think I want to hear this *now*?'

'You're wrong!' Kay's voice rose. She couldn't help herself.

Matt pinched the bridge of his nose hard. 'Why don't you just go?' he suggested, looking back at her, the pain in his eyes piercing her heart like a knife.

'Matthew, wait!' She called out after him, but he had whirled around and stalked away.

CHAPTER FORTY-TWO

Fear crackling through her like ice, Kay watched Matt stride off, banging through the staff doors at the other end of the corridor that would take him into the depths of the hospital. She had to go after him. She *had* to make him believe that it was him she loved. That it had only ever been him.

Where was he going? Nausea churned afresh inside her as she considered what his options might be. He wouldn't leave the hospital, with his father here and so ill. Holding onto that hope, she raced back to reception. The two women at the desk swapped curious glances as she burst through the doors. She guessed they might have heard Matt and her arguing.

Scanning the reception area, she ground to a halt, her heart pumping with a new kind of fear. They weren't here. Poppy and Jason weren't where she'd left them. Her throat constricting at the thought that Poppy might be ill, she flew back to the desk. 'Excuse me,' she called, a frantic edge to her voice. 'The little girl who was here with her uncle …?'

'She needed the loo,' one of the women said with a reassuring smile. 'Through the main doors,' she nodded her that way, 'turn right down the main corridor, and right again at the bottom.'

Kay wasn't sure whether to feel relieved or not. Thank God Poppy wasn't missing, but what if her need for the loo was an indication of an infection? 'Thank you.' Smiling weakly, she turned towards the doors, praying as she went that Jason hadn't heard their argument. He would be bound to ask questions. Quickening her pace, she rounded the corner and ran smack-bang into him.

He reached out to steady her as she stumbled back. 'That was close enough to be enjoyable,' he quipped.

'Clumsy Mummy,' Poppy chastised her, glancing up from where she was hanging on to Jason's hand.

'She is a bit, isn't she?' Jason smiled down at her, and then back at Kay. 'We'll forgive her, though, hey? She seems to be in a bit of a rush.'

'I was worried, wondering where you were,' Kay said, looking at Poppy rather than keeping eye contact with Jason, who was searching her face curiously.

'I needed the loo,' Poppy provided. 'Uncle Jason guarded the door while I went in, didn't you, Uncle Jason?'

'I did indeed,' Jason confirmed. 'She's decided I can have a job as her bodyguard. I'm not sure Matthew would be too thrilled about that, though. Is he still with Dad?' he added, before Kay had time to comment.

'I think so,' she answered vaguely. 'He had a call. A colleague he wanted to confer with, so I thought I would come and rescue you from my daughter.'

'No rescuing required. We're getting along like a house on fire, aren't we, Poppy?' Jason assured her. He was smiling, but his eyes were narrowed.

'Uh huh,' Poppy concurred. 'I helped Uncle Jason find the Play Store on his phone, didn't I, Uncle Jason?'

'You did.' Jason's gaze was fixed unwaveringly on Kay, making her feel uncomfortable. 'She's obviously pretty savvy. I'm tempted to employ her as my technical adviser.'

Poppy's eyes widened excitedly. 'Can I, Mummy? Can I?'

Wishing Jason would stop scrutinising her, Kay smiled indulgently. 'Maybe, when you're older,' she said. She glanced at him. 'We have to go. It's past Poppy's bedtime.'

'Oh *Mummeee*.' Poppy's face fell. She'd clearly bonded with him. Kay's heart plummeted. She couldn't bear to imagine what Matt would think of that.

A prickle of apprehension ran the length of her spine as she noticed that Jason was still steadily watching her. He must have heard the argument. She prayed he wouldn't comment or sympathise. She was perilously close to tears.

'Right, well, we'll catch up soon,' he said, 'and then we can finish our game, hey, Poppy?'

'I bet I'll beat you,' Poppy exclaimed, her face lighting up again.

'We were playing My Very Hungry Caterpillar. I think mine's starving,' Jason told Kay with a rueful smile.

'Can Jason come to tea one day, Mummy?' Poppy asked with a little jiggle, and Kay's heart dropped another inch.

'Maybe,' she said, looking away from him. 'We'll see.'

'Better check with Matt,' Jason suggested. 'Wouldn't want to do anything without consulting him, would we? He might think we're up to something behind his back.'

Kay's blood ran cold. *Stop, Jason*, she begged silently. *Please just stop.*

'I should get back to Dad,' he said, as she forced herself not to react. 'Catch you later.'

He waited, presumably for Kay to look back at him. She did so with an effort, smiling guardedly. She had no idea what she would do if he turned up at her house uninvited again. No idea what Matt might do … if he even came home. The possibility that he might not hit her, and she almost reeled under the weight of it. 'Say bye, Poppy,' she encouraged her, wanting to get away from Jason before her tears spilled over.

'Bye, Uncle Jason,' Poppy obliged gloomily as Kay took hold of her free hand.

'Bye, little niece,' Jason responded.

Panic spiralling inside her at what Matt might do, where he might be, Kay hurried on down the corridor. Then she stopped abruptly, her heart hurtling full force into her ribcage as she saw someone emerge from a door at the top of the corridor and head for the main doors into the hospital reception.

It was *her*. She was sure it was. *Amelia.* There was no mistaking that tangle of jet-black hair. And since she was wearing a nurse's uniform, she obviously *did* know Matt. She'd lied to Kay. Bare-faced lies. When she was talking about affairs and secrets that day at the university, she knew *exactly* what she was referring to. Matt had lied to her too – consistently, cruelly. And now he'd come out with this concocted claptrap about *her* supposed failings, digging the knife in and twisting it hard. Amelia was the nurse Jason had witnessed him with on the stairs. A graphic image of the two of them imprinting itself on her mind, Kay felt bile rise in her throat.

Why was he doing this? Her world shifting further off kilter, she pressed a hand to her forehead, and then stifled a laugh at her own stupidity. Because he wanted to be with Amelia, evidently, and had invented a reason to blame Kay. Maybe he wanted a new life, to build his family again with *her*. Was that why poor, *lonely* Amelia had tried to get close to her? So she could get close to Poppy? Kay didn't know how long he'd been seeing her, whether Amelia might even be Olivia's birth mother, but one thing she did know was that she would kill her before she let the woman anywhere near her child.

CHAPTER FORTY-THREE

Amelia

Widening her eyes, Amelia carefully applied her favourite Urban Decay eyeliner. She'd never considered herself as beautiful as her sister, but with a little make-up she looked reasonable. The mushroom shade certainly enhanced the colour of her eyes – her best asset, she felt. Applying a subtle sweep of nude lipstick, she stood back and scrutinised herself in the mirror, wanting to make sure she hadn't overdone it. The last thing she wanted to appear was tarty. Men who were looking for serious relationships, she'd found, much preferred women who had an air of vulnerability about them.

Reminded again of her little sister, who'd been as physically and emotionally vulnerable as a woman could be, her throat tightened. If only she could have been there for her. She *should* have been. Turning her gaze to the ceiling, she blinked back the tears that were threatening to ruin her make-up. There was no point looking back. She'd cried an ocean, tears racking her body until she'd thought her heart would break; she'd felt so guilty and bereft she'd barely been able to get out of bed, let alone function. And then she'd made up her mind, realised there was no point looking back, wishing she could have done things differently. She couldn't change the past. She had to look forward. She had a goal in mind, and that gave her a reason to get out of bed now, to paint on her smile, to function.

Giving her appearance a final check, she turned from the mirror, took several calming slow breaths to prepare herself for the day ahead and then went to the bedroom to get dressed.

She was grabbing her bag and heading for the door when her phone alerted her to a text. She fumbled the phone from her bag and cursorily checked it as she hurried to her car. Then she stopped, her pulse quickening.

He's made the payment, she read, and felt a flood of adrenaline rush through her. Then overwhelming sadness, followed by raw anger. This proved he was guilty, as guilty as sin, and justified all that she was doing. She'd wavered occasionally, but now she felt strong, empowered, hugely relieved.

She hadn't been sure the woman would take the bait initially, until Amelia had met up with her and shown her the photograph of her tiny seventeen-year-old sister, his arm draped proprietorially around her. What had finally swayed her, though, was when she showed her the text. The last text her little sister had ever sent her, a desperate plea for help that Amelia hadn't seen until it was too late. Much too late. She'd decided by then that she would honour her sister's wishes by not interfering in her life.

He's trying to take her. I don't know what to do was all it said. Amelia could only imagine how desperate she must have felt when she'd typed it.

Seeing that, the woman had been furious, judging by the flash of contempt she'd seen in her eyes. She didn't want to have anything to do with him, but she'd clearly decided he should pay.

CHAPTER FORTY-FOUR

Matthew

She was walking away. Matt tried to follow. Her progress was slow, unhurried, but no matter how hard he ran, the distance between them only seemed to grow wider. Hearing again the distressed cries of a baby, he stopped, indecision and fear twisting inside him as the melodic sound of his wife humming a soft lullaby to the child she had nestled to her breast floated back to him.

His gaze flicked to his side. He'd passed it several times, but still the room was there, a suffocatingly dark room, now revolving around him, the ceaseless cry beckoning him. His wife's humming grew fainter. The baby cried louder, raucous, desperate pleas for its mother, tiny arms and legs flailing above the rim of the pram it had been left in. His urge was to go after Kay, his instinct to go to the child. Terror gripped him as he approached, his heart thrashing. The baby's sobs slowed as he shushed it. 'It's okay,' he whispered. 'It's okay.' His hand shook as he reached out to free the child's face of the shawl that had been kicked over it. And then he froze, his blood running cold. The pram was empty, no bereft crying baby there, nothing but a dog-eared teddy bear.

'Loser!' His brother's voice – taunting, triumphant – permeated the darkness …

Matt's eyes snapped open as he felt it, his heart being ripped from his chest as the door to the room closed, the click of the lock sealing his fate, trapping him in his worst nightmare for ever. *No!*

He tried to call out, but couldn't get the words past the parched lump in his throat. The dull beat of his heart now thrumming prophetically at the base of his neck, he tried to oust the images and sounds from his head. Unable to move, he couldn't escape the baby crying, his wife humming, pushing the pram now, wheels trundling. Sensation returning, his hands and arms tingling, he strained to lift his head, tried to define the dark shapes around his bed, alien silhouettes illuminated by the light of the moon. No blinds at the window. It wasn't his window. This wasn't his room.

It wasn't the squeaky wheel of a pram he could hear, it was a hospital trolley. The silhouettes were intravenous stands, out-of-use monitors. *Christ.* Emitting a strangled laugh, he jerked himself upright and ran his hands over his face. Remembering why he was here, sleeping in an unoccupied side room after drinking himself into near oblivion, his chest twisted with pain and anger. She'd been lying to him. All these *years.*

She'd relied on him to be exactly who he was, dependable, there for her come what may, for Poppy. His throat constricted painfully as his thoughts went to his little girl, how all this would affect her. He hadn't been there for her tonight, hadn't said goodnight to her. Maybe Jason had, he thought, a toxic mixture of anger and jealousy churning inside him. Now that his brother was back, re-establishing himself in Kay's life, there was no reason why he shouldn't just step into Matt's shoes.

Fuck it. Getting shakily to his feet, he dragged his hands through his hair, wincing as his fingers caught the gash under his hairline – a physical scar inflicted by his dear brother to add to the mental scars Matt had tried so hard to shake off – and then headed for the basin to throw water over his face. He needed to pull himself together, think rationally. Decide what to do, what he could do that wouldn't rock Poppy's world further. She needed him, not some self-serving prat who would walk away the second he'd got what he wanted.

Trying to still the nausea swilling inside him, he pulled in a breath, and headed for the corridor. He should check on his father. David might not have been the greatest father to him growing up, but he'd made an effort with him lately. Did he know? it occurred to him to wonder. It was possible, entirely possible, that he knew what his shit of a brother had done. But then Jason wasn't entirely responsible, was he? It took two to tango.

Swallowing back the bitter taste in his throat, he walked into his father's room to find him conscious. 'How is he?' he asked one of the nursing staff, who was on his way out.

'Good,' the nurse informed him. 'Vital signs are all stable and no excessive bleeding. He wasn't in too much discomfort, but he's had a painkiller just in case.'

'Great.' Matt smiled his appreciation. 'Thanks, Adam.'

'No probs.' Adam smiled back and hurried on to his next patient, leaving Matt alone with his father, who, even as ill as he'd been, managed to glower at him – with good reason.

'How are you doing?' Matt asked, tentatively approaching him.

'I think I've felt better,' his father replied drolly, and attempted to ease himself up.

Matt reached to stop him. 'Better not,' he advised. 'I can call the nurse back to help me raise your bed and sit you up if you need to.'

His father shook his head. 'I'm fine,' he said. 'No need to fuss.'

'Right.' Matt wasn't sure what else to say, given why his father was in hospital and the part he'd played in it. 'You should only be here for a few days providing you continue to make good progress,' he managed, hiding behind his professional persona.

'A few days is too long with a business to run,' his father responded, disgruntled. 'What were you thinking, Matthew, charging in like that?'

That I'd quite like to break his neck, Matt didn't say. 'I wasn't, clearly.' He shrugged apologetically.

'Whatever it was you were arguing about, you must know that Kay thinks the world of you.' His father eyed him incredulously. 'She's in love with *you*, man. You'd have to be blind not to see it.'

He did know, then; something at least. Matt looked away.

His father, however, wasn't about to let it drop. 'Jason was up to his usual tricks,' he said, his voice edged with despair. 'I can't believe you've been letting this eat away at you for … how long?'

'Too long,' Matt said, then quickly changed the subject. 'You'll need to take it easy for a while, once you're discharged.'

'I gathered,' his father muttered.

Matt hesitated. 'Do you think it might be a good idea to look at slowing down? Semi-retirement maybe?' he suggested, and felt his gut tighten. This was exactly what Jason wanted, to slip into his father's shoes too. He wouldn't give a damn that the man had lived for his work since their mother died.

David shook his head. 'I'm not ready to hand the reins to Jason yet. I'm concerned he might be too impulsive. He's been spending money lately like it's going out of fashion. Now I'm thinking it's *you* I should be concerned about.'

Spending money? Judging by his reluctance to shell out on health and safety issues, Matt thought Jason had been doing the opposite. 'You don't need to worry about me,' he assured his father. 'I overreacted. I'm sorry. It won't happen again. I'm fine now, honestly.'

'Hence the smell of alcohol?' His father raised an eyebrow. 'Don't torture yourself, Matthew. Life's too short. Whatever gripe you have with your brother, don't let your marriage suffer because of it. Little Poppy needs you. Kay does too.'

'I know.' Matt glanced away again. He had to.

'Have you had the tests yet? The ones to find a suitable match should Poppy need a donor?'

'Tissue typing,' Matt supplied. 'We're about to.' He wondered how much he should say. Whether he should mention what the tests might reveal. He took a breath, then, 'Did you know, Dad?' he asked him quietly.

His father closed his eyes. 'No, son, not for certain. I had a feeling, but …' He sighed regretfully.

Matt pressed his thumb hard against his forehead. 'I should go. I have patients to see.'

His father nodded. 'Don't suffer in silence,' he said gruffly. 'I know we haven't exactly been close, but you can always talk to me if you need to.'

'Thanks.' Matt swallowed back a lump of emotion, wishing he *could* talk to him, about the past, the guilt he'd carried about the accident that had killed his mother, the guilt he was carrying now, feeling that somehow he was responsible for creating the nightmare scenario unfolding around him. But it was out of the question with him so ill. 'You need to get some rest.'

His father answered with a tired nod. The conversation had clearly exhausted him.

'I'll stop by in the morning.' Matt reached to place a hand on his arm. His dad had never been overly fond of shows of affection – unless from Poppy. Matt's stomach twisted as he thought about how her relationship with her grandfather might be affected. Had Kay thought about that, about the long-term impact of what she'd done? Obviously she hadn't.

'Go home,' his dad said behind him as he turned for the door. 'You work far too many hours. You'll burn yourself out and be no good to anyone.'

Would that he could go home. Matt suddenly felt dangerously close to tears.

'On my way,' he called back, his throat tight.

A combination of guilt and despair churning inside him, he walked slowly to the foyer at the end of the corridor and called the lift. His father was right. He would do no good here. David had smelled alcohol on him. He could smell it on himself. He'd been drinking to excess. He'd lost his temper, become the kind of person he detested. He'd almost killed his own father. His mind shot back to little Leo Cooper, how he'd struggled to pass the endotracheal tube down the baby's throat. He might have been responsible for his death too. He shouldn't be here, where vulnerable patients needed him to do a job he clearly wasn't capable of doing with his thinking clouded, his reactions slow. He needed to go. Where, though, he had no idea. He would call and check on Poppy, but he couldn't go home, not yet. He simply couldn't face Kay.

He was wondering distractedly about nearby hotels when the lift doors opened. Seeing who was on the other side of them, he moved back in surprise.

'I was looking for you. I was so worried when I didn't see you around.' Rachel stepped out and promptly wrapped her arms around him. She was too close, much too close. Matt's head reeled, the cloying scent of her perfume adding to his disorientation. He shouldn't be doing this. She shouldn't. 'Rachel …' He reached up, easing her arms from around his neck.

She stepped back. 'Are you all right?' she asked, scanning his eyes worriedly. 'Is your father okay? I thought he might—'

'He's doing fine, yes,' Matt said quickly, very aware of where they were, how this might look, who might see them. 'Thanks for asking.'

She nodded. 'I wondered whether you fancied some company,' she said. 'It might help take your mind off things. We could grab a coffee from the vending machine and find a quiet space, or just take a walk around the grounds if you prefer?'

Matt searched her eyes – striking grey eyes, flecked with worry – and felt bad. He was in danger of being curt with her. Yet she'd done nothing wrong. 'A walk would be good,' he said, thinking it might at least clear his head.

'Brilliant.' She beamed. 'There was actually something I wanted to talk to you about.'

'Oh yes?' Matt stepped into the lift with her.

'I'm doing this course.' Rachel's gaze flicked hesitantly to his as she pressed the button for the ground floor. 'I'm having a few problems, and I could really use your advice.'

CHAPTER FORTY-FIVE

Kay

Kay snapped her eyes open and jerked upright, waking from a dream so real she could still feel his hands on her body. They'd been making love, she and Matt, but he hadn't been Matt, not the Matt she knew. He hadn't been gentle, intuitive and caring. He'd been rough, demanding. *Oh God.* She buried her face in her hands, stifling a sob that seemed to come from her soul. What was happening to them, to him? He'd been behaving so oddly, she wasn't sure any more whether it was calculated cruelty or whether he might be having some sort of breakdown. He worked so hard, so many hours.

Shivering, her vest top clinging damply to her skin, she glanced at the alarm clock, which showed some ludicrously early hour of the morning, then threw the duvet back and climbed out of bed. She checked her phone to find he hadn't returned any of her calls or texts. *Where are you?* Fear like a cold stone inside her, she closed her eyes, praying that she would hear his key in the lock, which might allow her to breathe again.

Please come back, Matt. For Poppy, if not for me. Her overriding fear was for her daughter. It had taken an age to coax her into bed, another to soothe her to sleep after checking her protein levels, taking her temperature, soothing her worries about why her daddy hadn't kissed her goodnight and making sure she wasn't hiding her symptoms. The reality was, though, that beyond a certain point, Poppy would be in so much discomfort she couldn't hide it. If her kidneys started to fail, if her small body started to retain fluids, the outward symptoms would soon become obvious – the swelling, her ankles and face all puffed up. Kay didn't think she could bear it without the man she'd always thought she could depend on by her side.

Going to the door, she padded out of the room and along the landing, goosebumps prickling her skin, a cold hollowness spreading through her as she wondered again where he was. She still had no idea what he imagined she'd done to deserve to be treated so badly. Did he honestly think she was in love with his brother, carrying on something that had meant nothing compared to what the two of them had? Clearly it wasn't just her who was a bad judge of character. She couldn't quite believe that the man she'd spent so many years with didn't appear to know her at all.

Easing Poppy's door open, she crept inside, her fear abating a little as she found her sleeping, softly breathing, her eyelids flickering as her mind chased her dreams. Carefully she drew the duvet higher over her, tucking a tiny arm under it, wishing to God she could do more to protect her daughter. She would give her life for her. If it meant her baby could be safe and happy, she would do that in a heartbeat.

Going quietly out to the landing, she returned to her own room, wrapping her arms around herself and standing stock still in the middle of it, uncertain what to do. She didn't want to go back to bed without him, longed to feel his arms encircling her, making her feel safe, at least for a short while. Her Matt, the gentle man she knew him to be, not the monster in her dream, not the man he seemed to be turning into. She could smell him, the subtle citrusy undertones of his aftershave; the essence of him permeated every room. Had she lost him?

Walking across to his wardrobe, she opened the doors. Gliding her hands through his clothes, she finally extracted one of his work shirts. It was a poor substitute, but she needed to feel the closeness of him. She pushed her arms into it, pulling it on over her vest top, tugged up the collar and pressed her face to it as she headed back towards the bed – and her blood froze. This wasn't the subtle smell of Matt's aftershave. It was sickly and sweet. *Jasmine and honey* … Her heart fractured, each piece piercing her chest like an icicle. This was the scent of another woman. *Amelia.*

CHAPTER FORTY-SIX

She wasn't sure why she'd come here. To think things through, she supposed. Decide whether she should even try to fight for Matt. How could she compete with someone younger and undeniably prettier, someone he must be so in love with he couldn't see the pain he would cause an innocent little girl who needed him to be there for her? It was a tranquil spot, overlooked by the church, surrounded by trees and serenaded by birdsong. She usually found solace here, enabling her to put her chaotic thoughts into some sort of order, her worries into perspective. She didn't think she would achieve that today.

Uncaring of the damp grass, she lowered herself to her knees, reading the inscription on the headstone in the shape of a simple crescent moon, a child's teddy bear draped sleepily over it.

WE HELD YOU IN OUR ARMS FOR A PRECIOUS SHORT WHILE.
WE WILL HOLD YOU IN OUR HEARTS FOREVER.
WE LOVE YOU. SLEEP SAFE, LITTLE ANGEL. MUMMY AND DADDY

Glancing heavenwards, she swallowed back her grief, which seemed to have taken on a new bitter piquancy. If he'd given his heart to someone else, was there still room in it for his children? Wiping a hand across her eyes, she reached to rearrange the small bunch of purple freesias and white roses she'd brought with her. It looked like a wedding bouquet, she thought sadly. Breathing in hard, she waited for the unbearable heartache to pass. She doubted it would. Ever.

Her thoughts were on Matt, the soft glint in his eyes when he'd made his wedding vows, promising to forsake all others and love her completely, when she sensed someone behind her. Her heart jolted as he came alongside her, almost as if she'd conjured him up. 'I called at the house,' Matt said, 'to check on Poppy. Stephanie said you were here.'

Her heart fluttering nervously, Kay half rose to her feet.

'Stay,' he urged her. 'Take a minute. There's no rush.'

He crouched beside her as she sank back down, his arms resting on his thighs, his hands clasped, his head bowed as if in prayer. They didn't speak for a while, both unsure what to say that wouldn't escalate into an argument, she guessed. What was going on? How *long* had it been going on? She needed to know desperately, but couldn't ask.

She glanced at him. He looked so tired and dishevelled, unshaven, his collar askew, definitely not the Matt she knew. He might not pay the same attention to his appearance his vainer brother did, but he was always immaculately dressed. He would always shave, even at the hospital. It reassured people, he said. Parents who were relying on him to care for their little ones wouldn't want to think he might be struggling with his workload.

'Can we talk?' he asked at length. 'Not here,' he added, pressing his thumb to his forehead – a sure sign he was upset – and getting to his feet. 'I thought we might do better to walk.'

He waited while she stood. He would normally help her, extending his hand for her to hang onto, not because he thought she needed it, but because that was just the way he was, courteous and thoughtful. The way he had been.

Gathering her things, she walked with him along one of the paths leading to the older part of the cemetery, past stones worn by the elements and wingless cherubs that brought a fresh lump to her throat. It was as if time had forgotten them.

After a while, he stopped, turning towards her. 'I thought that would be us,' he said, nodding reflectively past her. 'That we would grow old together.'

She followed his gaze to a headstone dedicated to a husband and wife, both in their eighties, just one year between their deaths.

'What happened, Kay?' he asked her, his voice hoarse.

Kay looked back at him, tears blurring her vision. There were a thousand questions she wanted to ask, but she had no idea how to ask them. 'I've no idea,' she said eventually. 'I'm still the same person I always was.'

She waited, hoping he would pick up on it, that he would admit that he'd changed, admit something, rather than dream up unfounded accusations to hurl at her. He didn't. In a way, she was glad. Doing this here would only sully their son's memory.

Matt dropped his gaze, massaged his forehead. 'We need to take the tests, Kay. Both of us. As soon as possible. You know that?'

Kay nodded. She knew they did. Would they go together, or separately? she wondered, a deep loneliness enveloping her.

'I've spoken to the renal department about some dates,' he said. 'I'll let you know once they confirm.'

Her heart slowed to an aching thud as she wondered whether he would let her know in person or simply text her. He'd said he'd 'called at' the house, as if he didn't live there. Would the next time be to collect his things?

'There's something else I need to talk to you about,' he said, bringing his gaze warily back to hers. 'A woman I know at the hospital, she—'

'What woman?' Kay snapped before he'd finished.

'A nurse,' he said, causing her stomach to plummet. 'We both know her, apparently.'

Kay's emotions reeled. He *was* going to do this here, wasn't he? Clearly he didn't think it was inappropriate, with the child they'd made and lost together lying just a stone's throw away. She stared at him with a mixture of incredulity and excruciating hurt.

'She's a student on your course,' he went on. 'Rachel. Rachel Jones.'

Rachel? But her name wasn't Rachel. She was Amelia Jones. She was obviously using a false name. In case he let her name slip? she wondered, fury rising inside her. While *they* were making love? That thought caused her stomach to roil.

'How well do you know her?' she asked, a wobble to her voice, despite her determination not to allow the tears that were sitting too close to the surface to fall.

Matt's gaze flicked away. 'She's a friend,' he said, with an awkward shrug.

'I asked you how well you *know* her,' Kay reiterated. 'Don't pretend you don't know what I mean, Matt.'

Clearly knowing *exactly* what she meant, he drew in a terse breath. 'She's a colleague, that's all. She works nights at the hospital. But that's beside the point.'

Kay felt her world shift. *Don't.* She closed her eyes. Willed herself not to fly at him. 'And?' She met his gaze, hoping he could see the hurt and contempt in her eyes. 'You were about to tell me something about her, presumably?'

He ran his hand over his neck, looked momentarily indecisive. Not like Matt. Not like Matt at all. 'She says you're making life difficult for her.'

'*What?*' She stared hard at him.

'She thinks you've taken a dislike to her, that you're making it difficult for her to finish her course. The thing is, I'm not sure I believe—'

'She's a liar!' Kay laughed, absolutely incredulous. 'It's *her* who's making life difficult for *me*.'

He narrowed his eyes. 'Why would she do that, Kay?' he asked quietly.

'*Why?*' She almost choked. 'Why do you *think*? She's trying to split us up!'

Matt nodded slowly. 'I see,' was all he said.

'She's possibly lost me my job,' Kay continued, feeling desperate, besieged emotionally. 'She manipulated a situation, complained about me, *knowing* it might cost me my job.'

Matt regarded her thoughtfully. He really was, wasn't he: defending Amelia – Rachel, whatever her bloody name was – over her. Kay swallowed back the excruciating lump of hurt in her throat. 'Why are you doing this?' she asked him shakily. 'Why are you letting *her* do this?'

'I'm not doing anything, Kay,' he said, unbelievably. 'I'm simply trying to find out what's going on.'

'It seems pretty obvious to me what's going on.' Kay swiped at her cheeks. 'You're *fucking* her. Having some seedy, disgusting little affair with her!'

Matt shook his head, closed his eyes, then opened them again. 'What's wrong with you, Kay?' he said. 'I've done nothing but try to do my bloody best. It wasn't enough, obviously. I get that. But what you've done … Did I *ever* really know you?'

'Did I ever know *you*?' she countered tearfully.

He sucked in a breath, breathed it out slowly. 'For the record, I'm not having an affair, seedy or otherwise. But it really doesn't matter, does it? I can't change things, whatever I say.' He studied her for a long, hard moment, and then turned away from her. 'I can't do this, Kay.'

'Nor can *I*,' she threw after him. 'You two *deserve* each other!' Her world rocking violently, she watched as Matt wavered. She felt the foundations give way beneath her as he deliberated for the briefest of seconds, and then walked away.

CHAPTER FORTY-SEVEN

Feeling disorientated, as if she'd been dropped from a very great height, Kay let herself through her front door. Glancing in the hall mirror before going through to the lounge to see Poppy, she barely recognised the woman looking back at her. She'd never imagined she could feel like this, be this person, vitriol rising up inside her she had no idea what to do with. She might have forgiven him an affair. Somehow she might have found a way to do that. The way he was plotting and planning, though, trying to put the blame on her when she'd done nothing wrong, all but gaslighting her – how was she ever to forgive him that?

And Amelia? What was *her* ultimate goal, apart from to steal Kay's husband? Had she enrolled on the course purely for the satisfaction of tormenting her? How *could* Matt? With someone like *that*?

Resting her head against her hand, she closed her eyes, her mind drifting to precious moments with her husband that would be captured forever without need of a photograph. Matt cradling Poppy in his arms, his face filled with love and apprehension as he studied her perfect features. His eyes – she would never forget the look in those, the awe she saw there. He'd loved her on sight, completely. He'd sworn he would kill to keep her safe. Kay knew he would. She *did* know him, and she still loved him, God help her, but she loved the man she'd married, not this distorted version of him. A whirl of emotions churned inside her: anger, grief and confusion. How could she not have known he was cheating on her? How could they have appeared so happy together? It seemed their whole relationship had been precariously built on a bed of lies, like a house made out of cards. One card wobbled, and the whole house tumbled, their marriage crumbling along with it.

'Everything okay?' Stephanie asked, poking her head around the lounge door, causing her to jolt.

Collecting herself, Kay nodded weakly.

'Oh dear …' Stephanie stepped into the hall, looking her over as she closed the lounge door behind her. 'You're not a very good liar, Kay. Your face looks like a wet weekend in Bognor.'

'Thanks.' Kay laughed wanly, then glanced quickly down, cursing the tears that sprang again to her eyes.

'Come on.' Stephanie was by her side in a flash, taking hold of her arm. 'I think a medicinal wine might be in order. And you should eat something, too. You really are as pale as a ghost.'

Kay glanced towards the lounge as Stephanie marched her past. 'Has she been okay?' she asked worriedly. 'I should just pop in and check.'

'She's been fine. I would have rung you if she hadn't been. She's heavily into *Waffle the Wonder Dog* on TV at the moment. Grab a second while you can.'

Realising her friend wasn't about to take no for an answer, Kay allowed herself to be led. Sitting at the table, as instructed, she glanced around her kitchen, the kitchen she and Matt had planned together, both wanting a homey farmhouse feel to it. Her eyes fell on Poppy's innocent paintings adorning the fridge, and the tears welled afresh. Matt had pinned one of his drawings next to one of Poppy's, a stick dog, drawn deliberately badly. He'd penned 'First Prize' on Poppy's drawing, 'Booby Prize' on his own. He was a good man, with a heart of gold. She *knew* he was. How had she allowed someone else to steal that heart?

'God, Kay.' Stephanie came across with the wine she'd fetched from the fridge. 'Your eyes look like two pee holes in the snow,' she announced unceremoniously. 'Come on, spill. Whatever it is that's worrying you to death, you can tell me. We're friends, aren't we? I promise you it won't go any further.' Sitting down, she reached across the table for Kay's hand.

Kay took a tremulous breath. Steph would find out soon enough anyway, when she and Matt were no longer a couple. Her heart twisted painfully at that thought. How would she ever bear waking up to find his side of the bed permanently empty?

'Matt's cheating on me,' she whispered, her throat feeling as if she'd swallowed sand.

Stephanie's mouth dropped open. Kay might have laughed but for the fact that she felt like sobbing. Her friend looked like a startled guppy.

'Matt?' Steph finally gasped, staring incredulously at her. 'You're joking?'

Kay ran a hand under her nose. 'I wish I was.'

'Matt? *Your* Matt? *Cheating?* I don't believe it.' Stephanie was clearly struggling to digest the news, and no wonder. Matt really was the last man on earth anyone would imagine cheating on his wife. Kay had never imagined he would, yet here she was.

'Who? When? Where?'

Stephanie wanted details. Naturally she would. Kay couldn't blame her. 'I don't know where or when,' she answered unsteadily. 'He obviously hasn't been attending as many late-night emergencies as he would have people believe, though.' Have *her* believe. And she had, never once doubting him. Humiliation settled heavily inside her, exacerbating her grief and anger. 'As for who …' She caught her breath, a sudden image of Matt with *her* – his mouth on hers, his tongue tasting hers, his hands tracing the contours of her body, touching her, bringing her to the same sweet orgasm he did Kay – causing her stomach to clench painfully. 'It's someone

I know.' She dropped her gaze, unable to meet her friend's eyes, not wanting to see what would undoubtedly be there: the pity, the disbelief.

Stephanie snorted wine down her nose. 'You *know* her?'

'One of my students,' Kay provided, her voice small. She wanted to curl up inside herself.

'Now you really *have* to be joking,' Stephanie blustered. 'Oh well done, Matt. Shit on your own doorstep, why don't you?'

He had, Kay realised. He'd known, quite obviously, judging from the conversation they'd had, that Amelia was one of her students. Yet still he'd carried on. Had that turned him on? Had he got some extra kick out of the added deceit?

Stephanie squeezed her hand. 'I'm sorry, Kay,' she said. 'If there's anything I can do … like hire a hit man …'

Nice idea, Kay thought. But possibly not legal.

'What I don't understand is *why*,' Stephanie went on. 'I thought you two were really good together. I know you've had your problems, God *knows* you have, but you seemed so together. I honestly never thought Matt capable of that kind of …' She stopped, clearly realising from the tears now plopping down Kay's cheeks that she wasn't being very diplomatic. 'God, me and my mouth. Sorry, Kay. I'm not helping much, am I?'

'It's okay.' Kay swiped at her wet face. There wasn't much anyone could do to help. She had to pull herself together, get over it, if she was going to be the strong woman her baby would need. But God, she felt so squashed right now.

Stephanie was silent for a second. Then, 'So Olivia,' she ventured, 'she presumably is—'

'I've no idea.' Kay cut her short, a sudden violent anger sweeping through her.

'Sorry,' Stephanie said again. 'Sore subject, I gather.'

'Very.' Kay heaved herself to her feet. 'Would you do me a favour and stay a little longer, Steph?' she asked her.

Stephanie looked her over worriedly. 'Of course I will. But where are you going?'

'I have to pop into the university. I shouldn't be too long.'

Summoning all her strength, Kay headed to the hall. She couldn't allow herself to feel like this. There was no way she could wallow in her grief, no matter how much it hurt. She needed to fight. If there was no point fighting for Matt, so be it. But she needed to fight for her daughter, for her own self-esteem. She needed to stay standing.

CHAPTER FORTY-EIGHT

Kay wasn't sure she would be welcome at the university. She knew that Amelia would be there today; she would be in her Creative Non-Fiction class about now. Faltering at the main entrance, she wondered whether she should be doing this. Wouldn't she be more likely to hold on to her self-esteem if she acted with dignity and did nothing? But that would allow Amelia to totally diminish her in the university's eyes, in Matt's eyes. No, she simply couldn't walk away. That he would even imagine she would intimidate a student, discriminate against a student, was incredibly hurtful. Did he really think she was that sort of person? Her heart faltered. He'd obviously been all too ready to take *Rachel's* word over hers. That thought serving to fuel her anger, she steeled her resolve, pushed through the entrance and took the lift up to the third floor.

Her legs leaden beneath her, she made her way along the corridor. Approaching the classroom, she glanced through the glass and saw her immediately, sitting at the front of the class, her long legs crossed, her pretty head tilted to one side. She looked as if butter wouldn't melt. Kay's stomach roiled. The woman was on the wrong course. She should have applied to acting school. But then she was clearly already an accomplished actor.

Breathing hard, she stood to one side, her heart banging as she waited for the class to end. Minutes later, the door opened, students milling through the door. Finally Amelia emerged.

Kay stepped directly in front of her, causing the woman to step back. 'Why didn't you tell me you worked at the hospital?' she asked, trying for some level of calm.

Alarm flitted across Amelia's features, but she soon composed herself, her perfectly made-up eyes holding Kay's for a second before her forehead creased into a convincingly troubled frown.

'You *do* work there, don't you?' Kay's heart sank as she realised Professor Simons was approaching along the corridor, but her gaze never wavered.

Amelia laughed uncertainly. 'Yes. I work there part-time.'

'And you didn't think to mention that fact?' Kay's throat tightened with mounting anger.

The furrow in Amelia's brow deepened. 'Why would I have done? The subject never came up.' Splaying her hands as Professor Simons reached them, she glanced bemusedly at him. She was clearly attempting to garner his sympathy.

Kay's jaw clenched. 'But it did, didn't it, *Rachel*?'

Undoubtedly wondering what he should do, Professor Simons took a step closer. 'Kay … I don't think this is quite appropriate, is it?' he said, his tone apprehensive. 'Why don't we—'

'Rachel's my middle name. I use it because there's another Amelia on my ward.' Amelia was looking astonished now. 'I've never made any secret of the fact that I work at the hospital, Kay. I have to, to make ends—'

'Bullshit,' Kay hissed. 'You talk about *my* husband, making it obvious that you know him, and then deny it? You're a *liar*, Amelia.'

'I'm *not* lying!' Amelia countered tearfully. 'It's a big hospital. I didn't make the connection before. Obviously I do now, but … *Why* would I lie, for God's sake?'

Why? Kay felt the band of tension between her temples snap, launching her towards the woman. She wanted to gouge her calculating grey eyes out. 'You scheming *little*—'

'That's *enough*, Kay!' Professor Simons reached for her, one arm around her, physically restraining her, as students looked on with audible gasps.

'Do you see?' Kay's gaze swivelled desperately to him. 'Do you see what she's doing? She's manipulating me. Manipulating *you*. You must see.'

'What I'm seeing is that *you* appear to be very distressed,' Professor Simons responded shakily.

Kay laughed, disbelieving. 'I *am* distressed. Don't you think I have every right to be?'

The professor scanned her face, his own etched with concern. 'Please leave, Kay,' he said, quietly but firmly. 'We'll have a chat later and—'

'She's having an affair with my husband!' Kay shouted. 'She's obsessed with him. She's trying to *destroy* my marriage. Surely you must be able to—'

'You're insane.' Amelia pushed past her.

'You're fucking my husband!' Kay yelled after her.

Amelia turned to face her. Appraising her coolly, she said nothing for a second. Then, 'You should go home, Kay,' she suggested. 'Look after the daughter you think is his.' Spinning around again, she walked away, leaving Kay shocked to the core.

CHAPTER FORTY-NINE

Matthew

Feeling guilty, Matt headed home, wondering what he was going to say to Kay. What he could say that wouldn't open up another argument. Apart from the odd work conference, he'd never stayed away before, and he felt homesick. He realised the feeling was familiar to him – he had felt it as a child, when his home was no longer a home without his mother there. He shouldn't have stayed away, but he simply hadn't been able to face coming back last night. He shouldn't have brought up the subject of Amelia at the cemetery yesterday either. That had been tactless and unfeeling. He hadn't meant to be that. He simply needed to know what the hell was going on.

Approaching the house to find a car in front of the drive, he parked in the first available space he could find, then braced himself and climbed out. A yard or so off, he heard childish chatter drifting towards him. Poppy's voice, unmistakably – he could pick it out in a crowd – and another little voice. Her new friend? he wondered. Poppy was naturally shy. They'd both been concerned that her self-esteem might suffer because of her illness. From the sound of it, that wasn't the case.

Rounding the tall conifer hedge that separated the drive from the road, he stopped, squinting. The front door was open. He couldn't see from where he was standing, but Kay was in the hall presumably, talking to the woman on the doorstep. Poppy was crouching on the lawn, dancing one of her Barbie dolls towards the little girl in front of her. The drive was long; he was a good few yards away. It was possible his eyes were deceiving him, but … He felt his gut turn over. Not possible. Not unless he was hallucinating in broad daylight. The two girls weren't just similar in colouring. The friend Poppy was playing with could almost *be* her. They were like matching bookends. Feeling as if he'd been hit by an express train, he stepped back before the children saw him.

'Right, come on then, girls, inside. Liv's mummy has to get off.' Kay's voice reached him as he tried to do the simplest thing in the world and just breathe.

'Coming,' both girls said in unison, which winded Matt further.

'I'll be back in an hour, Liv. Be good for Kay,' the woman called.

Matt hurried back to his car and climbed inside. The two mothers had obviously arranged a play date. He tried to think through his confusion. From the outside, all would appear perfectly normal. But then, he supposed, it was for anyone but him. Feeling the foundations of his world swaying violently beneath him, and swallowing back his bewilderment, he waited while the woman climbed into her car, then started his engine. He should have just walked up to the house, fronted it out. Smiled cheerfully, swept his daughter up and said, 'Hey, who's your little twin?'

Jesus Christ, what the *hell* was happening here? How long had Poppy known this child? How long had *Kay* known? Why the *hell* hadn't she told him?

But he knew why. She hadn't told him because she would know what he knew: that the chances of even his brother and him producing two children who were so similar were infinitesimal. It was possible that it could be some fluke of nature, but if so, it would be a miracle. The children must have the same biological father.

Now it was beginning to make sense: Kay's sudden odd behaviour, her evasiveness, avoiding eye contact. He guessed she would have been stunned when she first met this child. She would have suspected that she'd been fathered by the same man as Poppy. She would have tried to prevent Matt seeing her, knowing that one glimpse of the child – a child most definitely not fathered by *him* – would have confirmed his darkest fears. He closed his eyes, recalling Poppy's delight as she told him about her new special friend. *Mrs Weaver thinks we're so close we could be sisters.* He recalled how she'd as good as *told* him, her eyes dancing with excitement. Quelling the nausea now clawing its way up his windpipe, he felt his heart splinter. What had been going through Kay's mind then, he wondered, as she'd stood there saying absolutely *nothing*?

Fuck it! Sucking in a breath, he tried to take some consolation from the fact that she at least cared enough for her daughter not to have tried to break the friendship up. Selfishly, he couldn't.

Driving at a safe distance, he followed the woman. He had no idea why, or what in God's name he would say to her. But if Kay wasn't going to be honest with him …

She didn't live far away. Matt supposed she wouldn't, since the girls were at the same school – which, it occurred to him, was why Kay hadn't been keen for him to do the school run. The *lengths* she'd gone to. Why? Why not just tell him she didn't want to be with him, rather than weave this elaborate web of lies?

Parking a discreet distance away, he waited until the woman had climbed out and gone inside her house, then pushed his door open and followed. He was heading towards her front door when he was thwarted by a woman emerging from the property next door and apparently heading towards the woman's house.

'Excuse me,' he called, thinking fast as he approached her. 'I'm an emergency doctor on call from the City Road Hospital.' He flashed his identity tag. 'Does Sarah Thompson live here?'

'No,' the woman said, looking suitably concerned. 'Nicole Taylor lives here. I've never heard of a Sarah Thompson. Sorry.'

'Not to worry. I think I have Claines Road and Claines Drive mixed up.' Matt smiled and turned back to his car. He had her name and address. It was a start. He had to find out more about her, and he doubted very much Kay would be forthcoming.

CHAPTER FIFTY

Kay

Watching the girls playing happily out in the garden, Kay tried to still her nerves. Nicole had said she'd been delayed in picking up Olivia. After the conversation she and Matt had had at the cemetery yesterday, she didn't imagine him being in any hurry to come home, certainly not at this time, but she decided to ring him anyway. She still wasn't ready for him to see Olivia. She felt as if she were lost in a maze full of doors, and if she went through the wrong one, it would close on her past life for ever. What had Amelia meant: *Look after the daughter you think is his*? Was she Olivia's birth mother? If she wasn't, she could only have known about Olivia if Matt had told her about her. If that were the case, it would be impossible to go back. Because what she'd thought she and Matt had together, the shared trust, had simply never existed.

Would he answer her call? she wondered, her emotions raw as she selected his number. Her heart catapulted into her throat and she whirled around when his phone rang out right behind her. 'You made me jump,' she said shakily. 'I wasn't expecting you.'

'Clearly.' Sweeping his eyes over her, Matt came towards the window she was bobbing hopelessly in front of, trying to prevent the inevitable. Her heart now banging a frantic drumbeat in her chest, she watched him glance out onto the patio. *Say something*, she willed him after an agonisingly long minute. *Anything*.

He didn't. Another hour-long minute ticked by, and Matt didn't utter a word. Instead, his face chalk-white, he simply stared at Olivia, a picture of innocence as she danced her Barbie Ballerina across the garden table – apart from the fact that she was almost a mirror image of their own daughter.

'Matt?' Kay placed a hand on his arm, willing him to talk to her, to acknowledge this child, as she'd had to, as *he* had to, and then snatched it back as he shrugged her off and stepped back from the window.

'Say something, Matt,' she said, her stomach feeling as if she were freefalling over a precipice. He could hardly lie about this, could he, with the evidence before their very eyes? 'Let's not argue,' she pleaded. 'Can we not just talk sensibly?'

Massaging his temples, he stayed where he was, and then finally he brought his gaze to hers, and Kay's blood froze. His eyes were as cold as glaciers. What had she done to deserve *that*, apart from stumble across his illegitimate child and live with that knowledge killing her slowly every day since?

'I need to ask you something.' He finally spoke, his tone flat. He paused, still eyeing her so icily Kay felt the hairs rise over her skin. 'How long have you been seeing him? Jason. How long have you been seeing him?'

She felt the breath leave her body. 'Don't do this, Matt,' she begged him, tears brimming. 'I haven't. You know I—'

'Before he went off to conquer America?' he went on, his tone scornful. 'Were you having sex with him then?'

'No!' Her heart rate ratcheted up.

'Was it a regular thing, Kay? You had free rein, after all, didn't you, with me working all hours – out of necessity, incidentally. I suppose I could have left patients to die while I popped home to check that my wife wasn't so lonely she was fucking someone else, but, you know, it didn't really occur to me. It obviously should have done.'

'Matt, stop.' Kay felt sick to her soul. She'd never seen him like this. He was scaring her.

'Are you having sex with him now?' he asked, his face taut with fury.

'No! Matt, for God's sake. Is that what he told you? He's *lying*. I promise you, I—'

'Did you sleep with him because he could give you what I couldn't? Or was it more than that?'

'Matt …' Kay shook her head, bewildered. 'This is insane. Please don't—'

'I mean, the anticipation of illicit sex with hotshot Jason has to be more of a turn-on than mundane sex with a man who couldn't give you the child you craved, doesn't it?'

'What?' Kay struggled to answer. This was complete madness.

'Who's the woman who dropped her off?' he continued, firing questions at her.

Kay struggled to keep up. 'I … don't know,' she answered, flustered. 'I …'

Matt eyed her with obvious disdain as she trailed hopelessly off. 'You really are weaving an intricate web, Kay. Did you never imagine you might get ensnared in it?'

'She's adopted,' Kay blurted. 'I wasn't sure whether you knew. I didn't know how to tell you.' She studied his face. He looked utterly bewildered. He didn't know about Olivia. He truly didn't.

Matt fell silent, scanning her face in turn.

'The mother abandoned her,' she went on more quietly, hoping to open the door for him to be honest with her.

He shook his head, clearly trying to assimilate this information.

'She left her at the hospital,' she continued, filling him in on what she was sure now he couldn't have known. 'She hasn't been heard of since. They tried to trace her, but …'

'City Road Hospital?' Matt's eyes were filled with confusion.

Kay nodded. 'Apparently, yes.'

'Why didn't you tell me about her?' he asked, his voice tight with emotion.

Kay felt for him, ludicrously. Whatever he'd done, she couldn't imagine he would ever knowingly abandon a child. 'At first, I don't know. I was scared,' she tried to explain. 'I wanted to speak to her mother, obviously. And then I thought she might be a possible donor for Poppy, and—'

'What?' Matt stared at her, astounded. 'Jesus Christ, Kay. Can you hear yourself? You'll stop at nothing to get what you want, will you?'

Seeing the disillusionment in his eyes, Kay's heart turned over. 'It's nothing to do with what *I* want,' she countered, not quite able to believe he wouldn't understand why she would consider the possibility. 'It's to do with what Poppy *needs*. I would have told you. I—'

'When?' Matt asked stonily. 'When would you have told me?'

Despair sweeping through her, Kay dropped her gaze. She didn't answer. She had no idea how to. She'd been quietly holding onto the sliver of hope that their marriage could survive. But now … She should ask him to go. She couldn't do this, couldn't defend herself. She wouldn't argue with him, not with those two innocent children in earshot. 'I'm not doing this, Matt,' she started. 'You need to—'

'I know, Kay.' He stopped her. 'I've always known.'

Her gaze snapped up. 'Known *what*?' Was he talking about Olivia? About Jason and her supposed long-standing affair with him? What was *wrong* with him?

'When were you going to tell me about that, I wonder?' he asked, his eyes burning with anger. 'When were you going to let poor gullible Matt know that the daughter he loves with his whole fucking *heart* isn't his daughter?'

CHAPTER FIFTY-ONE

Matthew

Matt arrived unannounced at Biochem. He wanted the element of surprise; not to kill his brother and end the misery he seemed to be determined to make his life, but to talk to him. Kay had denied everything, seeming broken-hearted that he would imagine she would do such a thing to him. She'd demanded to know where his proof for such a devastating accusation was. Matt had none. He'd never done a DNA test. He'd never wanted to. She clearly didn't realise how desperate he was to believe that Poppy was his. She clearly didn't realise, either, how broken he'd been inside for years. She would have her proof soon enough. He wasn't sure how she'd planned to deny it once the tissue tests were back.

Going into reception, he noted that Laura was still there. He'd been hoping she might already have left for the day. He'd spoken to her on the phone since his last unfortunate visit and apologised for his abysmal behaviour. He knew he'd shaken her badly, but she didn't look too perturbed to see him, smiling when he walked in. 'Working late?' he asked her.

'No choice,' she answered with a disgruntled roll of her eyes. 'He's cancelled the work on the side of the building, leaving yours truly to try to find a new contractor.'

He being Jason, Matt gleaned. He'd expected as much. 'Isn't it urgent?' he asked, aware of the highly combustible nature of the material that needed replacing.

'It is if we want to pass the fire risk assessment. David was worried about it, you know, from a health and safety aspect, but Jason says it's only a matter of ticking boxes to ensure that fire compliance is met. He said it wasn't a priority, and took it upon himself to cancel the contractor we finally decided on because the quote was too steep. I've been contacting a few other companies, but since we had three quotes in the first place, I can't see how anyone is going to do it any cheaper.'

Jason really was cutting corners, wasn't he? Why? As far as Matt knew, there was no cash-flow problem. 'Is he in?' he asked, though he knew he was. He'd seen his status symbol parked outside.

'Upstairs.' She made eyes at the ceiling. 'Making sure the accounts are up to date in David's absence.'

'Ah.' Matt nodded. As in making sure the accounts added up? he wondered.

'Have you come to finish the job?' she asked him.

Unsure what she meant, Matt eyed her quizzically. He got the drift when she made pistol shots with her fingers and then blew the smoke from them. 'No,' he assured her, his mouth twitching into a smile. 'Just to chat.'

'Pity.' She sighed, turning back to her PC. 'I won't bother to tell him you're here. Presumably you're going to go up anyway.'

'Cheers, Laura.' Matt headed for the stairs, glad that she hadn't got him down as the aggressive Neanderthal he seemed to turn into whenever he was near Jason.

There were still a couple of people working in the outer office, he noticed, sweating over phones and PCs. No doubt they were attempting to avoid Jason's wrath as well as hold onto their jobs. Talking into his desk phone, Jason glanced up as Matt approached his office. His look was one of weary resignation.

'I have to go. Talk later,' he said, ending his call and pulling himself to his feet. He'd probably decided he'd be better standing than sitting after their last meeting.

'Anyone I know?' Matt nodded towards the phone.

Jason scowled by way of an answer. 'Do you want something?' he asked. 'Apart from to attack me when you get the random urge, I mean? Because if that's what you've come to do, you should know it might not be a good idea.'

'No,' Matt ruminated, his fingers going to the wound on his head. 'I guess you could say we're even on that score.' He looked back at his brother with a short smile.

Jason shrugged grudgingly. 'Maybe.'

'I hear you sacked the cladding contractor,' Matt said casually.

'You can't sack someone who hasn't started the job,' Jason pointed out. 'The quote was too high. I'm trying to save the company some money, something you wouldn't understand.'

'Right.' Matt noted the condescending tone and counselled himself not to react.

'So you're here because …?' Jason arched an eyebrow half interestedly.

Matt waited, wondering whether he might think to ask after their father. He didn't. Why didn't that surprise him? 'Just to grab some stuff for Dad. Notes from the last board meeting,' he lied. He'd come for the sole purpose of talking to Jason. 'Laura's going to sort it out for me.'

'Right.' Jason checked his watch. A busy man, clearly.

'Have you been in touch with Kay lately?' Matt asked.

An irritated frown crossed Jason's face. 'So we're back to that again, are we? You know, I think you must be stuck in a time warp, little brother. How many times do I have to tell you: what I said God knows how long ago now was a *joke*. And while we're on the subject of who's seeing who, what about you? Had any more intimate liaisons with that pretty little nurse lately?' he asked with a supercilious smile.

Matt swallowed back his contempt. 'Do you know about Olivia?' He cut to the chase.

Jason looked at him askance. 'Who?'

Matt studied him narrowly. He seemed genuinely clueless. Or was this bullshit? Jason had mastered the art of looking innocent since before he could walk. 'Olivia,' he repeated. Pulling his phone from his pocket, he selected the photo he'd taken of the girls in the garden.

His face mildly curious, Jason glanced at it, and then did a double-take. 'Bloody hell.' He blew out a low whistle. 'That's a bit close to home, isn't it?'

Matt ignored him. 'Is she yours?'

'Mine?' Jason emitted a stunned laugh, then looked at him, deadly serious. 'No,' he assured him categorically. 'No way.'

Matt pulled in a tight breath. 'I need to know, Jason,' he said, making sure to hold his brother's gaze. 'Is Poppy mine?'

Jason took a second, causing Matt's heart to stall in his chest. 'You are kidding, right?' He stared at him, astounded. 'Is that what all this shit is about? Why you've been holding a grudge for God knows how long? You should talk to Kay, Matthew, because you are seriously barking up the wrong tree.'

'What happened to the girl you were going out with back then?' Matt asked.

'When?' Jason turned his attention to his PC, logging off and hurriedly grabbing his jacket from the back of his chair.

'You know damn well when.' Matt waited.

'Oh come on,' Jason said irritably. 'We're talking five, six years ago. I went out with several women then. You don't seriously think I kept tabs on them?'

'So you're saying none of them might have been pregnant?'

'To my knowledge, no.' Tugging his jacket on, Jason held Matt's gaze for a second and then glanced away. 'Are we done here? Because as pleasant as it is chatting to you, Matthew, I have a pressing appointment.'

Collecting up his car keys, he walked past him, pausing at the door. 'Maybe you should concentrate on your own past encounters, little brother,' he suggested, regarding Matt coolly. 'Seems to me there might be a few seeds you might not have realised you'd sown.'

Don't. A potent mixture of anger and hurt churning inside him, Matt willed himself not to follow as his brother sailed on out. Jason would only play the victim, attacked by his aggressive brother again, then move in on Kay now that he knew their marriage was in trouble.

Wiping a hand over his face, he breathed in, attempting to compose himself, and went across to the window. Trying to think what to do next, he watched his brother walk out of the building, heading towards his car – the expensive company car that seemed an odd choice given the cost-cutting mission Jason appeared to be on. A tax write-off? he wondered.

He should leave. Laura was probably wondering where he was. Tiredly he walked back across the office, and then stopped. His brother's PC was still showing the log-off screen. Glancing towards the door, Matt hesitated, and then seated himself in front of it. He wasn't sure what he expected to find accessing the company accounts, but what his father had said about Jason's extravagant spending didn't tally with the cost-cutting he knew was going on. Something just didn't add up. Was Jason dipping his fingers in the till? If so, why? Where was the money going?

Guilt wedged like a brick in his throat, he flicked through the spreadsheets, unsure what he was actually looking for. Realising he was possibly sinking as low as his brother, he was about to give up when a single payment jumped out at him. His heart stopped beating as he read the name of the recipient of the sum of ten thousand pounds. Scrolling through the spreadsheet, he found another payment, and then another, both double that amount. A total of fifty thousand pounds had been paid out, each payment signed off by Jason and all made recently. It was irrefutable proof. Jason knew all too well of Olivia's existence.

His brother was hiding something, trying to keep something from coming out. What was it that was worth risking his reputation for, his future with the company? Clearly it wasn't something Jason had felt able to approach their father with.

A new worry niggled away at Matt as he closed the PC down and headed out of the office. Where was Olivia's mother? Had she truly walked away, deciding she would have no contact with her child? There was only person who might be able to answer that question. He needed to talk to Nicole Taylor.

CHAPTER FIFTY-TWO

Deep in thought, Matt headed towards the renal department the next morning to check on his and Kay's appointments. Why had Kay continued her relationship with Jason, which their contact with each other seemed to indicate she'd done? He couldn't get his head around any of it. Had his brother been trying to manipulate her? He couldn't believe that Kay would allow herself to be coerced, unless Jason had some kind of hold over her. He smiled ironically. Of course he had: Poppy, the child he'd fathered with Kay, whilst also fathering a child with another woman with no care in the world for the consequences. Might it have been Kay doing the initial manipulating? he wondered. She'd been desperate for a child. Jason would have leapt at the chance to fulfil the role Matt couldn't. Losing out over him where Kay's affections were concerned must have been a bitter pill for him to swallow.

And then into the mix came Rachel, and suddenly she was embroiled in their lives. How much of a coincidence was it, her working at the same hospital as him and also attending the university Kay lectured at? If Kay was to be believed, she was in danger of losing her job because of a complaint Rachel had made about her making her life difficult, something Kay had vehemently denied, and which in truth Matt could never imagine her doing. How had he become so involved with Rachel? It seemed ludicrous, but he couldn't help feeling that somehow she was playing them off against each other. On the other hand, given his lack of sleep, Poppy's deteriorating condition and his world disintegrating around him, it was possible he was edging towards paranoia. He needed to get some rest.

About to go through the doors into the department, he stopped as someone called to him along the corridor. He glanced back and saw Jess, the police officer, hurrying towards him.

'I thought you'd never hear me,' she said breathlessly. 'You were miles away. Nothing too worrying, I hope?'

Matt shook his head. 'No, not really. Problem?' he asked.

'Since when are drunks not?' She rolled her eyes in despair, and he smiled his commiserations. 'I was just going to grab a coffee.' She nodded in the direction of the café. 'I wondered whether you wanted to take five and join me?'

'Better not. I have something I need to check on,' Matt declined apologetically. 'Maybe next time you're around.'

'Which will no doubt be too soon.' Jess heaved out a sigh. 'Catch you later.'

'Look forward to it. Oh, Jess …' Matt stopped her as she turned to head off. 'Sorry to eat into your coffee break, but I wonder if you could do me a huge favour?'

She narrowed her eyes warily. 'Depends.'

'Are you able to check the file regarding a baby abandoned here at the hospital?'

'Damn, and there was me hoping you wanted my body.' She sighed wistfully.

'Er, no.' Matt smiled. 'I would, obviously, but to be honest, I'm knackered,' he joked, knowing she was ribbing him. It was true, anyway: he'd slept badly in the spare room and then had to organise arrangements for his father's discharge.

'You look it.' She eyed him curiously. 'Things are a bit rough, I take it.'

He dragged a hand over his neck. 'A bit,' he admitted. 'It's my daughter. Her prognosis is worse than we'd hoped.'

Jess looked him over sympathetically. 'Sorry, Matt. If there's anything I can do …'

He nodded his thanks. There was nothing she could do. He could hardly ask random people if they would consider getting tested and, if found compatible, part with a kidney, but Christ, sometimes he felt like it. He hadn't asked Jason yet. For obvious reasons, he was finding that difficult. There was no question he was going to have to. His damaged pride mattered little measured against Poppy's health. What Jason's reaction would be … He was going to have to cross that bridge when he got to it, and pray to God he could hold on to his temper if Jason refused.

'So, what do you need?' Jess asked, bringing his attention back to her.

'I need to know whether you ever managed to trace the mother of a certain child.'

'No problem,' she assured him. 'I'll get on it asap.'

'Great. Thanks, Jess.' Matt gave her the details, having already found the record relating to the abandoned baby. At the time, he'd been on leave after Poppy had been discharged from hospital. He recalled that the baby had been just weeks old. According to the colleague who'd called him for advice, she'd appeared to be well cared for, warmly wrapped. On examination, she'd been found to have bronchitis caused by a bacterial infection. He remembered wondering why it hadn't been picked up earlier. Talking to a security guard who still worked here, he'd discovered there'd been no usable hospital CCTV footage of the baby being abandoned. It had to be Olivia, though.

'I'll call you,' Jess promised, checking her radio and heading off with a wave.

'Cheers,' Matt called after her and pushed on through into the renal department.

The guy on reception was on the phone but nodded a greeting as he came in. 'I've got something for you,' he said, one hand over the mouthpiece, and handed him a Post-it note.

Matt read it, and his chest constricted. The tissue typing was set for tomorrow. They would probably take a sample for testing for the faulty gene too. He needed to let Kay know. He should do it in person. Would she tell him then? She would have to. She would have no choice, but could he bear to hear it?

CHAPTER FIFTY-THREE

Kay

Having asked Stephanie if she would mind watching the girls while she stocked up on healthy snacks for Poppy, Kay pushed her way through the front door and made her way straight to the kitchen. Dumping her shopping bags on the table, she went to put the kettle on, trying hard to appear as if everything were perfectly normal for her daughter's sake. But things weren't normal. They never would be again. Poppy would soon pick up on it. She would realise her daddy was rarely coming home, that he was angry whenever he did. Her world would start crumbling. Kay couldn't let that happen. She had to speak to Matt, beg him to stop seeing that *creature*, to not do this to Poppy, not now.

With anger burning white-hot inside her, she'd come so close to hitting Amelia when she'd confronted her at the university. The thought terrified her. She was losing her grip. Why had Matt done it? Why had he chosen *her*, a woman Kay actually knew? Her chest heaved, her stomach along with it, as her mind played over images of them together, making love, making a child. She saw them walking together, cooing and fussing over the gurgling baby they pushed in the pram before them, Poppy and Olivia skipping along hand in hand behind them.

She'd had the dream again, and awoken, weeping, with the feeling of hands gliding roughly over her body, a mouth pressed hard to hers, a tongue probing and poking aggressively. In the dream, Matt had left her and his brother had climbed into her bed.

Why was Matt doing this? Why had he deserted her? She needed him. Her hands trembling, her mind heavy with fatigue, she pulled her phone shakily from her bag. She had to ask him to meet her, beg him to tell her honestly where they went from here.

You have it all wrong, Matthew. I love you, Poppy loves you. If you love her as much as you swear you do, please come home. She needs you. I need you.

Aware that it might make her look as if she didn't care what he'd done, as if she would have him back at any cost, she hesitated, read the text again, then hit send as Stephanie came through to the kitchen.

'God, Kay.' She studied her worriedly. 'You look terrible, as if you haven't slept for a week. Sit,' she instructed her. 'I'll get you a coffee. Unless you fancy something stronger?'

Kay declined. 'Thanks, Steph, but alcohol would probably finish me off altogether. How is she?'

'She's fine, although she did feel a bit hot earlier,' Stephanie answered, her brow knitted. 'Nothing to panic about,' she added quickly. 'I would have rung you if I'd thought it was. They're playing upstairs. Olivia has to be home by …'

She trailed off as Kay flew to the hall. Poppy had a *temperature*. She shouldn't have left her. She would never forgive herself if something were to happen. Her heart banging, she raced up the stairs, careless of Steph calling after her that Poppy really was fine. She wasn't fine. Nothing was *fine*. Her heart wrenched painfully as she considered what Poppy's future might hold: the tests, the dialysis, the hospital stays, surgery. All this without a stable family around her. Apart from for her to be well, that had been all Kay had ever wanted for her little girl. Feeling the absence of her own mother so profoundly sometimes she couldn't breathe, the loss of her tiny baby boy so much her heart physically ached, that had been her dream. She'd imagined her and Matt growing old together, always being there for each other, for Poppy. He'd ruined it, broken everything.

Bursting through Poppy's bedroom door, her heart stopped dead in her chest as the girls slithered off the bed to greet her, both looking up at her with painted faces.

'Do you like our make-up, Mummy?' Poppy asked excitedly. 'We're ballerinas like Barbie, aren't we, Liv?'

'Uh huh.' Olivia giggled and performed a little pirouette.

Kay simply stared at the girls, stunned. Pulling her daughter to her, she studied her face, confounded. It was Amelia she saw looking back, her pupils so large as to make her eyes almost black, her eyelids meticulously made up. *Mushroom-coloured eyeliner.* A pulse thrummed prophetically at the base of her neck. How had Poppy got hold of it? Her mind shot to the silver four-leaf clover she had been given in the school playground. Amelia had access to her child? *Oh dear God!*

CHAPTER FIFTY-FOUR

Matthew

Matt read the text Kay had sent and felt his heart crack. She wouldn't tell him she loved him if she didn't. He knew that. But how could she have done what she had if she did? She must have lived in constant dread that one day he might find out. It didn't add up. Nothing added up. He thought of Poppy. He loved her so much it hurt. Every night he would creep into her room, whispering how much he loved her as she was sleeping. Every morning he told her he loved her. He hadn't this morning. He'd left before Kay had come down. Had Poppy noticed? Was his baby hurting? He had to go back, tell Kay about the tests and then … pray, he guessed. Without honesty, their relationship couldn't survive, assuming she wanted it to. And him? Did he want it to? It was all he'd ever wanted. His work was important, but his family mattered more to him than his life. He wouldn't know how to be without them.

He was climbing into his car when he received the second text. *You need to come back now!* Kay had sent. *Her temperature is off the scale.*

Putting a call through on his hands-free, Matt swallowed back his panic and skidded out of the hospital car park. 'Is she in bed?' he asked as soon as Kay answered.

'Yes. I'm not sure what to do, Matt,' she said, her voice small and shocked. 'Please come back.'

'I'm on my way,' Matt assured her. 'Make sure she has a light cover or sheet over her, nothing too heavy.'

'Should I sponge her down?' Kay asked. She was working to keep her voice calm. Matt could hear her in the bathroom, running water.

'No, don't do that,' he said quickly. 'There's a danger of making her too cold. Give her a cool drink, small sips only. I'll be there soon.'

He swallowed hard. He should never have left this morning without checking on her, telling her he loved her. What the *hell* was the matter with him?

Ending the call, he drove like a man possessed. Finally, after what seemed like an eternity, he parked his car askew on the drive and raced to the front door. 'Where is she?' he asked Stephanie, almost colliding with her and the little girl, Olivia, as he burst into the hall.

'Upstairs.' Stephanie gestured that way. 'Kay's with her.'

'Poppy's hot.' Olivia stopped him as he took a step towards them. Her huge blue eyes were so like Poppy's as she looked up at him, he felt another piece of his heart fracture. 'Are you going to make her better?'

'We are, sweetheart.' He felt his voice crack.

Stephanie caught hold of his arm as he swung towards the stairs. 'Matt, I'm not sure what's happened between you two, but you should know that whatever it is, it's breaking Kay's heart. She *loves* you. Poppy needs you. They both do. Sort it out, Matthew. You need to be together now more than ever.'

Matt didn't answer. He knew they needed him. He also knew he needed them. Nodding, he sucked in a breath and continued on up.

Pausing at the main bedroom door, where he could hear Kay reassuring Poppy inside, he drew in another tight breath, attempting to compose himself. To be the man Poppy knew him to be, competent and in control. He wasn't in control; he'd never been so frightened in his life. Competent? He wasn't that, either. He should never have let things reach the point where he and Kay were incapable of communicating.

'Hey, gorgeous girl,' he said, forcing a smile as he pushed on in. 'How are we doing? Is Mummy being a good nurse?' His eyes flicked to Kay's as she rose from the bed. He could feel her fear. His heart cracked another inch as he realised they were finally united in something.

'Uh huh.' Poppy nodded. 'She's taken my temperature and she's making sure I don't drink too fast, and she's telling me a *story*.' She added the last as if that were the most important item on the list. 'She said she was going to call a doctor, but I reminded her you are one, didn't I, Mummy?'

'You did, sweetheart.' Matt saw Kay's visible intake of breath as she leaned to press a soft kiss to Poppy's cheek. She would have needed reminding, he thought agitatedly, his anger all with himself. He might be a doctor, but he wasn't able to help his daughter. Poppy thought he was going to make her better. She had faith in him, her father. Some shit father he'd turned out to be. Not being a suitable blood match, he couldn't even put himself forward as a direct donor.

Walking across to the bed, he pushed his self-pity aside to concentrate on her. 'Did I ever mention I love you?' he asked her as he lowered himself gently to sit next to her.

Settling back on her pillow, Poppy smiled. 'Bigger than the universe.'

'And all the stars,' Matt added, going through the ritual he couldn't believe he'd forgotten this morning. 'Tired, sweetheart?' he asked her, smoothing her curls from her forehead.

'A little bit,' she replied with another small nod, and closed her eyes. Matt noted that the flesh around them was definitely swollen.

Kay came across to him as he grazed his thumb softly over Poppy's cheek. 'I thought it might be the make-up,' she said, clearly having also noticed the swelling.

Matt glanced curiously at her.

'They were playing Barbie Ballerina. They made each other's faces up. I'm not sure where they got …' Pressing the back of her hand under her nose, Kay trailed off.

Guessing she was trying to contain her emotions in front of Poppy, Matt nodded and turned his attention back to the little girl. 'Do you mind if Daddy takes a quick look at your ankles, sweetheart?' he asked her softly. Kay would have checked, but still he wanted to make sure.

'I'm cold,' Poppy answered, a frown crossing her little face.

'I'll take a peek under the bottom of the sheet. I won't let much cold air in,' Matt promised, working to keep his own emotion in check.

Finding swelling, as he'd guessed he would, he kissed her toes and tucked the sheet back over them. 'I just need Mummy to show me where something is in the bathroom, honey. Will you be okay for a second?' he asked her.

She responded with a weaker nod this time, a slight movement of her arm as she pressed her dog-eared Luna Lamb comfort toy closer. A knot like sharp gravel in his throat, Matt indicated the door and led the way out.

Once they were on the landing, Kay closed the door quietly behind them. Her face was ashen, he noted as she looked at him, her pupils dilated with fear. She was petrified. Whatever she'd done, he had to be here for her. He simply didn't know how not to be. 'Her urine output is decreased, I take it?' he asked her.

She closed her eyes and nodded tightly.

'Has she been nauseous?' he checked.

Again Kay nodded, and swallowed. 'Breathless, too. She tried to do a pirouette, but …' She stopped, swiping at a tear that squeezed from her eye.

He needed to take her blood pressure, check her heartbeat for irregularities. He tried to think through the panic rising fast inside him. They could do that at the hospital. 'We need to get her in,' he said, grappling his phone from his pocket.

'Straight away?' Kay searched his eyes, bewilderment in her own.

'An ambulance might be best. They can monitor her on the way.' Matt thought out loud and jabbed 999 into the phone. He would need to ring the hospital direct, alert her consultant.

'Oh God, no,' Kay murmured.

Matt looked back at her to see tears now streaming down her cheeks, and his heart hitched painfully. She looked drained, dark shadows under her eyes, her wild blonde hair in disarray. She was beautiful. He loved her. God help him, how was he supposed to just *stop*? He hesitated, and then, whether or not it was him she wanted, reached out and pulled her to him. 'She'll be okay,' he whispered.

CHAPTER FIFTY-FIVE

Kay

'She's being really brave, aren't you, Poppy?' The nurse who was preparing Poppy's small arm for an injection of local anaesthetic looked across to Kay with a reassuring smile.

'That's because I'm getting used to needles now,' Poppy said maturely, glancing nervously down at the syringe nevertheless, and then away as the needle went in.

Kay didn't miss the wince flitting across her little face, and her heart wrenched for her baby girl. Because it was an emergency, they were going to have to insert a neck line, Matt had said. It was just a small tube fed into a vein in her neck in order to start the haemodialysis, which would filter the waste products from her blood. They would create a more permanent method, something called a fistula, in her arm at some point, connecting an artery to a vein. He'd outlined the procedure carefully, trying to reassure her. She wasn't reassured, though. She was terrified, her own blood turning to ice as she imagined all her baby had to go through. *Please God, don't let her be in pain*, she prayed silently. Poppy didn't deserve any of this. She was *five* years old. Just an innocent child. It was beyond cruel.

'There. All done.' The nurse gave Poppy a bright smile. Poppy managed a smile in return, while Kay bit back her tears. She had to be strong. She had to stay positive, for Poppy. *How?* How did the parents she'd seen on her many visits here, parents with children suffering so much, not just break down and sob?

'It will be about half an hour before it takes effect,' the nurse advised. 'The renal consultant will be around shortly to have another quick word with you.'

Kay nodded and managed a tremulous smile. 'Thanks,' she said, grateful for the intrinsic kindness that all the staff on the ward seemed imbued with. She wouldn't be able to do this job. How on earth did Matt do his with all that was going on? Because he had to. Because people depended on him to put his personal problems aside. That was what he'd always done, and she loved him for it. She couldn't believe he didn't seem to know how much.

'Mummy …' Poppy snapped her attention back.

'What is it, sweetheart?' Determined not to shed a tear, which would only destabilise her, Kay gently squeezed the hand she hadn't yet let go of.

'Could I have Luna Lamb?' Poppy asked, her voice small and uncertain for the first time since she'd been rushed in. 'I think he'll be lonely all on his own.'

Her snuggle toy. Of course she would want him. She never went to bed without him, despite her insistence that now she was big enough for school, she was only keeping him company. She was clearly in need of the comfort the bedraggled lamb would offer her while she was here. Kay prayed again, begging God to let her daughter get well and come home. She knew she wouldn't get well, that the miracle couldn't happen, but she prayed anyway. It was all she had.

'Absolutely. We can't have him feeling lonely, can we?' She looked suitably concerned. 'He's in her bag in the car,' she said, casting a glance at the nurse.

'Ooh, gosh, you'd better go and fetch him then, before he gets cold.' The woman widened her eyes in pretend alarm. 'Poppy can keep me company for a while, can't you, lovely?'

'Thanks.' Relieved, Kay got to her feet. 'I won't be long, I promise,' she said to Poppy, smoothing her hair back to kiss her forehead, and then hurrying to the door.

She was a short way down the corridor when she saw Matt coming towards her, carrying Poppy's bag. She wasn't surprised that he'd already thought of it. That was the type of man he was, thoughtful and caring. She'd never known him to be anything but. Could he find that caring within him now? she wondered. For Poppy's sake, could he put everything that was going on behind him and stand beside her, as she so badly needed him to?

'I thought she might want Luna.' He offered her a small smile.

'She does. I was just coming to fetch him.' Kay smiled back, wanting to lean into him, bury her face in his shoulder and cry all her tears out. He'd wrapped her in his embrace back at the house, when they'd realised the time they'd been dreading had arrived. He'd held her so close for one precious moment, she was sure she could feel the frightened thud of his heartbeat. Had it just been an instinctive reaction? Would he hold her now, as he had then, if she reached out? She couldn't bear it if she sensed reluctance, distance between them, not now. She didn't feel strong enough.

'I've had a word with the renal department,' he said. 'They said they can squeeze us in. They're going to rush the results through.' Handing the bag to her, he scanned her eyes, his own guarded.

Her stomach tightening, Kay answered with a small nod. She knew what he was thinking. She also knew what those results would prove. Would that bring some kind of resolution? Could they begin to heal? She still didn't know what his feelings were, whether he'd simply stopped loving her, whether it was Amelia he loved. 'Could I ask you to do something?' she said, struggling to hold his gaze.

Matt nodded, his expression cautious.

She summoned her courage. 'Could you stop seeing her? At least for a while? We need to focus on Poppy right now, and I'm not sure how I'll cope if I'm constantly wondering ...' She trailed off, a lump of emotion rising so fast in her throat she feared she might choke on it.

'Stop seeing ...?' Matt furrowed his brow. 'Kay, for Christ's ... You don't seriously believe *I'm* having an affair?'

Kay's heart dropped. 'Don't, Matt,' she whispered, inhaling hard to hold the tears back. She didn't want to discuss this now. Desperately didn't want to argue with him, not here in the hospital corridor. She had no fight left in her. Surely, he could see that? She just wanted to get back to her daughter.

'Don't *what*?' Matt looked at her incredulously. 'Am I supposed to not deny it? Stand here and say *nothing*?'

Kay avoided answering. 'I was hoping we could put everything aside and be there for Poppy,' she said, as calmly as she could. 'That you would do that for her, if not for—'

'Kay?' Matt took a step forward, took hold of her arm and led her to the side of the corridor. 'I have absolutely no idea what you're thinking, but I can assure you I am most definitely *not* involved with—'

'Matt, please!' Kay cut across him, a surge of anger running through her. She really did not want to do this, but she couldn't bear that he was standing there brazenly denying it. Wasn't it bad enough that he'd chosen to do this with *her*, the woman who'd now undoubtedly lost Kay her job and driven her half out of her mind with her innuendo and lies? It was incomprehensible. Could he honestly not see that the last thing she needed now was him adding insult to injury by lying to her? 'She told you I was making her life difficult at the university. She knew I was your wife. I saw a text from her on your *phone*.'

'Text? What *text*?' Matt looked at her askance. 'I've never—'

'"*Thanks for last night. Looking forward to seeing you again soon*".' Kay reminded him of the text she was never likely to forget. 'It was signed off with an "A", *and* two kisses, which I think indicates it was personal. Please don't deny it.' She stopped, her chest heaving, her self-control teetering on the brink as her anger rose, fuelled by her panic about Poppy.

Matt shook his head, looking confounded for a second, and then he squeezed his eyes closed. 'It was from Anna, my cousin. She had a baby recently. I met up with her—'

'And you didn't mention it?' Kay widened her eyes in disbelief.

'Because I didn't want to bring the subject of the bloody wedding up,' Matt pointed out irritably. 'Look, Kay, none of this is how it seems. I…' Sighing expansively, he trailed off.

'No.' Kay smiled sadly. 'Of course it's not.' His explanation was feasible. But the fact that Anna was having a child, would he really not have mentioned that?

She glanced down. She couldn't deal with this now. She had to focus on Poppy. 'There's something you should know.' She looked back at him. Whether she believed him or not, she needed to share with Matt her instinct that Amelia was dangerous – deranged, possibly with some sort of personality disorder. She needed him to understand the kind of person he'd got himself involved with. 'The make-up Poppy was wearing. It was Urban Decay, mushroom-coloured, an unusual colour. Someone gave it to her. A woman in the school playground.' She pulled out the eyeliner she'd taken from Poppy and held it in the flat of her hand. 'A pretty lady, apparently, with messy black hair.'

Matt looked down at it, his expression now one of confusion. She could see he'd made the link, though. She hoped so. 'At the school?' he asked shakily.

'Yes, so Poppy and Olivia said.'

He snapped his gaze back to hers. 'When?'

'I don't know. All I know is that my little girl was wearing it, and she certainly didn't go shopping for it. She was also given a silver four-leaf clover, I suspect by the same mysterious woman.'

Matt's expression was now troubled, extremely.

'I need to go back. Poppy will be getting anxious.' Kay turned away.

'Kay …' Matt called after her. 'I'm not seeing her. I swear I'm not. I'm guessing you don't believe me, but I'm not. I'm trying to put as much distance as I can between us after what you told me happened at the university. I didn't believe her. It seemed odd, too much of a coincidence.'

As in, not seeing her now? Kay didn't know. She just hoped that he realised he was being manipulated. That much was as plain to Kay as the nose on her face. If he'd ever imagined any kind of happy-ever-after with *Rachel*, he'd been sadly misguided. The woman had had an agenda from the outset. This latest twist, though, approaching Poppy – with what aim, Kay didn't know, other than to win her over – that was a miscalculation on her part. She should know that Kay would claw her deceitful grey eyes from their sockets before she would let any harm come to her daughter.

CHAPTER FIFTY-SIX

Matthew

There had been no way to talk further to Kay at the hospital. Once he'd collected himself and gone in after her to spend as much time with Poppy as he could, they'd exchanged glances, both of them silently agreeing to put everything aside to concentrate their emotions on their daughter. They'd always been able to communicate their feelings with a single look or a gesture. They would signal to each other to leave a mind-numbingly boring social event. When they were both of a mind to make love, there were never any words necessary. One sizzling look between them was enough. When they were amused or alarmed by some remark Poppy came out with, they would swap eye contact, checking that they were both on the same wavelength as to how to respond appropriately. They'd done that not so long ago, though they'd both been floored at how to respond that time. She'd been in her room, talking to her Worry Monster soft toy. 'We can make a wish,' she'd said, looking at it earnestly, 'but it's not magic. Doctors have to make it happen.'

Guessing what it was she'd wished for, Matt had felt his heart break inside him that day. He'd felt it break another inch every day since. He couldn't work magic. Couldn't make his little girl's wishes come true. All he could do was look at every possibility in the hope of locating a suitable donor for Poppy – which was what Kay had been doing, he realised, and regretted bitterly what he'd said to her. He'd accused her of being selfish. She hadn't been. She'd been secretive because she hadn't known which way to turn, believing the child who might be a good match was *his* child, a child he either didn't know existed or else had abandoned. Christ, she must have been devastated imagining that.

He didn't know whether Kay had told Olivia's mother how serious Poppy's condition was, whether she'd broached the idea of Olivia being tested – there hadn't been a chance to ask before he'd left the hospital. Either way, he knew he had to come here, talk to the woman and hope that she might think about what Poppy's future might be without the help she needed. That she might at least consider getting her child tested. There was something else he needed to approach her about, and he would, but somehow he didn't think the questions he had would help sway her regarding the tests if he asked them now.

Making a mental note to find out from Kay whether that was why she was in contact with Jason – a hope he was now holding on to, whatever had happened between them in the past – he slowed his car as he approached the school, looking for a suitable parking space. Finding one diagonally opposite that gave him a view of the gates, he placed a call to the police station in hope of getting hold of Jess. He'd tried her a couple of times, only to find she was out on patrol. Thankfully, though, she was there this time. 'Hi, Matt,' she said, coming to the phone. 'I tried to get hold of you at the hospital earlier, but I'm guessing you were tied up with a patient.'

'I was – my daughter,' he confirmed, his gut wrenching, as it did every time he thought about his baby girl looking so small and vulnerable as she lay in a hospital bed intended for an adult, waiting for her daddy to make her wish come true. Never in her wildest dreams would she imagine him letting her down. That was what fractured his heart into a million pieces.

'Oh no.' Jess sounded gutted for him. 'I'm sorry, Matt.'

'She's doing okay,' Matt said, praying silently. 'She should be able to go home once she's had her procedure.' He didn't go into detail. The renal unit were looking at organising home dialysis for her. That wasn't going to be easy to manage. The load would inevitably fall on Kay's shoulders. Whatever happened between them, he had to be there more for her, for Poppy. He hoped to God that they could somehow find a way to get through all of this.

'Fingers crossed,' Jess said. 'She's bound to feel better once she's in familiar surroundings.'

Matt hoped so. He and Kay would need to work at containing their emotion, however fraught things might now be. Poppy would need that security, to feel that her home was a safe place to be. Everything else had to take second place. At least for the immediate future.

'I have that information you needed,' Jess offered.

'Great.' Matt tried to focus his attention on the purpose of his call. 'Cheers, Jess.'

'The mother never came forward,' she went on. 'And from what I can see on the file, she was never traced.'

Matt had guessed as much. 'Were enquiries made regarding women who'd recently given birth?' he asked.

'They were, but they didn't offer up much. All babies accounted for. There was just one where they never had eyes on the child. Hold on a sec. I'll pull up the notes.'

Matt waited, keeping a watch on the school gates as he did. 'Here we go.' Jess came back on. 'The mother was out, it says here, but the uniformed officers who called spoke to her sister. She said she would ask her to contact them once she got home.'

'Was it ever followed up?' Matt asked.

'Possibly not,' she answered with a sigh. 'The officer in charge has moved on, and I can't see anything on file.'

'Right.' Matt had pretty much expected that. He took a breath. 'It's a big ask,' he said, 'but you couldn't let me have the mother's name, could you?'

Jess hesitated, obviously concerned about confidentiality. 'Are you thinking you might know her?' she asked cautiously.

'Possibly.' Matt kept his response vague. 'It might be nothing, but …'

'This didn't come from me,' Jess said at length. 'It's Kelsey. Kelsey Jones. A young mum, apparently. Seventeen when she gave birth, which means she must have been sixteen when she conceived. You do wonder, don't you, why kids …'

Matt had stopped listening. His heart had stopped beating, his head reeling as soon as he heard the surname; also Rachel's surname. *Slow down*, he cautioned himself, trying to think rationally. It was a common name. It might have nothing to do with Rachel. Right. Just a coincidence. Like all the other coincidences. No fucking way. Olivia had to be Jason's child, meaning he'd gone out with Rachel's sister – a sixteen-year-old girl, for Christ's sake – got her pregnant and then claimed to know nothing about it. Was it Jason who was at the root of whatever Rachel was up to? She had appeared not to know him when she'd met him at the hospital, but was that all part of some manipulative game Jason was playing? Had Rachel gone out with him too? Had he used her, coerced her to come between Kay and Matt, smoothing the way to move in himself when their marriage fell apart?

There was the possibility he hadn't known about the pregnancy, of course, treating his encounter with this Kelsey as just another notch on his bedpost. If that were the case, he wouldn't have known anything about her family – including Rachel, assuming she was her sister. That would be feasible, apart from one small detail – the fact that Matt had found evidence indicating that Jason was very much aware of the existence of the child he'd walked away from.

Matt wasn't sure what the hell was going on with his delightful brother, but he would find out if he had to shake the information out of him.

CHAPTER FIFTY-SEVEN

Seeing Olivia come out of the school gates with Nicole, Matt calmed himself and climbed quickly out of his car, only to end up dodging an oncoming vehicle as he raced across the road.

'You look like a man in a hurry.' Gathering Olivia close to her side, the woman eyed him with a mixture of curiosity and apprehension as he approached them.

'I am. Sorry, I didn't mean to startle you. I'm Dr Young—'

'Poppy's daddy.' Olivia finished the introduction before he could.

'That's right.' Matt smiled down at her. 'We've met before, haven't we, Olivia? Matthew,' he said, extending a hand as he looked back at her mother.

The woman didn't take it, instead easing Olivia closer, her expression wary. 'Nicole Taylor,' she said. 'Whilst it's interesting to meet you, Dr Young, as I told your wife, Olivia and I are perfectly fine. We don't require any involvement from the …' she paused, glancing protectively down at Olivia, 'shall we say, paternal element.'

Really? From what he'd discovered, she was already involved. She was concerned, he assumed, that he was here to question her about the money. He would, but not here. Right now, he wanted to appeal to her, not antagonise her. 'No, I can understand that,' he said with a short dip of his head. 'I'm not here to pursue that.

I, er …' Grappling for a way to explain with Olivia looking on, he took a breath. 'Poppy's in hospital. She's doing okay, though,' he added quickly, smiling reassuringly again for Olivia's benefit, as he could see she was alarmed. 'She'll be home soon.'

Nicole assimilated this information, nodding slowly. He wasn't sure how much Kay had told her about Poppy's illness, but he guessed she must have mentioned something. She would have had to if Poppy had spent time at her house. 'I'm sorry,' she said. 'Please give her our love.'

Matt nodded in turn, and then breathed in hard. 'She *might* need some assistance.' He said it as it was, and prayed. Would she at least consider it? He shouldn't be asking. Seeing this child's face, her features so similar to Poppy's, the obvious fear in her eyes for her best friend, he knew he shouldn't, but what was he to do? There was a chance Kay might be a match, a chance she might not. And Jason? Matt had yet to ask him, though he wasn't sure how he would bring himself to do it, particularly knowing now how contemptible his brother was. In reality, he wasn't holding out much hope that Jason would agree to being tested. Clearly he didn't think he had any responsibility to anybody.

'I know.' The woman sighed heavily, her expression agonised. Clearly she did have a conscience, and was struggling with it. 'I've had this conversation with Kay. I made my feelings quite clear. I'm afraid I can't do what you want me to do. It's just not possible. Olivia means more to me than my life.'

As Poppy did to him. Matt understood, completely. It didn't make what she was telling him any less painful.

'Would *you*?' she asked him. 'If the situation were reversed, could you?'

Matt's gaze went again to Olivia. He'd already asked himself that question. His answer was that he wouldn't easily offer up his own daughter. Poppy being so ill was obviously clouding his thinking, hence his coming here.

'Possibly not, no,' he conceded. 'I'm sorry, I shouldn't have come, accosted you here.' He ran a hand wearily over his neck. 'It was unprofessional, thoughtless. I …'

'Felt desperate?' She contemplated him thoughtfully. 'I think I would have done the same,' she said after a second. 'I'm afraid my answer still stands, though. I just can't consider it. Please accept my apologies.'

'Accepted.'

She smiled.

Matt managed a smile back. He'd been judging her, wrongly, it seemed. It was possible that she'd judged Jason correctly, hence the route she'd decided to take. Though why Jason would agree to go that route, he had yet to find out. 'I should let you go.' He offered her his hand again.

She shook it this time. 'Best of luck, Dr Young,' she said.

'Thank you.' He swallowed. 'Bye, Olivia,' he said, making an effort to give her a smile too.

'Bye, Dr Young,' Olivia replied, regarding him with curiosity. She was clearly wary of him too. Matt's stomach constricted as he realised she had every cause to be.

He turned to go, his throat tight.

'Can I come and see Poppy at the hospital?' Olivia called after him.

Matt hesitated. And then turned back. That wasn't his decision to make. He eyed her mother questioningly.

She took a minute. Matt guessed she might be reluctant, and understood why. 'I don't see why not,' she agreed at last. 'We could make her another get-well card.' She squeezed Olivia's hand. 'Would you like that?'

'Yes!' Olivia jumped excitedly on the spot.

'Thanks,' Matt said hoarsely, guessing the woman understood that though Olivia couldn't help her physically, Poppy would need her special friend emotionally, now more than ever. He was grateful for that much.

CHAPTER FIFTY-EIGHT

Kay

Kay was aware that Matt had barely slept since yesterday. He'd slipped back into Poppy's room after attending an emergency during the night and settled down in the chair on the other side of her bed, but she hadn't seen him once close his eyes. It was more than either of them dared do. He'd tried to get some rest during the course of the morning, but had again been contacted by colleagues, this time to assess an urgent referral. She was surprised he was able to function.

Easing herself from the cot one of the staff had thoughtfully provided when she'd said she wanted to spend the night, she glanced at Poppy, who was sleeping for the moment, thank goodness, then went across to where Matt was sitting, his elbows resting on his knees and his head buried in his hands.

He jumped when she reached out to him. He'd clearly been miles away. She scanned his eyes as he attempted to focus on her. They were raw with lack of sleep, ringed by dark shadows. His face was tight and white. He looked haunted, and utterly exhausted, jaded to his bones. 'Why don't you have a lie-down?' she whispered. 'I'll keep an eye on Poppy.'

He shook his head, his mouth curving into a semblance of a smile. 'I'm okay,' he answered quietly.

Kay was unconvinced. 'You look dreadful. You'll scare the patients,' she chastised him.

'I'm scaring myself,' he admitted throatily. He ran his hands over his face and got to his feet. 'We need to have a talk … about what we were discussing yesterday,' he said, his expression a combination of guilty and guarded.

Kay nodded shortly. Neither of them had brought the subject of Amelia up since their conversation in the corridor. He'd said the text was from his cousin. She didn't know whether she believed that, but she simply hadn't got the energy to pursue it. 'But not here.' She glanced at Poppy.

'No, not here. Not now. But soon.' He kneaded his temples tiredly. 'If only there was something I could do. I feel so bloody useless.'

Feeling for him, a doctor who could do nothing to help his daughter but rely on other people, she tentatively pressed a hand to his arm.

'She thinks I can make her wish come true,' he said, his voice taut with emotion. 'I'm not sure how I'll cope knowing she thinks I've failed her.'

Watching his expression change to one of soul-crushing sadness as he moved towards Poppy, Kay felt an overwhelming love for this man, tinged with unbearable, palpable pain. It felt as if her heart might tear apart inside her. He hadn't failed Poppy. She worshipped him.

Hesitantly she reached to place the flat of her hand on his back. He stiffened visibly, and she felt overwhelmed with hurt all over again. Would there ever come a time when they could hold each other, comfort each other? Would they ever look into each other's eyes without seeing the pain there? Amelia had obviously been aware there were problems between them. Because Matt had told her? Kay didn't know. She did know, though, that the woman had been playing psychological games with them, her aim to push them further apart, and she'd won. Matt had succumbed to her devious charms.

Dropping her hand, she gulped back the lump expanding excruciatingly in her chest. 'I'll fetch us some coffee,' she said, in the absence of anything else she could say.

'I'll go.' Matt turned, meeting her gaze, but only briefly before his eyes skittered away again. 'I need to check on a patient in neonatal anyway.' Nodding towards the door, he offered her a small smile and headed that way.

Kay watched him kneading the back of his neck as he went, trying to ease the tension he was carrying through his shoulders. She would have done that just a short while ago, and he would have reciprocated, soft, sure strokes, expertly relaxing her muscles, working his way down her spine until he found that place in the small of her back that melted her completely. Those were the times he would orchestrate their lovemaking. Tenderly, each of them perfectly tuned to the other, they would move in perfect synchronicity, his gaze never leaving hers, until that one sweet moment when his eyes would close briefly. They would lie together afterwards, limbs entwined, hearts beating as one, as she nestled close to him, her head resting on his chest, listening to the steady, reassuring thrum of his heartbeat. Would they ever have that again? Be in tune with each other again?

Glancing at her daughter, she willed the tears back. She couldn't give in to them, not here. Easing the sheet Poppy had kicked aside over her small body, she gave her a reassuring smile as her baby's eyes flickered open. She needed to freshen up but would wait until Matt got back. After a mild sedative, Poppy was drifting in and out of sleep. She didn't want her to wake and find no one here.

She was sitting on Matt's chair, gently stroking Poppy's arm, when the door squeaked open. She glanced up, and was surprised to see Nicole poking her head tentatively around it. 'I hope it's okay,' she said. 'I know it's probably difficult for you under the circumstances, but Olivia's desperate to see how Poppy is.'

Poppy answered for her, lifting her head from the pillow as Olivia squeezed between her mum and the door frame. 'Liv's here!' she exclaimed, a brighter smile on her face than the weak ones they'd seen up until now.

'Of course it's okay.' Standing, Kay gestured them in. Olivia didn't need much prompting, immediately dashing across to the bed. 'I made you another card,' she said excitedly. 'This one's got bigger hearts and kisses and lots of sparklies, see?'

'Careful, Liv,' Nicole warned her, noting the mattress dipping as Olivia leaned to show Poppy the card.

'It's fine,' Kay assured her. They'd removed the neck line early this morning ready for fitting the fistula. For now, Poppy was tube-free and comfortable. Dismissing the pang of fear as she considered Poppy's next procedure and how uncomfortable that might be, she walked across to Olivia. 'I'm sure it will be all right for you to sit next to her, as long as you're careful not to bounce around too much. Would you like that?' she asked the little girl, who wouldn't know the heartbreak simply looking at her caused. And nor could she ever. None of this was her fault. She could never sense that it might be.

'Yes!' Olivia replied gleefully, lifting her arms and allowing Kay to sweep her up.

Once the girls were tucked up – like peas in a pod, Kay thought sadly – she smiled at Nicole, whose expression was nervous. Kay guessed why it might be. 'Grab a seat,' she said, indicating the chair she'd just vacated. 'Matt's gone to check on a few things and grab us a coffee. I'll give him a ring and ask him to fetch you one too.' She didn't want the woman to feel guilty. None of this was her fault either. She could never blame her for the decision she'd made.

'I'm good, don't worry. I've not long had one.' Nicole smiled appreciatively, but Kay could tell by her gaze drifting down and back that she did feel guilty. 'Kay, I …' she started, then stopped, frowning curiously as raised voices reached them through the open door from the corridor.

Kay walked across to close it, glancing out towards the nurses' station as she did, and then froze. Amelia was here. Right here on the floor her baby was on. Her stomach lurched, icy fingers trailing the length of her spine as she realised that one of the raised voices was hers, and that the person she was screaming at was Matt.

CHAPTER FIFTY-NINE

Matthew

'For Christ's sake, Rachel, what the …?' Growing extremely concerned for her, having noted the bruising on her face, Matt moved towards her. 'I just want to make sure you're all right.'

Rachel backed away from him. 'I don't want you near me!' she cried, to the astonished looks of the staff gathered there. 'Just leave me *alone*.'

Stopping in his tracks, Matt splayed his hands in confusion. 'Have I done something to upset you? You're obviously distressed. Rachel, please calm down.' He took another step. 'I only want—'

'*No*. Stay *away* from me!' She whirled around, only to crash into an equipment trolley parked against the wall behind her.

One of the staff raced to her assistance, casting a worried glance at Matt as she did.

'Tell him to leave, *please*,' Rachel sobbed, wiping a hand across her nose as the woman put an arm around her.

'I think you'd better—' the other woman started, only to be interrupted by the clinical lead, Angela, calling fiercely from the corridor, 'Dr Young! My office, please, immediately!'

What in God's name …? Stunned, Matt glanced around as Angela stalked off, hoping someone might enlighten him, only to meet yet more worried glances. Suspicious glances? *Jesus Christ.* His gut turned over. Were they thinking that *he* …? Had she …?

No way. He suspected she was trying to come between him and Kay, which had to have something to do with Jason, but she wouldn't do this. Would she? Shaking his head, he met her gaze as she glanced towards him, and far from fear in her eyes, her look was one of quiet triumph.

Stupefied, he walked past her. His insides turned over as he heard one of the male nurses ask her, 'What happened, lovely?'

'I don't know.' Rachel's voice was small and tearful. 'He lost his temper, and …'

Hearing her gulp back a sob, Matt clenched his jaw hard. *He*, as in *him*? No *fucking* way! Banging through the doors at the end of the corridor, he went straight to Angela's office, knocking perfunctorily on the door and going straight in.

'Would you like to tell me what the hell's going on?' he demanded.

Angela was standing behind her desk, her arms folded across her chest. 'I was about to ask you the very same question.' She glared furiously at him.

She bloody well had, hadn't she? Matt felt sick. This had to be a joke.

'Close the door, Matt.' Angela nodded towards it.

He stood stock still, too stunned to move.

Angela marched past him, slamming the door shut, then strode back to her desk. 'Sit down, please.' She nodded to her visitor's chair, her face stony.

Still Matt didn't move. It was all he could do to breathe. 'Is this what I think it is?' he asked shakily.

'Which is what, Matthew?' Angela batted the question back, a flash of palpable agitation crossing her features.

Quelling the nausea now clawing its way up his windpipe, Matt felt his heart go into freefall. 'She's made a complaint, hasn't she?' He stared at her, disbelieving.

'Correct,' Angela confirmed, dropping heavily into her chair.

Jesus. Every sinew in his body tensed. 'Is she actually saying that I *hit* her?'

She scanned his face, and then looked away. 'I'm afraid it's worse than that,' she muttered, shuffling paperwork on her desk, picking up files, putting them down.

Matt's blood stopped pumping. '*Worse?*'

Clearly reluctant to meet his gaze, Angela hesitated before answering. Finally, she looked back at him. 'She says it was sexually motivated,' she announced, causing Matt to reel back.

Christ, this could not be happening. Fear tightened his stomach like a slipknot. *Please don't let this be happening, not now.*

'Did you do it?' Angela asked, bluntly.

Matt baulked, shocked and utterly incredulous. 'No I did *not* bloody well do it.'

She studied him, a long, searching look. As if considering him *capable?* Christ almighty, she was judging him. They all were. Swallowing back the hard knot of panic climbing his chest, he glared back at her.

She dropped her gaze. When she looked back at him, her fury had given way to a sliver of compassion. 'You need to take some leave, Matt,' she said, dropping another bombshell. 'As in, immediately.'

'*What?*' Matt swiped at his forehead. He could feel the sweat soaking the shirt on his back, the foundations of his world rocking beneath him, his life slipping away like sand through a timer.

'You're overdue some leave anyway.' Her gaze flicked away again.

'Not happening, Angela,' he answered, his heart banging unsteadily in a combination of fury and incomprehension. 'My *daughter's* here, for Christ's sake.'

'I know.' She sighed heavily. 'You can come and see her later. Tomorrow would probably be better. But check with me first.'

Matt looked her over for a long, hard moment. 'You know if you do this, I might as well hand in my notice?'

'Matt …' She pressed the heels of her hands to her desk, pushed her chair back. 'You're exhausted. You're already in danger of not being able to do your job properly. And now, with this—'

'It's bullshit! You know it is. You *know* me. There is no way I would *ever* do anything like this.'

'I have to remain impartial.' Angela dropped her gaze.

'Right.' Matt was getting the gist. He was guilty until proven innocent. 'So, *she's* being asked to take some leave too, I assume?'

Angela didn't answer, which Matt guessed was confirmation enough. 'There's no way it won't look like an admission of guilt. You know that, right?' His heart slid icily into the pit of his stomach.

Steepling her hands under her nose, Angela drew in a terse breath. 'You've been involved with her, Matt. I—'

'*Involved?*' He shook his head hard.

'You've been seen walking with her, talking to her—'

'About *work*,' Matt pointed out, struggling hard to hold on to his temper.

'On numerous occasions,' Angela added, hammering nail after nail into his coffin.

'We *work* together.' He tried to get his head around it. Why she'd done it. What had driven her to do something that would completely destroy him?

'You should have known better,' she threw back at him. 'Fraternising with a young, pretty nurse was bound to lead to speculation. My God, Matt. What were you thinking?' She exhaled wearily. 'The department could really do without this.'

'The *department*?' Matt repeated, truly scared now – for himself, for his daughter. For his wife. Rachel had done the same thing to her. He recalled Kay's frightened disbelief when he'd repeated what Rachel had told him about Kay supposedly making life difficult for her. *She's trying to split us up! She manipulated a situation, complained about me, knowing it might cost me my job …* Why was she doing this? Dear God, what was her agenda?

CHAPTER SIXTY

Kay

'But it's not true! None of it is true. You *know* Matthew. Some of you have worked with him for *years*.' Kay looked around at a sea of embarrassed faces. No one spoke. Not a single word was uttered in Matt's defence.

She stared at the staff who'd congregated at the nurses' station, no doubt keen to catch up on the juicy gossip. She couldn't believe it. So many times Matt had said he needed to be here when he should be at home. So many times he'd said he needed to do his job to the best of his ability because his colleagues, as well as his patients, depended on him. If there was an emergency, he would drag himself back to the hospital, exhausted, whatever time of the day or night, often rising again at the crack of dawn the next morning.

Where were they when he needed *them*? Turning their bloody backs on him. Not one of them prepared to stand up and condemn that woman for the vicious lies she'd told. Instead, they condemned Matt, even knowing what kind of person he was, that he simply wasn't capable of the heinous crimes he was being accused of.

'This is wrong,' she cried, shaking with anger. '*All* wrong.'

'Kay, leave it,' Nicole said behind her, placing her hands gently on her shoulders and easing her away. 'Come on, let's go back to Poppy and Olivia. It'll be sorted out, I'm sure. This won't do any good.'

Kay turned towards her. 'Someone has to stand up for him,' she argued, aware of the wretchedness in her voice, the desperation. 'She's *lying*! It's obvious she is. She …'

Nicole pulled her into a hug as she choked out a sob. 'You're upset. You're bound to be. Let's go back and collect ourselves, shall we?' she suggested softly, steering her back towards Poppy's room. 'We'll take a breather and see if we can find out what's happening.'

Feeling the strength drain from her body, Kay allowed herself to be guided. Why had Amelia done this? There couldn't be any truth in it. Kay might have been shocked that Matt had got involved with the woman, that he'd had an affair with her, but she knew he would *never* have abused her. Never. 'He wouldn't,' she murmured.

Nicole simply nodded, to placate her more than in agreement, Kay suspected. She'd never felt so alone in her life. Pausing outside Poppy's room, she breathed deeply and attempted to pull herself together.

'Okay?' Nicole smiled kindly.

Kay nodded gratefully. Poppy would need her now more than ever. She must have heard something. She must be wondering what on earth was going on.

A semblance of a smile on her face, she stepped into the room. And stopped. 'Poppy?' For one blood-freezing moment, she stared at the empty bed where her daughter should be. 'Poppy!'

Nicole caught her as her knees buckled.

CHAPTER SIXTY-ONE

Matthew

He'd left Kay at the hospital, feeling he had to leave immediately, rather than risk being escorted out by security. His one solace had been that Poppy's consultant hadn't looked at him with condemnation as he'd stopped by his office. The man had promised to keep him informed regarding her progress. Matt appreciated it. The guy knew him from way back, but if there was one lesson life had taught him, it was that you could never truly trust anyone. You couldn't know what was going on behind the facade. His brother wasn't the man he pretended to be. Kay ... Once he would have trusted her with his life. Now, knowing what he knew about Poppy, that the nightmare he'd tried so hard to dismiss was actually his reality, how could he bring himself to trust her again? He'd become wary of Rachel, though not initially. She certainly wasn't what she'd seemed.

Abandoning his attempts to make coffee in lieu of the whisky he'd been sorely tempted to tip back, he slammed the kettle down, scalding his hand in the process but barely acknowledging it. What was a surface burn, after all, compared to the suffering his little girl had to go through? *His* little girl. She would be lying in her hospital bed now wondering where her daddy was, the great doctor who would make her wish come true. He'd sworn he would always be there for her, and he wasn't. His family was being ripped apart.

Running his hands through his hair, he wondered what the hell he should do. He supposed he should be thinking about ringing his union about the inconceivable complaint made against him. He had no clue why Rachel was doing this. It was obviously something to do with Olivia's abandonment. She could be the little girl's aunt, in which case – assuming she was of the same opinion as Matt as to the identity of Olivia's father – she might have some gripe with Jason, but why choose to destroy *him*? Why choose Kay? Try as he might, he couldn't make sense of any of it. All he could do was hold on to the hope that the hospital would launch a full investigation. Had she reported him to the police? Would the hospital be obliged to? Christ, he prayed it didn't come to that.

Swallowing back the bitter taste in his throat, he headed for the hall for his phone. Jesus, he couldn't believe he was actually having to do this. Who did one contact when accused of a sexual assault? Still numb with shock, he guessed he should google solicitors. Should he consult with the HR department as well as his union, as Angela had suggested? No doubt they would have a protocol in place and would be able to inform him what the procedure was, and the chances of his career surviving if such a complaint were upheld. He didn't dare go there. He had no idea what he would do with his life if he wasn't a doctor. His job was part of who he was. He'd wanted to be a medic since he was a small child, and had never even thought about doing anything else.

He should call Kay first. He should have done it earlier. His thumb hovering over her number, he prevaricated. What would he tell her? The truth, he guessed, for what it was worth. He was about to place the call when someone hammered urgently on the front door, causing him to jolt.

Steadying his heartbeat, he turned towards it, panic climbing his chest as he realised that this might even be the police. His stomach tightened, cold fear creeping through him as he braced himself to answer it. He had no choice. He couldn't run away from this – as Rachel would have known he couldn't.

Heaving in a breath, he pulled the front door open. His world reeled violently as he saw Jess standing there. His throat dry, his gaze went from her to the officer at her side. Jess's expression was sympathetic. The guy with her looked almost apologetic.

'Can we come in, Matt?' she asked.

Matt frowned, a combination of fear and confusion running through him. Were they here to arrest him? Something didn't feel right. 'Of course.' He stepped back, eyeing Jess curiously as she stepped in.

'I'm sorry, Matt,' she said. 'We have some bad news, I'm afraid.'

Matt felt the hairs rise over his skin as he noted her eyes filling up. 'What news?'

'Poppy …' His heart skidded to a stop in his chest before she'd got the words out. 'She's missing.'

CHAPTER SIXTY-TWO

Matt banged into the ward, Jess and her partner close behind him. 'Where is she?' he asked a member of staff.

'I'm so sorry, Dr Young,' the man replied, his face awash with concern. 'We've no idea how the children could have wandered from the ward. Angela has security on it, and as you've gathered, the police are involved. I'm sure we'll find them.'

Children? His heart hammering like a freight train, his legs weak beneath him, Matt tried to assimilate this information and failed. They wouldn't find them. Poppy hadn't wandered off. She'd been taken, for fuck's sake. Wasn't it obvious by whom? 'Where's my *wife*?' he bellowed, pushing past the man. He needed to speak to Kay. He needed to know what the hell had happened. *Now.*

Dear God, he needed to know where his baby was. Scanning the ward, seeing a multitude of stricken faces looking back at him, he spotted Kay, his chest almost exploding with relief as she saw him and came running towards him.

He caught her as she launched herself at him, wrapping his arms around her, squeezing her hard. 'What happened?' he asked as she clung to him, trembling, dry sobs emerging from her throat.

'They were on the bed,' Nicole said behind her. 'Olivia and Poppy, we left them on the bed. We came out here when we heard the fuss.' She closed her eyes. Her face was grey, her eyes tortured.

'When we went back in … they weren't *there*. How?' she asked, glancing feverishly around. '*How* could they have just disappeared?'

He heard someone calling his name through the horror unfolding in his head: his baby out there somewhere, her wounds still open, her kidneys failing. He hadn't been there for her when she'd needed him.

'Thank God you're here,' Angela went on, coming towards them. Matt bit back his contempt. 'We're pulling up all CCTV footage,' she said, her normally officious tone tremulous. 'We have security guards on all the exits. We're searching the hospital, the grounds too. Everyone is looking for them. We will find them, I promise you.'

Matt tried to force his brain to think logically. How could two tiny children be missing from a ward full of people? How had no one noticed them leaving? Unless they had been taken by someone in uniform.

'When, Angela? When will we find them?' He hoped she would understand his meaning without him having to spell out in front of his wife what might happen to Poppy without the medical care she needed. Holding Kay close to him, he physically supported her as they followed Nicole towards the relatives' room.

'It's Amelia, isn't it?' Kay asked, her eyes wretched with fear as he helped her into one of the chairs there.

'I don't know,' he said, his voice hoarse. Though he did. She was involved in this, though to what end, he had no idea. He knew now that the debacle earlier, her devastating accusation, had been nothing but a distraction. There could be no other explanation.

Pouring Kay some water from the jug on the table, making sure she took a sip, he sucked in a breath and turned to Nicole. 'You need to talk,' he said.

The woman paled further, if that were possible, her eyes growing frantic and wide.

'You can tell me, or you can tell the police.' He paused, locking his gaze hard on hers. 'Why are you blackmailing Jason?'

'Oh God.' She pressed a hand to her mouth, seeming to wilt where she stood.

'Blackmailing?' Kay shot to her feet.

Matt held up a hand, stilling her as she took a step towards the other woman. 'Talk to me, Nicole,' he warned her.

Nicole sank into a chair by the far wall. 'He's Olivia's father,' she whispered, her voice barely a croak.

Matt nodded. This much he knew.

'That woman, Amelia, she got in touch with me,' she went on shakily. 'She'd seen me with Olivia. She said she hadn't been sure at first, but that Olivia looked so like her sister. She asked around at the school, found out she was adopted and … she contacted me.'

She stopped, looking up at him and then to Kay beseechingly. 'She knew I was in debt,' she said, glancing away. 'I think she broke into my house, saw my accounts. She told me that Jason was well off. She also told me he'd destroyed her sister, her family; that he wasn't the kind of man I would want in Olivia's life. She said he should pay, and I …' She paused, and wiped a slow tear from her face.

'Decided to extract payment,' Matt finished, quashing the anger bubbling up inside him. Burning fury at his brother, who'd never breathed a word of this. Who might have prevented this. Poppy was *missing*. The clock was ticking.

'How?' he demanded, causing Nicole to jump. 'What hold did you have over him?'

Swallowing tightly, she looked back at him. 'Amelia said to send him a message.'

Matt waited.

'She said to say "I know what you did", that was all.'

'And it worked?' Matt was incredulous and astonished in turn. What in God's name had Jason done that he would be so desperate to hide? What could have been serious enough to panic him into paying out thousands of pounds?

She nodded, her face filled with shame. 'There's something else,' she said, as he pulled out his phone, scrolling through it for Jason's number. 'He said he wanted to see her. Olivia. I said no. I also said that if anything were to happen to me, a letter would be sent to the police.'

'Dear God …' Kay whispered hoarsely.

'I was desperate.' Nicole looked from Kay's shocked face back to Matt. 'I was in danger of losing my *house*. I—'

Matt's heart flipped over. Calling Jason's number, he exchanged terrified glances with Kay. He could see they were thinking the same thing: that Jason and Amelia might be in this together. That their aim might be to take the children away.

'Shit!' he cursed as Jason's phone rang out.

CHAPTER SIXTY-THREE

Stopping for no one, Matt raced through the hospital, throwing himself in his car when he reached it and screeching out of the car park. His heartbeat ratcheted up as he drove, adrenaline forcing him on. *Please God, let my daughter be safe.* He prayed desperately, wiping the perspiration from his forehead with the back of his hand, attempting to focus on the road rather than the fear gnawing away at his insides. He had to find her. He tightened his grip on the steering wheel. He had to get hold of his *fucking* brother.

Was Jason involved with Amelia, as he'd now come to know her – a name that stuck in his throat? It seemed insane that he would want to reclaim his children now, but Matt couldn't think of any other reason any of this would be happening. Was Amelia in love with Jason? That was infinitely possible. Jason had the looks, the charm … until you got to know him better. And love drove people to all sorts of madness. Matt knew that well enough.

His heart slammed to a stop in his chest as the thought occurred that Jason might even have organised for them to fly back to the States.

Shakily he tried his brother's number again. Reaching his voicemail, he took a breath and called his father, hoping he might have some idea of Jason's whereabouts.

'Matthew, how are you?' David asked when he picked up.

'Fine. I'm just between patients,' Matt lied, attempting to calm himself. The last thing he wanted to do was panic his father. 'How are you doing?'

'Good,' his father assured him. 'I was just about to have a potter in the garden, deadhead a few roses. That's pretty much the extent of my exercise regime at the moment.'

'Don't overdo it. You need to take it slowly,' Matt warned him.

'Ever the doctor.' His father sighed good-naturedly. 'I won't,' he promised him. 'So, are you ringing just to check up on me, or was there something else?'

'Er, it's actually Jason I wanted to talk to,' Matt said, as casually as he could. 'You don't have any idea where he might be, do you? I can't get hold of him on the phone.'

'Jason?' His father sounded surprised, as he would be considering the hostility between the brothers. 'Don't tell me you two have finally called a truce.'

'Not quite. I'm trying to be less reactive, though,' Matt assured him. 'It's actually work-related, a medical order I needed to check with him.'

'Ah.' His father sighed, no doubt resigned to the fact that there would never be a truce. 'You'll find him in the office. He rang me from there about ten minutes ago. He's going to be working late. You two have probably got more in common than you realise.'

At Biochem? But that made no sense. If Jason was involved in Poppy's disappearance, that would be the last place he would be, surely? 'I'll try him later,' he said. 'I'd better get to my next patient.'

CHAPTER SIXTY-FOUR

At the Biochem offices, the security guard waved him through once he'd checked with Jason, who presumably told him it was okay. That surprised Matt. It also tightened the terror unfurling inside him. Would Jason have agreed to see him if he was involved in the girls' disappearance?

His brother rose from his desk as Matt walked through the outer office, opening his door and coming out to meet him. 'What's up?' he asked, his expression wary. Because he knew why he was here? Matt couldn't be sure.

'I needed a word,' he answered vaguely, not wanting to alert him until he knew more.

Eyeing him quizzically, Jason nodded and indicated his office. 'Is this something to do with Kay?' he asked, leading the way. 'She texted me. Said she wants to meet. She sounded desperate.' He glanced back at Matt over his shoulder.

'Don't, Jason,' Matt warned him. Whatever this bastard was up to, one thing he did know was that Kay wasn't part of it. There was no way she would have helped him take the girls.

'Oh, for fu—' Jason turned at his desk. 'Matt, you really need to change the record.' Plunging his hands in his pockets, he glanced up at the ceiling, shaking his head despairingly. 'Look, this is ridiculous. It's time to bury the past, don't you think? Why don't you just sit down? I'll grab us a coffee, and we can—'

'Where is she?' Matt asked, his voice tight. He hadn't got time for this. Poppy hadn't got time. Did Jason not realise that, for Christ's sake?

Jason squinted at him, his expression now perplexed. 'What are you talking about?' he asked.

Was it an act? He'd certainly done a bloody good job of keeping his relationship with Kay under wraps until now, hadn't he? His temper simmering dangerously, Matt cautioned himself to stay calm. Losing it would achieve nothing.

'I just need to know where she is,' he said. 'We can talk about the rest later.'

Jason looked at him in bewildered astonishment. 'What in God's name are you on about, Matt?'

'Just answer the fucking question, will you?' Matt shouted, moving towards him. 'I need to know she's okay!'

'Whoa, back off.' Jason took a step back, only to collide with his desk. 'I honestly haven't got a clue what you're talking about,' he insisted. 'You're talking in riddles, Matt, and you are genuinely scaring me.'

Matt narrowed his eyes. Was he telling the truth? His complexion was sheet-white. That was likely if he thought Matt might be here to break his neck, which right now, he felt very much like doing. His eye contact, though, was direct.

Jason sighed. 'Look, I know what you think, but I didn't sleep with her.' His expression was somewhere near contrition, for the first time ever. 'There was no affair. Nothing happened between us. Kay wouldn't, don't you get it?'

Matt stared at him, confounded for a second. Then his contempt for the man rose off the scale. 'Meaning you tried, you bastard.' His temper frayed with exhaustion and worry, he exploded, lunging before he had time to counsel himself not to.

Jason, though, was ready for him, barring him with his arms and shoving him backwards. 'You need to wise up and stop blaming everyone else for what's wrong in your marriage, little brother,' he spat as Matt tried to keep his feet. 'If she's left you, have you considered the fact that it might not be anything to do with me, and everything to do with *you*?'

His heart banging erratically, Matt locked eyes with his brother. Jason didn't look away. He really didn't know what Matt was talking about. He didn't have the girls. Jesus Christ. How much time had he wasted? He needed to leave. He needed to find Poppy.

'You could try checking local hotels,' Jason suggested behind him, his voice now edged with his usual sarcasm. 'My guess, though, is that maybe she doesn't want to be found.'

Matt breathed in hard, yanked the door open and hurried across the outer office, pulling his ringing phone from his pocket as he went. *Kay.* He'd asked her to wait for the CCTV footage. Praying that it had picked something up, he hit call receive. 'Anything?'

'Nothing,' Kay said, her voice tight with the same panic he felt. 'There's no direct view of the door to her room, no sign of anyone leaving through the ward doors with two children.'

'Right.' Matt felt helplessness wash through him.

'I'm approaching the Biochem building,' she went on as he tried to think what the hell to do next. 'Have you spoken to Jason?'

His breath hitched. She shouldn't be here. Neither of them should. They should both be concentrating their efforts on giving the police any assistance they could. 'They're not here,' he said. 'Go back to the hospital, Kay. There's no point you being here. I'll be right behind you.'

He heard her draw in a shuddery breath. 'Please hurry,' she said.

'I will,' he assured her, his heart breaking afresh. This would kill her. 'Keep strong, Kay,' he urged. 'Poppy's going to need you to be. How's Nicole doing?'

'I'm not sure,' Kay answered uncertainly. 'I haven't seen her since you left. She's joined the search, I think.'

'I'll be with you soon. We'll find them, Kay, I promise.' Finishing the call, praying hard again, he reached to pull open the outer office doors – and reeled back.

CHAPTER SIXTY-FIVE

Kay

Kay slowed the car to a stop. Numb with shock and fear, she sat unmoving for a second, then clamped her hands hard over her face. She'd hoped Poppy would be here, prayed she would be. She hadn't understood half of what Nicole had said, why Jason would be paying her money. She didn't want to understand. She just wanted her baby.

She tipped her face up to scream at the heavens. 'Where *is* she?' There was no answer. The sky was grey and unyielding, the dark fast descending. *Please bring her back. Please let them find her*, she prayed, as she'd already prayed over and over, though God clearly couldn't hear her.

She pushed her foot down on the accelerator, lurching the car forward. 'Dammit!' She tried again, her hands shaking as she shoved it into reverse. Matt was right. She needed to stay calm. She needed to stay strong for her child.

Swinging the car around and attempting a three-point turn, she tried to concentrate, impossible when all she could see was Poppy's face, her wide blue eyes, so like her father's, filled with innocence. *Please don't let them be filled with fear. Please don't let her be scared or hurting. Dear God, please let her be alive.*

After five manoeuvres, she finally succeeded in straightening the car on the lane. She had to talk to Nicole. It was all linked, she knew it in her heart: Amelia and the awful things she'd done were somehow connected to Jason and whatever despicable thing he'd done. She had to find out what it was all about if she was to find Poppy.

Taking a breath, she blinked hard against the tears clouding her vision and eased the car forward. *Concentrate*, she willed herself. She would find her. *I'm coming, sweetheart. Mummy's coming.*

Running her hand under her nose, she stifled another sob, gripped the steering wheel hard and drove on. She'd gone just a few yards when her eyes snagged on something in her peripheral vision. A scarecrow? she wondered, squinting through the rain slashing against the side window. Not a scarecrow, she realised, her heart jumping as the lone figure moved.

She could see it was someone small. Slim. A female. Why would a woman be out here in such hostile weather in the middle of nowhere? But it wasn't the middle of nowhere. It was a stone's throw from the Biochem building. From Jason.

Amelia. Who else would it fucking well be?

CHAPTER SIXTY-SIX

Amelia

After making her way across the fields towards the Biochem premises, Amelia stood for a while feeling the rain lashing her face, the wind whipping her hair. It made her feel more alive, made her feel … something, other than the emptiness and grief she'd carried around like a cold stone inside her for almost five years. And the anger, that the police had refused to listen to her. He'd been out at a restaurant that night, they'd told her, the night the little parcel had been delivered to the City Road Hospital. There'd been twenty-odd witnesses to that, including his father, who'd given a statement to confirm it. Of course he would have. They were family. Amelia felt a new wave of grief crash through her. She felt it deeply, the loneliness of being alone, of having no family to call her own. She still had her mother, but only in the barest sense, and had long ago grieved the loss of the woman she'd known. No doubt she would grieve again, though, once she'd gone.

She stayed where she was for a while, contemplating what could have been if he'd never come into her sister's life. She didn't put down the bouquet of pretty peach roses she'd brought with her, but plucked off the petals instead, sprinkling them softly over the ground.

She didn't feel good about what she'd done, far from it, but she'd achieved what she'd set out to. The Young family weren't a family any more. They were estranged, broken, each of them in their own personal hell, as she'd been, wondering how they got there. She didn't feel sorry for any of them, bar one: Kay. She actually could have liked her, perhaps been a friend to her, but for the link to the family that had taken her own family away. But then, she'd slept with *him*, hadn't she? Dear little Olivia and Poppy being so alike confirmed that. She must have had an affair with him, seeing him behind her husband's back. Matt's eyes had needed opening to that fact. He would hate his brother now, want nothing more to do with him. His father would, too, once he realised Jason had been using company funds to keep his secret safe. He would be alone, on his own, just as she was.

Matt had been a casualty. It was a shame. Amelia swallowed back a lump in her throat as she thought of his dear little daughter's bewilderment once she realised her parents were separated and that her daddy wasn't coming home. She could empathise with that. She'd grieved the loss of her own father, a loss so deep she wasn't sure how her child's heart had borne it, knowing that he'd taken his own life rather than be with her.

Matt quite obviously loved Poppy, though, and would never voluntarily leave her. She'd seen tears in his eyes as he'd talked about her. She'd thought he was a bit of an enigma, given the circumstances of Poppy's conception, which he must be aware of. But then she'd also seen lust in his eyes. He tried to hide it, but she was sure he would have been tempted if she'd pushed it. Didn't he deserve it too, then, to have everything he loved taken away from him?

'Perhaps we won't lose too much sleep over Dr Young after all, hey, my lovely?' She spoke out loud, knowing there was no one to hear her.

Her heart jolted violently as she realised she was wrong.

CHAPTER SIXTY-SEVEN

Matthew

'What the hell …?' Jason gasped, stepping out of his office door.

'Stay there!' Matt shouted, pressing an arm to his face and attempting to make his way back across the main office. The lights had gone out. The air was thick, acrid smoke burning the back of his throat since he'd opened the outer office doors. *The bloody cladding!* Jason had cancelled the contractor, glibly putting people's lives at risk. Little had the selfish prick realised that he would also be endangering his own life. Matt's too.

Reaching the fire door to the stairs, he grasped the handle, and tugged it. *Jesus.* Surely it wasn't locked? Cursing, he tried again, pushing at the door. It wouldn't move. Trying not to think about the consequences of what his brother had done, the horrendous death they would suffer by fire or from smoke inhalation if they couldn't get out, he tried to shift it again. It still wouldn't budge. *Jesus Christ.* His gut turned over.

'Open the door, for God's sake!' Jason shouted frantically. 'What the *hell* is the matter with you?' Blundering out, he shoved his brother aside and grabbed hold of the handle. He pulled at it, and then curled both of his hands around it, shoving at the door, ramming his shoulder and then his whole body weight against it. 'Give! You fucking thing!'

'Leave it.' Matt glanced around, trying to think what to do. There didn't appear to be any other exit.

'Leave it?' His brother gawked at him, his face deathly white. 'And *burn* to death? Are you *insane?*'

'I said, *leave* it,' Matt yelled. Panic breaking through as he realised the door might well be keeping the fire out, he wrapped an arm around Jason's shoulders and yanked him physically away from it. 'We need to get back.'

'Get back *where?*' His brother struggled to break free of the grip Matt had on him. 'There's nowhere to *go!*' His voice was shrill, bordering on hysteria.

'Your office.' Matt tightened his hold. He would bloody well carry him there if he had to.

'We'll be *trapped.*' Half walking, half staggering with him, Jason looked around wildly, dragging a hand repeatedly across his smarting eyes as they made their way blindly back the way they'd come.

We are *trapped*, Matt didn't point out. 'We need to buy some time,' he said, trying to quell his now rapidly escalating panic. The fire was underneath them. He could feel the heat rising, the deadly toxic fumes along with it. How much time did they have?

Dear God, how much time did Poppy have? He needed to get *out* of here. Manhandling Jason along with him, he bundled him into his office before closing the door behind them, praying that the walls were made from safety glass. He sucked air into his lungs, choked a breath out. Christ, what now? His eyes streaming, he blinked hard and turned back to survey the door. The gap beneath it wasn't much of a gap, but … Tearing off his jacket, he shoved it against the bottom of the door, then turned to his brother.

Jason had dropped to his haunches, his back against the outer wall, his body shaking, his face ashen as he looked pleadingly up at him. 'What do we do?' he croaked.

Jabbing 999 into his phone, Matt snatched his gaze to the wall his brother was leaning against. The whole thing was glass. Glass everywhere, but ... 'Are there any windows?' he yelled. 'Do they open?'

Jason didn't answer. His arms wrapped around his knees, as if attempting to make himself small, he stared through the glass out to the main office, his eyes wide and petrified.

Matt followed his gaze and fear sliced through him like a knife as he saw what Jason was seeing: flames licking and curling around the frame of the main office doors, smoke billowing underneath them. *Fuck!* He snapped his focus back to the glass wall. Dammit, there had to be some component of it that opened. His gaze travelled along it, relief crashing through him as his eyes snagged on the section at the end.

Quickly he moved towards it, assessing it. It appeared to be another emergency exit of sorts. He hesitated. They were two floors up. It was doable if they climbed out and dropped down backwards. They had no choice, he realised, bracing himself. *He* had no choice. He wasn't going to die here. His wife and daughter needed him. The choice was stark. They could either succumb to the fumes, which he had no doubt were noxious enough to kill them excruciatingly painfully, or risk breaking their legs. In Matt's mind, the latter was vastly preferable. 'We need to get out,' he rasped, his throat and lungs already burning. 'Jason!' he barked, his gaze flicking towards him. 'We have to get out!'

Jason didn't respond. Alarm flooding his features, he shrank back as Matt headed towards him. 'Jason, move it! We don't have much time.'

He shook his head. 'I can't.'

'We need to go. Now!' Matt grabbed hold of his arm – and then, seeing the undiluted terror in his brother's eyes, he stopped. Christ almighty, his vertigo. He was scared of *heights*. Now what in God's name did he do?

He glanced towards the window, then back at his brother. There was no way he could bring himself to leave him behind, no matter what. Cautiously, aware of the time ticking, the inferno they might soon be engulfed in, he crouched down. 'We have to go, Jason. We don't have an alternative,' he explained, careful to keep his tone calm.

His brother closed his eyes, shook his head again hard. 'Don't leave me,' he murmured, a sob escaping his throat. 'Please don't leave me.'

'I won't leave you,' Matt promised thickly. 'I'll be right with you, I swear.'

Jason looked back at him, a sliver of hope in his eyes. Then his gaze skittered to the window and he closed his eyes again fast.

'It's just two floors,' Matt tried to encourage him. 'I'll help you climb out. I'll hold onto you until you're ready. You just need to turn around and drop from the window. There's no other way.'

Jason dragged a breath in, coughed hard, looked back at him. 'What I said … about Kay,' he said falteringly. 'It's true. She didn't want to. She—'

'Now's not the time.' Matt's jaw clenched. 'We need to move.'

'I have to tell you!' Jason's voice rose. 'I *have* to! You need to know.'

'For fuck's sake, *move!*' Matt bellowed, getting to his feet. He didn't want to hear it.

'You're not listening.' Jason stayed put. 'She didn't *want* to! She was drunk. We both were. She was crying, upset. She—'

Matt's heart boomed loud in his head. 'Did she say no?' His throat tightened; his head swam.

Shrinking back further, Jason didn't answer.

'Did she say *no*, you bastard!'

'She … passed out. She was unconscious. She … I was drunk, Matthew. I swear I didn't mean—'

'You piece of fucking scum!' Matt clutched his brother's throat hard. Blind fury driving him, he squeezed tighter, feeling Jason's Adam's apple bob in his throat as he dragged him bodily upwards.

He was seconds away from choking the life out of him when a warning bell kicked in. He couldn't live with it. But this piece of human flotsam could. He wasn't going to die. Not today. Matt wouldn't let him. The bastard could suffer slowly.

He was almost at the window, Jason sobbing and sniffling along with him, when he felt a tremor run through him. It lasted no more than a few seconds, like the aftershock of an earthquake, the ground readjusting. A rumble deep in the belly of the fire, he realised, as it belched through the main office doors and hurtled towards them.

CHAPTER SIXTY-EIGHT

Kay

'Where's my daughter?' Kay twisted the fistful of raven hair tighter, prepared to rip it out by the roots if the woman didn't tell her where her baby was.

'Kay, *please* …' Amelia whimpered, trying to pull away from her. 'You're *hurting* me.'

Hurting her? Did she not realise she would *kill* her without compunction if she'd harmed a single hair on Poppy's head? But she already had. Without her mummy or daddy with her, Poppy would be scared. She would be bewildered and in pain. She might even be *dying* while Kay was here listening to the heartless lies that spilled from this twisted bitch's mouth. She shook with a raw anger she hadn't thought herself capable of. 'Where *is* she?'

Amelia squirmed as her hair was twisted still tighter. 'I don't *know*. I don't know what you're *talking* about. I would never, ever do anything that might harm a child. I'm a *nurse*. Kay, please, let me go. Let me help you find her.'

'Do you *honestly* expect me to believe you?' Kay screamed. 'You've torn her world apart! Caused her so much confusion and pain. You *callous*—'

'I don't know where Poppy is,' Amelia yelled over her. 'I swear on my sister's grave I don't. Please, let me go. I know the hospital. I know all the nooks and crannies. I can help you.'

Kay's head reeled; her heart pounded with fear. Was Amelia actually telling the truth? Was it possible that someone else had taken the girls? But who? And why? Her insides twisted, nausea climbing her throat as she considered the implications.

'You're wasting time here,' Amelia went on. 'You need to *find* her.'

She was right. Kay shouldn't be here. She should be out there looking for her daughter. She wavered, her grip slackening, and Amelia took advantage of it in an instant.

'*No!*' Kay's rage spilled over as the woman tried to scramble away from her, slithering and crawling in the mud. Adrenaline driving her, Kay went after her.

'Don't stand there!' Amelia cried as Kay loomed over her. '*Please*, if you have any compassion at all, don't stand there. There's a mound there. You might be walking on *top* of her.'

Kay looked at her uncomprehendingly, then glanced down to the ground beneath her. Nausea almost choked her. Amelia had been on her knees, sprinkling rose petals here. *Dear God!* Sick comprehension dawned. 'There's someone *buried* here?'

'Not Poppy!' Amelia scrambled further away. 'It's not Poppy,' she said again frantically. 'It's my sister. Please … don't stand on her.'

Kay stared in complete disbelief as the woman looked up at her with tears cascading down her cheeks. 'You *killed* her?'

'*He* killed her!' Amelia blurted. 'She's here somewhere. I know she is. He killed her and buried her here while the building was being constructed. It was him who left her baby at the hospital. I *know* he did.'

Kay felt an ice-cold chill run the length of her spine. Surely she didn't mean—

'I thought they would look for her. I thought the police would find her and he would get the punishment he deserved. They didn't believe me because his fucking *father* lied for him. He gave him an alibi. They said my sister abandoned her baby. But she *didn't*. Kelsey would never have done that. She *loved* her.' She was talking fast, gabbling it out, a ludicrous, unbelievable *lie*. 'He killed her! And he got away with it!' Her eyes were full of incandescent rage. Her gaze didn't flinch as Kay stared hard at her.

It wasn't a lie. Kay's stomach roiled. She was telling the truth.

'He's a bastard!' Amelia yelled. 'He destroyed my family, my sister, my mother! And *you're* sleeping with him. You had a baby with him. How could you have done that? Treated your husband like that? *How*, Kay?'

Kay shook her head, trying desperately to keep up with her. She hadn't slept with Jason – not since they first went out together. Matt had obviously told Amelia she had, or else … Had she been watching her? Had she seen her meeting with Jason? Jason coming to her house? Matt obviously believed she was having an affair with his brother. He truly believed that Poppy wasn't his child. But … Olivia? She was Poppy's half-sister. She had to be.

Her head thumped, confusion doing battle with the anger raging inside her. Swallowing back the painful lump rising in her throat, she glanced down. As disorientated as she was, still she felt compelled to step away from the grave she might be desecrating.

She watched as Amelia got slowly to her knees and then pulled herself stumblingly to her feet. 'How could you have done that to him, Kay?'

Kay stood frozen to the spot. 'I didn't. I wouldn't.' She tried to make sense of the bewilderment in her head.

'I prayed he would get justice. Every single day, I wished he would burn in hell,' Amelia said quietly. 'Do you think if you pray hard enough wishes come true?'

Kay squinted as Amelia nodded past her, a satisfied smile curving her mouth. Twisting to follow her gaze, her heart jolted violently. She'd smelled smoke when she'd arrived. She'd thought it was farmers burning their fields. The smell had been thick, cloying, almost like burning rubber. Her attention had been on Amelia, on following her across the fields, her mind on her daughter. An icy dagger of foreboding pierced her heart.

Oh God, no. 'Matt!' Seeing flames lapping like hungry tongues up the side of the Biochem building, primal instinct kicked in, and she ran. 'Matt!'

'Kay! Over here!'

Matt? She looked around frantically to see him limping towards her from the woods at the perimeter of the field, half carrying, half dragging his brother along with him, blue lights rotating beyond them. Choking, he lowered Jason to the ground as Kay flew towards him.

'Don't!' Amelia screamed behind her. 'Don't let him go! He killed her! He's getting away.'

'Her sister,' Kay gasped, her hands on Matt's shoulders, her gaze on Jason as he rolled over, coughing and spluttering and trying to heave himself to his knees. 'She thinks—'

'He killed her!' Amelia screamed louder.

Matt locked his gaze on her for a second and then grabbed his brother, closing his hand around the back of his neck and heaving him to his feet.

'He buried her here,' Amelia cried tremulously.

'I didn't!' Jason yelled. 'I *didn't*! For fuck's sake, she's insane! You're not seriously going to—'

Matt cut him short, squeezing tighter and shoving him forwards.

'Where *is* she? Tell me!' Amelia flew at him, punching and pummelling him as he fell back to his knees. 'Tell me! You *killed* her, you bastard!'

'I didn't!' Jason tried to protect himself as she tore at his hair, his clothes. 'For fuck's … It was an accident!'

Amelia stopped, stunned.

'It was an *accident*,' Jason repeated, looking from her to Kay, then beseechingly to Matt. 'The car crashed. I swear to God, I didn't mean it. I'd been drinking. I … didn't know what to do. I was due to fly out. The flight was booked. I was … I didn't know what to *do*.'

His expression inscrutable, Matt simply looked at him. Then he stepped towards him. 'On your fucking feet,' he growled, a telltale tic playing at his cheek as he clutched a fistful of Jason's shirt and heaved him back up to face the approaching police.

CHAPTER SIXTY-NINE

Angela

Her department in chaos, Angela sat at her desk frantically trying to imagine how the girls had gone missing. She picked up the phone again, then slammed it down. There'd been no news. No sightings on the CCTV cameras. They'd searched every inch of the hospital right down to the bowels. Scoured the car parks and the grounds. They were nowhere to be found.

Dear God, those poor children. Where were they? Who would do such a thing? How could anyone have just walked out with them? It was inconceivable that no one had seen them. Her reputation would be in tatters, her career ruined, but that mattered little, she realised, against the lives of the patients who should be able to trust in the hospital's absolute care. Poor, poor Matt; how much pain must he be in right now, a man who'd cared deeply about every single one of his patients? She'd turned her back on him when he'd needed her to stand by him. She wasn't sure she would ever forgive herself for that, or that Matt would be able to bring himself to.

Burying her head in her hands, she debated what to do. She would have to check in again with the powers-that-be, she supposed, give them an update.

Pushing herself away from her desk, she walked to the door, leaning tiredly against the frame as she surveyed the department:

people rushing around, alarms and monitors pinging, phones ringing. It had always been chaotic, always would be, with perpetual targets to meet and cuts to funding, but she'd prided herself on meeting those targets, on making damned sure it was organised chaos. At least she would be credited with running a smooth ship, she supposed, when she handed the reins over.

Taking some solace from that, she went back to her desk, drew in a long breath and picked up the phone. As she dialled the number for the chief executive officer, she sensed someone hovering at the door, and snapped her gaze up.

'Poppy's poorly,' the little girl said. 'I think she might need her daddy.'

Angela leapt up and flew towards her. 'Where is she, darling?' she said. 'Can you show me?'

'Uh huh.' The little girl nodded and turned to point to the main corridor doors. 'She's in the cupboard where all the sheets are. We were hiding because we got scared when we heard people shouting.'

CHAPTER SEVENTY

Matthew

Three weeks later

Matt willed the traffic ahead of him on. He'd almost told the doctor who'd rung him from one of the smaller local hospitals that he was attending another urgent appointment. He should be. He should be at his daughter's bedside, not sitting here in traffic. What else could he have done, though? There'd been no other neonatologist available within reasonable driving distance, and the baby was in desperate need of evaluation. Born at just twenty-two weeks, way before her tiny body was ready to leave the womb, her important organs – heart, lungs, stomach and skin – weren't mature enough to function. They'd resuscitated her, but she would need surgery to switch her two transposed major arteries around. Matt had left her stable, with an initial care plan in place, and reassured her family as best he could, but right now, he needed to be with his own family.

'Come on, hurry up, for Christ's sake.' Sliding his window down, he craned his neck to see temporary traffic lights ahead. *Typical.* Blowing out a breath in frustration, he raked a hand through his hair. Poppy would be being prepped for surgery by now. He was desperate to see her before she went to theatre, to assure her that he would be keeping an eye on things, as he'd promised her he would, which she'd seemed comforted by. He wanted to see Amelia, too. He was still reeling with shock that, unbeknownst to him, she'd put herself forward for testing and then for transplant surgery. He wanted her to know that whatever she'd done, they would always be grateful to her for that.

Jason was a different matter. Amelia claimed not to have set the fire that had engulfed the Biochem building. Matt wasn't sure he'd believed her, until the fire investigation report had concluded that a cigarette carelessly discarded in the long grass at the foot of the wall had caused the cladding to ignite. The grass was dry, protected from the elements by the overhanging roof above it, which was used occasionally as a shelter by smokers. Laura had confirmed that the last visitor to leave that day had lit up as he left. The security guard also smoked, but was adamant he hadn't stepped out for a cigarette that evening. With no CCTV on that side of the building, it had been impossible to prove intent rather than accident.

In Matt's mind, it was Jason's negligence that was to blame, end of subject. He almost wished he had left him in the burning building, but supposed that in dragging him out, at least he wouldn't have to live with his conscience. He wasn't sure he would ever be able to bring himself to see his brother again. He struggled to look his father in the eye now, knowing that he had covered for Jason. And when he'd told Kay exactly what kind of contemptible bastard his brother was, and what he'd done to her, he'd had to witness the unbearable pain in her eyes. He didn't know whether she believed how much he loved her, or whether that love would be enough to help her through this, along with the counselling. All he could do was reassure her on a daily basis, be there for her, listen to her and remind her that now that Kelsey Jones's body had been found where Amelia had insisted it would be, Jason would get his justice in prison, where he would rot for a very long time.

His father's medical history meant he might be spared prison. Matt wasn't certain he should be. He'd thought he might miss his family, such as it was, but his real family was Kay and Poppy. He would never let his insecurities put what they had together at risk again. He'd promised Kay that.

Finally. Breathing a sigh of relief as the queue of cars in front of him began to move, he picked up speed, hoping to get through the lights before they changed again. His heart faltered as he noted an incoming call from the hospital. It started beating again when he realised it was the colleague he'd asked to fast-track the paternity test he'd taken.

'Hi, Paul,' he said. 'I'm driving, on my way back to the hospital. Can you make it quick?'

'No problem,' Paul assured him. 'I have those test results you wanted. Thought you might want to know.'

Matt braced himself. 'And?'

'Okay, I've sent you a text, but just to confirm, the paternity test concludes that Jason Young is the biological father of Olivia Taylor. It also confirms he's the biological father of—'

'Jesus Christ! What the …?' Matt's gaze swung to the side window, his heart stalling in his chest a terrifying heartbeat after the car slammed into his driver's-side door.

Unable to move, he couldn't escape the deafening silence that followed. Silence so complete he swore he could hear the soft beat of a bird's wing.

Then all his senses assailed him at once: searing pain in his ribcage, a cacophony of noise, too loud in his head. Horns blaring. People shouting. Sirens plaintively wailing. Someone screaming, high-pitched, hysterical.

Then he heard nothing. Saw nothing but his mother's eyes, not blaming him, but quietly beckoning him.

CHAPTER SEVENTY-ONE

Kay

They would never be the best of friends – that simply wasn't possible after all she'd done – but Kay was grateful to Amelia and slightly in awe of her putting herself forward for testing without breathing a word. She would save Poppy's life. Was it her way of trying to make amends? Kay wondered. Amelia had never said as much; they hadn't really had any in-depth conversation about why she'd set out to destroy them – Jason's family, as she saw it. If only she'd realised how fractured his family already was. Kay would never understand why she'd made those accusations against Matt, which she'd since withdrawn, confessing that the bruising she'd claimed he'd caused was self-inflicted.

He'd told her about the incident Jason had witnessed on the stairs, Matt supposedly being intimate with Amelia. She'd said she'd been attacked in the grounds. She'd been upset, convincingly enough that he didn't doubt it was the truth. He'd tried to comfort her. She supposed Amelia had hoped it would lead to more than that, her initial aim to entice him into an affair, which would certainly have had dire consequences for their marriage. Kay could only guess that she'd made the subsequent allegation against him, because he'd never succumbed to her charms. Had she known Jason was there, possibly that he was interested in her? It wouldn't have taken much to entice him to follow her to the stairs where he would witness the exchange between her and Matt and use it to stir up trouble between them.

Matt seemed to be able to move on. Kay wasn't certain she could. She was having to take it one step at a time, cross each bridge as she came to it. With Matt by her side, she hoped she could learn to live with what Jason had done, and the deep humiliation and self-blame that swept crushingly over her every time she thought about it. She still had the nightmares. Matt held her whenever she woke, her heart palpitating and sweat coating her body. Strangely, though, they came less frequently now that she knew the source of them – perhaps *because* she did.

Bracing herself, she pushed through the door to the side ward Amelia was on. 'Are you doing okay?' she asked, approaching the chair she was sitting in after being prepped for her surgery.

'A bit nervous,' Amelia said, glancing up at her. She struggled to hold eye contact, Kay had noticed, always looking nervously down, a deep sadness in her pretty grey eyes. Kay hoped she would hold her head up again one day. They would both have to learn to do that – maybe together. She reminded herself that since losing her mother, Amelia was all alone in the world. Could Kay offer her some kind of friendship? She hoped she would be big enough to do that in time.

'Thank you,' she said, reaching to take Amelia's hand. The words would never be enough, but hopefully knowing Poppy would thrive because of her would be.

Amelia glanced up, some of the embarrassment gone from her eyes. 'No problem.' She smiled. 'I can't bring my sister back, but I can do this, give another person a chance to grow into a beautiful woman and live a full life.'

Kay felt her heart swell. It was enough. She decided she would do her best to be a friend to Amelia, and to be there for her. 'Can I bring you anything in?' she asked, realising the woman might not have many visitors after her surgery.

'A bottle of vodka?' Amelia suggested. 'We never did go for that drink.'

'Maybe not such a good idea.' Kay smiled. 'We will, though. As soon as you can. I'd better go,' she added. 'I told Poppy I would only be a minute.'

Amelia nodded, apprehension flitting across her face. 'Will you give her my love?' she asked.

Kay hesitated, then, on impulse, leaned to press a soft kiss to her cheek. 'I will,' she promised.

Her thoughts on Poppy, fear in her heart as she worried about the outcome for her baby, she tried not to pay too much attention to the trolley that was being rushed at breakneck speed towards her. Some poor soul seriously injured, she gathered from the rich crimson stains seeping starkly through the white sheet draped over it.

Trying to avoid seeing too much, she stood back, squeezing herself against the corridor wall to allow the trolley and the flurry of medical staff accompanying it to pass. It must be bad, she realised, seeing the panic-stricken face of the nurse holding an IV drip aloft. It didn't register immediately that the arm the drip was attached to was familiar; that the wedding band on the third finger of the left hand matched her own.

CHAPTER SEVENTY-TWO

Matt had once said that sometimes, when he'd exhausted all options with a vulnerable baby, he prayed. She knew he did. He'd prayed for their tiny boy, asked God to keep him safe in the embrace of an angel's wing, spoken the words out loud at the small funeral service they'd had. He'd prayed for Poppy as they sat together keeping a constant vigil over her. He'd broken her heart in a different way that day. It was beyond broken now. She didn't think it would function again without him.

Bowing her head, Kay prayed now for Matt. Her hand seeking his as she sat by his bedside, she begged with her heart and soul for God to have mercy on her husband, a man who'd saved so many lives, who would have given his life in a heartbeat for his daughter, the little girl he'd unquestioningly believed was his, even when suspecting she wasn't. When he'd received the results of the tissue-typing test, proving he wasn't her biological father, he'd barely reacted, pulling Kay to him after a second and simply holding her. Words, she'd sensed, were superfluous. She'd discovered that one of his colleagues had been calling him with paternity test results when he'd crashed his car. Kay had reassured the man that that hadn't been the reason he'd crashed. He'd already known. It hadn't mattered. Nothing could change his love for the little girl he thought of as his own. He didn't deserve to have his life taken away in the blink of an eye for no fathomable reason.

Her chest feeling as if it might burst with the weight of her pain, she squeezed his hand gently, prayed harder. There was no reaction. No movement of his eyes. She studied his profile, willing him to give her a sign that he would come back to her, the smallest flicker of his impossibly long eyelashes. Did he realise how jealous of those eyelashes she was? Did he know how much she loved him? So much, she would never be able to bear the pain of losing him.

'Poppy's out of surgery,' she whispered, working to stop her voice from quavering. 'She says she's going to come and give you a cuddle as soon as she can, so you're going to have to shuffle over and make room for her.'

She stopped, attempting to draw a breath past the excruciating lump in her chest. Would he ever shuffle across their bed again to make room for his baby girl, allowing her to snuggle into the crook of his arm, where she would rest her head on his chest and listen to the reassuring thrum of his heartbeat as Kay herself so often had?

While trying to digest the results of his CT scan, Kay had barely heard anything the neurosurgeon had told her beyond 'subdural haematoma' and 'surgery'. They'd performed something called a craniotomy to remove the haematoma, secured the section of the skull back in place with plates and screws. It had been successful, the neurosurgeon had since assured her, but … Kay's heart had folded up inside her at that point. 'Buts' were rarely a good thing. Now it was a waiting game, it seemed. The bleed was extensive, he had explained carefully. Matt might make a good recovery. Equally, there could be complications: memory loss, weakness in his limbs. There was the possibility he might never recover fully. The surgeon was preparing her, Kay knew, to cope with whatever the outcome was. She would cope willingly. What frightened her was that Matt might not. That he might not want an existence coping, not doing what made him fundamentally who he was.

Would her love be enough for him? His daughter's love, which she knew without any shred of doubt was precious to him; would that be enough to sustain him through those first crucial weeks?

If he woke up.

Wake up, Matt. Please come back to us. We need you. Suppressing the sob that rose in her throat, Kay got to her feet. She had to go back to Poppy. Matt wouldn't want his little girl fretting, least of all now.

Carefully she leaned towards him, pressing a soft kiss to his cheek. 'A kiss from Poppy,' she whispered. 'She says she's as lucky as she can be having you for a daddy, so she's saving all her wishes up for you.'

That was when God sent her a sign that he hadn't deserted her. That was when she knew that somehow miracles happened and wishes came true. The movement of Matt's eyelids was almost imperceptible. If she hadn't been so close, she might have missed it. His fingers curling softly around hers confirmed it. In that second, she knew that he would find a way to be there for his little girl. He always had.

EPILOGUE

Five days later

After checking on Matt, Kay headed back to the ward Poppy was on, where she'd left the two little girls chattering excitedly. Nicole had brought Liv in. She'd been twice already, and each time she'd hardly been able to look Kay in the eye, disappearing soon after delivering her daughter to grab a coffee or make a call. Kay needed to make time to talk to her. There had been no repercussions regarding the blackmail – something Kay had never imagined Nicole capable of, though she did understand to a degree why she'd felt she had no choice but to go that route. She suspected that Matt's father had decided not to pursue it. She could only imagine that Jason hadn't said anything to the police because it would implicate him further. He might still, though, when he realised there was nothing to gain by staying silent. Kay would have to offer Nicole her support. Olivia was Poppy's half-sister, which made her part of her family. She would do all she could to make sure the little girl was safe.

First, though, she had to concentrate on her own daughter, on her husband. Somehow she would find the strength she needed to get them all through this. As she went into the ward, her mind was on the treatment and recovery plan she'd been discussing with Matt's consultant. He'd told her there appeared to be significant brain function improvement. Importantly, there was no swelling after his surgery, which could have produced potentially fatal pressure inside the skull. The next thirty days were crucial. Physio and occupational therapies would follow. But they weren't at that point yet. There was a possibility he might have seizures. Reminding herself to cross her bridges as she reached them, she pulled in a breath and arranged her face into a smile for Poppy.

As she approached her bed, she realised that Amelia had wheeled herself into the ward. Liv was on the foot of the bed, and both girls were clearly engrossed in the story she was reading them. It sounded like *Toto the Ninja Cat and the Great Snake Escape*, another one of Poppy's favourites. Kay had to smile. Amelia had given the cat characters different accents, and was making their nocturnal adventures eye-poppingly exciting, judging by the girls' transfixed faces.

'Where's Nicole?' Kay mouthed as Amelia glanced at her.

Amelia made coffee signs and carried on reading. Seeing the girls were obviously in safe hands, Kay decided now might be an opportunity to break the ice with Nicole. To tell her that she was there for her and Olivia should she need her to be.

A quick scan of the tables in the café told her Nicole wasn't there. Perhaps she'd popped to the loo? Kay checked the toilets, and then, wondering whether she'd decided to grab a coffee from the vending machine in the main reception area, headed that way. Nicole, though, was nowhere in sight. Strange. Kay had assumed she would meet her on the way back. Perhaps she'd gone to the hospital shop. It was Kay's own regular port of call for supplies.

She might as well grab herself a hot chocolate while she was here, she supposed. The evenings here tended to be long, the nights longer, but she doubted they would be as long as nights spent in an empty house on her own. As she extracted her cup from the machine, she looked up and glanced through the glass in the exit doors.

Seeing Nicole standing outside, her back towards her, her arms wrapped tightly around herself as if she were cold, Kay was taken aback. She wasn't sure why she should be really, except … Leaving her drink on top of the machine, she went outside. 'I didn't know you smoked,' she said curiously.

Nicole jumped, jerking the cigarette she was about to take another draw on away from her mouth, tossing it quickly aside and spinning around.

Kay noted where it landed: on the grass verge to the side of the ramp they were standing on. There was no danger, the grass was short, and it wasn't close to the building, but … Her pulse thumped, blood racing through her veins as she recalled how the fire at the Biochem building had started. *No.* It was a ludicrous idea. She wouldn't have. She *couldn't* have. Her gaze snapped from the discarded cigarette back to Nicole. The petrified look on the woman's face said it all.

'It was an accident,' Nicole blurted. 'I went to see him. I knew he was there. I rang the company, spoke to the receptionist. She confirmed he was working late. I had a cigarette before I went in, and I … I didn't *mean* for it to happen.'

Her eyes wild with desperation, she took a step towards Kay. 'I didn't know what to *do*. The fire caught so fast, and I … I was *scared*. I ran. I shouldn't have. I know I should have said something, but … I'm so sorry, Kay. So, *so* sorry. I didn't mean for it to happen. Please believe me.'

'You left the hospital?' Kay took a bewildered step away from her. 'When the girls were missing, you left the hospital?'

'I had to, don't you see?' Nicole's expression was now distraught.

Kay didn't see. It was incomprehensible. 'The girls might have been in there *with him*!' she whispered, her insides turning violently over. 'Matt was inside the building! He might have suffered the most unbearably painful death, and you ran away and *left* him?'

'I didn't know he was there, I *swear*. I parked in the lane. I
didn't know his car was in the car park. Please believe me, Kay. I
knew the children weren't there. Obviously I knew that. I would
have gone in after them. I would *never* have left them. You must
know I would never have—'

'*How* could you have known?' Kay cut her off. 'You couldn't
possibly have known.'

'I did!' Nicole insisted, her voice wretched.

Kay scanned her face, stunned. 'You knew where the girls
were, didn't you?'

Dropping her gaze fast, Nicole said nothing.

'*You* told them to hide,' Kay went on, sick realisation creeping
through her. 'All the time we thought they were missing, taken
by God knows who; all that time we were imagining our baby
in pain, terrified that she might even *die*, and you knew where
they were! For God's sake, why would you *do* such a thing? To
provide yourself with an alibi?' She grappled for an explanation,
any explanation. 'A distraction, so that you could—'

'I *had* to,' Nicole cried. 'I had no idea what else to do. He
insisted on seeing Olivia; not once, several times. He wanted to
confirm she was his. He would have had access to her, that *monster*.
I couldn't allow it. I couldn't undo what I'd done, and … I was
scared.' Tears streaming down her face, she trailed off with a sob.
'I was scared, Kay, for Olivia.'

Kay studied her, appalled and bewildered in turn. What should
she do with this information? Who could she ask? She felt a sob
catch in her own chest as she thought of Matt, the person who'd
always been there for her, steadfast, no matter what. *What would
you do?* she asked him silently.

'I needed to keep my little girl safe,' Nicole went on tremulously.
'Poppy too. Knowing what I did about your husband's brother, that
was my first priority. I thought I could talk to him, offer him the
money back. Somehow persuade him that it was best his family

didn't know about Olivia. I know you'll never be able to forgive me for what I put you through, but there's part of me that doesn't regret the outcome.'

She held Kay's gaze, and now Kay glanced down, trying to process everything. For what he'd done to poor Kelsey, who at seventeen was not much more than a child herself, Jason Young was where he belonged. For what he might have done to Olivia, for his constant persecution of Matt, his undoubted manipulation of his father, he belonged in prison. For what he'd done to *her*, Kay quietly hoped his stay there would be torture meted out on a daily basis.

'What will you do?' Nicole asked.

Kay looked back at her. Nicole was shaking, petrified for Olivia, Kay didn't doubt that. 'We should go back inside,' she said quietly after a second. 'The girls need us.'

A LETTER FROM SHERYL

Thank you so much for choosing to read *The Liar's Child*. I really hope you enjoyed reading it as much as I enjoyed writing it. If you would like to keep up to date with my new releases, please do sign up at the link below. Your details will never be shared and you can unsubscribe at any time.

www.bookouture.com/sheryl-browne

I can't believe this is my ninth book published with the fabulous Bookouture. I'm thrilled to bits to be sharing it with you, my lovely readers who inspire me to keep writing. I love writing psychological thrillers looking at family dynamics, delving deeper beneath the surface to seek out what drives people, what secrets they might keep, what challenges they might have to overcome to keep their families safe. *The Liar's Child* looks at an ordinary couple striving to do their very best for their child under extraordinary circumstances. Little Poppy has a kidney disease. Kay and Matthew are determined to give their precious daughter her best life possible. Will secrets, breeding feelings of jealousy, doubt and mistrust, thwart their efforts though? Will lies and manipulation impact on Poppy and cause the safe walls they've built around her to crumble and threaten her future?

The book covers some sensitive topics and Poppy's story in particular might touch parents of children with chronic illness. It is a subject close to my heart and I hope I've done it justice. In the book, Poppy's father, a neonatal specialist, strives to see the child, not just the illness. I'll leave it to you to judge whether Poppy's personality shines through.

As I pen this last little section of the book, I would like to thank those people around me who are always there to offer support, those people who believed in me even when I didn't quite believe in myself. To all of you, thank you for helping me make my dream come true.

If you have enjoyed the book, I would love it if you could share your thoughts and write a brief review. Reviews mean the world to an author and will help a book find its wings. I would also love to hear from you via Facebook or Twitter or my website.

Stay safe, everyone, and happy reading.
Sheryl x

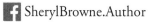 SherylBrowne.Author

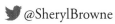 @SherylBrowne

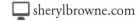 sherylbrowne.com

ACKNOWLEDGEMENTS

As always, massive thanks to the fabulous team at Bookouture, whose support of their authors is amazing. Special thanks to Helen Jenner and the wonderful editorial team, who not only make my stories make sense, but make them shine. Huge thanks also to the fantastic publicity team, Kim Nash, Noelle Holten and Sarah Hardy. Thanks, guys, I think it's safe to say I could not do this without you. To all the other authors at Bookouture, I love you. Thank you for being such a super-supportive group of people.

I owe a huge debt of gratitude to all the fantastically hard-working bloggers and reviewers who have taken the time to read and review my books and shout them out to the world. It's truly appreciated.

Final thanks to every single reader out there for buying and reading my books. Knowing you have enjoyed my stories and care enough about my characters to want to share them with other readers is the best incentive ever for me to keep writing.

Printed in Great Britain
by Amazon